OTHER BOOKS BY
COLUMBUS CREATIVE COOPERATIVE

While You Were Out
Short Stories of Resurrection

Across Town
Stories of Columbus

Overgrown
Tales of the Unexpected

Origins
An Anthology

COLUMBUS

PAST, PRESENT AND FUTURE

Proudly Presented By

COLUMBUS
CREATIVE
COOPERATIVE

WWW.COLUMBUSCOOP.ORG

Edited By
Amy S. Dalrymple, Brenda Layman
& Brad Pauquette

Pauquette ltd
dba Columbus Creative Cooperative
PO Box 91028
Columbus, OH 43209
www.ColumbusCoop.org

DEVELOPMENTAL EDITORS
Brad Pauquette & Brenda Layman

COPY EDITOR
Amy S. Dalrymple

PRODUCTION EDITOR
Brad Pauquette

PROOFREADER
Mallory Baker

Cover design by Michelle Berki.

ISBN 978-0-9835205-7-3

Printed in the United States of America
1 3 5 7 9 10 8 6 4 2

To the people of Columbus, from Lucas Sullivant to
the newest baby at St. Ann's hospital.
Happy 200th Birthday!

CONTENTS

1812

1912

2012

CONTENTS

2012

2112

2212

Illustrations

*Biographies of contributing artists can be found
on pg. 311.*

COMMONS CAROUSEL
Doug Oldham

FOREWORD
Columbus Mayor Michael B. Coleman

On behalf of the City of Columbus, let me officially introduce you to *Columbus: Past, Present and Future*, the Bicentennial Columbus anthology. The talented writers who have contributed to this anthology continue to tell the story of Columbus through short stories that honor our past, celebrate the present and envision our future.

This year is one of epic proportions for the city of Columbus as we celebrate our bicentennial. Those who were here in 1812 when the General Assembly created Columbus to be our state capital, and those who came in those first few years after—I think they would give us high marks for taking their ideas and vision far beyond anything they ever dreamed of.

Those ideas and vision are firmly rooted in such a way to take us into a healthy and prosperous future. As a city big on collaboration, we are working together to pull people out of poverty, give our youth opportunities, attract more jobs, revitalize our neighborhoods, provide options for alternative transportation, and be more environmentally responsible; and we are doing all we can to encourage and support a robust creative class.

But, we don't want to stay in the past—or even the present, for that matter. On its 200th birthday, Columbus is poised to move ahead to continue making strides for its residents in virtually every area. As the largest city in the state and the fifteenth largest city in the United States, we should be proud of our growth and the fact that we are making decisions about Columbus that make it a city where people want to live, make their careers, and raise their families.

Each of you is a contributor to our success. When people describe Columbus as friendly, welcoming, supportive, eco-conscious, beautiful, clean, energetic, and creative—that's because of you. Without a doubt, our people are our greatest asset—the best representation of what Columbus is all about. Throughout these pages you can see just a sampling of what we have to offer.

We've accomplished much as a city, and there is still much to do. But, every day as I work with individuals from the public and private sectors, as I shake hands with our residents and listen to aspirations of our youth, I am more determined than ever not to rest on our laurels, but to continue the work that was started 200 years ago and continues fervently today.

Happy Birthday, Columbus!

Mayor Michael B. Coleman is the fifty-second and current mayor of Columbus, Ohio. First elected in 1999, he is currently serving his fourth term.

INTRODUCTION

Wolves were a real problem in Columbus in 1812. I'm not kidding—wolves. Columbus folklore has it that in the first couple of decades after Columbus's founding, the men would take their guns to church and if a pack of wolves was spotted near the town, the call would sound and the men would rise from their seats to go hunt them down like dogs, literally.

I haven't lost any livestock to dangerous predators recently, so I think it's fair to say that life is different now than it was 200 years ago. And it will be different still 200 years from now. When Lucas Sullivant settled Franklinton more than two centuries ago, who can say what bizarre and ludicrous predictions of magic and technology he might have made for the year 2012, let alone 2212.

This book of fictional short stories examines our past, sometimes seriously and at other times with a wink, inspects our present, and extrapolates our course two centuries into the future.

This book holds short stories written by twenty-three of Central Ohio's best authors. In addition, fifteen artists have contributed work to this anthology, and resources have been assembled from the Library of Congress and the Columbus Metropolitan Library.

The stories in this book are set between the years 1812 and 2212, from Columbus's founding to a day 200 years in our future. You'll find that some of the historical fiction is well researched and documented, while other stories stretch your imagination to the limits of what might have been. Some of the stories set in the future depict a world that seems as inevitable and real as the increasing price of gas, while other prophecies stretch the inconsistencies of our present day to their least logical but most hilarious end.

We've done our best to assemble the most variety possible for this book. You'll find hints of every genre in this anthology, from adventure

1

to romance, comedy to science fiction, thriller to drama, and everything in between.

I believe that each and every story included in this collection is an excellent example of work in its particular genre, and each story is intriguing and entertaining.

When you read this anthology, you're not just getting a fantastic piece of art and entertainment, you're also supporting something important. Publishing opportunities are few and far between for writers and visual artists alike. By coming together as a local community, we can give deserving individuals, artists who in a more equitable world would be at the top of every publisher's list, a chance to showcase their work.

These stories and this artwork have been provided by students and retirees alike. These tales have been written by your bus driver, your lawyer, your barista and your IT guy. Each story has been carefully selected to represent a specific time period in Columbus's past, present or future.

In addition, the Columbus Historical Society will receive a significant portion of the proceeds from this book, which will help them to continue their mission of sharing and protecting Central Ohio's unique history. By purchasing this anthology, you support the work of this important institution.

This anthology begins with historical fiction, from a comedy about the founding of Columbus, Ohio by the state legislature, to a heartfelt and moving story about brothers in the civil war, all the way through the changing social world of the 1970s.

The present day section begins in 1982 and will take the reader through some of the icons you'll recognize around Columbus, complete with humor, drama, the occassional touch of the supernatural and just the right amount of nostalgia.

As you move into the future section of this anthology, you'll find that each author has been given complete freedom in their depiction of our days to come. Some predict a barren world of hunger and depravity, while others portray a booming and prosperous metropolis. Unlike our historical fiction which must move forward along a predictable and real line, we have made no attempt to resolve the future stories with one another. Each should be considered as an independent work of imagination, with little relationship to its anthological neighbors.

We had a fantastic time putting this book together. Such a vast amount of phenomenal material was submitted for consideration, and the selected stories have merged into a beautiful anthology. We hope that you enjoy reading it and cherish this book and this unique time in the history of the City of Columbus as much as we do.

Thank you, reader, for beginning your journey through the history and future of Columbus. And thank you to the Columbus businesses who have sponsored this project and made this anthology a reality. We couldn't produce materials of this caliber without the support of the entire community—readers, writers and businesses alike.

An opportunity to publish a book like this only comes once every 200 years. Here's hoping we didn't blow it.

-Brad Pauquette
Director, Columbus Creative Cooperative

A special thanks to Barbara Perrin,
who first told me about the wolves.
May she rest in peace.

WILLIAM HENRY HARRISON
Ninth President of the United States of America
Provided by the Library of Congress

1812
A WHISKEY MAN
By Brad Pauquette

I walked into Shae's pub at the usual time, sat down at my usual bar stool, threw my hat in the usual place and downed the whiskey that Willy Shae had waiting for me. I stomped my leather boots on the ledge that ran underneath of the wooden bar, and Willy and I listened to the mud crumble off and patter against the floor.

"You couldn't stomp them outside, you sorry old bastard?"

I looked beneath me, where dust and grime coated the rotting floorboards. "If you can come over on this side and show me a single piece of dirt amongst all the others that I brought in tonight, I'll give you my boots." I had bet Willy my boots at least twice a week for the past four years, and I'd never gone home barefoot.

"Just stomp 'em outside next time, Lucas!" he refilled my glass. "What would I do with your boots anyway?"

I shrugged. "Pour yourself one, a tip from your favorite patron."

Willy reached for a glass, then stopped himself. His eyes narrowed as if I were trying to trick him, and his hands found their way as usual to his dense red beard.

"Can't, mum says I can't drink when I'm on duty anymore, got to serve the customers."

I scoffed. "You're nearly forty, and you're still taking orders from your mother like you were twelve years old?" I made an act of looking around the place. There were four tables in the tiny shack of a bar and not a soul at any one of them. "I think you'll be able to handle the crowd."

"Aye, but we left the lantern burning when we fell asleep on the floor last night. She thinks I'll burn the place down."

I nodded. "Tell you what, Willy, if we leave the lantern on tonight, I'll give you my boots, and a kiss for your mum, too." I laughed heartily as Willy smiled and picked up the bottle.

"Damn you, Lucas," he grabbed a glass from under the bar.

"To the finest liquor establishment in Franklinton that was built in your mother's barn, too close to the river," I raised my glass.

"Aye, to that." We both threw back the brown liquid, and breathed deeply as the fire rolled through our sinuses.

"At least you know now what you're serving," I chided him. "If your mum comes around, you can tell her I forced you."

"What I wouldn't give to be out from under this place, Lucas," Willy leaned forward and whistled. "You wouldn't believe. Comes a time when a man's got to move out of his mum's house, stop drinking every night in his mum's barn like a damn youth. Ready to make my own way …"

"You better make it fast," I clanked my empty glass against the bar.

He filled both of our glasses again, and suddenly the door burst open. Willy looked up, and I could tell by his wide eyes he expected it to be his mother. Instead, four young men stumbled in, stomping the mud off their boots as they made their way to a table.

"Stomp your boots outside, boys!" Willy yelled over the roar of merriment they'd hauled in with them. "You don't have to sweep the place—"

"Apparently, neither do you," the first one through the door shouted as he kicked up a cloud of dust from the broad-planked wooden floor. The last boy through the door pulled off his leather top-boots and threw them back out the door before it could swing shut.

"For you, Willy," he shouted, and his compatriots laughed. He walked to the bar in his bare feet. "It's Samuel's seventeenth birthday, 1812's been a good year, sir."

I looked at Willy and shook my head.

"Let's make a deal, you and me, Willy," the boy continued. "My father's goat just had kids, and they belong to me for tending them. I'm feeling generous, I give you a goat, everybody in the bar drinks on me tonight."

I perked up from my newfound gloom for a moment while Willy considered it. "I don't know, Ezra, bar could fill up, then where would I be?"

"Fill up with who? Mr. Grubb's your only regular. If not for the four of us, in a couple of hours you two'll pass out by yourselves on the floor with the lantern still burning."

Willy just shook his head.

"Fine," Ezra sighed, "if more than one other person comes into the bar tonight, I'll give you one of my young layers, too."

Willy bit his lip to fight back a grin. He'd made a fine deal, a goat and possibly a chicken for beer and whiskey for six people. Ezra Brooks was known around town, had a way of being generous, making a deal, but there was usually a catch and it was usually the next morning.

"When do I get the goat?" Willy asked through a menacing grimace.

Ezra smiled. "Soon as I feel well enough again to bring it over!"

His buddies laughed and I chuckled. Willy's eyes narrowed.

"You'll have it by tomorrow sunset," Ezra assured him, "or I'm not a whiskey man!"

This time Willy laughed too, and shook his hand. "Samuel's seventeen, eh? A man starts with whiskey." He walked around the shabby bar, set four glasses on their table and filled them generously with three fingers of the only whiskey in the house.

"Guess you can put your coins away, Lucas," he told me when he returned. "What'll it be, whiskey or beer next?"

I just stared at him as he grabbed a beer glass … and filled it halfway up with whiskey. "That'll do," I told him. "That'll do."

The sun was beginning to set when Willy insisted that everyone switch to a round of beer. The golden light filtered in around the door and through the cracks in the wooden siding of the former barn.

Out the shanty's only window, which looked to the east and over the river, a peaceful darkness was settling over the swamp and the forest beyond.

The boys died down a bit with the beer. Beer has a way of bringing out the prophet in a man, the way that red wine brings out the poet and whiskey awakens the gambler. I pretended to carry on my own conversation with Willy, but in a tavern with four tables, six stools and only five patrons, there was only ever one conversation in the room.

Samuel, the birthday boy, hadn't said much up to that point, but as he sucked the foam off of the top of his glass, his tone turned serious and he looked out the window.

"There's the capital, friends," he announced, looking over the river. "The capital of the finest state in the Union."

Willy looked out too. "Which capital do you mean, young Samuel, the forest or the swamp?" Willy chuckled with me, but his friends waited for him to continue.

"They'll build something soon. You just wait and see. The legislature's already making plans for an assembly hall that takes up ten acres." He took a long drag from his glass, and his eyes grew vacant. "Some day there'll be thousands of people over there.

"There'll be buildings a hundred feet tall," he continued. "We'll have three or four bridges across the river to connect us with them, and paved roads on either side."

I just grinned at the drunken kid, and I drifted away in my own memories of hopeful youth as he talked, but his friends seemed to draw closer to him with every word.

"Some day, there'll be a college on the other side of the river where people from all over learn to be doctors and lawyers and ministers. Only it won't be like the one in Athens, there'll be hundreds, maybe even a thousand young men that go there. They won't just learn the same old things we've always been taught, but they'll learn new things, too. They'll think up things that have never been thought before, and discover things that never existed."

Samuel finished off his beer and Ezra rested his head on his fist while he listened. Willy filled up new whiskey glasses for the two of us.

"Aye, Samuel," Willy goaded him. "And there'll be women on every street corner with their knickers up and their bosoms popping out."

Ezra and the other two broke from their trance and hooted with Willy, but Samuel continued, unfazed.

"There'll be trains crisscrossed all over the city that will take you from here to Zanesville or Chillicothe in a half day. Every respectable man will have a horse, or maybe even something better, something we've never even considered before."

"Like what?" I asked. I'd had too much whiskey, and for a moment I mistakenly began caring what the young man had to say.

"I don't know, could be anything," he said. "Something with steam maybe, like a carriage machine."

"Or like a small sailboat for the land ..." one of the others chimed in, and they nodded in agreement.

"Aye, or maybe some kind of machine that stomps forward on legs like a mechanical horse," Ezra suggested, to more agreeable nods and verbal praise.

"Right, and I'll have an oxen with two heads so that I can go in both directions at once," I shouted out. The boys laughed and pounded their fists on the table.

Just then, the door opened cautiously. In walked a gentleman I'd never seen in Franklinton before, which is a notable occurrence for a settlement of 400. The man walked to the bar and sat down, his stately clothing offset by the slump in his shoulders and his reluctant gait.

"You're two feet away from owing me a chicken," Willy called out to Ezra, who simply waived him off and dramatically sucked down his beer.

"That'll be another round then, Willy," he shouted.

Willy delivered four more beers while the stranger sat down and removed his hat.

"Welcome to my tavern," Willy stumbled down the bar with a warm smile and welcomed the man. "What'll you have, gent? Whiskey or beer?"

"I've never been a whiskey man," the solemn man answered slowly. "I'll take a beer."

Willy poured a beer from the tap. "No charge tonight, we're all drinking on young Ezra's tab."

"Aye, that's a start," the gentlemen raised his glass and nearly smiled. "To Ezra then."

"Not to me," Ezra smiled kindly. "For my friend Samuel's birthday here!"

"And not with a beer," I chimed in. "A proper toast comes with whiskey. Pour him a finger, Willy."

Willy put the glass he'd just prepared for himself in front of the newcomer.

"All right then," the man spoke elegantly but without conviction, "I, William Henry Harrison, toast to the great honor of young Samuel's birthday—may your life be peaceful and long."

A mutual chorus of appreciation met the roof and we all took a hearty drink from our glasses. The man threw the liquid into his mouth and then coughed.

"I'll say, that's really something," he said with more energy than he had spoken with before. "That'll get the troops marching. Make it another, my good man." He accepted his second drink, but then returned to his brooding.

The boys had taken up a game of Doubloons, and other than the thwack of coins bouncing off the table, the tinkle against glass when they hit their target and the occasional outburst of celebration, the tavern took on a melancholy reserve.

"Tell me mate," Willy finally leaned towards the stranger. "Why so glum? Can't be so bad …"

He sized Willy up, then spoke. "Well, if you must know, I have just been given complete and utter control over the Northwestern Army of the American States. Now I have what they call an 'army' in this region, a ragtag band of farmers with muskets with scarcely a whole uniform amongst them, and I'm supposed to fight British and Indians." I swallowed hard. Willy and I nodded. Then I looked around. The place was quiet and all eyes were on the newcomer in that shack of a bar.

"Exactly," he said. "Some problems *can* be so bad. They offered me second in command, and I politely declined. I'm not one to sign up as any man's second, after all. Then they fired General Winchester and told me that since I insisted, I can have the whole blasted army to myself!" He leaned forward onto the bar with his head in his hands. "Now I've got an army and no place to put them."

"Well, you should ask Samuel," Willy brightened up. "He's full of ideas tonight. You should hear what he's got in mind for the swamp across the river." The tavern chuckled nervously.

General Harrison took a long drag from his whiskey. "Very well then, Samuel, what do I do with my army?"

Willy, Ezra and his friends laughed while I turned from General Harrison to watch the young man ponder the question.

Samuel cocked his head and looked General Harrison in the eye. "The British took the Village of Detroit. Take it back."

General Harrison nodded his head, but Willy barged in. "Ahh, not Michigan, the British can have 'em!" The boys laughed again. "I've met some of those fellows from Detroit," Willy continued. "A worthless bunch, the lot of them. They'll take a savage to bed just as quick as their sister, been out in the cold too long, those ones have."

"Aye, it's true, dumb as rocks, too," I agreed. "You could probably even convince them to open a factory for Samuel's blasted steam carriage." I downed my remaining whiskey while everyone laughed.

"No," General Harrison pronounced when the laughter died down. "He's right. The first order is to stop the advance, reclaim what's ours. They may be from Michigan Territory, but Michigan is ours since 1794, and they're a hell of a lot better than the British. Very well Samuel, then what?"

"Wait, let's slow down." I jumped in. "A good idea such as this deserves to be honored with a bit of whiskey, wouldn't you say?"

Willy agreed and the boys abandoned their table, saddling up to the remaining stools at the bar.

Over the next several hours, a plan was formed. Such a perfect plan as can be formed only amongst seven suddenly close friends of no account socializing with one another on a dark night in a candle-lit tavern with a seemingly limitless supply of free alcohol at the ready.

As it turned out, Samuel was full of good ideas. We'd fortify the Maumee River in Northwestern Ohio—a shot was taken. We'd train the recruits in Franklinton—another shot. By the time we got to reclaiming Detroit and then invading Upper Canada, the boys were nearly falling off of their stools.

Before I began falling asleep on the bar, thanks to Willy's half pint of whiskey earlier in the evening, I was at one point to be a captain in General Harrison's army, with Willy as a colonel and second in command, and the young men as freshly commissioned lieutenants.

I suppose Willy was too old to be a lieutenant, and his recurring joke that he "hates Michigan, but not as much as the goddamn British" must have convinced General Harrison that he had the gumption, and complete lack of experience, to be a high-ranking officer with virtually no responsibilities. He was the perfect kind of ass to be second in command.

"Damn the British to hell," General Harrison exclaimed at one point in the evening. "And I'll be damned if I'm not a whiskey man!"

It must have been at this time that one of us, probably me, fueled by the high spirits of a whiskey high threatening to crash, convinced Willy to burn his mother's tavern down.

"It's too to close the the river and little more than a barn," I do remember specifically shouting.

Willy somberly considered the idea while the others made their arguments.

"Aye, we'll need the space to train the lieutenants," General Harrison agreed.

"Aye, it's a hazard as it stands now," Ezra contributed. "It'd be damn irresponsible to leave it standing, what with our mission we won't be able to stay here and keep an eye on it."

"Who knows what your mother will do with it while you're gone," I drunkenly whispered.

"You're right," his eyes caught fire. "My time and this space have better futures."

A mighty cheer shook the building and we ambled outside with our mugs of beer and a lit candle.

"To duty, and to my country," Willy held up the candle. "And to my mother, she can shove it up her ass."

"No, no! Wait!" I yelled and ran back inside to grab all of the whiskey bottles. I brought them out and sat down next to a rock, trying to convince my eyes to look straight ahead instead of in opposing circles.

As I concentrated I saw why our new friend William Henry Harrison was the general and my old friend Willy was only to be the colonel. "Wait, wait, boys," he called out to them before Willy lit the place. And at once it was an officers' exercise. Together the four boys followed Willy's instructions, which were supplied by General Harrison, to find the weak points in the structure. Together, on Colonel William Shae's order, the four young men who would lead their compatriots into battle pushed at the old structure, which collapsed into a ragged pile of roughly hewn barn siding and sycamore posts.

Without hesitation, William Shae ceremoniously fetched the candle from Harrison, marched dutifully to the heaped remains and set it ablaze.

As we basked in the warmth of Shae's tavern, burning brightly in the scantily lit night, the future city of Columbus, Ohio, then just a forest and swamp, was illuminated behind the flames and sparks reaching ever higher towards the sky.

In the eerie and majestic crackle of the fire, Willy stared into the blaze, awed and dumbfounded, as General William Henry Harrison congratulated his young officers. "Mr. Samuel," he slurred his s's badly. "I promote you to Captain of the Northwestern Army for a stimulating, no—" he staggered just slightly, "what's the goddamn word—an impersonating performance in the face of great hardship and better whiskey."

Samuel's friends slapped him on the back amiably, their friend a captain in the army at only seventeen.

"But I was the captain," I mumbled to my rock, but no one else heard.

"And to you, Ezra Brooks," Harrison continued in his drunken cadence. "A lieutenant you shall remain, but I have a feeling, a good feeling in my—in my heart, that in the future, the future that your friend Samuel sees over in the forest across the river in the place that will one day be Columbus, Ohio ... I have a feeling Mr. Ezra Brooks, that you will be forever known as a man who makes bizarre and sometimes wonderful things come to fruition on dark nights amongst friends."

Ezra's friends cheered as he shook the General's hands, and together they all turned to leave.

"I'll be a captain in my own army," I jeered as I watched them, oblivious to me, turn and march into the darkness. Willy led them in boisterous song, and they leaned on each other greatly as they stomped off.

As the sound of their singing faded into the distance and the burning tavern began to cool, Mrs. Shae, Willy's mother and owner of the barn pub, came running. She gasped and fell on her knees before the smoldering ashes.

"What happened? Where's Willy?" she shrieked, rousing me with a slap to my face. "Where's my sweet baby boy?"

"Gone to make it on his own," I mumbled. "Now where will I drink?"

"What?" was all she could gasp.

I did my best to gather my thoughts and stop the world from spinning. But before I passed out completely, there was only one phrase that my whiskey-battered brain could place together to summarize the occasion for poor Mrs. Shae.

"Muck ... Fichigan." And the world turned to black.

Brad Pauquette is an independent web developer and freelance writer in Columbus, Ohio. He lives in Woodland Park, a neighborhood on the east side of Columbus, with his wife Melissa, son Theodore and dog, Harvey. You can find more information about Brad on his website, www.BradPauquetteDesign.com.

William Henry Harrison gave away shots of whiskey during his campaign to become Ohio's first U.S. President. Although he gave the longest inauguration speech in U.S. history, he served the shortest term, dying of pneumonia only 32 days after taking the oath of office.

During the War of 1812, General Harrison did train troops in Franklinton, Ohio, did fortify the Maumee River and did eventually recapture the Village of Detroit from the British.

AMERICANS, CAMP CHASE
Chase Cemetery, Columbus, Ohio
Paul Binder

1863
THE CONFLUENCE
By Heidi Durig Heiby

October, 1863
2nd Lieutenant William W. Ranney
Camp Chase Federal P.O.W. Camp
Columbus, Ohio (Confluence of the Scioto and Olentangy rivers)

Oddly, all I could think of when I first saw George was that clean, ragged piece of flannel that I had torn haphazardly from our bed after he fell from the McIntosh tree many years before. I had been fifteen at the time, the eldest of six children, and I had not panicked in the least but had expertly cleaned the seeping wound with water and lard soap before wrapping it. George, newly six, had been difficult to calm but had eventually lain shuddering with the shock of the experience in my lap until Father returned from town. Thank the heavens no bone was broken in the fall, and the large scrape healed quickly and well, leaving only the faintest scar in the shape of a "Y."

Now, eighteen years later, my younger brother lay silent in his pain, curled up with it, having very much surrendered to it. How I wished he would scream out, if only to warrant my comfort. My stomach lurched anew at the sight. My God, what condemnation was this? How had we gotten here? I was glad that our father had succumbed to fever in his forty-seventh year and would never know of this.

But what if he didn't make it? I had not dared think of such a scenario before, despite the death all around us. George had seemed in fair enough health to this point, as far as I could tell. His injury had been improving slowly, and he appeared somewhat mobile and even quite jovial from my hidden vantage point. As an Officer of the Guard, I was tasked with overseeing the prison camp as a whole, organizing the guard and security details and pacing the wall several times a day, but only rarely entering the grounds or barracks. The latest was that George had felt unwell and developed fever, indicating infection or maybe even

15

Yellow Fever, which was claiming dozens of lives a day. If the worst were to happen, and if I made it home, I would tell our mother only that her boy had fought and died bravely, which was true, and was buried honorably, which was most likely not to be true. George was the enemy here, and Confederate remains were being interred quickly and without decorum in a neighboring field.

"Damned if this is not putting you between shit and sweat, Sir," Sergeant Talbot Moore, the only trustworthy of my men at Chase, had commented carelessly at the news. He had been Sergeant of the Guard in the mess where my brother was being held, and he kept me quietly informed of goings on for the four months George and I had both been there, prisoner and guard. So this time, hearing of George's acute distress, I erred purposefully from my prescribed path at approximately 22:30 and entered his mess in Prison Number Two. I stood, allowing my eyes a moment to adjust. The acrid smell of sweat and filth was overwhelming. Probably near twenty men occupied twelve narrow stacked bunks that were themselves mere boards; at least George was one of the few who had not had to double up. Some still had short coats, some longer, mounted artillery capes, and others only their worn shirts and trousers. There were no blankets, and being that it was mid-October, the night air had turned damned cold. Each cradled whatever canteen or haversack he may have still had, the sum of his worldly possessions. I could discern where George lay only because of the fierce red of his auburn hair. I walked cautiously toward him. He had been given the bottom-most bunk on the back left side, probably because he had fallen ill. The partial lameness of his left leg also made it likely that he could not climb. He lay on a threadbare cape that still bore the rust stain where his leg had been nearly shot off.

"Georgie, Will is here," I rasped from an aching throat as I stood over him. He blinked confusedly. I wanted no one to hear these terms of endearment.

His cracked lips moved but no sound came out. Then, "I believe …" George began tentatively. "I believe you may have been right." The words burst suddenly from his mouth like they had been pushed by a gale.

"No!" I shrieked. I crouched down next to him, oblivious now to the others who were waking at my intrusion, and stroked his fine hair, noting the unnatural heat of his forehead. "There is no more 'right'," I cried quietly.

"Shiloh …" was all he could manage thereafter. So he had known.

I shushed him while trying to hold back choking sobs, but there was no keeping my sorrow at bay. Others would hear me now and see my breach of conduct. It was strictly against regulations to come into contact with or even speak to the prisoners except for reasons of security. This was the first time I had spoken to George since he had been brought here as a prisoner in the spring just after I began my stint as a Lieutenant of the Guard.

Sentinels and guards were to be as neutral as possible in all things; prisoners did not need to know their names, and vice versa. Our main task was simple: shoot to kill for any infraction. Prisoners under my watch had been killed for simply misunderstanding the strict rules of conduct or getting too near the dead line, one having been accidentally shot when a sentinel thought he had struck a match past lights out and it had turned out to be moonlight filtering through the beams of the barrack walls.

I could not remember the last time I had allowed myself tears. I sensed the night watch guards stopping their pacing. I almost felt as if no one breathed as my grief spilled, unchecked. I know I heard sighs and prayers as other prisoners ceased their thrashing and moaning. The chaotic sounds of suffering are ever present in such a place, even in the dead of night, but there was a sudden stillness in that barracks that I will never forget, and it underlined our pathetic circumstance.

"A clean flannel!" I barked. No one moved. Finally, Sergeant Moore peered in and abruptly spun on his heels in retreat. Of course there were no clean flannels to be had, not for these boys, but the sergeant would no doubt get the hint and have someone "borrow" from the officers' supply. I would take full responsibility. When he came back what seemed an eternity later, he held an uneven length of flannel that he reached down to me. His face was like stone.

"Sir," he said and turned. I had uncovered George's bandaged leg carefully, taken aback by the split just below his knee that still seemed barely healed, and wrapped it in the clean flannel. He did not make one sound. Then I put my thick jacket over his chest and drizzled water from my canteen into his mouth. I pulled George to the floor and held him in my lap that way, the other guards widening their beats to cover mine. I stared at the crude dressing on his leg, so much less than our own torn bed flannel and lard soap, when so much more was needed. Our linens back home had been—ironically, blue and gray check—and so soft. Always clean. Always smelling of Mother's lemon verbena and the sharp spice of lye. Such simple things.

So I sat, praying rambling prayers over this wayward brother of mine, hoping against hope that it was but a mild ailment that would pass. Those who shared George's meek quarters did not stir nor inquire my purpose there. I must have fallen asleep, slumped against the back wall, because when a hand pressed my shoulder I had to squint from the slivers of low sun spilling between the rough, timbered walls. George slept, and I knew I had to leave. I heaved a sob at the chill of his skin and lay him down in his bunk gently. He felt as angular and light as a bird. No one mentioned a word about it, and no higher up reported a theft from supply. When I heard that George had failed to cue for roll call and then morning rations, I finally went to Major Zinn and requested that my brother be allowed to see a doctor. He eyed me silently.

"I will see what can be done," he murmured. I thanked him and waited for dismissal. "And you are being transferred immediately," he added. "Now return to your barracks, Lieutenant Ranney. Before evening call you should have your personal items readied. Have I made myself clear?" I had no choice but to acquiesce, salute and leave without further comment, hope held tight in my chest that George could still be saved; it mattered not that my otherwise spotless record had been marred by this incident.

September, 1861
Mr. William W. Ranney, Jr.
The William Ranney Household
Livermore, Kentucky (Confluence of the Green and Rough rivers)

Two years before that terrible night at Camp Chase, I would never have imagined how all our lives were about to be altered. We were sharing Sunday dinner at our home, and George and I had a moment to speak. The lucidity in his blue eyes, so much like Father's had been, startled me. He had never been easy to talk into or out of things once he got them into his brain, and this would be no exception. I was already a married man at his age, running Father's mercantile, but George showed no signs of wanting a settled life. Now that the war had begun, he had become increasingly restless. Our usual brotherly chats had become politically-charged. He disagreed with the rest of our fervent belief that the Union be preserved at all cost and of the wisdom of President Lincoln.

"You, of all people, should know how *disparate* the needs of our states are," he argued to ruddiness. "Is Massachusetts in the *least* like Kentucky?" he demanded, pounding the dining room table.

"I see your point, George, but you are missing the larger context." I tried to remain as calm as possible, but he never let me finish.

"There is no larger context! We cannot be controlled like puppets!" He used baby William's arms, who sat enraptured in his uncle's lap, to imitate the jerky movement of a marionette. I then watched him gesticulate each point of the Southern succession argument once again, his handsome face set. "We are Kentuckians, Brother," he had concluded. "Our interests are southern interests."

"*You* are a Kentuckian," I reminded him, trying to lighten the mood. "Not me." He chuckled at last. George and our younger siblings had all been born in Kentucky, but our older sisters and I had begun our existence in Massachusetts, where our father and his brother had built their booming merchant business in the port town of Newburyport. Then our father and uncle had taken themselves and their entire families to Kentucky and another port town, Livermore, in the spring of 1839 in the fever of exploration of the "Great West" and its new opportunities.

"We are both *Americans*," George had countered. "And this is about preserving the rights of all Americans within their own circumstances, as it should be." And there was that look in his eyes, the one that warned me of his steadfastness in the matter. I had tired of arguing with him just as dinner was brought and the family assembled. After the blessing and the filling of plates, George wasted no time in making his unwelcome announcement.

"Colonel Hunt is asking for volunteers for mounted artillery," he began. Mother's head jerked up and we all paused eating. "And I have decided that, with my skill on horseback and as a marksman, I would be the ideal candidate to offer my service. I will muster next week on October first." We were all in shock. Certainly he would not abandon his appointment as head druggist. Certainly he would not fight for the South. Our youngest sister, Mariah, spoke first.

"You want to be a *Reb*?" she asked sharply.

"You cannot go!" Mother shrieked and put down her fork.

"It is done," George said smoothly, flashing his even smile as if he were conversing about the weather. "I turned in my signed promissory to enlist. I will die to defend the rights of the states, even the right to form an independent republic. If that is what a 'Reb' is then so be it. I am a Reb." I thought Mariah's eyes might pop out of her head and Mother's mouth hung open.

"You have an obligation to the family business and to this family," I began icily, my hands gripping the table.

"I have a responsibility to no one now that Mother is remarried and you so expertly manage the store. I will live *my* life now." He chewed appreciatively on a roll and no longer looked my way.

"Father would never have approved of this," I added carefully, watching Mother bury her face in her hands. Our parents were northerners, having grown up in Connecticut, and even in the earliest days of the talk of secession of southern states, Father had been against it. He would undoubtedly support the Union if he was still alive, and George knew that.

"Do not bring Father into this!" he bellowed. "I am my own man, Will." He promptly took another bite, wiped at his mouth and looked directly at me when I continued.

"You must not do this, George. You will betray this family and all we have worked for. And there is plenty here to keep you occupied."

"This is *not* for my amusement!" He countered angrily. "Brothers cannot always be of one mind. I love you all," he made sure to interject before going back to his roast, "and I will take care to keep myself well. I am a trained druggist, after all. You have made sure of that." No one could speak. Mother left the table. Although I did not doubt that he loved us, the last comment had not been necessary. Mother and I had practically forced him into his apprenticeship when he had looked into joining the Navy and then a team of explorers heading west into the territories to map uncharted Indian land.

"I beg you, George," I said weakly. "At least wait until spring. See how this great conflict plays out and practice your skills in the meanwhile. Then if men are still needed, you can find a proper replacement at the store and you will be truly ready to make an informed decision." I said this only to stall him in the hopes that the war would not last long, as many predicted. He ignored me entirely except to point out that Charlie, our youngest brother and three years his junior, was more than ready to take over for him, which was probably true. I waited, saving my last, best weapon. "And what of Sarah?"

He looked up. "What *of* her?" he answered blandly, and went back to his plate, but that was the only moment I saw a hint of hesitation in his eyes, a possible trace of dark regret. I had spoken to him many times about wedding the comely, flaxen-haired Sarah, with whom he had been friends since childhood and who adored him completely. He insisted he was not ready, but we all knew how much he cared for her and how patiently she waited for him. Thereafter I held my tongue. If he were not willing to soften for the main object of his affection, nothing I could say would move him. I felt such sorrow at that moment, such impotence. We all finished eating without another word, Mother returning to the table after a short while, and the deep fear that this was the last meal we would share with our dear, fearless George supped with us.

July, 1863
2nd Lieutenant William W. Ranney
Camp Chase Federal P.O.W. Camp
Columbus, Ohio (Confluence of the Scioto and Olentangy rivers)

It was two months before George fell ill when, at a bit of prompting and the strong hand of the flask, I finally spoke of it openly. It was a night as hot as we imagined hell, and there was nothing to do but sit, fanning ourselves between shifts using a copy of the "Harper's Weekly" we passed between us. The whole group of guards lamented being stuck there when others were riding to nearby towns like Zanesville to intercept Morgan's renegade Confederate invaders. I, however, had had enough of warfare.

I based my decision to join as a Second Lieutenant the spring before entirely on a feeling of deep obligation to my country. The Union was struggling in the wake of a chain of Confederate victories, and I could not sit by and do nothing to help turn the tide. And Charlie had turned out to be a fine druggist and expert consultant at the Mercantile. I left the business in good hands. My first engagement after joining the Twenty-sixth Kentucky Infantry and being attached to the Army of the Ohio, Fifth Division, was on the Tennessee River near a place called Pittsburgh Landing. It became known as the Battle of Shiloh. Ten thousand men from each side fell in two days, upwards of 3,500 dead from what we had heard. I was not surprised at the numbers, judging by what I had seen that godforsaken day in April. My injury was not nearly as grievous as George's, as I was lucky enough to get hit narrowly in the foot, but I would always favor my left side and probably always have a slight limp.

As we wiped our brows and drained the watered whiskey, we eventually tired of bashing politicians and our superiors and turned to the all familiar comparison of combat experience. I had remained tight-lipped during these boasting sessions, stating only that I had indeed served under General Buell in General Crittenden's Fifth Division, directly under Colonel William S. Smith, Fourteenth Brigade. Being that I was always somewhat reserved, no one had asked more before. Only a few knew that my own brother was one of our prisoners. No one knew the rest of our story.

Lieutenant Mabry scratched nervously at his beard, which grew in wily tufts of auburn. He was barrel-chested and always had the last word, an Ohioan with the stout stub of his left arm tied to his chest. He turned to me abruptly.

"Tell us about Pittsburgh Landing," he said simply. I shifted in my chair and paused.

"It sits on the Tennessee River," I began, "approximately eighty miles east of Memphis, a marshy hellhole of a docking ..." I was interrupted with such a strong pounding to my back I could not continue.

"Clever bastard," the Lieutenant laughed. "You know we are not interested in geography! You are hiding something. And how is it that each of us does not have something to hide?" Now there was a challenge in his eyes, a scrutiny that asked what I guarded when all the others had spilled their often gut-wrenching stories without so much as a thought. "What is it? Did you get shot in the *heel*?" Lieutenant Mabry accused. The others laughed. The implication of a betrayal like that was more than I could bear, even though I knew it was a gaffe.

"I saw my brother," I said, with a calm that surprised even me. "I faced his regiment directly that second day, across the Hamburg-Savannah Road." I examined my hands in my lap. "There was so much chaos," I continued, "but I saw the guidon for the Sixth Kentucky, borne by what looked to be a boy of twelve or thirteen. Then I knew." I looked back up. Everyone gawked. Lieutenant Mabry had been silenced and he frowned, stroking his beard again. Even if they were not familiar with the details of the Union victory at Shiloh, all now knew that my own brother was a Johnny. "I saw him after my first 'fire' order, helping to carry a wounded officer out of the fray. Then I shouted to charge against their advance, as I had to. I did not see him again, but heard later from our mother that he had almost lost his leg in the fighting that day. And now I have seen him every day for better than two months, even though we have not spoken." I sighed deeply to steady my voice.

"I am sorry, William," Lieutenant Mabry finally said, humbled. "A brother is a brother. No politics can change that." I chafed at his sudden attempt at sympathy.

"That is '*Sir*' to you," I shouted, standing. I never tolerated

Mabry's presence well anyway, and he was still immediately below me in rank. "And not a word of this to another soul," I commanded to the group as I turned to leave. "It would severely compromise our security." It made for an uncomfortable truce.

June 5, 1896
Judge William W. Ranney, Jr.
Confederate Cemetery, former Chase P.O.W. Camp
Columbus, Ohio (Confluence of the Scioto and Olentangy rivers)

It was difficult for me to fathom that nearly thirty-three years had passed since I had left Camp Chase. I had not known at first who "R. R. Bailey" was. His letter had been delivered just three weeks after my transfer. I had actually received a telegram from Mother about a week before, just a few days after George's passing, that we had lost him. Robert Bailey had turned out to be the good-natured, ebony-haired Corporal who had become like a brother to George during his time as a P.O.W. Guards often commented on this pair, who regularly lead games and practiced slight of hand with cards, good enough to trick even the sutler, to the great amusement of their fellow inmates.

I stood in the cemetery, holding Robert's letter again after over thirty years had passed, daring to read the devastating lines for only the second time:

Your brother ... was taken sick on the night of the fourteenth ... but we thought not serious. On Friday the doctor pronounced it the ty-phoid pneumonia and ordered him to be taken to the hospital. There he received the closest attention of Dr. Norris from Owingsborough, who did all in his power to make him comfortable. We still thought that he would recover, but, alas, God had willed it otherwise. At seven o'clock this morning He in His infinite wisdom called him from this world of sin and sorrow to enjoy the rich blessings of a never ending eternity. We have been prisoners together ever since the twentieth of May, and I am happy to say that I not only found him a pleasant and agreeable companion, but a young man that won the respect and esteem of every one who knew him. And while his friends at home mourn his loss, we as brothers in the same cause deeply regret that he has been called away, feeling that we have not only lost a true friend and a good soldier whose place it is hard to fill, but one whose life had it been spared would have made a bright and shining star in society. I also would remark for the consolation of his friends that he was fully prepared for the summons, and quietly resigned himself to his fate. He retained full possession of his senses to the last. Yours with respect, R.R. Bailey.

I had remained in touch with Robert Bailey over all those ensuing years, both of us having lost a brother, and having become brothers ourselves through correspondence, even though we had never met. He recounted with flair and humor all of George's war-time stories that I had never been able to hear, all the ways he had been a hero to his fellow enlisted comrades and a model soldier to his superiors. I recognized, in these frequent installments, the boy I had known so well growing up, the George who was witty and talented and unbelievably brave. I, in turn, sent Robert return post with a successive account of George's boyhood adventures, beginning with his fall from the McIntosh tree and the only time I ever saw him cry past babyhood. This exchange of letters filled a void in me, as I believe it did in Robert.

That original feeling of despair had come once again when I learned of how, many years later, the field where George had been buried, where I had seen so many young men hastily interred in mud and rocks, had been allowed to grow over into nothing more than a bramble patch, the few wooden markers in various states of disrepair and decay. Now, thanks to Mr. William Knauss, a former Union Colonel retired and living in Columbus, and the government grant he was able to procure, the cemetery had been cleaned up and mown. The wooden markers were being replaced with simple stones, and a fence had been constructed to contain the grounds.

So the day had come, and it was a contrarily beautiful morning. I slid the letter back into my pocket and meditated on the sight of my brother's name carved in stone for the first time, feeling the rush of wind that caused my long jacket to flap slowly against my back and the miniature flag next to his marker to wave gently. I felt again as I had so many years before, holding George on that barracks floor. I felt myself a failure as a brother. I felt a deep, searing sadness. I held a hand across my mouth to keep the weeping quiet, breathing as well as I could though my fingers. I begged God, and George, to please forgive my shortsightedness. I tried with little success to stem the tide of my anguish, when I felt a hand on my shoulder. He had come after all.

"William," he said simply, eyes already brimming when I turned to face him.

"Robert," I almost whispered. I reached my hand out to shake his, and he pulled me to him, embracing me briefly. "Here he is." I indicated the stone at our feet.

"Oh, but he is not," he affirmed gently. "He rests with our Lord, and lives in our hearts and our words." By 'words' he was referring to our many years of letters, I understood immediately. I nodded.

"Indeed," I said. I let him stand quietly for a moment, two intimate strangers side-by-side. Instead of feeling a renewed wave of sorrow with George's comrade next to me, the one who had been with him at the end, I felt instead a sudden blanket of peace rest over me.

"He told me about Shiloh," Robert finally said. It had never been mentioned in our letters, but I had no doubt that he knew.

"What did he say?" I asked.

"He said that he heard the gossip as they marched north from Corinth that second day that General Buell's men under Generals Crittenden, Wood, and McCook were fresh to battle and heading to cut them off. He said that a letter from your mother had informed him of your enlistment and then another of your service under Crittenden. He said he looked for you, but the rain and the mayhem of battle made it nearly impossible to see, despite how close you most likely came, his own regiment under Colonel Trabue facing yours in the last. He said he felt you in some way, thought he heard your voice. He knew you were there."

I could not speak and we stood in silence for several minutes. I was numb. Finally, he added, "He was not angry or disappointed in the least, not even in that horrible moment." I could see Robert swipe a hand through his still thick hair and continue. "He knew how well you must have commanded. He spoke highly of your character and was pleased to see you living your convictions. He had nothing but good things to say about his older brother and was never ashamed of having family serving honorably for the North."

We stood for another silent moment, until I could find my voice, knowing that *I*, on the contrary, had felt very ashamed of him at one time.

"I could have helped him here at Chase," I said. "But I did not. I was a damned stubborn fool. *That* is what tortures me." My voice caught in my throat.

"You acted as soon as you knew he was unwell," he insisted. "And if you are talking about buying him favors or bribing someone for extra rations or protection, he did not need it. You know how very clever he was." I could see Robert glance at me. "He had everything he could have gotten one way or the other. And if you had tried to help him, he would have refused it, anyway, I can assure you. He did have his pride." I actually felt a grin tug at the corners of my mouth. Of course he was right. I turned to Robert and embraced him again, for the first time noticing on his lapel the insignia he wore as a Confederate veteran. I had never seen one before. When he saw me looking at it, he reached a hand into his pocket and produced another such button, resting it in the dirt against George's stone.

I felt a weight lifted, and wished I had pursued these topics with Robert in our letters years before, but this was not something that could have been properly conveyed through post. I needed Robert there, next to me. My purgatory had been necessarily served this way.

"The ceremony is about to begin," Robert noted. "Let us go celebrate our service and that of all of these fallen."

"And of all of the fallen in this war," I added. Robert nodded and slid a hand behind my back to guide me toward the front of the field where people were slowly gathering.

A cart had been brought in by a local farmer to use as a speaker's stand, and many neighboring farms had graciously supplied flowers to adorn each and every one of the 2,200 plus graves: dahlias, peonies, roses, and daisies of all colors were being handed out freely from overflowing baskets. Robert and I took as many as our arms could carry to help with the distribution, including going back to George's grave. Both men and women took part, probably close to a hundred in all. Veterans formerly of the blue and the gray shook hands and engaged in brief exchanges, talking in hushed tones in the codes of armies and regiments they had served with. They were calling it "Decoration Day," and from what we heard, it had not come without controversy. There had been threats from throughout Ohio to cease and desist investing in and recognizing the graves of traitors to our great nation, but Mr. Knauss would not be deterred.

The crowd reconvened in front of the makeshift podium, where wooden chairs had been set up. Lightened faces looked out over the newly trimmed yard, framed by a lovely dark iron fence, and a virtual sea of flowers upon which the new stones seemed to float, free. American flags had been planted at every one, adding to the scene. Mr. Knauss, who was almost solely responsible for the restoration of the cemetery, took the stand first after a brief benediction. He described his horror at moving to Columbus and finding the graves of these soldiers completely neglected, and then his crusade to bring a measure of respect back to this place. He also mentioned his intention to have this Decoration Day happen annually into the future.

"My friends and American citizens," he began, "about us and within this enclosure are buried *American citizens* ... who died in a cause which they believed was right." The crowd gave a loud burst of applause. Of course, I could not help but think of the last conversation I had at home with George. We had seen America differently at that time, but we had still seen America as worth fighting for.

Several other speeches came after Mr. Knauss, two by former Union Generals who stressed "malice toward none and charity toward all." A former guard at Chase, a Colonel Cook, gave his recollections of camp life and mentioned a touching story that had been passed on about two brothers, one prisoner and one guard. Robert and I exchanged looks. Finally, "America" was sung by the crowd, led by a Mr. Nolan, which left nary a dry eye. At the conclusion of the ceremony, Robert and I agreed to go into town, to Wagner's Tavern, to share supper and a drink or two before our trains left Union Station later that afternoon, one heading north and one heading south.

One further question still burned in me, something that I had pondered over the years. It was clear that George had remained firmly faithful to the Confederate cause to his last minutes. According to Robert, he had never faltered in his beliefs. I often thought that maybe it had been fever that had induced his ramblings on that fateful night at Camp Chase, but I still could not stop wondering what George insisted I had been "right" about. Over a frosty pint and good feelings, I finally asked Robert if he would know what that could have meant. He thought over it for only a few seconds, and the answer was one word.

"Sarah," he said, looking up to me from his mug. "He told me that last evening in the hospital that he regretted not having married Sarah, that he might miss out on having a wife and children. It really was his only regret." I had to stop to compose myself yet once again.

"So that is the only advice his older brother gave him that was 'right'?" I asked, trying to lighten the mood.

"He told me that you had warned him that he should not wait to marry, and that you had tried to use Sarah as a way to get him to change his mind about enlisting. He had almost changed his mind in the end." Of course, I knew that. "Do you know what became of Sarah?" he asked finally.

"She married our brother, Charlie," I admitted. I could not help but smile at the thought of how happily married they were and the nieces and nephews they had given us. "She had grieved George horribly at first, as we all did, but something made her turn to our quiet, introverted Charlie, and they have made a good life together." At that, I took a long drink of ale. Now Robert smiled.

"Did you know that George wrote Sarah a letter his last night?" he asked. I told him I did not, and he continued. "In it, he told her that he feared his time was short and that he could not bear the thought of her grief over him. He begged her, if he were not to return, that she should become acquainted with Charlie, who was the same age as she and a better match anyway. More settled. More suited for marriage." We both grinned. We were quiet again for a moment, the peripheral noise of the pub allowing a safe lull in conversation. So George himself had brought Sarah and Charlie to each other. As far as I knew, it was the only letter George wrote from the hospital.

"It is a wonder how things come together," I commented, more sober. Robert nodded as he drank. He knew what I meant by it, but I meant it about so many things. Everything, really.

We never made it back to another Decoration Day in Columbus, but I learned years later that a stone arch had been placed inside the gate of the cemetery. On the arch, below the statue of a Confederate private is etched a single word: *Americans*.

"Prisoners of war did not die amid the roar and crash of battle, where soldiers go to death with heart aflame and blood on fire; but, heart-sick and weary, they sank to rest far from home, far from shrill of fife or beat of drum."
William H. Knauss, *The Story of Camp Chase*

Sources:

Information about and quotations from the first official Decoration Day ceremony (etc.) were taken from the book, *The Story of Camp Chase*, by William H. Knauss
Nashville, Tenn., and Dallas, Tex.
Publishing House of the Methodist Episcopal Church, South
Smith & Lamar, Agents
1906

Excerpts from the letter written from R.R. Bailey to William Ranney were taken from the book *Middletown Upper Houses*, by Charles Collard Adams, found on www.ebooksread.com.

Information about the Ranney brothers and their military service, were taken from *The William Ranney Papers*, 1858-1927, 1858-1895 (bulk dates), 1F59M-170, AAP0240LM, Special Collections, University of Kentucky, Lexington, KY.

Heidi Durig Heiby is a stay-at-home mom who works part-time for ZeroChaos/Google, Inc. from her home in Zanesville, Ohio. Her family includes her husband, Fritz, her daughter, Anna, and two zany cats. Heidi's passion is writing short fiction. You can find out more about her at her website, www.heididurigheiby.com.

Chase Cemetery, located on present-day Sullivant Ave. in Columbus, Ohio, holds the graves of more than 2,200 Civil War soldiers. George Ranney's head stone can be found in row 2, number 33, grave 55.

Decoration Day is held at Camp Chase annually.

The Fixer
Jeff Ockerse

1898
COLUMBUS HIDES A MURDER GREAT
By Casey McCarty

T he meeting was set. The help had been discharged hours ago. The stately manor house was hushed, just as one might expect at this hour of night. Those who had been summoned arrived discretely—ducking into the dimly lit rear entrance typically reserved for deliveries and waitstaff. If anyone saw these distinguished gentlemen meeting at the residence of the Home Office Commissioner, the society page would surely be abuzz the next morning. Inside, the gentlemen waited anxiously in the den for one last arrival. Fine gold pocket watches attached to fine gold chains were retrieved from superbly-cut suit coats, examined, and replaced. The Commissioner paced in front of the fireplace, while his associates fidgeted in overstuffed wing-backs, swirling scotch or bourbon, puffing nervously on imported cigars.

"Where the devil is he?"

"Are we still sure we can trust that blasted Irishman?"

"No. You can never *really* trust the Irish. But he is a necessary evil," the Commissioner assured them. "He'll be here."

Outside, the man they knew simply as MacArthur discharged his Hansom wordlessly, with a paltry tip to its geriatric driver. The driver was quick to pull away from this dubious man who seemed to unnerve the horse.

MacArthur straightened his faded topcoat, adjusted his hat, smoothed his trousers, and took one last draw from his cigar. He dropped the butt and ground it intently into the cobblestone beneath his feet. He ascended the few steps of the stoop, rang the bell and tapped his finger against his leg, impatiently awaiting an answer. One of the nervous men from inside cautiously opened the heavy door and invited him in with a silent nod. The other gentlemen froze momentarily when MacArthur entered the den, now smoky from nervous puffing. The Commissioner broke the silence with a labored throat-clearing and a dry reproach.

"You're late, MacArthur."

MacArthur ignored the remark. Instead he sauntered directly to the decanter, poured himself a scotch and swirled it in his snifter a couple times before downing the entire drink in a single gulp. He wiped a dribble of scotch with his coat sleeve and let out a sigh. Finally he turned towards the group and snorted disapprovingly.

"This rich bastard scotch will make you weak, ladies." MacArthur's coarse language punctuated with decidedly lower class Irish overtones made the prim English gentlemen grimace.

"Has it been ... done?" A meager voice piped in from one fidgety gentleman. The others glanced between him and the Commissioner.

"Yeah."

"Care to elaborate, MacArthur?" the Commissioner demanded. "Or have you traveled all the way back here to be coy with us?"

"Maybe next time you'd care to take care of your own dirty deeds?" MacArthur growled in contempt. He glared at each man in turn, but none dared rebuke the insult. "There are no more loose ends. It's over," he confirmed.

"Then we're done here," the Commissioner stated. He nodded to his silent associate, who dug into his breast pocket, retrieving a thick envelope. He tossed the envelope to the Irishman, who snatched it clean out of the air.

"You'll forgive me if I don't trust the English," MacArthur chuckled, as he tore open its flap and fanned through the stack of crisp notes, before plunging the payment deep into his pocket. "Pleasure doin' your dirty work for yeh' as always," MacArthur chimed, stressing his accent again.

MacArthur turned on his heel and strode out the way he had come. He disappeared into the darkness, swallowed up by the roving fog outside. The gentlemen breathed an uneasy sigh of relief and silently prepared to leave; the transaction was over.

* * *

Oliver Randall James was the third-born son of a wealthy Massachusetts shipping magnate who had made his fortune during the Great War between the States. Young Oliver had come of age amid the postwar flourish of Yankee industrialization and his father built an empire from a once- modest enterprise. Oliver was disinterested in the family business, however. He longed to escape the shadow of lofty social expectations that accompanied his family name and privileged status.

His family had his life planned out for him since his childhood, which seemed agreeable just until Oliver became aware of the infinite alternatives that lie just outside the reach of his little world.

When he could tolerate the monotony of finishing school and Governor's balls no longer, he struck out to explore the vast expanses of territory which seemed daringly untamed to a sheltered young New England socialite. He eventually found himself, quite unintentionally, in the middle of Ohio.

Oliver had, on a whim, followed the suggestion of a fellow train passenger to stop in the relatively young but thriving city of Columbus, home to universities, hospitals, newspapers, and even massive asylums and penitentiaries, the largest of the region.

How exciting, asylums! He at once found the concept deeply intriguing. Many letters of protestation followed from his dear mother as her youngest boy reported his relocation to Ohio, then his studies at the heretofore unknown Willoughby Medical College of Columbus, and finally announced his first position as a psychiatrist in some asylum. But by then it was done, and there was nothing to do but tell her society friends that her son had become a doctor and avoid the specifics.

Oliver might have won his appointment to the great Central Ohio Lunatic Asylum without the congratulations of fawning parents, but he brimmed with pride for weeks. He wrote to his mother that the asylum was the largest in the region with over 1,300 (crazy!) patients. His mother shuddered at the thought; indeed taking to her bed for nearly a full week when that letter arrived.

Oliver set up his ill-lit, meager office, which consisted of a few dusty bookshelves, a scratched desk, and a lockable cabinet which could secure supplies and medication. He was unceremoniously deposited at his doorway by a tired-looking nurse whose sagging eyes interrupted her otherwise neat and crisp uniform. To Oliver, however, the tiny room was his, a reward for his years of medical studies, and he couldn't have been happier.

He commenced at once wiping away the months of neglect since its last occupant, tidying and unpacking his small crate of personal effects: some golden-edged reference books which revealed the modern state of psychiatry, a fountain pen set sent to him by his father to acknowledge Oliver's graduation, and a handsome embossed leather journal of remarkable craftsmanship which Oliver had purchased as a treat for himself and with which he intended to capture the crux of his patients' diseases and treatments. Perhaps one day, he mused, he would be able to turn such anecdotes into a reference book of his own.

Four days into his employment with the asylum, Oliver was assigned his very first patient, one Ezra Bennett, aged thirty-eight, who had been an inmate for the last six years and whose most recent doctor had succumbed to bilious fever.

According to his file, Ezra had been admitted to the care of the asylum July 8, 1891, by a cousin, Victor Hardlow, who represented the family's interests. Once admitted, neither this cousin, nor any other family members were ever heard from again. Ezra was in the later stages of syphilis and often delirious. Von Jauregg's cutting edge malaria therapy was applied, with decent results, although the patient suffered more than the usual subsequent malarial fever, and was infrequently lucid after that, the notes read. Of late, the nearly skeletal patient seemed to be recovered from the recurrent fevers, and did indeed seem coherent, although clearly delusional, recounting tales of murder and intrigue to any who would listen. Ezra had since been isolated for fear of upsetting the other patients.

The patient file was spotted with glaring omissions, missing paperwork, and indecipherable scribbles, but Oliver waited excitedly to meet his first psychiatric case. Another tired-looking nurse appeared wordlessly with Ezra and disappeared. Ezra was frighteningly thin, not uncommon in the asylum, but he had retained his bright eyes and dark hair, now peppered with streaks of silver. His face was pock-marked from various infections suffered during his stay, and part of his jaw seemed alarmingly sunken, the result of losing many teeth, probably from malnutrition during his malarial treatment, Oliver theorized.

"Please, have a seat. My name is Doctor Oliver James. It's a pleasure to make your acquaintance. I've been given your records, and you'll be seeing me now for your treatments." Oliver rose, gestured to the uncomfortable-looking wooden chair on the other side of his desk, and waited for Ezra to sit before again taking his own chair.

"Now Mr. Bennett, how have you been feeling? I can't seem to locate any notes on the progress of your treatment after the pyrotherapy. Where did you and Doctor Engles leave off?" Oliver flipped nervously through the chart, then peered across his weathered desk to the silent Ezra. He hoped his patient would speak soon. The silence was decidedly awkward.

Then Ezra's hands gripped the arms of his chair tightly and he leaned forward, staring the young doctor in the eyes with an intensity that made Oliver lean backwards. Ezra exploded: "There ain't been no treatment, as you say, since that one Doc gave me the fever that damn near killed me!" His cockneyed accent had been softened by years of living in the States, but he was clearly not a local. He paused, rocking himself gently in his seat, scratching his forearm.

Without looking up he continued, "I can't take it anymore! Sit 'n my cell, eat slop, yard time, then more slop, and more sittin'. It's maddening, just *maddening*. I keep trying to tell them I ain't sick no more but they don't even *pretend* to listen. Just ... *maddening*." He pounded the arm of his chair and met the surprised gaze of Dr. James, but then averted his eyes. Ezra winced as he rubbed his forehead, which now ached.

Oliver just stared at Ezra. At first he felt as though this must be an example of the delusional outbursts noted in his records. Yet Oliver really could sense genuine frustration, and frustration and insanity were not the same.

Oliver attempted to tease out the purported delusions. "Mr. Bennett, they tell me you've been having some outbursts. They tell me you think you were brought here against your will, as some sort of 'cover up,' to quote you. That's why you're seeing me."

"I *ain't* crazy. I was dragged halfway 'cross the world by the Fixer—that's what we called him. No, I don't know his real name. He stuck me in here to keep the ugly secrets of what they had us do ..." Ezra drew a circle in the air with his finger, "...over there." He began to rock and scratch more vigorously.

"Over where?" Oliver coaxed.

"In London. In Whitechapel. It was awful. Surely you Yanks heard of it here."

"I'm afraid I'm uncertain of which events you speak."

"*Whitechapel*, son! That doesn't mean a thing? The Whitechapel murders!" Ezra looked at Oliver incredulously as though Oliver had told him he hadn't heard of London itself. "That was us," Ezra continued, raising a palm, "And I've had to make my peace with God Almighty for my role in helping those horrors come to pass, but I swear on the souls of my poor children, it was against my will!" Ezra began to break down; he shook his head, slouched uncomfortably in his chair, and covered his face with his hands in shame.

It took awhile before it dawned on Oliver. "You mean the whole Jack the Ripper thing? All those murdered women in London?" Oliver stifled a chuckle. "You're telling me you believe you are Jack the Ripper?" Oliver scribbled furiously. "Fascinating," he muttered.

"There was no 'Jack the Ripper.' The Fixer invented him, and those men at the papers ate it all up," Ezra insisted with a straining voice. "It was all set up by the Fixer. Or by whoever hired him. He told us where, and when, and who." Ezra gulped, and rubbed his eyes as if to erase the image of something horrible. "He told us what to do *after*, and where to put 'em." He hung his head. "That was my job. What happened after. It was just ... so ... awful. The blood, the ..." Ezra trailed off. Eyes and nose running now, he wiped his whole face on his dirty sleeve.

Oliver continued to pen his observations. Despite the obvious upset of his clearly ill patient, Oliver became stuck on the image of Ezra using his sleeve as a handkerchief and the resulting fresh layer of snot. He felt mildly queasy for a moment. Oliver's excitable stomach was one reason he had pursued psychiatry rather than surgery. His mind wandered for a moment to the time he nearly passed out cold when they introduced the cadaver. He was none too concerned about the content of Ezra's delusions, other than to wonder if the symptoms indicated a return of the syphilis.

"I see. Well, I can tell you're very upset by something, Mr. Bennett. But you are not Jack the Ripper. You were brought here by your first cousin, a Mr. Victor Hardlow, who represented your family's interests in taking care of you when they became unable. It says in the notes that you had lived alone with your mother, who had taken ill herself, so Mr. Hardlow came down from Athens to bring you here." Oliver paused for a moment, looking up at Ezra, who did not meet his gaze. Oliver sighed, stopped writing his notes, clasped his hands on the desktop and made a concerted effort to soften his tone.

"Sometimes, patients think they've done something awful to have made their family bring them here. But that is not the case, Mr. Bennett, Ezra, if I may. You just needed more help than your poor mum could manage," Oliver said as sympathetically as possible.

Clearly the delusions were some manifestation of guilt or confusion as to why he had been removed from his home. Perhaps he got his hands on some old newspapers at the time the delusion was formed and he built this fascinating story around those headlines.

"Don't worry; we'll help you get comfortable. It will be alright, Ezra. We'll have you feeling better again!" Oliver tried to sound cheery.

Ezra just looked through him, utterly deflated, and shook his head. "Waste of bloody time," he muttered, and then asked if he could go back to his room. Oliver nodded, made another diminutive statement of encouragement, and walked him to the door.

In the hall, a nurse chatted softly with an orderly, twirling a blonde curl. Oliver bade the nurse to return Ezra to his room, and scribbled his instructions for some sleeping syrup to be given at the evening meal. Oliver went back to his desk, finished his notes, and prepared for the next patient.

At the conclusion of Oliver's duties for the day, he neatly packed up his journal, straightened his desk, pushed in his chair, snuffed out the lamps, and made for the exit—cheerily bidding good evening to all he passed. It was wonderful to be doing such meaningful work! Outside, he drank in the cool summer evening air and the bustle of the city. He walked several blocks, deciding to take in the sights instead of hailing a Hansom.

Farther up High Street sat the M. Trope Saloon, run by a Russian immigrant family. The place was utilitarian in its simplicity: the saloon offered sturdy but unadorned wooden tables and chairs, a few faded photographs peppered the otherwise bare walls, and dusty gas-lit sconces that flickered gently. The dark cherry bar was dull and marred but kept fastidiously clean under the watchful eye of the silent but attentive barkeep. It wasn't particularly cozy, but it was quiet and convenient with a limited but tasteful selection of local brews. It would do as a new haunt, and Oliver never really had such a spot to call his own.

Saddling up to the bar, he waved to the barkeep, ordered a cheap gin and tonic and looked around for a friendly face. A couple seats away sat a fashionably dressed young man with an eager face and sandy blonde curls just barely escaping from under his camel-toned derby. When he caught the glance of Oliver, he nodded and flashed a broad smile. Chipper greetings were exchanged; the young man slid off his stool and came over to Oliver, offering a firm handshake.

"Haven't seen you before! The name's Eagan Hart," volunteered the young man. His bright eyes, genuine smile, and contagious energy made him seem quite the affable fellow.

"Oliver James," the doctor replied. "This is my first time here. Right on my way home from the hospital. Seems nice enough, I could fancy myself a regular!"

"Hospital, eh?"

"The lunatic asylum, actually." Oliver specified.

"Ah! The local Bedlam! Tell me, what's the battiest thing you've seen in there?" Eagan took a swig of lager, wide-eyed, adding, "I could use a good tale!"

COLUMBUS CREATIVE COOPERATIVE

"Well, truthfully, I just started. In fact, saw my first patient today. I'm their newest psychiatrist."

"Congratulations, Doc!" Eagan raised his glass, gulping down a swig before waiting for a return toast. Oliver smiled and returned the gesture.

"How'd it go then?" Eagan asked.

"I think it went fairly well, really."

"Well, that calls for another round," Eagan summoned the barkeep with a nod. Oliver switched to the house brew, and thanked his new friend for the drink. Eagan continued, "So, what brand of crazy did you see today?"

"Surely you don't care to hear the details! What do you do for a living, sport?" Oliver wasn't sure he should be talking about his patients at the pub.

"Oh, of course I want the details, I'm a reporter! For *The Evening Dispatch*. I'm pretty new in town myself, so I'm not getting the real dirt yet, but once I make my bones ..." he grinned, raising his glass as he trailed off.

The two continued their chat. Young men of about the same age, having both struck out for a new life far from the homes of their youth, a bit renegade in their chosen professions, they had plenty in common. As the evening hours slipped by, Oliver eventually shared the story of how his first patient believed himself to be the famed Jack the Ripper. Eagan, through his gentle prodding was able to draw out as many details as his increasingly inebriated curiosity desired.

The seeds of a meaningful friendship were planted by the time Eagan and Oliver eventually decided to retire, and they vowed to meet at "their" pub again soon.

* * *

Weeks passed, and sessions with Ezra grew darker as the days grew shorter and summer acquiesced to fall.

Oliver encouraged Ezra in the telling of his story, hoping the pressure to provide intimate details would force him to acknowledge his delusion.

"Tell me again, who paid you to do these deeds?" Oliver inquired in a voice of kind sincerity, pen poised to capture the response in his leather notebook, which now showed some wear.

"Already told ya' Doc. I don' know the names. The Fixer, that's what we called him, made sure we didn't know their names. But I can tell ya' they were important, with money a'plenty, that's for sure."

"Political leaders?"

"If I had to guess. They had their reasons for what we did and when."

"Such as … "

"Well, this anarchist fellow, set up shop in the Jewish neighborhood, started something like 'The Worker's Educational Club,' or some such thing. But really he was gettin' everyone worked up about unions an' worker's rights and all that." Ezra looked towards the floor, shaking his head, inhaling deeply on the cigarette Oliver had provided him. "Then next thing you know, we get the order to leave a body in the yard of that place." Another drag. "You know, to shut him up. Police and the paper men started thinkin' maybe he had something to do with all these murders, see? Then he didn't have so much time to be causing all that trouble."

Oliver continued to press for details, but Ezra could go on at great lengths—never faltering even when Oliver tried misdirection or pretended he'd forgotten specifics Ezra told him weeks prior.

At another session Ezra described how he came to be recruited, along with the others. He had been increasingly ill, and knew he would leave only debt to his wife and three children. In an alley on the way home from a grueling shift at the meat market, he was offered a handsome figure for a job that would be temporary in nature but would require the utmost secrecy. If he did as he was told, there would be plenty of money for his family, but if he told anyone anything, the whole lot of them would lose their lives. He did as he was told. The others petitioned for the crew had their own weaknesses—gambling debts, facing penitentiary time—and a couple of the men seemed to just plain enjoy the violence.

The job had been fairly straightforward. He was to use his skills as a butcher to do things to bodies that were brought to him. The specifics Ezra preferred not to share. Someone else would then take the bodies elsewhere, just as someone had brought them to him in the boiler room of a dingy foundry long after workers had gone.

But as Ezra's illness had progressed, he sometimes lost control of his tongue and had been observed to utter bits and pieces of the horrid acts and soon after, he was spirited away by the Fixer. He reported he had drifted in and out of febrile consciousness on voyage to America. That was the last he had seen his wife and children in London.

* * *

The sessions took their toll on the young doctor, and the after-work meetings with Eagan at the pub became more frequent. Oliver rubbed his temples as his head hung over a tall lager at Trope's. He had never been so relieved to see Eagan's face as the ambitious young reporter ducked into the pub, collar turned up against the wind and a light rain.

"You look rough, mate," Eagan observed as he removed his coat and hat, hanging them nearby. "Bad day at the farm?"

Oliver snorted. "I just can't wrap my head around this case." He waited for Eagan to settle into the seat next to him before continuing. "You recall my 'Ripper' patient?"

"Yeah, sure," Eagan nodded, waving to the barkeep for his usual. He scooted his chair closer to Oliver's and leaned in intently. A subtle smile parted his lips.

"Well I just don't know. I've been trying for weeks to catch him on something, to trip him up. I've been asking him to repeat very specific things, answer all these questions, and then answer them again. I thought his story would break down, and we'd have some kind of breakthrough." Oliver looked to his friend with an expression that begged for consolation.

"But ..." Eagan prompted, nearing the edge of his seat. Of all Oliver's tales of the asylum's colorful patients, the Ripper character was obviously his favorite.

Oliver dreaded hearing the words come out of his mouth even as he said them. "I just don't know." He dragged his admission out longer with another drink, and then one more for good measure. "It's just that, he's unshakeable. He can recall all of these things, time after time, and he seems so ... genuine." Oliver kept his gaze averted, afraid his friend would erupt into hysterical laughter at him.

"So, you're thinking he might actually be telling the truth?" Eagan was almost salivating. "You know," he said in a low, hushed tone, "the paper has contacts with the London papers, and with the Home Office itself. Wouldn't hurt to send out a few letters of inquiry. Just to put your mind at ease."

Oliver nodded. "Sure. Just so we know. Probably nothing, but ..." he trailed off with a shrug.

Eagan slapped his melancholy friend on the shoulder, "Buck up, mate! We'll have some answers soon enough."

* * *

A month passed. Eagan tried to busy himself with his local beats but thumbed through his mail delivery excitedly each day. Oliver seemed more relaxed, with an end to the great mystery in sight. The longer it took for Eagan's inquiries to be returned, the more likely there was nothing to this whole scheme. Meanwhile he gently steered the interviews with Ezra toward the mundane: how he passed the hours, was he social with any of the others, did he catch the cheery traveling show the administrators had arranged?

The dispatching of the letters gave them permission to forget, however superficially, the wretched plot.

* * *

As the letters reached their London destinations, chilled nights foretold the harsh winter to come. An early snow had turned to cold, dirty rain which streaked the city's coal ash layer down the sides of every building and the dreariness was reflected in the expression of all who had to trudge the muddy streets to their destinations.

The inquiries made their ways across many desks, some landing no farther than the waste bin, with the snicker of lower editors. In at least one instance, another eager lackey had rescued it, on the off chance there could be a lead. Telegraphs were sent. A couple meetings requested. Largely the inquiries of some American pursuing a wild goose chase received little sincere attention, but when one landed upon a certain desk in the Home Office, it caused nothing short of panic.

A courier was summoned to deliver a hastily penned note to the Commissioner: *Inquiries circulating with details of WC from American in Ohio. Appointment urgently required.*

The recipient of that message was known to be stoic, if not stern, at all times, but even his heart skipped a beat with that news. He forced a couple slow breaths before issuing a reply to the courier: *Meeting ill advised. Remain calm. Will bring to his attention immediately.* To whose attention did not require explanation.

* * *

Three mornings later, the Commissioner sat, nose buried in the *London Times,* as the train rocked gently. By his dress and manner, it was obvious he was a gentleman of impressive standing, but clear out in Cromwell it was unlikely any of the early morning passengers would recognize him. He appeared almost relaxed with the ride through the countryside of sloping hills, low stone walls and huddled sheep. It would have been a pleasant escape from his daily business was it not for the purpose of the trip.

As the train lurched toward the next station, he grew visibly uneasy. No longer able to concentrate on the news, he shifted in his seat, and wiped sweaty palms on his handkerchief. An Irishman boarded the train and walked towards the back of the car. His jacket and cap suggested he was working class, and he smelled of bourbon, even at the early hour. He seemed gruff even in silence, his brows fixed in a scowl, his mustache unkempt. He settled casually next to the gentleman and they exchanged the courtesies of strangers.

After a brief silence, the Commissioner removed an envelope from his breast pocket and slid it discreetly to the other.

"You'll find a letter. A reporter in Ohio seems to have discovered our old friend, the butcher. It seems his illness has resolved, and he has been quite talkative." The Commissioner paused. He leaned in closer to the Irishman. "You assured us there would be no … surprises down the road, MacArthur. That was why we agreed to send him away. At considerable expense, I might add."

MacArthur glared at the Commissioner—his fists clenched, knuckles popping audibly. He stared directly into the Commissioner's eyes, his grinding teeth flexing his wide jaws. His eyes flashed a hostility so evident the Commissioner shrank away from him, pushing his shoulder as far towards the window as possible, and both men sat in silence as if reflecting on how they arrived at this moment.

The fateful summer of 1888 in Whitechapel, London, a prostitute had been found dead in the streets, a nameless victim of a random act of violence. The stir it made in the papers, however, brought several days of peace and quiet to the Commissioner's office, which had recently been implicated in several incidents of corruption and incompetence.

"What we could really use is another dead hooker!" the deputy Commissioner had chuckled as they arrived at the office late one night to rid the Commissioner's office of incriminating papers. The Commissioner took the crude joke as a solution to their problems, however, and MacArthur was hired.

One more body gave them enough time to dispose of and re-write records before an official investigation could be launched. Another body and the group of protestors that gathered each evening outside his office became just a note on page two. It was just too easy.

"They're throwaways anyway," the Commissioner had said of the women who would be the victims. Drunkards, prostitutes, and other ladies of ill repute that no one would miss—there would be no grieving families sobbing for photographers, just the media frenzy of a serial killer on the loose. No formal investigation ever came to pass in the midst of the Whitechapel mayhem, and the Commissioner grew addicted to the results. Union-organizing anarchist disrupting his foundry-owner friend? A body appeared in his yard and took care of the problem.

But when the gruesome jobs were done, the Commissioner had wanted to renege on the payment and security he promised to the crew. "Why not just take care of the loose ends right now? Save us a few pounds, and the worry of loose lips?" the Commissioner casually asked MacArthur as the summer came to an end.

"I will not!" MacArthur snapped. "You promised these men payment for their deeds—you certainly couldn't have done this on your own." MacArthur took out a hunting knife he always kept on hand, and twirled it menacingly—digging the tip into the Commissioner's desk. "You don't pay a man, that's bad business. And folks who send bad business my way don't have the chance to make that mistake twice." With money in hand, MacArthur grinned just slightly as he left the Commissioner trying to drink his Scotch with shaking hands.

MacArthur offered a friendly warning to the crew that they take their money and the next train out of London. Ezra was a family man, however. He didn't want to just disappear, and then he got sicker, and his loose tongue drew attention to him once again. MacArthur again refused to murder him, but agreed to deposit Ezra as far away as his vast network of contacts reached—a cousin, an orderly at a large asylum knew just the place.

The Commissioner finally broke the tense silence. "Are you drunk, you idiot? Did you hear what I told you?"

"English bastard," MacArthur fumed in a low, deep voice, "you rich and powerful types always think of everyone as tools at your disposal—things to use an' discard as it pleases you. You know I could snap your neck right here an' now and nobody would lift a li'l finger to stop me?"

The Commissioner looked around the train car anxiously. There were only a couple other passengers up front. MacArthur heaved a sigh and sat back in his seat. "Besides, he's been locked away for what, six years? Do you really think he's credible at this point? Tell me, who is he going to convince?"

The Commissioner bristled at the Irishman's dismissal. "Credible enough a reporter has been flooding half of London with his inquiries. I—we—want you to take care of this."

"It's goin' to have a price."

"Doesn't it always? Take care of it this time. There is enough for your travel, and then some," the gentleman nodded towards the envelope. "Let us know when it has been done. You'll have the rest then."

MacArthur nodded as he rose, tipping his hat in an exaggerated manner. The Commissioner rolled his eyes, adjusted his spectacles, checked his pocket watch, and returned to his paper. He waited for MacArthur to turn his back before he pulled out his handkerchief and dabbed his forehead with trembling hands. MacArthur passed into the following car and waited for the next stop.

* * *

Oliver and Eagan planned to meet at Trope's as usual one particularly frigid night. It was the middle of December, and despite the poor weather, the approaching holidays imbued the atmosphere with a sort of conviviality amongst fellow pedestrians. As the two men removed their overcoats and scarves and settled in at the bar, the tone of their candid chatter was light and jovial, in part because of the season's festivities and partly because they no longer mentioned the letters, which had largely gone unanswered.

Eagan had received only two replies—one terse reproach for his gullibility and another, more gentle assurance that all reputable leads had been given due diligence by the finest of Her Majesty's investigative minds.

Oliver, by contrast, had been quite relieved. He slept better knowing the man had not been wrongly confined to the asylum. Even more comforting was that such a plot surrounding the most notorious unsolved serial murder was not, in fact, his responsibility to expose. Oliver had confronted Ezra with the findings, and the topic of Whitechapel and its hidden horrors was not again breached. Oliver encouraged Ezra to find meaningful work or hobbies—Ezra went through the motions with a diffuse indifference which was regarded as "significant improvement of symptomology."

At Trope's, Eagan spoke of his current assignments and proudly recalled his recent exposé on Dr. Samuel Brubaker Hartman, yes, *the* Dr. Hartman of Peruna Elixir fame. Oliver mentioned his successes with new patients and amusing anecdotes of his elderly wards perpetually accusing orderlies of thieving off with their prized knick-knacks in the night. Drinks and hearty laughter flowed freely.

They did not notice the somewhat disheveled-looking man alone at a table in the rear. The flickering shadow of a nearby sconce covered half his face as he drank alone, pipe in hand. He had the distant expression of a man who could often be found smoking and drinking alone.

Behind the stoic face was a sinister plan, however. It had taken only a tidbit of cash and a complement to entice a homely nurse to point out one Doctor Oliver James. It was even easier to follow the oblivious young man to his favorite pub where he would meet his journalist friend.

The barkeep, who had been eyeing the weather, was restless. It had been snowing for some time, though his patrons were unaware. "It's snowing steady now, boys. Might think of headin' home before the drivers retire for the night."

"Well mate," Eagan sighed, clapping Oliver on the back, unsteadily sliding off his bar stool, "we best be off then, I suppose." Oliver nodded.

Outside, the icy wind blew stinging snow in their faces as they peered up and down a desolate High Street. "We'll never find a driver at this hour in this mess," Oliver told his friend. "You best just stay with me tonight. We can make it on foot, and maybe not catch our deaths if we hurry!"

Eagan nodded in agreement. They cinched their coats, tugged their hats as far over their ears as possible and tied their scarves around their face until only a slit was left through which to see. Fists deep in pockets, the two jogged as fast as the slick streets and their inebriated state allowed. Through their heavy breathing, curses and laughter, the two remained unaware of their silent observer, who was not too far—or too near—behind.

At Oliver's door, he fumbled awkwardly for the key, and cursed again that the nearest streetlamp had been snuffed out by the wind. The surrounding narrow brick town-homes were pitch black inside as well. Finally the heavy wooden door opened and the two spilled inside. Oliver at once turned up the gas heaters and started a fire in the small fireplace. Soggy coats, scarves and hats were peeled off and hung.

Once reasonably dry, Eagan sat in a faded wing-back he pulled closer to the fire while Oliver prepared some warm brandy. He handed Eagan a cup and pulled up a wooden rocker to the fire as well, wrapping himself in a quilt his mother had sent for Christmas. Eagan pulled a blanket over his lap, wrapping his hands around the warm cup. The two quietly chatted, but with plenty of alcohol in their blood and the exertion of battling the elements, they were soon fast asleep in their chairs, basking in the warmth of the crackling fire.

Later that night, neighbors awoke to the sounds of two small explosions and shattered glass. The men of the houses, still in their night clothes, poured out of surrounding homes to see the modest two-story of Dr. James fully ablaze, thick smoke billowing out windows into the night sky, the snow-covered ground covered in glass shards. Inside the conflagration, more pops, booms, and hisses shied even the bravest bystander from approaching the unstable dwelling.

The neighbors' wives led bundled children and armfuls of special belongings to friends' homes across the street, in case the fire should spread to their own residence. Witnesses hoped aloud the Doctor had not been home, and a couple ventured around the back to see if anyone had escaped. By the time the fire brigade horses had made it through the snow, little remained of the James house.

The following morning the *Dispatch* reported the devastating fire at the residence of Doctor Oliver James, which had exploded into flames likely due to an undetected gas leak. Sadly, it was not a particularly uncommon event during the long Ohio winters, and the *Dispatch* reminded its readers to exercise all proper precautions this season. The *Dispatch* continued, with the utmost condolences, that it was believed that one of their own junior reporters, Eagan Hart, had also perished in the fire, according to a neighbor who observed the friends arriving home late in the night. So concluded a police investigation, though curiously, no remains of any body had actually been found among the remnants of the James house.

Two days later, a freshly clean-shaven and kindly-appearing gentleman with the faintest hint of an Irish accent appeared at the admissions desk at the Asylum with the good news that their patient, Ezra Bennett, could be cared for in his family home again. The receptionist summoned Dr. Harris, the medical chief of staff on duty, who examined Ezra's file, concluded the patient had no dangerous condition which would necessitate confinement, and signed the discharge slip releasing

Ezra to the care of his relative, a Mr. Victor Hardlow. The two shook hands, and Dr. Harris ordered a nurse and an orderly to go get the patient packed up and changed into regular clothes. Mr. Hardlow took a seat in the waiting area, graciously accepting a cup of tea from the secretary, and made pleasant small talk.

Ezra sat dumbfounded, mouth agape, head tilted when the nurse announced that he would at last be going home. The nurse smiled warmly and placed a neatly folded pile of clothes next to him on the bed. She touched his shoulder and repeated the news. Ezra shook himself aware, stood, and giddily answered, "Sure, ma'am. Whatever you say."

He dressed quickly, ran a comb through his brittle hair, and checked himself several times in a cracked hand mirror. He packed his few possessions in a satchel the nurse provided—a few letters he had penned to his wife which remained unsent, some watercolor sketches he had painted in the courtyard one spring. He took one last look around the room and nodded to the nurse that he was ready. They escorted him down the hall. He looked around the hallway at the patients, nurses and orderlies that dotted the aisle. All were going about their regular, rigid routines. Ezra smiled ever so slightly as they walked closer to the exit.

Ezra followed the nurse and the doctor through a set of double doors, followed by a silent orderly. As the doors swung open, he was nearly blinded by the bright sunlight that streamed in from the two-story-tall atrium windows. He squinted as the light bounced off the polished checkered marble floor, and vaguely made out the figure that rose upon seeing the party.

"Cousin!" the figure boomed in a merry tone. "It is truly wonderful to see your face again!" Mr. Hardlow walked towards Ezra, arms open wide. As Ezra made out the man's face, he stopped dead in his tracks, his heart skipped a beat, and his lungs failed to inhale. His arms flailed and he back-peddled for the doors but ran promptly into the barrel-chested orderly, who instinctively grabbed Ezra and held him in a bear hug which only increased Ezra's opposition, kicking and writhing in an effort to wriggle from the orderly's snare.

Ezra screamed out: "No! No! Don't let him get me! You can't let him get me!"

This wild display had caught the staff completely off guard, and now they panicked as they tried to get Ezra under control.

"What is it, Ezra? What is the meaning of this?" the doctor demanded. The nurse tried to reassure Ezra, "I know leaving here can be scary, but it will be better for you to be amongst family!"

"That man is a murderer! He is *not* my family! He will *kill* me, don't you understand? KILL me!"

The doctor and nurse exchanged exasperated glances. "Stop this. Stop this at once. This is just part of your sickness," the doctor scolded. "No! No! Ask Doctor James! He knows all about it. Where is Doctor James? Doctor James!" Ezra bellowed frantically. He had since been brought to his knees by the orderly who looked to the doctor for instructions.

"I'm afraid Doctor James passed away earlier this week. There was an accident at his home," answered the nurse regretfully.

Upon hearing that news, Ezra locked eyes with the man he knew only as the Fixer back in London. Hardlow grinned wryly, a silent exchange no one else saw.

Ezra grew weaker. He continued to push against the orderly, but his arms and legs dangled heavily between each attempt. Ezra breathlessly puffed incoherent snippets, "Whitechapel ... murderer ... Ripper ... " to which the nurse gave a puzzled look towards the doctor.

"It's part of his ongoing delusion," Dr. Harris answered her unspoken question. "Look here Mr. Bennett ... oh *never mind.* Nurse, get me ten milliliters paraldehyde," the doctor instructed as another orderly appeared with a wheel chair. Ezra's arms and legs were strapped to the chair, and he was wheeled out of sight.

The doctor straightened his white coat and turned toward Mr. Hardlow. "He has this ongoing delusion. Most of the time he's fine; surely the stress of this unexpected discharge has set him off again," the doctor apologized. "We'll just give him something to help him relax and in a few minutes, he'll be composed again. He should give you no trouble on the train home, but it may take ... there may be an adjustment period, you understand," Dr. Harris advised.

"Seein' family again will bring him back to us, I'm a'sure of it," Mr. Hardlow said with a convincing smile.

One-half hour later, an orderly wheeled a virtually limp Ezra through those double doors once more. Ezra's head tilted back awkwardly. His mouth gaped open and shut slightly like a fish too long out of water—no longer able to flop, a mere twinge and flutter from death.

The nurse gently covered him with a blanket, and told Mr. Hardlow it wouldn't be missed as the orderly lifted Ezra into the back of a Hansom; Mr. Hardlow bade farewell as he slid in next to him. And away they rode down the brick driveway, the Hansom gently rocking as they pulled farther away from the great marble walls of the asylum.

Dr. Harris broke the silence as the nurse and orderly returned to the atrium, "Nurse, would you help me go through Dr. James' office?"

"Certainly, Doctor," she replied courteously. "It's such as shame about Doctor James, isn't it?"

"Indeed."

In the office of the late Doctor James, Dr. Harris set about collecting patient records and anything else that would need to be passed along to another psychiatrist, while the nurse collected a few personal effects.

"What of his things, Dr. Harris? Will we be sending these to relatives?"

"I believe his family is back East. Just put his personals in a separate carton for now. We can put them in the store room until we receive instructions."

She nodded. "What a handsome diary," she muttered to herself as she gently placed a well-loved leather journal into the carton among a few gilt-edged reference books and set of fountain pens.

Casey McCarty is the creative director of Sine Metu Designs, a family-owned business specializing in decorative and fine arts found online and in Columbus boutiques. She is involved in the local arts community and buy-local movement. Casey is a Columbus resident, with her husband and two daughters. Find out more at www.sinemetudesigns.blogspot.com.

The Central Ohio Lunatic Asylum, in its first incarnation on Broad Street, burned to the ground in 1868, killing several inmates. A new asylum was constructed on 300 acres of land donated by William Sullivant in the Hilltop area, and the facility reopened in 1877. Today, the site is home to the Bureau of Motor Vehicles and Department of Transportation buildings, although the cemetery still remains.

THE FRANKLINTON FLOOD, 1913
West Town Street, Columbus, Ohio
Provided by the Columbus Metropolitan Library

1913
HOPE ALSO RISES
By Deborah Cheever Cottle

The year 1913 made us all take notice, right from the start. January and February were bitterly cold, with blizzards that howled for days. Some of those blizzards pulled ice storms behind them, leaving a crystal layer over the snow and making it impossible to walk the streets of Columbus without slipping. When March came in like a lamb, we all rejoiced.

No one could remember a March that had been so warm and gentle. Trees budded weeks ahead of time, and even the lilacs made an early appearance. "We've skipped right over spring and gone straight to summer," neighbors said by way of greeting. Of course, we all knew it would never last. What we didn't know was how bad it would get.

Good Friday was a gray and dreary day with non-stop rain pouring from the sky.

Rain continued to beat a sad lullaby against the roof as I fell asleep that night, but by morning, the sound had stopped. Leaping from bed, I dressed quickly in my skirt and blouse and headed downstairs.

For years I had been too old for Easter egg hunts, but had pretended I wasn't and Mama pretended it, too. Now that I was thirteen, the pretending would stop and I would be helping Mama set up the fun for the young ones. It was a sure sign I was growing up.

Mama gave me her wicker basket and I set off for the grocery to buy eggs and a red onion. I breathed deeply of the freshly washed air and carefully stepped around the puddles in the street. The day was already warm and alive with the beauty of spring. My mind danced with happiness, and if I hadn't reminded myself that I was now a young lady I would have skipped my way to the store.

Mama already had a pan of water boiling when I returned. She showed me how to add eggs along with a little vinegar and the skins of the red onion. When the eggs were cooked, the fragile shells would be a brownish shade of red.

From time to time we had to shoo my little brothers out of the kitchen. Two-year-old Micah was too young to pay attention to what we were doing at the stove, but five-year-old Eli just might make the connection between the eggs in the red water and those that would mysteriously appear around the house tomorrow morning.

As I fished the dyed eggs from the cooking water and layered them carefully in Mama's special crock, Mama set a second pot of water to boil. "I need you to go and bring me some dandelion greens," she said. Dandelion greens, she explained, were the secret to Easter eggs the color of grass and new leaves.

"I thought green was a Christmas color," I replied.

Mama tapped my nose with her finger and smiled. "Green is the color of hope. Each spring we hope for health and happiness."

I took a kitchen knife and went outside, hoping not for health and happiness, but for Easter candy. Even though I was too old for the Easter Bunny story, I hoped that Mama would have a candy egg for me, the kind that was sky blue like a robin's egg, with tiny white speckles.

The small square of yard in front of the house had a few thin patches of grass, but most of the green came from weeds. The ground squished under my feet and everywhere there were puddles like little lakes. It was a sign that the ground had already taken in more water than it could hold, a fact that didn't really register in my mind. I was too busy trying to keep my skirt out of the mud as I sawed off the dandelion leaves.

I left my shoes at the door when I came back inside. Mama helped me dunk the dandelion greens up and down in a bowl of water as if we were washing a pair of Papa's work overalls from the livery stable. When a layer of dirt had settled at the bottom, we dropped the greens and the remaining eggs into the boiling water and watched as the white shells turned a delicate emerald color.

The rest of that day seemed to fly by with the baking of a special apple cake for tomorrow's breakfast and the readying of our Sunday clothes for Easter services. There hadn't been money enough for a new Easter outfit for me this year, but Mama had let out the hem of last year's dress and added red trim around the placket. She had also wrapped the wide brim of my Easter bonnet with tulle and pink ribbon rosettes, which made it especially beautiful. The boys would be wearing their usual Sunday best, but their clothes still needed to be pressed and, as always, there were buttons that needed replacing and torn seams to mend.

Papa came home early that afternoon, sending Eli and Micah running to hug his legs and wait for turns to be tossed into the air. At Papa's suggestion, we all went outside for a walk. It was even warmer than it had been that morning, the air pressing full and heavy against us. Papa said it was the sun trying to soak up all the rain that had fallen. When we passed a beautiful lilac bush, Papa plucked off a sprig of blooms and tucked it behind Mama's ear. She smiled and blushed and then scooped Micah up into her arms as we headed for home.

Before Mama tucked the boys into bed for the night, she gave them each a clean shirt. Eli took his shirt and formed it into a small bundle on the kitchen floor, pushing the middle down to make a tiny circle. Micah followed Eli's lead until there were two small nests where the Easter Bunny would leave a special treat. As Mama led the boys to their bedroom, she turned and gave me a nod. I took two eggs from the crock and gently laid one in each of the boys' nests. I then started to hide the rest of the eggs around the house for tomorrow's hunt.

Papa took a green egg from the crock and disappeared outside. I ran to the window to see where he was going, but he waved me away. Minutes later he returned and, with a teasing grin, announced, "That one, Pumpkin, is for you."

When Mama returned from upstairs she had a smile on her face. She added a candy egg to each of the nests and then turned and held out a sky blue egg to me. She had another egg for Papa and, I was happy to see, she also had a yellow egg for herself. "I think the Easter Bunny expects us to eat these eggs right now," she said, and we each took a small nibble of our treat.

The crunchy outer covering cracked beneath my teeth, and the sweet sugar filling melted like magic in my mouth. I had never felt as grown-up as I did at that moment, sharing an Easter treat with my parents. I wondered if life would always be this good. Looking back, I can see how naïve I was. I had yet to discover that everything can change in an instant.

* * *

I woke to the whisper of raindrops on the roof. When I went downstairs, I saw that Mama had already set two umbrellas by the door for our walk across the Broad Street Bridge to Trinity Church. Within seconds the boys were down the stairs and squealing with delight when they saw their nests. Mama let them eat their candy eggs before breakfast, and then they set off on their search for the hidden eggs. Micah trailed along behind Eli, clapping his hands each time Eli found an egg, as if it were his own discovery. I could tell by the sound of the rain that my own hunt outside would have to wait.

When all the eggs had been collected, Eli and I peeled them and put an egg in each of the eggcups that stood by our plates at the table. We all held hands as Papa gave a special prayer of thanks and praise on this Easter day and then Mama served up thick slabs of the apple cake, almost as good as a candy egg.

Suddenly a clap of thunder, louder than anything I had ever heard, shook the house. We all jumped, and Micah started to cry. Torrents of rain lashed the roof and windows.

While Mama tried to sooth Micah, Papa and I headed outside to stand on the covered wooden stoop. Thick, damp air wrapped around us, making it hard to breath. Water came down in sheets, so hard we could not see the houses across the street. From time to time, lightning parted the skies and thunder rumbled. In the east, where Easter sunrise should have been painting the sky, strange purple clouds rolled and tumbled against each other.

Papa and I turned as one and headed back inside. Papa closed the door, leaning his weight against it as if keeping out something evil. "We're going to have our own Easter services, right here," he said. I felt my heart sink a little, but I knew he was right. There was no umbrella large enough to protect us from that downpour.

Mama got the large family Bible from its place on the shelf. She opened it carefully, turning each of the thin, crackly pages slowly and gently. When she found the right spot, she began to read the Easter story. Eli stood on one side of her and Micah on the other. From time to time, Mama reached up and hugged them just a little bit closer.

After the story, Mama led us all in singing, her voice soft and sweet as an angel's. When we got to the song "Onward Christian Soldiers," we all smiled as Eli and Micah began to march around the room. As if on cue, thunder exploded and sent the boys scurrying back to Mama's side. Strangely, the thunder did not stop.

For the rest of the day, there was a constant rumble of thunder, as if Columbus was under siege from enemy cannon fire. We had never heard anything like it, and never have again. By the time night rolled around, everyone was nearly mad from the sound of it. We never imagined there were far worse sounds to come.

* * *

The rain continued to pour without let-up through the night. It was still pouring Monday morning. I ran to the window when I got up. Weak morning light shone on the horizon, and I could see that our house had become an island. The yard had disappeared underwater and that same lake had swallowed up the street and the yards on the other side.

When I went downstairs, Papa was holding his shoes in his hands. His socks peeked out from the pocket on the bib of his overalls and the pant legs were rolled up past his knees.

"No school for you today, Pumpkin," he said cheerfully, but in his eyes I saw a worry that was not like Papa at all. "You help your Mama with the boys, okay?" I nodded, feeling a thread of panic weave its way through the excitement of a day off from school.

The sound of the rain intensified as Papa opened the door. "We need to keep an eye on that river," he said, tipping his head upward towards Mama. She nodded and then Papa was off to work, off to take care of the horses at the livery. I watched while rain poured off his umbrella as he waded through water past his ankles.

I helped Mama with the boys that day, teaching Eli to play jacks while at the same time keeping the tiny jacks out of Micah's hands. I told the boys stories and rocked Micah to sleep at nap time. And I kept an eye on the river, even though that assignment was not meant for me.

I imagine that today, buildings would block the view, but in those days I could see a sliver of the Scioto River if I stood at the upstairs window and looked to the north. The river looked angry and swollen. I was looking out the window when I saw Papa coming home from work, even though it was only noon. Water was up to his knees as he walked and the bottom rolls of his pant legs were wet.

"I'll go back later tonight to check on the horses again," Papa said, "but there's no point my spending the afternoon at the barn. It's not safe to have the carriages or horses out in this weather."

After a quick lunch, Papa leaned back in his chair, catching Mama around the waist as she went past and pulling her onto his lap. "You know, I never did get to see my girls in their Easter finery yesterday," he said. "I think it's about time for an Easter Parade."

Mama laughed and kissed the top of Papa's head. "Carrie Ann might want to get dressed up, but I don't have a new outfit to show. Last year's clothes are still just fine."

Papa caught my eye and I had to put my hands over my mouth to keep the words from tumbling out. In all of yesterday's excitement, I had completely forgotten the surprise we had for Mama. I ran to my room and climbed up on a stool so I could reach the back of my closet shelf. There, hidden behind a pile of blankets, was Mama's hat with the two beautiful Mephisto feathers that Papa had ordered special from F&R Lazarus. While Mama was at her ladies' group at church last week, I had sewn the feathers, rising like two scarlet plumes, to the back of her hat.

I watched Mama's mouth fall with surprise when I brought the hat out and laid it on the table in front of her. "It's beautiful," she whispered.

"Put it on," Papa encouraged, and we all took up the chant. Mama blushed with pleasure and carefully set the hat in place. She stood and gave a little twirl that ended with a curtsey and a round of applause from us all.

"You really shouldn't have," Mama declared, but the look on her face said that she was ever so glad that we had. I thought of the pictures we had seen in the paper of ladies boarding the steamship *Titanic*—it was hard to believe it had been almost a year ago. So many of them had been wearing hats just like Mama's. I was sure that most of those hats had been lost at sea, but fortunately, Mama's hat would stay safe and dry until next Sunday when she wore it to church. It would be as if our rainy Easter had never happened at all.

* * *

I slept fitfully that night. The wind had intensified, shaking my bedroom windows and howling under the eaves like a wild animal. When I opened my eyes Tuesday morning, I could hear the rain heavy and endless, hitting the roof in a continuous downpour. I pulled my pillow over my head and tried to block out the sound.

It was no use. I could hear Mama and Papa speaking in whispers in the kitchen. I slipped out of bed and went to join them. When they saw me, the whispering stopped but they weren't able to hide the frightened look in their eyes.

"Still raining," Papa announced, as if I didn't know. He was putting on his wool coat and his knit hat. "It got cold again overnight."

Papa's bare foot splashed as he stepped onto the stoop and he quickly closed the door behind him, not even taking the time to say good-bye.

Mama's hand was a comfort on my shoulder as we stood together at the window and watched Papa push against the wind and water as he headed out to check on the horses. I didn't know that I might never see him again. I wondered why Mama had tears in her eyes.

As the morning wore on, that window became my portal to the world. The water was rising higher and higher. It now covered the entire stoop and rippled across the front yard.

A horse, belly deep in water, struggled to pull a wagon as it traveled past our house down Starling Street. I watched in disbelief as it fell and fought to get upright. The wagon driver jumped down just before the entire wagon tipped sideways. It took five men, along with the driver, to get the whole mess straightened right again.

From time to time I went upstairs to keep an eye on the river. Water spread like a creeping vine under everything, continuously stretching into the distance. When I saw twigs and branches and even a big piece of lumber floating like paper boats across our yard, I knew that the yard and river had become one.

Papa didn't come home for lunch, and no one felt like eating. The boys were cranky, and I was both terrified and bored. The rain drummed monotonously against the roof, and the wind shrieked as if it was calling for us. While Mama took the boys upstairs for their afternoon naps, I tried to read, but my eyes seemed disconnected from my mind. I gave up and closed the book, not even bothering to mark my place.

Suddenly, a terrible roar rose above the storm. I jumped from my chair and flew to the door to see what could cause such a noise. Without thinking, I stepped outside and felt the instant bite of freezing wetness up to my knees as my skirt fanned out in the water around me. People and animals alike were half-running, half-swimming down the street as the roar grew louder. A six-foot wall of churning yellow water was racing towards me. Before my eyes, two men disappeared beneath it.

The sitting room windows burst inward as I ran back into the house. Torrents of muddy water raced across the floor, knocking me off my feet. Water surged over me, and the coldness took my breath away. I called for Mama, but the words were washed from my mouth with dirty water. Coughing and choking, I tried to get my head above the current as I tumbled along with the water's flow. With a sense of grateful surprise, I realized the water had carried me to the stairs.

Hanging on to the banister with all my might, I began to pull myself hand-over-hand up the stairs. Mama ran down and wrapped her arms around me, and together we scrambled to the landing. Safely on dry footing, we turned and looked back down into the room that had been our sitting room. Chairs and plants floated and bobbed, and water lapped at the mid-way point of the stairs. With sinking hearts, we turned and headed up to the second floor rooms.

I quickly changed into dry clothes and joined Mama and the boys in the little bedroom where they were stationed. The boys were playing with a toy car on the floor. Their faces were red and swollen, and I knew they had been crying. Mama stood at the window. "You won't believe this," she said softly as she motioned for me to join her.

A boiling river raced past, the water level just below our second floor window. A steady stream of casualties—tables, chairs, a grand piano, cars, and even whole houses—flew by, swept along with the raging current. We saw scores of horses, which caused my heart to race with fear and worry as I thought of Papa. Some of the horses were dead and some were still alive, their eyes bulging with terror as they struggled frantically to keep their heads above the swirling water.

As if not to be outdone in this parade of oddities, we saw the long, low lines of a chicken coop, the chickens sailing along as passengers on the roof. In the very middle, a stack of chickens rose—one on top of the other, three chickens high—like a feathery chimney. Mama and I both pointed to it at the same time and we started to laugh. I have since wondered how we were able to find any humor on that day, but I realize now that moment of laughter was as vital to us as the air we breathed.

After a while, Mama called me away from the window. I imagine she thought there was only so much awfulness a young girl should take in. She asked me to read Eli a story, and the two of us settled down together on a rug. As we finished a second book, I noticed that Eli looked concerned. "I didn't wet myself," he stated defensively. I shifted my weight on the rug and cringed at the feel of a soggy sponge beneath me.

"Mama," I shrieked, pointing to the water seeping through the floor.

"Oh, dear Lord," she said, and I could tell she was saying a prayer. The water was coming in rapidly now. It had already covered my shoes and I could feel it working its way past my ankles.

Mama struggled to open the window and then leaned out, looking upward. "I think you can reach the eaves, Carrie Ann," she said to me. "And if you can reach the eaves, you can pull yourself up onto the roof." She stated it as a fact, but to me it was a very big question.

With shaking hands, I pulled myself through the window, pressing against the glass on the other side. As I stood on the narrow sill, I felt the strength of the raging current, just inches below my feet.

The wind flailed against me, and my heart caught in my chest as I lost my balance. Instantly, Mama's hand grabbed my legs, supporting me and giving me confidence to continue.

I carefully walked my hands up the glass as I reached higher, standing now on tiptoe, until my fingers grazed the bottom of the eaves. Encouraged by this success, I stretched even more, cheering inside as my fingers locked around the edge of the roof.

Mama pushed against the bottom of my feet and I pulled and pushed my weight against the eaves. It felt as if my arms would leave their sockets, but I could move no higher.

The wet fabric of my skirt pulled at me like a weight, and my fingers started to slip. Desperately, I kicked away from Mama's hands. As if pumping a swing, I drew my legs in and then swung them forward until my feet rested against the top of the window frame.

Pain burned from my fingertips down through my arms. Gathering all my strength, I pushed off against the frame with my legs while my arms bore down on the eaves. Miraculously, I moved higher, my upper body rising above the rooftop.

From this position I was able to pull myself the rest of the way up. I lay, savoring the solidness beneath me, until I no longer gasped for breath. Then I turned around, and lying flat, reached back over the roof's edge. Mama handed Eli up to me and I grabbed his tiny hands in mine. I saw sheer panic in his eyes as he started to thrash against my hold.

"Eli, be still," I commanded him, and he listened. I pulled him up and wrapped him in my arms, hugging him to me as if my heart would break. I showed him where to sit and then angled myself downward once again. This time it was easier. I lifted Micah from Mama's outstretched arms and delivered him to Eli. "You need to hold him still," I instructed, and I shuddered to think I had just given a five-year-old responsibility for his brother's life.

Mama didn't want me to try to pull her up, and she was right. I was not strong enough to do that. Instead, I lay looking over the roof's edge, ready to offer encouragement. Mama was able to get out of the window with relative ease and as she locked her fingers around the eaves, I felt sure that she would soon be with us. But she made no further progress. I could see the effort and struggle on her face, the muscles that tightened and strained, but she lacked the strength in her arms to pull her body weight upward.

The wind whipped her dress into a tangle around her legs, and she swayed slightly from side to side, dangling above the current. The tips of her fingers turned blue where they held to the eaves and I knew it must be painful. I offered my hands, but Mama shook her head. I wanted to grab her wrists, but I was afraid I would break her grip and she would slip away into the churning water.

I could tell that Mama's energy was rapidly fading. Her mouth formed the words, "I can't," and the storm swallowed the sound. A strange look filled Mama's eyes. It was not a look of fear, but rather of profound loss and I knew that in her mind, Mama was telling us all goodbye.

"Mama, please," I shouted, and we both turned our heads in unison and saw a huge oak tree racing towards us with the current. The branches of the tree spread out in a giant arc, ready to sweep away everything in its path.

A scream tore through my throat and, instinctively, I reached down to grab Mama under her shoulder and pulled with all my might. At the same time, I could feel her body surging upward, and I knew Mama had found her own well of strength. As the tree raced by with branches crushing against the house, we were all safe, for the moment, on the roof.

We moved to the uppermost peak and Mama gathered us, like a brood of chicks, huddled together under her arms.

The rain still poured, stinging like little stones as it hit us. We were soaked. Our clothes clung to us like a second skin and made us even colder. Across the street I saw my best friend, Cynthia, perched with her family on the roof of their house. We waved to each other as if we were meeting to play.

The roar of the water still surrounded us. Another sound mingled with the roar. A loud, cracking sound like gunshots—the sound of trees and telegraph poles snapping off like toothpicks.

The steady flow of debris continued to pass by. From time to time a house sailed along with people clinging to the rooftop. They reached out their arms to us as if we could pluck them off to safety. Their faces were wild with fear and their mouths moved in screams we could not hear.

From where we sat, there was a clear view in all directions. I could see the beginning of the Broad Street Bridge and I could also see the spot where it had washed away. I knew that Papa was across the bridge and I prayed this was the reason he had not returned home. On the other side of the bridge, I could see the downtown buildings, rising up above the water that spread like a dirty gray blanket over the land.

All around us, other people sat on their roofs and waited for whatever would happen next. A few houses away, I saw a huge elm tree with people clinging to the branches like Christmas ornaments. I counted the people and there were thirteen. I hoped that thirteen would not be an unlucky number for them. I hoped that thirteen would not be an unlucky number for me.

* * *

I can feel my heart racing with fear, even though it has been decades since I sat numb and shaking on that rooftop, surveying the city and the probabilities of life. Much has changed during those years, but one thing has stayed the same—I relive it all, each and every time my memories turn in that direction, just as if it was happening again.

The rooftop was the worst. I don't like to let myself linger there long.

We clung to that rooftop as hunger gnawed from within and thirst parched our throats until we were tempted to sip from the filthy water that surrounded us. We clung to that rooftop as daylight faded away and total darkness closed around us like an angry fist. We clung to that rooftop as a new day dawned and the rain lessened, mixing itself with snowflakes that sparkled like specks of diamonds when the sun peeked through. We clung to that rooftop as we looked for a rainbow that never came.

As soon as the currents weakened, a rowboat appeared and saved us from the rooftop. And as the boat turned and floated across our backyard, there on the floor of Eli's tree-house was my green Easter egg—the one Papa had hidden. It was one of the few trees left standing in the neighborhood. I have always thought that somehow it was the presence of that little egg that had saved it. In any case, there it was—round and green and full of promise. I hoped for health and happiness for all of us, and especially for Papa. I hoped so hard it was really more of a prayer.

We made one more stop, fitting an elderly mother and her daughter into the boat before heading to a relief center where we could get dry clothes and food and water. We had only been there a few minutes when I heard Papa's loud voice calling our names. "I was hoping I'd find you here," he said as he wrapped us in his arms.

My story ends with hope, for if there is one thing I have learned it is this—there is always hope.

Deborah Cheever Cottle lives in Westerville, Ohio with her husband, David. Their son, Aaron, lives and works in Seattle. Deborah is currently a freelance writer. Her story "The Ant Doctor" appeared in the CCC anthology *While You Were Out* and she has recently completed a suspense novel. Deborah can be contacted via email at debbie.cottle@gmail.com.

The Flood of 1913 has been called "Ohio's greatest weather disaster." Approximately 100 people died in Columbus, mostly in the Franklinton area where the Scioto River surged through the streets at depths of up to 17 feet.

THE SOUTHERN THEATRE
Melissa Pauquette

1927
THE GHOST IN THE SOUTHERN THEATRE

By Leslie Munnelly

Isadora spent every afternoon dancing in The Southern Theatre. On-stage in the dark, she whirled and arched before hundreds of empty seats, accompanied not by music, but by the tap of her feet against the boards. Why she'd been sentenced to spend eternity in Columbus, Ohio was a mystery she had yet to unravel—the one time she'd danced there before she'd been subject to a lackluster response and poor reviews—but what she *did* know, from firsthand experience, is that the line between the here and the hereafter, wherever it happens to be, is tenuous at best.

Isadora's sudden death had come to her as a complete surprise. It was a freak accident, one that made headlines across Europe and the United States: *The Great Isadora Duncan, Dead at 50!* and *Mother of Modern Dance Dies in France!* One moment, she'd been careening through the streets of Nice, en route to the apartment of a handsome young Italian (not an uncommon occurrence for her); the next, she'd been jerked from her seat and catapulted to the ground, her scarf wound tightly around her broken neck and the rear axle of the motorcar.

"*Mort*," declared a passerby who'd stopped to help, his fingers releasing her wrist to let it fall by her side. "*Absolument.*"

"*Mio Dio*," said the Italian, his expression shocked but not sorrowful. "What a way to go!"

"Save me, *s'il vous plait*," Isadora pleaded silently as her spirit waned. "I'm not yet ready to leave this world!"

The men could do nothing; her life and death were beyond their control, and so she stepped from her body and rose above the accident scene, watching as the doctor came, and then the ambulance, an awkward-looking carriage pulled by two draft horses. She lingered on awhile as two orderlies loaded her body into the back and turned toward the morgue; then she closed her eyes and prepared herself for heaven.

There was a rush of cold air accompanied by a howling that was

65

louder than a thousand wolves. Isadora felt herself thrust into a current that pulled her forward, faster than a motorcar. She felt as though her spirit was plunging headlong through a tunnel without end and kept her eyes tightly clamped as she hurdled through space toward her fate.

When she felt her feet settle at last, she opened her eyes and stared about. Instead of white clouds, harps, and St. Peter, she was alone on the stage of a darkened auditorium. It was not the famed stage of her beloved Théâtre des Champs-Elysees, or the Teatro Municipal; not even the Metropolitan Opera House.

"This cannot be heaven," she whispered as she realized where she'd landed. "It's a mistake. It has to be!" She raised her eyes to the ceiling, then gazed around the dim cavern in dismay. She'd materialized in the Southern Theatre in the city of Columbus, Ohio.

Day after day, she sent her misgivings skyward and waited patiently for transportation to another resting place—a theatre in Avignon perhaps, with an adoring crowd to cheer her on and a large suite overlooking the Mediterranean Sea; or Paris, with waiters to deliver Dom Perignon and chocolates to her room and handsome escorts to entertain her whims—but her wait was in vain. Finally, after one long week, bored and dejected, Isadora decided to take matters into her own hands. If God would not restore her to France, she'd just have to get there herself.

No one noticed as she pushed the door of the Southern Theatre open and stepped onto the sidewalk. Not a head turned or hat tipped as she strode purposefully south. At the end of the block, she stopped. There was an obstacle there, at the curb's edge, invisible but impenetrable. While women of flesh and blood passed through it undeterred, the imperceptible shield stopped Isadora cold. Turning on one stiletto heel, she stalked north, where she met with the same fate. East and west proved equally fruitless.

"What do you want from me, God?" she cried, throwing her arms skyward dramatically. "Why am I here? Have you abandoned me?"

There was no answer. She walked the block again. The shield remained firmly in place.

Isadora sighed. She knew when she was beaten. Her alternatives gone, she returned to the theater and settled down to wait. If God, indeed, wished for her to remain in Columbus, he must have a plan. A year passed, and then two. Nothing further happened. It was vexing, an utter frustration, but one which she was powerless to change. Finally, she moved next door to the Great Southern Fireproof Hotel where she checked into room 113. She didn't much care for the number, but, like the Southern Theatre itself, number 113 was the only door that opened for her.

In her early dead days, lonely and homesick, Isadora was a rebellious ghost. Night after night she attempted to get herself evicted, thinking that banishment might solve her plight. She threw chairs, ripped pillows, and howled into the wee hours of the morning—all things that had worked successfully during her living years—but the staff of the Great Southern Fireproof proved tolerant. Instead of outrage, her antics were met with amusement; instead of fear, she created curiosity. Angry and frustrated, Isadora persevered. She howled louder and pounded the walls, scratched the mirrors and slashed the wallpaper. Still, she remained.

Every morning cheerful maids righted the furniture and vacuumed up feathers without complaint. Every afternoon, guests queued up at the reservations desk to request the rooms to either side of hers. No matter how incorrigible her behavior, nothing she did was bad enough to get her thrown out of the hotel. Ghosts, it seemed, while not good tippers, were excellent for business.

As time went by, Isadora's boredom increased. Unlike Paris and Nice, Columbus, Ohio hadn't much to offer her. There were no parties to keep her entertained or lovers to stroke her ego, and the arts scene was limited to what played next door. It was 1930 and America was under prohibition; there was no champagne. "*Mon Dieu!*" she cried. "No alcohol? It's barbarous; completely uncivilized!"

Aggravated, she expanded her nightly haunts to the hotel's hallways. This activity offered a bit more excitement. Prowling through the Great Southern's corridors, she'd search out hapless guests to tease; a pinch for this one or tangled foot for that. Seldom was she seen, but occasionally an unsettled victim would give a description of her that was spot on: they'd been accosted by a barefoot woman with long dark hair and flowing robes of indigo, who wore Chanel No. 5 and a blood red scarf; a graceful woman with sad eyes who'd left behind a breath of warm air as she'd passed by.

These guests, the ones who saw her, were the ones she returned to, following them into their rooms and spending long hours beside them while they slept. A lustful woman, she missed the human touch: the rough hands of Sergei, her dead and crazy husband; the sweet lips of

Mercedes, her poet lover. For a woman known for her scandalous affairs and brazen sensuality, the chaste evenings lacked spark, but without her mortal body they were as close to making love as she could get. Isadora knew her limitations; she lay beside these semi-clairvoyants and took what little comfort she could.

Eventually, Isadora eased up on rebellion and settled down to her fate. She developed a routine that helped to dispel the boredom of her endless afterlife that included sleeping late and dancing next door before the evening show. In the summertime, she sat on the roof and raised her face to the sun. In winter, she huddled close to the fire that crackled in the front lobby and watched the snowflakes fly. Spring brought the scent of flowers on the wind, and fall—crisp temperatures and skies of brilliant blue. These small comforts helped the time pass. It was not the heaven that Isadora had envisioned, but at least it was tolerable.

Outside her world, life went on. Musical tastes shifted from swing to pop to rock and roll. Kids played with Silly Putty and Hula Hoops. The computer was invented, the Atomic Bomb exploded, and color televisions became commonplace. Times were changing faster than fashion.

While its star attraction watched Walter Cronkite and sang along with Doris Day, Peter, Paul, and Mary, and The Beatles, the Southern Theatre went through a series of transformations of its own. Vaudeville transgressed to silent films in the 1930s and segued to second-run double features after World War II. Then, as flight replaced rails and man took to the sky, her stage played host to a weekly country music show. After that, in the seventies, it was back to B-rate movies.

Through it all, Isadora persevered. She remained as she had on September 14, 1927, a fifty-year-old woman with a zest for life that death had not extinguished. In the sixties, she discovered *Peyton Place* and *I Dream of Jeannie*. In the seventies, she watched *Sonny and Cher* and *The Partridge Family*. And, of course, she danced.

All the while the city changed. The population grew, and Columbus sprawled and spawned suburbs. Outside of Isadora's one-block perimeter, huge shopping malls cropped up sporting chain stores and megaplex cinemas that drew the masses with their abundance of choice. New venues for live entertainment opened in closer proximity to the shifting population, making an evening out on the town in the suburbs cheaper and more convenient than a trip to the city center.

What followed was inevitable: attendance at the Southern Theatre declined. The once-respectable neighborhood grew seedy as drug dealers and whores took up residence in the theatre's dark corners. Dust settled thick on the faded velvet seats where ladies and gentlemen once gathered for an evening of refined elegance.

It did not escape Isadora's notice how sparsely filled the seats became, or how the thick layers of grime discolored the carpet and gold paint of the auditorium; nor was she blind to the sketchy activities within the old theatre's walls. But aesthetics and law-keeping were not her business. She was an artist; her business was to dance. So, she turned a blind eye to the deterioration around her and continued with her calling.

In 1979, half a century after she'd materialized within its walls, the Southern Theatre was abandoned, and her doors were locked for good. Isadora waited for God to send her elsewhere, but again, nothing happened. So, every afternoon, she continued to mount the stage, ignoring the threadbare curtain and grimy walls as her feet beat a soft rhythm across the sagging floor. It appeared that God had forgotten about her; even the death throes of her final resting place were not enough to free her of the Southern Theatre and its host city, Columbus, Ohio.

1998

The men in the auditorium shifted slightly as Isadora glided down the aisle toward the stage. In her wake, she left warmth and the scent of perfume, proof positive that she'd passed. She sniffed the air as she pushed aside the curtain, a magnificent swath of deep purple, and stepped to center stage. Gone was the sour stench of decay of the past decades. Instead, the walls of the Southern smelled of fresh paint, and the woodwork, of varnish. Beyond the dais, the proscenium was illuminated with hundreds of lights that angled toward her where she bent and stretched. Beneath her feet, the clear maple floor gleamed.

It was the fourteenth of September in the year of 1998, the seventy-first anniversary of her death, and the Southern Theatre had just undergone a major remodeling. The project, an ambitious undertaking by the Columbus Association for the Performing Arts (CAPA), had been an expensive endeavor, setting its patrons back the better part of ten million dollars. It had been risky as well—the city of Columbus had three other functioning theatres to support, the Ohio, the Lincoln, and the Palace. When it began, there were as many skeptics to the plan as supporters, but in the end, even the most cynical among them agreed that the investment had been worth it; fully restored to the peak of her grandeur, the new Southern Theatre was no less than stunning.

Fourteen months before, when the work had begun, there'd been dozens of carpenters and painters milling about the place, but now it was down to a skeleton crew … nine or ten guys charged with miscellaneous chores necessary for the completion of the project: assembling the seats, installing hardware, hanging curtains, and other fine details that had been overlooked until last.

Street-side, framed fliers boasted of the talented entertainers who had played there throughout the years: Sarah Bernhardt, Lillian Russell, Al Jolson, W.C. Fields, and Lionel Barrymore, to name a few. Their faces smiled out from the newly painted front windows alongside current acts that were booked for the upcoming season.

Front and center, alongside the banner announcing the historic grand re-opening, was a life-sized portrait of Isadora herself. The day it was hung, she'd lingered before it, recalling the morning she'd posed for the picture, her arms thrust forward in a position the photographer had called "beseeching." She'd had to remain completely still for many minutes, an arduous ordeal, but the results spoke for themselves: the photo was timeless, compelling. It captured the essence of what she'd been trying to convey through dance without the movement … a catch-22 of sorts.

Shifting her attention, she studied the re-opening announcement more closely. The first performance at the Southern would feature four acts: Brian Bedford, The Canadian Brass, Dee Dee Bridgewater, and Fred Hersch.

Who the hell are they? she wondered. And what right, as entertainers, did they have to receive the honor of opening night in *her* theatre?

Back in her room, she flipped through the television channels searching the credits for the foreign names. Seven, ten, twelve, and thirty-two. Nothing. She settled the dial on MTV and watched into the late hours. There were plenty of acts on the station that she admired and would have enjoyed seeing take the Southern's stage: the Spice Girls, Back Street Boys, Mariah Carey, and her favorite, Celine Dion, but no one named Dee Dee Bridgewater or Fred Hersch; no Canadian Brass, nor Brian Bedford.

Frustrated, she turned off the light and sat in the dark, drumming her long fingers against the headboard. A grand re-opening should be a gala event with celebrities of the highest caliber. If the people of CAPA could not manage to snare a single international star, she told herself, she'd just have to help them out herself. She had not been officially invited, but as the theatre's longest performing artist she expected to be welcomed by the audience. After seventy-one years, she believed she was entitled to dance.

By the next morning, pictures of the unknown performers had appeared on a makeshift marquee by the concierge's desk. Isadora studied their faces intently. Brian Bedford, it seemed, was a British stage actor with Broadway credits to his name and a Tony under his belt. He wasn't Sean Connery or Michael Douglas, but, she decided, he would do. (Even Isadora, cloistered in her one block heaven, knew about Tony Awards.)

Next, she shifted her attention to The Canadian Brass. They were a quintet of horn players who'd played every major theatre in the country over the past thirty years. She shrugged. So, maybe they weren't Puff Daddy and the Bad Boy Family, but they had to be legitimate musicians to have been invited to so many venues.

Dee Dee Bridgewater was another surprise, a Grammy-nominated jazz singer who had long-established roots in France as well as the United States.

"France? *Incroyable!*" Isadora stared at her picture, committing her face to memory. The woman's dark hair was pulled back tight and her mouth was open in song. She wore a sequined dress of silver that accentuated the dark brown of her skin as she raised her arms to her audience. In the photo, she was accompanied by her pianist for the event, one Mister Fred Hersch.

"Jazz," Isadora muttered, shaking her head. "I thought that went out of vogue in the forties."

It had not been the easiest music to dance to and she'd been happy when tastes evolved. "Oh well," she sighed. "It looks like I've got some practicing to do!"

Back at the Southern, the standard radio station was off. Music from the upcoming performers was playing instead, piped onto the street outside to advertise the event. Isadora watched as people hesitated on their way by, listening. A few perused the flyer. Others bought tickets from a pony-tailed girl in the front booth. Maybe jazz hadn't gone completely out of vogue after all, she thought as she pushed through the front door and sashayed past the workmen.

Onstage, she began a series of moves. Some, she'd used before, others she'd learned from watching the dancers on MTV. Over and over, she tweaked her routine as she committed it to memory: bend, twist, leap, spin, and bend. Repeat. By the time she'd finished for the day, she was reasonably content with her choreography. The arts patrons of this age were different from their predecessors, more open-minded. Unlike theatre-goers of her era, she felt certain they would recognize the brilliance of her routine; after all, there were many dancers now who followed her style. *Modern dance*, they'd called it in the 20s. The name brought a smile to her lips. *Modern* dance …

The weekend of the gala celebration finally arrived. Isadora could sense the tension as the hotel filled with celebrities and their entourages. She dodged past couples in the crowded corridors and took the stairs to avoid the lines at the elevator, arriving on the first floor flushed with excitement. In the Great Southern's lobby, every chair was taken while receptionists checked in those waiting to register. The bar, of course, was full.

She lingered for a moment, taking stock of the faces, some familiar and others not. Many of the guests were regulars at the hotel, natives of the city who returned from time to time to visit family or carry out business within the city limits. Others she'd never seen before and assumed that they were concert-goers who'd come to Columbus specifically for the grand re-opening of the theatre next door.

At the concierge's desk, under the star's pictures, a program of the evening's events had been posted. Isadora stopped to read it. First on the docket was The Canadian Brass. They'd be followed with a comic monologue by Bedford and then the pianist, Hersch, playing solo. After a brief intermission, Bridgewater would take the stage. She was slated to sing from her newly released album *Dear Etta*, a tribute to Etta James that had already gone platinum and had the critics whispering "Grammy."

To round off the evening, all four acts would take the stage for a final tribute to the Southern Theatre and the people of the state. The last song to be performed would be the state anthem, "Beautiful Ohio". The words were printed in full on the program and the public was asked to join in. It was a perfect ending for the evening and the perfect moment to showcase her talent, she decided. "Beautiful Ohio," she would dance to that.

Isadora looked to the lobby ceiling and shook her head at God, a being she'd yet to see. "You have given me a gift and that gift is dance," she said. "What good is this heaven of mine, without people to share it with? If they cannot see my soul and gain pleasure from my work this time, I'll give it up completely."

Without waiting for a response, she wrapped her scarf tightly around her neck and stepped from the hotel lobby to the sidewalk.

Outside, the air smelled like fall. There was a bite to the wind, but the sun was still hot. Isadora pushed aside her anxiety and breathed deeply as she made her way down the crowded sidewalk to the theatre doors. The entire cast was expected to gather at three o'clock to run through the order of performance, and she would be there, too. Pushing past the ushers, she glided through the mezzanine and down the left-hand aisle, past the velvet covered seats and newly restored frescoes. Her heels were silent where they touched the plush warp of carpet, her fingers gentle as they trailed along the fabric. She reached the stage and took the steps two at a time, ducking beneath the dark plum curtain with its gold tassels and secreting herself in the shadows at the back.

An hour later, her fellow performers arrived. The director called them to order and waited for their conversation to die before repeating the schedule for the last time. As he announced each act, he indicated their stage positions and timing in a fast forward mock-up of the main event, rattling off the songs they'd play with staccato precision. When he announced the final song, Isadora took her place, front and center before the empty seats, and bowed, miming her involvement as she waved to an imaginary crowd.

"Very good," the director said. "Excellent! The show begins at seven thirty. Be here by six, not a minute later. And everyone," he added, "break a leg!"

With his final words, the performers dispersed. It was four o'clock and they had things to do: makeup to apply, costumes to don, last minute rehearsals, and perhaps a drink or two at Thurber's Bar. Isadora watched them leave as she dropped to the floor and began her warm-up. It was early still and she wanted one last practice session. Unlike them, for her the grand re-opening of the Southern Theatre was not a once in a lifetime experience, it was once in an *after* lifetime event, and one that she took most seriously.

The clock crept forward. At last it was showtime. Overhead, the lights blinked twice as last-minute arrivals took their seats and checked their programs. When they dimmed for the final time, all conversation stopped in anticipation of the show. Brian Bedford took the stage and stood in the spotlight as the curtain rose. Smiling broadly, he welcomed the audience, gave a small speech about the history of the theatre, and announced The Canadian Brass, who would start the evening off. Music rang through the auditorium to a huge round of applause. The grand re-opening was off to a good start.

Half an hour later the curtain fell as the Brit re-took the stage and began his act. Behind him, support crews pushed a grand piano into the corner and prepped the microphones for the pianist. No one noticed Isadora as she paced among them, her heart fluttering wildly. She hadn't been so nervous since she'd first played Paris, a century before.

When Fred Hersch had played his last note, there was a brief intermission. She continued to pace as bright lights illuminated the theatre and the lobby filled, the hair on her arms pregnant with goose bumps, her stomach a tight knot. She had been subject to many emotions while dead: anger, bewilderment, sorrow, and loneliness, but never, not once, had she been nervous. Now, standing in the wings before a full house with the gauntlet thrown, she was not only nervous, she was terrified.

After the break, the entertainment continued with Dee Dee Bridgewater and the jazz-savvy crowd went wild. They rose to their feet and applauded, loud and long, as the singer smiled and bowed. Isadora stopped pacing and stood in the wings, looking out at the rapt faces and waving arms of Bridgewater's fans. "That's what it's like," she murmured as she watched from the shadows. "To be truly famous … *that's* what it's like."

Afterward, Bedford took the stage for the final time. While he regaled the audience with a lighthearted rendition of the restoration of the Southern and its upcoming events, the rest of the performers waited to the left of the curtain for the grand finale. Isadora joined them, prepared for her own grand entry. Finally, he turned and gestured them forward; she followed them into the spotlight. Stepping to the front of the stage, she took her position.

"Beseeching," the photographer had said, posing her before him. "When I look through the lens, I want to see 'beseeching'." Overhead, the lights flashed on. Isadora stared out at the audience from the pose she'd held for the portrait artist so long ago. Behind her, the Brass quintet began to play. The opening notes of "Beautiful Ohio" filled the air to the cheers of the crowd as the spotlight settled upon her. Arms trembling, dark eyes pleading, she beseeched.

Isadora put her heart and soul into her performance that night. Her leaps were as high as a deer's; her pirouettes tight and smooth. Across the stage she traveled, her movements light and swift, accompanied by the soaring notes of the piano. The red scarf rippled like a ribbon in the wind behind her; her bare feet flashed against the floor boards without the weight of gravity. She was a bird, free and unfettered; a wave, high and breaking. She was nature and nurture, love and heartbreak, longing and triumph, sorrow and joy. For three short minutes, Isadora Duncan was everything in the world. For three short minutes, she was *of* the world.

As the last note faded away, she fell back into her opening position, beseeching, and waited.

The silence in the theatre was complete. Her heart drummed hard against her ribs. She felt her throat tighten, overwhelmed by the grim possibility of failure, as tears of disappointment filled her eyes. She had given God an ultimatum, and it seemed he was calling her bluff.

Then someone began to clap. The sound of hands echoed through the night and swelled as others joined in.

A rose landed at her feet, and then another. Isadora scooped them up, heart pounding. Her tears flowed faster and her fear turned to joy as she turned to indicate the rest of the performers. The spotlight illuminated each in turn and returned to rest upon her, sending a shadow across the stage. The crowd clapped louder.

They could see her; she was certain.

Cradling the blooms, she bowed deeply to a standing ovation, then straightened to look out on the people. They remained standing, their applause deafening. Isadora trembled as relief flooded her tired limbs. At last she knew where she truly belonged. Not in Paris or Nice, New York or Rio, but right where she was, in the Southern Theatre. God had not abandoned her after all, she realized. He'd given her the city of Columbus, and at last it felt like home.

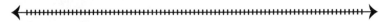

Leslie Munnelly, a Cleveland native, is married and a mother of two adult children. She's an avid reader, writer, and runner. Currently, Leslie has a second short story pending publication in the fall. She is also working with an e-publisher on the revision of her first novel.

Isadora Duncan danced in Columbus, Ohio during her U.S. tour in 1915. Slated for another venue, she refused to visit the city unless she was booked at the Southern, Columbus's theatre of choice. After a lackluster response, Isadora returned to Europe and founded a school of modern dance that kept her legacy alive, even after the tragedy of her death in 1927.

TOASTING WONDER BREAD
Don Slobodien

1951
DUKE ELLINGTON BLESSES THE WONDER BREAD

By Jay Fulmer

Robert Pete and I walked onto the loading deck. "You tellin' me Duke Ellington was over your house fo' supper last night and he played your daddy's piano again?" he asked me.

"We came by your place but you weren't home," I apologized.

"Well, I was attendin' t' Betty Jean, but had I known ..."

"He's coming back for supper this Sunday, so ask Betty Jean to join you at our house," I suggested as we slid open the back door of a truck.

"Well, that might be a bit too crowded on account a Betty Jean's husband, but I'll gladly join you and your family this Sunday, Frankie."

"Good. Oh yeah, bring your guitar."

"Oh, we'll see," Robert Pete said as he headed off to repair an oven.

Robert Pete was my best friend, and although he was from Louisiana, and he no longer lives here, he helped me make Columbus my home. I wasn't thrilled to call Columbus my home when we first moved here a few years ago from New York. Columbus was initially a backwater letdown as my dad moved us here from our friends and schools and the neighborhood I had known my whole life. I was twelve at the time, and my sisters Helen and Mary were fifteen and seventeen.

Dad worked for Columbia Records, and his job was to expand and manage the distribution of Columbia Records and their subsidiaries throughout the Midwest.

His territory was Ohio, Kentucky, and Indiana. Dad had heard from many of his musician friends that Columbus had become a hub for touring musicians. Since there were no major venues in Columbus, musicians could actually take a break from the road and spend a day or two gathering themselves back up for the next show or session.

We bought a big house on Arcadia Avenue; Dad loved it right away because the huge living room was perfect for our baby grand. Dad flourished at his job and was instrumental in expanding Columbia's distribution. As regional manager, Dad was also involved in arranging lodging for the label's touring musicians. Even though we had left New York, Dad still made sure that we were entertaining musicians as they passed through from Detroit to Atlanta and New York to Chicago.

Our neighbors gave us funny looks sometimes when we had musicians lounging on our porch in the mornings or rolling up late at night, but they soon got comfortable with our social habits. Life for my dad was still very exciting as my mom, my sisters, and I acclimated to the slow drip of Columbus, Ohio. The kids at my new school were friendly enough, and my next door neighbor Carl befriended me when we first moved in, but I still didn't feel settled. My sisters were both far south from happy with their new high school, but they eventually made lots of friends in the neighborhood.

Carl was with me when I first met Robert Pete. It was last summer and we were walking down High Street checking out the campus girls when we came upon Robert Pete standing at the corner of Fifteenth Avenue and High Street playing his Kay guitar, case open at his feet and singing blues like I had never heard. I was instantly captivated by the sound, and Carl as well, as we threw whatever cash we had into his case and sat down and listened to him play. After a while we got to talking and I did exactly what my dad would have done, I invited him to dinner. From that time till he moved on back down south, Robert Pete became one of the family.

Music has always been a part of my life, and I can play piano and Alto, but it wasn't till I heard the blues that music finally spoke to me. The blues took me to a very different place: music so enormous and powerful that it articulated the imagery of the soul. My life changed when I saw Robert Pete's posture while playing his guitar. His stance was that of a man braced for a hurricane. My life changed when this music he played resonated deep in my soul. Robert Pete knew everything about the blues, having lived them all his life. He saw how the music affected me, and he shared his knowledge and travel tales, building a desire to carry on this message.

Robert Pete could tell you where Lightning Hopkins toured in 1945, or where Arthur "Big Boy" Crudup recorded his last session, but he never volunteered information about himself or his past beyond that of being a traveling blues player. I remember when my dad asked Robert Pete his last name:

"My last name is America," was his fast reply.

I always wondered about his past, but I could tell that it wasn't a topic of discussion for him, so I was content to hear him talk about his travels and the blues men he had played with. He had been working as a maintenance man at Continental Bakery for a couple of years, and he had a little house on Chittenden with a garage out back where he worked on cars for side money.

He and my dad hit it off right away, both being living music encyclopedias. Robert Pete loved to go through and spin my dad's record collection, and he would bring over boxes of ten-inch blues records to play for us. Robert Pete and my dad would talk for hours about their records and the musicians and the origins of those sounds and melodies. The blues records became my favorite and I listened to them every chance I got.

The summer of 1951, Robert Pete got Carl and me jobs at Continental Bakery on Fourth Street. We rode our bikes to work at four thirty a.m. and unloaded trucks of yeast and flour till noon. After work, we slept under the trees across the street till Robert Pete got off, and then we'd go back to his house and listen to records or listen to him play.

Duke Ellington's current tour dates were scheduled between major recording sessions, and the locations put him back in proximity of our place. Dad made him promise that he'd come back for dinner, and Duke had stopped by Thursday night and was now coming back Sunday. I was so glad that Duke was coming back through—mostly so Robert Pete could meet him.

After church Sunday we all helped Mom get ready for dinner while Dad drove to Dayton to pick up Mr. Ellington. Robert Pete walked up with his guitar case, and we all came out on the porch to cool off. It was June and already in the eighties and humid. Robert Pete played "Key to the Highway" as my mom and sisters looked through the Lazarus fashion section in the local paper.

"Frankie, you know, you're a lucky young man. Your mamma and daddy bein' as kind as they are and your daddy givin' you the gift of music," Robert Pete told me as he tuned his guitar.

"You're the one with the gift for music."

"Baby boy, the blues ain't a gift. The blues is a helpin' hand when you're standin' there empty-handed after all the kindness been handed out." There was a clear destination in his eyes as he looked down the street.

"I mean, there ain't many folks who get t' know these men as they pass through your town."

"I want to be the one passing through town."

"No, you're better off helpin' sell them records like your daddy. Believe me, it looks much prettier from here."

The day was bright and sunny in the humid warmth, and Robert Pete's melodies blended in rhythm with the crickets and cicadas. The little spruce trees we had planted in the spring looked fluorescent green after last night's rain. Robert Pete finished playing "Standing at My Window" when my mom came up and hugged him and kissed his cheek.

"Robert, you are such a good man."

"Ah thank you Madam Marie."

Dad pulled up with Duke Ellington and they got out of the car laughing and carrying on like old friends as they walked up the steps. We all stood as they joined us on the porch, and greetings went around. Duke Ellington was his humble and gracious self, but this was the first time I'd seen him when he didn't seem worn thin. There was an aura about him, like a stage spotlight that somehow shined on him from within himself. Robert Pete shook Duke's hand.

"You must be Robert. Frank's told me about you."

"It's an honor t' meet you, Mr. Ellington."

Mr. Ellington shared stories of his current tour with us and all that goes into managing a traveling orchestra.

"Keeping all these guys out of trouble every night is a full time job. Now, the longer I can get them to practice the more rest they'll need for the next gig. Now look at you! You've grown since last year, Frankie."

"Yup. Wonder Bread now has a thirteenth way of strengthening my body; they've got me unloading trucks at Continental. Local fifty-seven!" I exclaimed and flexed my arms.

"Oh yes, even Howdy Doody is selling that Wonder Bread now. I should compose a suite to Wonder Bread. Maybe something like 'How White Thou Art'."

Everyone laughed, and Mom called us in for dinner. After we finished we all relaxed in the living room. Duke eyed Robert Pete's guitar case. "Frank told me that you can really play the blues, said he offered to take you down to King to record a demo."

"Yes sir, I know the blues, and Frank's offer's mighty kind, but the road I'm on now is takin' me back home t' see some things through." With this Robert Pete smiled kindly at my dad.

"Well, I'd like to play some blues with you, Robert Pete, if that's why you brought your guitar."

"It would be an honor t' play with you, Duke."

Robert Pete stood up and got his guitar out and walked over to the piano. Duke Ellington smiled. He went to the piano and started in on a slow country blues progression and Robert Pete picked it right up with "Motherless Children Have a Hard Time".

I could sense Duke's surprise and respect for Robert Pete even from behind, through his own posture and performance. They played through four or five different standards, some up tempo and others in the country blues vein. Robert Pete was standing tall, still postured as if weathering a storm while he played, but this time at the helm, his fingers digging into the mahogany fret board and turning out such sad and intoxicating notes. They ended with "Such Sweet Thunder," with Robert Pete playing the horn solos on his guitar.

My family was awestruck, and my eyes were watering from the majesty and mastery performed in our living room. We only caught our breath when they stopped and then we applauded until they made us stop.

Dad brought out a bottle of scotch and everyone got to talking. The bakery kept coming up in conversation and finally Robert Pete asked, "Duke, would you come down and bless the Wonder Bread?"

At first, everyone, including Robert Pete just laughed at this, but as the scotch began to disappear and the night dawdled on, the idea of Duke Ellington blessing the morning's fresh loaves became more and more important. So important that at four in the morning we all piled into dad's Continental Mark II and headed for the Continental Bakery. My dad and mom and Duke Ellington were in the front seat and Robert Pete, my sister Helen and I were in the back. My sister Mary opted for going to sleep, and I know she regrets it to this very day.

When we arrived, the first batches of loaves were out of the ovens, and the air was filled with the overpowering smell of fresh, warm bread. Everyone applauded as my dad and Robert Pete announced the arrival of Duke Ellington. About forty-five of the bakery's 215 employees were on shift, and I should have been getting ready to unload the trucks. Robert Pete led us all up on a catwalk above the oven room where Duke poured some of the sacramental scotch down on the top of a Vulcan-hot oven.

"Man cannot live on bread alone, yet man is alone earning his bread. May these loaves of wonder bring health and enrichment to everyone they touch. A toast ... to the toast," blessed the Duke. Then he took a drink of the sacramental scotch and handed the bottle to Robert Pete.

"To the toast," smiled Robert Pete, and he partook of the scotch and handed the bottle to my dad.

"Amen," Dad agreed and took a drink.

Seeing these three men, my dad and Robert Pete, the two most important men in my life, and Duke Ellington, perhaps *the* most important man in the development of modern music, united by the equality of expression and the reverence for that expression filled me with understanding and respect for purpose. I knew I had to share with the world the way these men shared.

I think we ate about four loaves of that blessed bread. It was the June eighteenth and nineteenth Wonder Bread supply for Columbus, Delaware, Mt. Vernon, Washington Court House, Lancaster, Zanesville, Chillicothe, Springfield, and Marion. I still have a bread bag from one of those blessed loaves in a trunk somewhere. I told everyone I knew about the blessing, but most people just looked at me as if I was crazy. I know there were hundreds of people who unknowingly ate the blessed Wonder Bread, and I wished that there was some way I could tell them about this communion, but alas, news of this event did not spread.

In September of 1951, Robert Pete told me that he had "heard the call" and was heading down south to help his people. I never saw him again. He asked my dad to look after all his boxes of blues records since he was traveling, and every time I play those records, Robert Pete comes back to me.

Jay Fulmer is a writer living in Clintonville, a neighborhood of Columbus, Ohio with his two children, Katie and Miles. He is currently seeking representation for his first two completed novels and is a part time ethnomusicologist. He can be contacted be email at jayfulmer@hotmail.com.

In the 1950s, Duke Ellington, as well as other great jazz performers like Miles Davis and Nancy Wilson, performed at the Lincoln theater in Columbus, Ohio. At the time, segregation was still prevalent, and the theater was a hub of African-American society. The theater was closed in the early 1970'.

The theater, which sits in the present-day King-Lincoln district on the near east side of the city, was reopened to the public in 2009, and currently holds events and performances on a regular basis.

REJOICE
St. Ann's Hospital, Westerville, Ohio
Debra Fitch

1963
AND A YEAR AND A YEAR
By Drew Farnsworth

She always crumbled when Harold told her the truth. He dreaded talking to her and imagined she felt the same. She looked rattled— her jaw locked, her fingers strained against their joints. When she got up from lunch a few tables over from him, he looked away. She was surely busy, on her way back to work in the pharmacy.

"Hello Dr. Fisk," she said as she walked past his table.

"Margie Needham," he acknowledged. He dropped his dollop of creamed spinach into his bowl. "Little Jack was well this morning." She didn't seem to be listening, but he'd already begun the conversation, so he felt he must go on. "The scar tissue from his last skin graft is almost healed. He might have full mobility in that arm."

This positive spin was a knife's edge. To be honest about her son meant such pain. To soft pedal meant lies. How does one tell a mother that the chances her son would survive, though better by the day, still met even odds?

Harold judged her expression momentarily but still couldn't read it. She had a caring, youthful face without a stern bone or sharp line. He continued talking. "You know I sent a letter to Tom Moorehead, our Congressman, and even to President Kennedy himself about those pajamas."

"Oh," Margie said. "Thank you Doctor."

Harold nodded. "I sent them an article from *Popular Science* about a kind of miracle fiber that might be ten times more fire resistant than the cotton flannel your Jack was in."

"That's wonderful," Margie said. She smiled politely at first, but when she actually looked into Harold's eyes she burst open with pity. "Are you all right, Dr. Fisk? You look sick. I know I've said this before, but maybe you should take the day off."

"Oh," Harold moaned, "I don't know about that." He pushed away his plate of cold greens and beef.

"You can take a break," she said. Then she leaned in, put her hand on his shoulder and whispered warmly, "The war's been over for ten years."

Harold bristled and flinched. Margie tittered reflexively. Without another breath or another moment's pause she said, "Come to the pharmacy if you need anything," and she glided away like a breeze.

She was right. The war was over. Yet every day Korea flashed him with grizzled effigies and hollow, tinny voices. The children there screamed with unfathomable depth, but at least Harold didn't know the words. He remembered the one girl lucky enough to jump into a lake after she'd been set ablaze. Beneath one little patch between her toes there was no burn. Yet the skin there seemed sapped of all life, even more than the char that went clear down to muscle.

That thought stayed with him. He noticed it more and more. Even babies burned only on one arm would die. Had they been normal wounds, had someone cut that skin out with a scalpel, those kids might have lived. No. These burn victims, they died with crushing imminence. They were beyond hope. He recognized death on their faces the moment he saw them. At least he had hope now. At least he'd kept the life on little Jack's face.

Harold finished his bit of roast beef and carefully placed his plastic lunch bowl back into its metal container. He stood and walked out of the cafeteria, through the long institutional halls of green linoleum to his office.

He opened the chart for the little boy, Jack. *Recommend six months burn treatment plus three months out-patient physical therapy. Parents Marjorie and Jason Needham. Six brothers. One sister. Six skin grafts completed. Two more scheduled. Admitted April 10. Immediately intravenous electrolytes: sodium, potassium, chloride and bicarbonate administered at room temperature.*

The electrolytes.

It was that little girl in Korea. Napalm hadn't been used before that war except a few times against Japan. In Korea they just dropped it from the air. It set whole villages on fire. They didn't use it often enough for it to make news, but Harold was there to attest to it. That little girl lived just long enough to spark a grand idea for him.

It wasn't the wounds that killed the burn victims. It was the shock. Their bodies suddenly went out of balance. They lost nerve function because of the shift in electrolytes. More important than tending to the burns was hooking up that IV to keep their nervous systems running.

Burn victim after burn victim. Death after death. It taught him.

Harold walked toward the pharmacy with his shoulders hunched forward. In the lobby, his shadow cast out across the gray linoleum. It fell on the statue of the archangel Gabriel that stood dead center in full marble glory. It had a child's face with a cleft chin and taut little dimples beneath its premature crow's feet. Harold loved that statue. He saw in its smiling face a fullness of life and beauty. It was very familiar, not like the dying masses that shuffled past him.

A few bland, sunken faces caught his eye, each sitting alone on one of the benches that lined the perimeter of the lobby. A woman chatting quietly with herself. A man slumped over a cane barely standing. Dead. All of them. Or dying. He'd seen enough to recognize it. That uncanny look of death. He knew it well.

When he reached the pharmacy he found the counter empty. No one noticed as he walked in. When Harold cleared his throat the only answer was an airy, distant sniffle. He took a quick peek behind the counter through the pharmacy curtains. Margie was sitting on the ground, spinning her wedding ring between her fingers. She hadn't noticed him yet. She breathed slowly and peacefully but sniveled gently from time to time.

Harold did the only thing he'd ever done in such a situation. He pretended he'd seen nothing.

The bell sounded louder than he'd intended as he stood by the counter looking vacantly at the vials on the back wall. He waited for a response from Margie.

"Dr. Fisk," she said from behind the curtain. The long pause before she emerged must have given her time to fix her makeup because she looked positively glowing when he saw her.

Harold's mouth flopped open, but no words came out.

"Do you need something?" Margie asked. "The Aspirin? I can get you a couple of them without a charge if you want."

Harold nodded feverishly. "A headache. I think there might be an occlusion in my nasopharynx." Which of course wasn't true and he felt awful lying.

"Nasopharynx?" Margie asked. "I'll bet that's in your nose. Isn't it, Doctor?"

Harold smiled. "Right. It's a silly way to say I'm all stuffed up."

Margie went back to grab the pills, talking over her shoulder as she opened the bottle. "Well at least your voice is all right. I know you doctors need to talk all day."

She handed over two pills along with a small paper cup of water. Harold looked down at them. He hated taking medication, especially when it wasn't required. "Thank you," he said. The pills tasted bitter as he choked them back.

"I didn't see little Jack yet today," she said as she put the bottle back on the shelf. She fumbled with it because she still held her ring in her hand. "I thought he might want to sleep in after this last operation."

Harold nodded. "He's well."

"That's my Magic Jack," she said. She touched her ring compulsively. "He'll be out of here soon, I hope, back with his brothers. Every Tuesday, after school you know, they all line up outside so he can see them out the window. He misses them."

"I wish they could visit," Harold mused absently.

Margie smiled and looked away. "Me too," she said. "I understand the parents only policy. Kids don't belong in a hospital making noise." She put her ring in a pocket and caught Harold's gaze. "I wish we visited more."

Harold leaned forward as Margie looked away. "You do well," he said. "Jack couldn't be luckier."

She poked at a tray of pills. "It was nice to see you, Dr. Fisk. I hope your head feels better."

Harold nodded. "It's feeling better already," he said.

He walked quickly back up to his office and checked the file for some information about Jack's father. It only said his name and birth date. He was fifty-two. For the amount of money spent on these treatments Mr. Needham must have been very successful. The phone number was listed, but the chances that Harold would reach Mr. Needham during business hours were remote. He decided to try the house anyway, chancing that one of the children was home.

The phone rang. It rang again. Harold felt his palms grow wetter against the receiver. "Hello," said the voice on the other end of the phone. She sounded portly and old. Probably the maid.

"Is Mr. Needham there?" Harold asked.

The woman answered earnestly. "Oh no. You haven't heard? He's at St. Ann's."

"St. Ann's Hospital?" asked Harold, stupidly. "Visiting his son?" he stammered.

"Well, no," she said. Then she filled in a silent moment with a very loud "umm ..."

"I'll just call for him there then," Harold said. "Thank you kindly."

He hung up and immediately dialed the operator and asked for Jason Needham's room. During the minute or so while the operator searched the files Harold had time to reconsider.

"Room 302 in the east wing," the operator said. Room 302. That was the psychiatric ward. Harold said his thanks to the operator and hung up. Normally St. Ann's only hosted women and children but in rare instances they'd house a well-appointed husband if he needed help. This was definitely a rare instance.

But first he had to do rounds. When he reached little Jack's bed he found the boy sleeping, nestled uncomfortably with his arms and legs tied down to prevent him from scratching at his wounds.

Little Jack always looked calm. Only the parts of his body that had been covered in the flannel pajamas had burned. His face was spared. Thank God. He wore the most eloquent expressions. The nurse exposed a few of Jack's sores. Some wept a clear liquid, but most had completely healed. The white-pink tissue showed no signs of infection. Two more skin grafts. The boy had more than a fighting chance.

The next girl, Sonja, ten years old, wasn't so lucky. She'd been brought in the night before. Burned on the face, down her throat. Today was her day. He knew it as soon as she'd entered his ward. She had perhaps five minutes until the end. The sallow vacancy tipped him off. That and something Harold could never explain. He'd said once before to a colleague that a patient would die in the next ten minutes. He couldn't believe the scolding. "You never write a patient off!"

Ordinarily one should never. But when one has absolute knowledge that death is inevitable …

While Harold made notes on Sonja's chart, she coughed. Her breath quickened. That only worsened the influx of fluids and scar through her system. Harold fought. He pounded at her chest and felt her silent heart reignite only to silence once again. Then she left him. He'd watched the veneer of life chip and crackle overnight. Just that tiny cough blew it clear away. Most can't see the difference between a living person and a dead one. To Harold it was as if she'd been translucent before and only now he saw her.

After he informed the family and filled out the paperwork, Harold took a brief stopover in the chapel and whispered a tearful prayer for Sonja. He'd known her not even a day but he felt her loss bodily. Despite her pain she'd laughed when he told his joke about the gargoyles favorite office supply. It's stationary. He'd never forget that laugh.

He finished his rounds. Then Harold walked with purpose to

the psychiatric ward. Harold and Dr. Wilson, the head of psychiatry, weren't on the best terms. Not that Harold harbored any resentment. No. When they'd met, the first thing that Harold talked to him about was his experience in Korea. They spoke for only a few minutes, but in that time Dr. Wilson had decided that Harold should not be practicing medicine in his current state. He said Harold couldn't cope. Said it was killing him. In confidence of course.

It was Korea's fault. Korea exploded. Korea pounded and ached. Every breath of Korean air choked, every bite of Korean food burned. The death everywhere. He knew death better than he knew life. Of course Dr. Wilson wouldn't sympathize with that. He hadn't seen a real wound since his residency.

Dr. Fisk reached room 302. Jason Needham sat in a leather chair with a thick leather-bound book perched on his lap. He scanned feverishly, finishing each dense page in just a few seconds. His broad forearms and monstrous hands dwarfed the book. His hair, mostly gone, had several distinct shocks of white. His chin dipped down on one side. He was dying slowly. He had ten years left at most.

Harold stepped carefully through the door but said nothing. He just watched Jason read. The shallow, tepid shores of Pacific isles glimmered with the same intensity as the blue in Jason's eyes. Miles deep or barely inches. Harold couldn't stand to look at them for long.

Instead he scanned Jason's face. As he read, Harold noticed that the orbicularis oculi muscle around his left eye registered no movement, while his right remained entirely expressive. He'd had a stroke. Other features led to that conclusion, like the way his constantly circulating jaw dipped as it moved to the left. His cigar smoldered in the ash tray. Jason focused entirely on his book. He hadn't noticed Harold yet.

"Psychiatric, physical, or spiritual?" Jason asked without looking up. His deep voice thrust smoothly and quickly like far off artillery, like a man who'd seen combat. Quick words. Short syllables. He drove forth like a tank.

"I'm Dr. Fisk," Harold answered.

Jason motioned with his eyes toward the other leather chair across from him. Harold sat. "Fisk?" asked Jason. "What's a man of English roots doing in a Catholic hospital? Of course I should ask myself that." He slurred his speech slightly and only on his esses. He sounded like Edward R. Murrow aside from that flaw. He stared right through Harold, unblinking. Entirely relaxed.

Harold's hands shook. This man scared him. Though doctors usually have the strength of title and austerity on their side, this man had a way of leveling that advantage immediately. "Your Jack, sir," Harold said. "He's in my ward, and he's doing much better these days."

Jason laughed. "Of course he is. Could you imagine a little thing like a burn taking my son's life? He'll live through anything."

"It was close …"

Darkness billowed into the room, and the air thickened as Jason bowed his head. He clenched his jaw and winced. The tendons in his neck buckled visibly. Anguish. "Thank you Doctor," he whispered, and looked up again. "You're a saint."

Harold's lip quivered. Despite being frightened by them, Jason's eyes pulled him in. Harold couldn't look away. As ferociously as he could, Harold said, "He still has a fight."

"He'll win," Jason said. Eyes vibrate when they stare straight ahead. They undulate with little quivers like a running motor. All eyes do this. But Harold swore that Jason's eyes were still. A glacial blue. He closed them only briefly after he'd spoken. "He's strong. It's in his face." He lilted to allow Harold an entrance. "Dr. Fisk …"

"Harold," he said. He usually didn't offer his first name, but he almost couldn't help it.

"Harold, I have an uncanny ability. I love life. I'm drawn to it. I feel it. I see it. Even in the dying I see the last glimmers of the soul. Even in my miserable state, I see it in the mirror. I've cheated death more than anyone you've ever known. In the war …" He trailed off and looked desperately into the distance. "Were you in the war?"

"Korea," Harold answered.

"No, I mean *the* war." Jason snapped his book shut without placing a marker. It crashed down next to his chair. "Pacific Theater. *USS Monterey*. Attacked eight times. Four ribbons. We had a typhoon slip two fighters off their cables. Along with six other officers, I stopped the fire, saved the ship." He caught a breath and then reached with leisurely slowness toward his cigar and took a mellow puff. "Munitions officer. We had over seventy tons of live munitions on that boat. Twenty thousand triggering devices. Some compound—two ways to blow you clear out of your shoes."

Harold scratched at his cheek. "I was a doctor," said Harold. "Medical unit."

"Not on the front lines?" Jason asked.

"About ten miles from the fighting," Harold answered. "But we had a few fighters find their way into camp. We had some shooting."

Jason sat back. "So you know what it's like to survive. Survival is everything."

Harold wrung his hands and tried to smile. Jason tapped his fingers on the table.

"I like your tie," Jason said warmly after a long pause. "You picked that tie out yourself, didn't you? Not your wife. It's not like the ninny ties these head shrinkers wear. Always paisley."

Harold laughed. "Is that what it's called? I think it's supposed to be soothing."

Jason snorted. "Most of these doctors have no taste. They talk to you like they know something but I'll tell you, there's nothing Mr. Freud said that wasn't said better in a fortune cookie. I've read *The Interpretation of Dreams, Totem and Taboo, Zur Einführung des Narzißmus.* Bullshit layered upon sauerkraut layered upon even more bullshit." They shared a quick laugh. Harold agreed completely.

Jason drew nearer to Harold. "You seem like you can read people," he said. "I should know. We can always spot our own type. But while I see the happiness in people, you see the sadness."

Harold took a deep breath. "I think your Jack is sad."

"What medical school did you go to?" asked Jason abruptly.

"University of Pittsburgh," Harold answered.

"Pitt?" Jason asked. He twirled his cigar in its ashtray with a Bogart smile. "You couldn't have learned how to do what you did from a place like Pitt."

"I'm a burn specialist," Harold said. "I'm the only one in Columbus. You're very lucky your son came to this hospital. He could have gone anywhere. St. Ann's just happened to be closest."

They sat in silence for a long moment as Jason puffed at his cigar. Harold looked out of the window toward the adjacent wing, a brocade of tiny windows digging into a solid brown brick wall.

"Korea then," said Jason grumpily, like he was disappointed. "You learned about burns in Korea."

Harold sighed. He'd found another shrink, this time an amateur. "That's right," Harold said. "Lots of burns. Mostly children."

Jason scoffed. "You treated the enemy?" He snarled into a full bear muzzle but his voice stayed tight and focused. The cadence of a train on a track. "When there were wounded American soldiers to help? You treated the China men?"

"I swore an oath," said Harold. "You can't imagine how devastating the napalm ..."

"Napalm?" Jason interrupted, suddenly composed and unencumbered. "You mean the incendiary? You mix naphthenic acid and palmitic acid and then stir in some petroleum?" He choked and bit into his cheek before continuing. "Operation Meetinghouse. I must have loaded ten thousand gallons. We used it for the first time out there in the Pacific. I fashioned a triple rig. One trigger split the first casing, it was a fifteen wire thermite charge. That let loose ten cluster bombs filled with the incendiary. Those split open with a C-17G pressure sensitive trigger about five hundred feet above the ground—ninety kilopascals. That spilled the incendiary fluid. Then my contribution. The last trigger was an aluminum and phosphorous igniter that only lit when exposed to air just a second before hitting the ground. I think it ended the war."

Harold's hand shook all the more. He bowed his head and said a quick Our Father to himself.

Jason spoke softly but with a pounding rhythm. Hypnotic. "The reason you were able to heal my son was because they used my bombs in Korea." He puffed his cigar. His muse drifted up toward the ceiling in swirls of smoke.

Harold felt sick. He watched the bomb's descent in his mind while Jason talked. He felt its guts open and spill that black fluid toward the world below. He felt that fluid light on fire and wash over hundreds of innocents. He couldn't bear to open his eyes. Yet as always, he remained as composed as he could be. "Were you there when your son was burned?" Harold asked.

"No," Jason answered. The left side of his face sagged even more. "I split time between New York and Chicago. Trading, mostly bonds, some commodities. You know, frozen meat futures are a sure bet. Mark my word." Yet again he smiled that sophisticated smile. "I work five days out of the month sometimes. Sometimes every day and all night for weeks on end. I come home when I can."

"Do you want to see your son?" Harold asked finally. He looked up and into Jason's eyes. They had such fire. Everything else about Jason had died long ago, but a spark remained in the dark of his impossibly blue eyes. Something fought feverishly to live.

Jason whispered to himself. "Magic Jack. What a boy."

"He has about a fifty-fifty chance at this point," Harold said. "It'll be an infection that gets him or some sickness due to his weakened immune system. That's if it happens."

"Are you administering topical antibiotics?" Jason asked.

Knowledge came out of Jason's mouth bolstered by his droll confidence. Harold almost couldn't answer. "Yes," Harold said. "Gramicidin."

"He'll be fine then," Jason said dismissively. "Working in munitions, people get burned. I've seen my share. I could fill a drawer with the number of fingers I've had to pick up off the deck." He took another puff of his cigar. "If we had live ammunition that was mis-triggered I had to go in there and defuse it. You talk about surgery. If you make one mistake ..." He cracked his neck and stretched the joints of his gigantic forearms. "I needed to be on top of my game. They had a good supply of Dextroamphetamine and Benzedrine on boat so I was fine. Never had any problems."

"And your wife works in the pharmacy?" Harold asked, putting certain pieces of the puzzle together. "That's why you're speaking so fast. Does Dr. Wallace know?"

Jason cut him off powerfully. "It's a good job for her." He twisted in his seat and heaved his chest. "I wanted her to stay at home but she thought she could see me more often if she worked here at the hospital." He grumbled. "And Jack, too."

Harold didn't believe that for a second. "Mr. Needham, why are you here?" he asked.

"Because I'm a drunk," Jason answered. "Look at me. Who else isn't sick but wears a bathrobe at two o'clock on a Wednesday? I'm trying to get dried out. I'm a good Catholic. I know it's not right for my sons to see their father bleary."

Harold looked at the book by Jason's foot. It was stamped along the pages, "Property of St. Ann's." Volume five of *Harrison's Principles of Internal Medicine*. Half the pages were dog eared or marked. The four preceding volumes were stacked in the corner. Three thousand pages at least. "How many times have you been admitted here?" Harold asked.

Jason stared through Harold. He'd stopped breathing. Red spider webs of veins shot toward his irises. "This time is different."

The room spun through hovering cigar smoke. Nothing Jason said mattered. Those kids. Those little charred bodies. The stink of singed hair and linen. It was because of him. Sickened, Harold curled forward. He focused on the patterned linoleum to settle his stomach. Harold wasn't sure how to feel, but he was certain that Jason deserved his full wrath more than anyone else he'd ever met.

Harold took a moment to clear his throat. "Mr. Needham," he began, "did you realize that your son never once asked to see you?" He choked. His heart felt as though it had stopped entirely.

Jason's face folded down toward his premature jowls. Suddenly he had no expression at all. That spark Harold had noticed, the ever-bright glint in the black of Jason's eye, it faded. For the first time in his life Harold was happy to see death on someone's face. He felt no guilt. He thought he should, but he didn't. He suddenly realized that despite those lively eyes, Jason had but two years left if he even had a day.

Harold gave his leave. He walked back to the pharmacy, the only place he could think to go. Margie stood behind the counter. She'd regained her customary smile. "How are you, Dr. Fisk?" she asked.

"I just wanted to tell you something," he said. "I talked to your husband. I won't tell anybody about this, but I want you to stop stealing pills for him. You're not doing him any favors."

It must not have been the first time she'd been caught and let off, because she had no reply. "Thank you Dr. Fisk," she said to his shoes. "I thank the Lord for you every night."

"Promise me that when little Jack gets out of here—little Magic Jack—promise me that you'll spare him from his father. Save him."

Margie nodded. "His brothers take care of him. Jason Junior, he's our oldest, he's already stood up to my husband." Then a tear ran down her cheek. It pulled with it some of Margie's makeup. For the first time, Harold caught a glimpse of the death that had begun to find purchase on her face. Slightly purple-green. Slightly flat. A recent bruise that left behind irreparable capillaries. She had a good long time left, probably forty years. For how many of those would Jason be strong enough to hit her like that?

None, Harold thought. Jason wasn't nearly strong enough, thank God. But just the thought ... Harold's gullet tightened into the pit of his stomach. His eyelids shook, and his skull reverberated with children's cries. "I'd appreciate another of those Aspirin if you don't mind," he said. "That headache is coming back."

She turned to get the pills. Harold couldn't stand to look at her since he'd seen a glimpse of her demise. He turned toward the pharmacy entrance, a window looking into that cold, dark lobby. He caught his reflection. It looked so sunken. He hadn't long to go. In his cleft chin and loose dimples beneath his sagging crow's feet, in his skeletal forehead, in his eye sockets drooping from decay, he saw his time was coming. A year. Two at most.

At least he knew that little Jack would make it. He'd seen it. He'd live on almost forever, despite the odds.

Margie brought the pills. "Here you go Dr. Fisk."

He smiled and took them. "Thank you, Margie," he said. "I'll say a Hail Mary tonight for little Jack. I'll pray to Gabriel as well. I don't know why the angels get left out of our prayers so often."

"They're too busy," said Margie. "For every angel there's a devil. They can't stop the fight long enough to hear our prayers." She took the paper cup back from Harold and dropped it in the trash. "But the angels win. I know they do."

"I suppose that's right," Harold smiled. "If they're not winning, I hope at least they'll take the devils down with them so that everyone else can live in peace."

Margie smiled and wiped the tear from her face, smudging her makeup. The little trail of death disappeared. Harold sighed his relief. Margie took that as a sign he wanted to go. "I'll see you tomorrow, Dr. Fisk."

"Absolutely," he said. "I usually don't say this, but I guarantee that little Jack will continue to get better. I promise you." He walked briskly back through the lobby toward the Archangel Gabriel statue. At least there were angels, even if they couldn't hear his prayers. At least there were angels. But first there was work. He'd neglected his filing for too long. At this rate he'd be up until eight scratching his pencil against the paper. But he'd make time to pray for the boy. He'd sleep at most four hours that night, just as he did every night, but he'd make sure to pray.

At home he scrawled out illegible notes across a sordid mess of papers. He'd gone through this same situation before. Laws were meaningless. The department of welfare was no help. He'd tried before.

He drew out his options. They all required parental consent. If Jason Needham didn't exist, Harold could have gotten help from the parish. He could have found space at Gilmour Academy or a boarding school in some other state. But in this world nothing, save for the breath of God, could have saved that boy from his father. Not a doctor. Not a burn. Not a plea for help. Not a priest. Not even a year in the hospital.

Harold made a note with his physician's scrawl. With a wide downward stroke he crossed out his treatment plan and began anew. *John Needham—age three—one year burn treatment plus one year physical therapy. In-patient.* He closed the file and laid his head on his desk to sleep, the best he'd had in years.

Drew Farnsworth came to Columbus, Ohio three years ago with his fiancé Colleen. He works with Green Lane Design as a data center systems designer. He is also currently developing film properties with his brother Gavin, a director, and his writing partner Anwar Uddin.

Mount Carmel St. Ann's hospital originated as St. Ann's Infant Asylum in 1908. The Mount Carmel hospital system also houses the first nationally accredited school of nursing in the country and the first free-standing emergency and diagnostic center in central Ohio.

The hospital admitted its first male patient in 1972.

FRESHMEN YEAR
The Ohio State University, Columbus, Ohio
Nick Coplen

1976
BREAKAWAY
By Brenda Layman

I cringed as far away from the scuffling pile of men as I could, plastering myself against the bus window. Rage gave the drunk strength, and it took three of them to hold him down. They had dragged his jacket down over his back, and his face was pressed against the bus floor. The man had threatened to kill us all, and I watched with fascinated horror as he mouthed slobbering curses into the filth. Bobby shifted his grip on the man's shoulder, and the maniac struck like a snake, trying to bite the strong hand that pinned him, barely missing. I cried out and was surprised to hear that my voice sounded like the yelp of a frightened puppy.

Bobby looked up and his brown eyes met my blue ones. He looked surprisingly calm.

Less than two weeks ago I had begun the first leg of this journey. It was the Wednesday before Thanksgiving, 1976, and I was a freshman at The Ohio State University on my way home to Kentucky for a long weekend. Waiting downtown in the Columbus, Ohio bus station, I was looking over the crowd of people who would be my fellow passengers when I saw a familiar face. Bobby Thomas, a high school classmate, was standing near me.

He looked a little different than when I had last seen him on our graduation day. Bobby, a football and track star, had sported an impressive afro then. I remembered how he used to squash it down when he put on his football helmet. Bobby had relinquished his trademark hairstyle in favor of a short crop.

I figured that, like me, he had discovered that a college student's schedule didn't leave a lot of time for fussing with hair. I wore mine in a Farrah Fawcett shag, and my natural wave made that an easy style for me to manage. I caught Bobby's eye and he gave me a quick smile and a lift of his head in recognition.

"Hey, Beth," he said.

"Hi Bobby," I answered. "How have you been? Aren't you at DeVry?"

"Yeah. How do you like OSU?"

We boarded the bus together, and Bobby took my bag and shoved it into the overhead space with his. We tucked our backpacks under the bench. I took the aisle seat, he slid in beside me, and soon the bus was on its way to our hometown. We hadn't been much more than acquaintances in high school, but our mutual friends and our college experiences gave us plenty to talk about.

Time flew as the bus rolled south down Route 23, and Bobby and I chatted and laughed together. I enjoyed listening to his funny stories, and it was good to hear someone speak in the soft Kentucky drawl we had both grown up with. Bobby's new haircut suited him, making him look older and more studious. His cologne wafted over to my side of the seat, not overpowering, but pleasant. When the bus warmed up, we took off our jackets and Bobby stuffed them both in beside our bags up above. He pushed his sleeves up his muscular arms and his blue sweatshirt made an attractive contrast with his chocolate brown skin. He didn't mention a girlfriend, but I was willing to bet he had more than one girl interested in him.

It was in Portsmouth that I noticed something happening. The bus stopped there to load and unload passengers. The people who got on gave us pointed looks as they walked by. One woman whispered something to her companion, and they both stared openly as they edged past us down the center aisle. For a moment I was confused, wondering what we had done. Then I remembered why Bobby and I had not been closer friends in high school. Appalachia in the 1970s was not a place where a blue-eyed white girl and a black boy could hang out together without causing a stir.

I could tell Bobby felt it too. We both fell silent. To break the awkwardness, I dragged my backpack out from under my seat, unzipped it, and pulled out a book.

"Well, I still have some studying to do, even though it's vacation," I said.

"Yeah, I should study too," he said, reaching down and retrieving his own backpack. We remained silent, with our noses in our respective books, until the bus reached its destination.

Bobby got up and pulled our jackets and bags down from above. He handed me mine without a word. We shuffled off the bus with the rest of the passengers. Bobby's brother was there to meet him. My classmate turned to me and stuck out his hand.

"Well, see you around," he said. "We'd offer you a ride home, but you know how it is."

I did know. I remembered the time a new girl at school invited me to go with her to the city swimming pool. It was the first time I had been there. My family belonged to a private club, and that was where I spent my summers. Club membership was by invitation only. There were no black members. A few days later, back at the private club with my old friends, I mentioned that I had been to the city pool. Silence. Then one girl sniffed, "I would never go there."

"Why? It was okay," I said.

"Because," she whispered, "they let black people in the water."

"But what does that matter?" I asked. "They weren't doing anything different than what we do. Just swimming and goofing off like us."

My friends looked at me and shook their heads. I was baffled, and yet I felt vaguely guilty for having broken the unspoken code. I went back to the city pool with my new friend a few times, and once we watched Bobby and some other boys do stunts off the high dive. I never mentioned it to my old friends at the club.

Memories of those visits to the city pool nagged at my mind all weekend. I had been able to get away with fitting in with both groups then, and I knew that I didn't want to have to make a choice. Our town wasn't a big place, but Bobby and I didn't cross paths again until we met at the bus stop on Sunday afternoon for the ride back to Columbus. We greeted each other, but Bobby was distant and aloof. He avoided eye contact with me and stood as far away as he could. Part of me wanted to walk up to him like nothing was wrong, but part of me still struggled with guilt. Whether the guilt was from breaking the unspoken code or from confronting my own cowardice, I didn't know. I only knew that my gut boiled with anger and shame. I wanted Bobby to make the first move, to take the responsibility, but he didn't.

We boarded the bus. I got a whole seat to myself near the front and Bobby walked past me without a look and took a seat somewhere behind me. With a lurch and a roar, we were off, on our way back to Columbus. I read for a while, but with no one to talk to and night coming on, I started to doze. My head kept drooping over my book, my eyes would close, and I would be nearly asleep until the bus hit a bump in the road and I was jerked awake.

When we reached Portsmouth, I decided to get off, stretch my legs, and buy a soda, hoping the caffeine would help. When I climbed back on the bus, I found Bobby sitting in the window seat I had vacated, with a sheepish smile on his face and a look of apology in his big, brown eyes with their curly lashes.

"I figured it would be okay now," he said.

"I'm glad you did," I said. I sat down beside him and pretty soon we were chatting and laughing like old friends again, telling each other all about our Thanksgiving weekend vacations while the bus rolled along up the dark highway toward Columbus.

A few new passengers had boarded the bus at Portsmouth. One of them, a dirty, disheveled man in dingy white painter's pants and a faded black windbreaker took the empty spot right behind me. His thin, fair hair hung down over his eyes, and he smelled of beer. He collapsed into the seat and promptly dropped off to sleep. I tried to concentrate on Bobby's spicy cologne instead of the stink coming from behind me.

Somewhere between Portsmouth and Columbus, the man woke up. He started to mutter to himself, shifting around as if searching for something. We could hear him growing louder and more agitated. Suddenly he rose to his feet and yelled,

"I'm gonna start shooting you people, do you hear me? Ain't none of you all gonna get off this bus. You all think you can just treat me bad, stare at me and stuff, but you can't. You hear me? I've got a gun."

Fear shot through me like an electric shock. I turned and saw the wild-eyed and red-faced man weaving from side to side, one hand gripping something in his jacket pocket. He was right behind me, breathing down on me as he swayed and clutched the back of my seat, cursing and yelling his threats. I closed my eyes and scrunched down in my seat, trying to make myself invisible.

The bus swerved, and I felt him stumble and nearly fall into the aisle, but he righted himself and continued his rant. I could smell his sour odor, like a pile of old beer cans, and feel his weight leaning on the cushion behind me. My heart was pounding and the palms of my hands dampened with sweat. No one else on the bus spoke as we sped down the road, the man lurching and cursing, threatening to kill us all for some imagined offense.

Suddenly Bobby's face was close to mine. He whispered, "You have to change seats with me."

"I can't," I whispered back. "I can't move. I'm too scared."

The man staggered again and grabbed the seat behind Bobby's head.

"You all think you're better than me, don't you? Well, you won't be thinkin' that for long," he slurred. I couldn't make myself turn around and look to see if his hand was still in the jacket pocket.

"You can do it," Bobby insisted. "I need the aisle seat. I'm going to count to three, and on three you're going to slide under and I'm going to slide over. Ready?"

I nodded. Bobby counted, "One, two, three." I slid toward the window, and Bobby moved over me to the aisle. I felt sweat trickle down my back. Had the man noticed us? Would he shoot Bobby? Would he shoot me? I fought back new terror when I looked up and realized that Bobby, the driver, and two men from farther back in the bus were signaling to each other in the driver's mirror.

It happened in a split second. The two men dove forward and Bobby spun out of his seat. The three of them grabbed the drunk, pinning his arms to his sides and forcing him to the floor. I watched Bobby's hands grip the man's shoulders and slam his face onto the scuffed and dirty center aisle, and I struggled to connect that with the soft-spoken, gentle friend who had been beside me for the last hour. Crazed with anger and frustration, the man swore and spit, kicking and struggling to get free. One of the men who held him reached over and turned the jacket pockets out. There was no gun, just a crumpled pack of cigarettes and a disposable lighter.

They fought beside me as I huddled against the bus window for what seemed a long time, although it could not have been more than a couple of minutes. I realized the bus was slowing down, pulling over onto the berm and stopping. The driver opened the door, and two state troopers climbed on board. In seconds they had put the drunk in handcuffs and marched him off the bus to cheers and applause from the passengers.

When Bobby returned to the seat beside me, I threw my arms around him and hugged him. Outwardly he was ice-cool, but he was sweating and with my head against his hard chest I could hear his heart thudding. The big hand that was lost in the curls at the back of my neck was gentle again. Suddenly embarrassed, I pulled back and looked up at him.

"How did you know he didn't have a gun?"

"I didn't. You okay?"

"Yeah, I'm fine," I answered.

"Cause you don't look okay," Bobby continued. "You are white, I mean really white, like white as a sheet. You're not gonna faint, are you?"

I had to laugh. Bobby looked like he was more scared of me fainting than he had been afraid of the paranoid drunk who maybe had a gun and might have shot us.

It seemed just a short ride the rest of the way. We pulled into the bus station in Columbus around ten o' clock. Bobby brought my bag and jacket down from the overhead bin and handed them to me, then he went back to get his where he had left them over the seat he had chosen at the beginning of our trip. As I started down the aisle, I felt someone tap me on the shoulder and I turned around. A middle-aged woman was smiling at me.

"Your boyfriend was very brave. You must be proud of that young man." I looked back at Bobby, standing taller than the people in front of him, waiting patiently for his turn to move forward, his big, chocolate brown hands holding his backpack and duffel.

"Yes," I answered her. "Yes, I am."

 **Brenda Layman** is a freelance writer and a member of the Outdoor Writers of Ohio. In addition to her stories in Columbus Creative Cooperative anthologies, her work has appeared in *Ohio Valley Outdoors*, *Pickerington Magazine*, *Ohio Game & Fish*, and *Trout*. She lives in Pickerington with her husband, Mark.

Despite the decline in bus ridership, the Greyhound Lines terminal in Columbus, Ohio remains open and continues to provide service across the nation.

Currently, Greyhound competes with another bus line in Columbus, Megabus, which provides express service from the capital directly to Indianapolis, Chicago and Cincinnati at discounted rates.

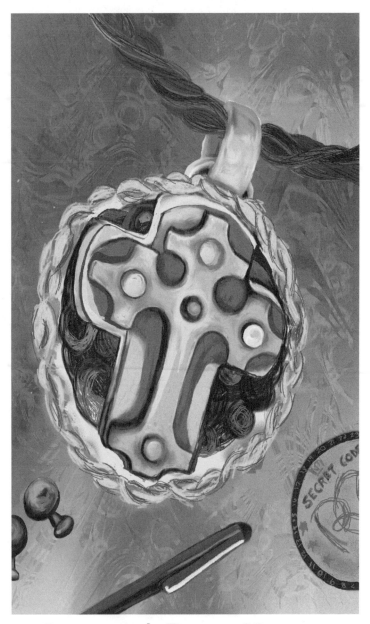

Callahan's Retail Museum
Adrianne DeVille

1982
CALLAHAN'S RETAIL MUSEM
By Amy S. Dalrymple

T he line at the Short North Jeni's was the longest I'd ever seen it, and by the time Charlotte and I reached the front—me with my usual scoop, Ugandan Vanilla Bean, and she with her Trio—the line snaked out the door and far down the block. Behind the counter, two trendy young ladies with their hair tied up in orange bandannas and their counterpart, a boy in tight jeans who wore his bandanna tucked in his back pocket served up sample after sample of new summer flavors and old favorites to the flushed, sweaty crowd.

But collective consciousness wasn't all that surprising that day—it was August, and the old-fashioned mercury thermometer outside my kitchen window read ninety-four degrees. It sure took me back, the stifling heat—took me back precisely thirty years to my worst summer, 1982. A lot has changed in thirty years. I'm an old man now, mostly watching it all from a distance.

I knew I should put the poor kid in my air-conditioned truck and drive her to the movies or to that indoor water park. I knew I had no business dragging her outside, but the last thing I wanted was for Charlotte to spend her last day in Columbus, her last day with her old grandpa circling 270 or packed into a movie theater like a couple of sardines with a bunch of strangers.

So, I left it up to her, and just like the classy kid she is, she said simply, "Let's go to the park." Goodale Park. Whenever Astrid, her mother, went missing all those years ago, I always knew to look there first, and I'd usually find her sprawled out on her stomach beneath some old oak, her nose in a book or maybe playing a game of chess against herself. And Tali, seven years older, could usually be found smoking behind the bathrooms, or draped over some picnic tables just looking morose with her punk friends.

I stood in line behind my lovely granddaughter, ghostlike and dressed in her grandmother's white tea dress, a 1940s relic even when my Lizzy wore it thirty years ago. It billowed around Charlotte's wiry frame, hiding her ankles and grazing the tile floor. Worried about her fair skin in the beating summer sun, I had allowed her to raid the old trunk in the corner of my apartment, its black leather peeling, brass buckles tarnished with years of neglect. It held all that remained of my old shop. She dove in headfirst, and I left her in search of sunblock, returning to find her wearing not only a wide-brimmed straw hat with a faded, fraying blush-rose ribbon, but also *the white tea dress.* My breath caught deep in my throat for a split second, and I felt a little dizzy, re-membering.

Charlotte earned a lot of curious looks in that dress, but this was the Short North, after all, where almost anything goes even still, more than three decades after I first set up shop here, although the landscape is much different. Callahan's at 714, it was called, but its true name was always changing. I liked to call it Cal's Retail Museum, because it really was like a museum, filled with wonderful things for inquiring minds.

Most of them I lost when the shop closed in '94, but standing there in that narrow ice cream shop, decorated with strands of brightly-colored flags and teeming with people, I could still see my shop, and my favorite things as if no time had passed at all. A Renaissance soapstone bust of an Italian lady wearing a knit skullcap, her head slightly turned to the left, her eyes downcast. A set of Babylonian tablets that I was eventually able to translate. It turns out they were just grain receipts, nothing special. No one ever believes me about them, but there are lots of things that escaped museums.

And my prized possession, a Civil War pistol, a funny thing to hold precious for a guy that tried pretty hard to evade the Vietnam draft. The engraving on it was still pristine—*H.E. Ashbrook, 55th Reg. OH Volunteers.* I used to keep it in the glass case, but I could never seem to part with it, and I finally moved it to a cabinet behind the counter. Well, I finally ended up selling the gun that summer, the summer of '82. I had to get it off my hands.

"Are you folks all set?" The young lady behind the counter woke me from my daydream, and I handed her a twenty and glanced down at Charlotte. The next morning, I would put her on a plane to meet her parents, who were waiting for her at their new home in Tokyo. They were gracious enough to allow me to keep her the whole summer. As-trid wouldn't stop talking about me visiting them, coming to stay, even, but she must have known the truth. I'll be seventy-five next year, and it's no time for a move all the way around the world, where I won't be able to earn my keep.

And Tali, my oldest, she's a Buddhist now. She lives at the Zen Center in California, grows all her own vegetables. I've been out there a fair amount to visit, and she always asks me to stay, but I don't really fit in there. No, I belong here, in my little apartment above the ice cream shop.

So that's where we spent our last day, Charlotte tagging along in that ethereal dress while I told my stories, grateful that she hadn't yet grown tired of them. Or stopped believing in them. I wish I had a nickel for every time some Sherlock Holmes type pointed out the inconsistencies in my stories, but every good storyteller knows you have to add in a little color when memories begin to fade into grainy oblivion. Specifically, I meant to tell her a story about one of her mother's last days with me in Columbus, thirty years ago. Maybe it was too mature a story for a ten-year-old, but there's far worse on television these days. And the Callahan girls have always been a little too precocious for their own good.

By some stroke of magic, two stools by the window opened up just when we needed them. Charlotte ate her ice cream gingerly, spooning just a baby-sized amount of each flavor—Icelandic Happy Marriage Cake, Whiskey and Pecan, then Juniper and Lemon Curd—into her mouth. I shot her a curious glance when she ordered the Whiskey and Pecan, but it was the juniper that caught my breath. The scent of juniper always makes me think of death and loss; it always takes me back to that day thirty years ago that I have tried so hard to bury. But just like the special things in my shop, it has a life of its own. If it was forgotten, it was only for a little while, and if it was buried, it would only be a matter of time before someone dug it back up, brushed off the dirt, and tried to sell it for cash.

I just stared out the window, briefly forgetting my ice cream. I always liked to meditate for a moment before the first bite, the first sip.

"Thanks for letting me borrow this dress, Grandpa," Charlotte said, flashing me a wide smile. She was a quiet kid, a little too shy, and her smiles were usually fleeting things you could miss if you blinked an eye, but this one lit up her whole face.

"Your grandmother loved that dress," I said quietly, not trying to hide the sadness in my voice. How Lizzy loved that dress, how she always conspired to find excuses to wear it.

"Sometimes we'd pop into Mike's or the Russian Tea Room, but we usually couldn't afford to go out. She'd just put on that dress, and we would go for long walks; we would take a little cheese and day-old bread and cheap wine from Christy's Market down to the park. We would walk back up High Street and try to imagine what it might look like someday.

"Things were really different back then, you know. It was a pretty run-down area. Oh, it was teeming with history, and all that beautiful architecture, but you wouldn't want to walk around much after dark."

"I guess she would like here it now," Charlotte said.

"Yeah, I guess she would." I sighed, and I finally took a bite of my ice cream. "Well, I think she'd like you to have it."

Charlotte's face lit up again, and she slid right off her stool and threw her arms around me. "Thanks, Grandpa!"

"You're welcome, kiddo. Now, finish your ice cream, I have something else to show you." I reached below the open collar of my linen tunic, grasped the soft black cord, and carefully pulled out the medallion that had been weighing heavily on me all morning—for many years, in fact. I slipped the cord over my head and held the medallion in my open palm. Usually, I kept it locked up, rarely touching it without soft white gloves. But sometimes it begged to be taken out, like a living thing deprived of fresh air. I always forgot how heavy it was.

Charlotte's eyes were wide with the question she didn't need to speak.

"Well, Charlotte, I think it's about time I told you about the lost medallion of Charlemagne.

* * *

I gave this old medallion to your mom when she was the same age as you—ten. It was just this time of year too, and hotter than Mount Vesuvius. It was the dog days, when I'd seriously consider chopping off this old ponytail, and maybe my beard, too, but I could never go through with it. I guess I'd just feel naked without it. We didn't have any air-conditioning then, either, in 1982. Oh, it was invented—your mom's not that old, but we couldn't afford it.

It was right before Lizzy—your grandma—left to take the girls to her sister's on Lake Erie, for their annual vacation, and—well, you're old enough, you know the ending, Char—I knew they weren't coming back this time.

Astrid helped me in the shop a lot that summer. Tali was seventeen and disinterested. She was sleeping until noon, spending the rest of the day and half the night out with her punk friends, and Lizzy was …

preoccupied. In bed, where she stayed most of the time in those days. In the beginning, when we first opened the shop, she kept the books; she did all the window displays. She was just as zealous as me about fixing up the Short North—in fact the shop was her idea. But she started to lose interest when it became difficult to pay the rent on time, when dinner was peas porridge cold for the ninth day in a row. Do you think old hippies are vegetarians purely for moral reasons? Meat is a lot more expensive than dried beans.

Your grandma started talking a lot about growing up in those days, as if we had failed to do so. "It's time to forget about those silly dreams we had when we were twenty," she said. "It's time we found a better school for the girls." She didn't like them traipsing around the Short North anymore—it wasn't changing fast enough for her. It was still gritty. Men would stumble into the shop, drunk as skunks—once one of them peed right on the floor and then stumbled right back out. Another time, this desperate looking fellow tried to sell me gold fillings right out of his mouth. You don't believe your old grandpa, do you? Well, he brought his buddy in with him, pliers in hand, ready to pull them out right then and there.

My stories can be verified—just ask your mom and your Aunt Tali. They were with me the morning they found an old drunk dead in the doorway next to Mike's Bar and Grill. Someone must have deposited him there the night before at closing time, thinking he'd sober up in the cold air. But he never did, and when I went over to him to give him a shake and see if he needed a coffee, he was cold and stiff. Astrid and Tali stood on the sidewalk with me, waiting for the police. The yellow police tape scared up attention, and we did pretty well in the shop that day.

So, Astrid had been filling in for Lizzy. She'd been running the cash register since she was seven, and she started keeping the books the previous summer when she was nine. You think she learned all those business skills in college? Well, she was sitting at the counter, poring over some paperwork when Beene came stumbling through the front door, his hair a frizzy mane going off in all directions, wire spectacles sliding down his nose.

"Uncle Beene!" Astrid screeched and bolted from her stool and vaulted right over the counter and into his arms, nearly knocking him over.

He was always Uncle Beene to the girls; he'd been a close friend since before they were born. He somehow managed not to get his

111

Ph. D. in Antiquities just a year or so shy of graduating, preferring to peddle treasures rather than write about them. He was overly fond of tweed for someone who hadn't made it in academia.

"Well, you're sure growing like a weed, Asteroid," Beene said with a grin, but I could hear tension in his voice, I could see dark circles underneath his eyes, and the way his lips were forced into a tight smile against their better judgment.

"Have a seat, Beene," I said. "Let me get you a drink." I disappeared around back and fixed us each a gin and tonic. When I returned with the drinks, Astrid looked up with such a sad, left-out look, and I could see how her curls were matted, her forehead shiny with perspiration that she wiped from time to time with a red bandanna without complaining.

"Why don't you go next door to Mike's and get yourself a drink?" I suggested. The bartenders over there knew Tali and Astrid well, and they served them a special Italian soda topped off with a maraschino cherry and a cocktail umbrella. I dug my hand deep into my right pants pocket, catching all the change, picking out the quarters—seven. $1.75 was enough for an Italian soda and more than one candy bar back then.

Lizzy didn't like me sending the girls alone into the bar—Mike's Bar and Grill—but Mike was an old friend, and there weren't too many options back then. Well, Astrid was gone in a flash—she really lived up to her nickname, although Beene was just about the only person she'd let use it. And just as soon as she was out that door, Beene's smile disappeared.

"I've gotta get back to L.A. as quick as I can, and I'm low on cash. I barely made a dime at the show."

I nodded but didn't ask questions. I would luck out with some good bargains today, thanks to Beene's bad luck. I just sipped my gin and tonic nice and slow while Beene heaved his big, soft leather bag onto the counter and carefully opened two brass buckles—shining, gleaming brass, even though the leather was very old. He'd polished those buckles, painstakingly.

He began pulling out small bundles wrapped in soft blue velvet. One by one, he placed them on the counter in neat rows. Then, he folded up the empty bag and set it on the floor next to his stool. He took a long drink of his gin and tonic, downed half the glass in fact, and then he began unwrapping the bundles, one by one.

This was the most wonderful part of my job, never knowing what treasure might walk in the door at any moment. That day I'm sure he brought me jewelry—silver and gold and precious stones were always guaranteed to sell.

He had a couple Orphan Annie radio decoder badges that caught my eye. I would've liked to keep one for Astrid, but they were more than forty years old, pre-World War II, and I just couldn't afford to give them away. A fourteen-karat gold pen with the Buffalo Bills logo etched along the edge. Two sets of sterling silver cufflinks with enamel settings etched with the silhouettes of Asian women.

"I bought those from the grandchild of a very wealthy Chinese lady who hid them away in her attic for God knows how long. She herself was the descendent of some dissipated dynasty."

There was a story like this for nearly every object. That's all I have left now, the stories, and they're just as vivid as they were twenty years ago. More vivid, maybe. You really start to remember things when you're old.

Finally Beene got to the last bundle, and as he began to unwrap it ever so slowly, I had this premonition. I not only knew what it would reveal, but I could *see* it. Not in my minds eye, no I *saw* that old familiar medallion, that old friend of mine before he even started to unwrap it.

"How much for the medallion?" I asked before thinking, before I could stop myself long enough to guard my tone, my expression.

"Oh no, this medallion is something special; it's not for sale."

It was something special all right—about twice the size of a silver dollar, nearly pure gold. It was missing the original chain and now hung from a braided black cord. Etched on the front was the cross of Charlemagne, surrounded by a circular knot. On the opposite side, there was a strange symbol in the center—possibly something Kabbalistic. Charlemagne was devoutly Catholic, but it was the sixth and seventh century, and there was still a lot of lingering mysticism. Etched around that strange symbol in a distinctive Latin script—Carolingian miniscule, I eventually learned—were these words: *Causa laetet vis est notissma.* "The cause is hidden; the result well known."

I broke the rules then; the glint of that old gold in my eye distracted me, and I knew my expression bespoke my want of it. I knew that Beene could read my face, so I didn't even try to make it up by feigning disinterest.

"I know that medallion—it was mine, more than once. It was the first precious thing I ever owned."

Beene sighed. "I'm sure you have an entirely believable story about it, Cal."

I let that one slide, and he continued, "Well, I wanted to hang onto it for awhile, but truth be told, it'd be somewhat of a relief to get it off my hands."

"What do you mean?" I felt a natural pang of curiosity, of course, but something else, too, something dark. I pushed the thought to the back of my mind and reached for the gin, filling each of our glasses with about a double without adding more tonic.

And Beene, he must have felt it too, because as he reached inside his tweed vest and fumbled for his cigarette case, I could see that his hands were trembling. He didn't speak until he'd lit up a Sweet Afton and taken a long drag.

I'm sure that what he told me next was the truth. Beene was one of my oldest friends, and I knew he couldn't lie to me. But I can't help wondering even now, if he left anything out. One or two crucial details could have changed everything. But I could tell he was down on his luck—we all got worn down once in awhile, and it's easy to let your morals slacken up a little when you're hungry.

"I can't really say, Jack. It's just that I've had a bad feeling ever since this medallion came into my hands. I don't even know much about it, where it came from, who it belonged to. I bought it from a young woman a few weeks ago. I usually only buy from other dealers and shops, and this girl—something wasn't quite right about her. I wouldn't have made the deal if I thought it was stolen at the time, but my doubts only grew and grew after she left.

"I just have this *feeling* about it, Jack. Sometimes objects are more than they seem. Every once in awhile I come across something, usually a piece of very old jewelry, and it's almost like it has power. It's special, all right, Jack, but I wouldn't be too sorry to see it go."

And that's when I noticed Astrid standing in the back, at the close end of the hall that led to my office. The little sneak, she'd come in the back so she could spy on us. I'm sure she saw the look I shot her, the look that said, you're in trouble, but she ignored it, bolted across the floor and behind the counter, and dragged her stool to face me and Beene and the three rows of treasure. She knew to pipe down while I was doing business. She just sat there gulping her Italian soda and wolfing down two Snickers bars so fast you'd've thought I was starving the poor kid. It took her a minute to notice the thick silence, the unspoken words hanging in the air between us like flies caught in a sticky trap.

But she gave nothing away save a glint of curiosity in her bright brown eyes and a hint of a sly smile on the left side of her mouth.

Subtle, but I could spot it a mile away—Tali, too, had that sneaky little grin, ever since she was a baby.

I swirled the ice around in my rocks glass, avoiding her gaze. "Well, how much for the lot?" I asked.

Beene shot a suspicious glance at Astrid—he was never quite comfortable discussing money in front of a child—and instead of replying, he took a dog-eared reporter's notebook from his pocket, and a mint-condition Parker 51 fountain pen and scribbled a number.

It was more than I wanted to pay, more than I should have. I should have haggled with him a little. A man should never pay the asking price—and neither should a young lady, remember that. But I just set my glass down and said without hesitation, "I'll give you the cash now if you throw in that old medallion."

And Beene, he just ran his fingers through his sweaty, snarled mess of hair, thinking hard, that deep frown line in his forehead furrowed into an impenetrable trench, like there was some private battle raging just beneath the surface.

"It's pretty important to you, Jack?" he finally said, and again I broke protocol—I nodded, and I didn't hide my eyes, which surely belied the God-honest truth. "That medallion came to me the day I buried my father when I was just seventeen, and I've lost it more than once, but it always comes back to me."

"Okay, then, it's a deal." Beene held out his hand and shook mine firmly. His hand was wet and clammy, and somehow I suspected, not just from the August heat.

I picked up the medallion with my right hand and clasped my fingers around it, holding it tight and remembering. It's funny how those memories all come flooding back at once, like a dream. Even the memories that were not my own seemed familiar, the ones where strangers in old garb and curly wigs spoke in languages I didn't know, in places I had never seen. Palaces and prisons. The medallion was always there, just a hint of gold peeking out from an unbuttoned white shirt or clutched tightly in a leather-gloved hand.

I opened my fingers and placed the medallion in Astrid's small palm. Her eyes were wide brown pools; her lips parted with a thousand questions on the tip of her tongue.

"Why don't you hold onto this, Astrid, and I'll go open the safe." I began walking to the back, and she called out, her voice unusually timid.

"Just—just until you get back?"

I turned around. "No, I think you should hang onto it for awhile."

Now it was Beene's turn for incredulity. "Well, I'd say you're a lucky girl today. You better not let your big sister catch wind of this."

I walked to the safe, turning that metal dial with a heavy heart. I knew that both my girls were leaving me soon—all three of my girls, actually, because Lizzy never stopped being my girl—and it didn't really matter which one of them had the medallion—the medallion that always managed to find its way back to me. I hoped it would bring them back, too.

That night, the night I gave Astrid the medallion, Lizzy and I left Tali in charge, probably not the best idea, Lizzy said, and I guess she ended up being right that time. You'll notice that this part of the story is hearsay, pieced together after the fact from what I could get out of Tali and Astrid. But I heard a lot of stories in my years at the shop, and most of them had one or two questionable details. There's no such thing as a true story, I always say.

Tali was a punk, can you imagine? She was about a decade too late for the best action, but she tried, anyway. She could've been Astrid's twin—they both had the same fair skin that freckled every summer, the same strawberry-blond hair, although Tali's was now jet-black with streaks of Manic Panic hair dye. Atomic turquoise blue. I remember the color because of the ruckus it caused when Lizzy found out.

But lately, Tali had been looking a little lonesome. Lately, she'd been on a quiet streak, hardly uttering more than a sentence at a time. Where's Mom? Pass the salt. I'm going out. And underneath all those baggy clothes, the ratty t-shirts, the too-big beat-up jeans and my old leather belt looped twice around her waist, the tattered pair of Victorian-era black leather riding shoes she'd salvaged from my shop—underneath all those clothes I could hardly tell what she looked like anymore. But I worried that her cheekbones were a little too pronounced, her wrists a little too fragile, her face too white against all that pitch-black makeup.

I still remember what she was wearing that night—this beat-up Clash t-shirt—do you even know who the Clash was, kiddo? Oh, that's right, you have the records—how could I forget? That last one cost me about half a month's rent. Well, she was wearing this Clash t-shirt that looked like it had been through the garbage disposal, even though I witnessed her tearing it up and safety-pinning it back together at the kitchen table.

RAP RAP RAP RAP RAP. A loud, impatient knock interrupted Tali from her brooding, and she pounded down the stairs, recognizing the pattern. Behind the big red front door stood two of her punk friends, dressed in pretty much the same uniform. Adam and Cory. Or was it Cody? I can't remember which one she liked either, but I'm sure it was Adam who started it, who said, "Hey Tali, Jessie's doing tattoos tonight—come on!"

Adam's beat-up Chevelle station wagon was still running in the driveway, the headlight shining through the waning summer light into the doorway, where Astrid stood behind Tali, wearing her summer nightgown, being nosy as usual.

I might not remember those kids' names, but how could I forget the car, the getaway car that didn't quite get away? How could I forget what my own daughters were wearing on the night I almost lost them? You're not the first person to accuse me of embellishing, Charlotte, but when you get to my age you have to fill in the blanks sometimes.

So, Tali was standing there, looking sad. "Not tonight, guys. I have to watch my sister."

"Jessie's driving back to New York tomorrow morning," Adam persisted. "We have to go *now*. She's not even going to charge us."

"Shit," she muttered. "I know exactly what I want, too."

I'd like to blame Adam or Cory, or at the very least Tali, but it was Astrid who egged her on, who looked at her with pleading eyes. In her defense, she'd been left abandoned quite a bit as of late. "Come on, Tali," she said. "I won't tell."

And to Adam and Cory, without hesitation: "We have exactly two hours."

She was always a good kid, Astrid—your mom—she'd never even been grounded. Once in awhile Lizzy would take her books away for neglecting her chores.

"Okay," Tali acquiesced, and Astrid zipped off in search of her shoes. She returned wearing tennies and her old leather bomber jacket over her nightgown, another treasure from the shop. I'd come across probably the smallest existing World War II bomber jacket—I don't know how that pilot's feet ever reached the pedals. Well, Astrid was never really into the old dresses, but she took one look at the bomber jacket and had to have it. It hung loose on her despite its small size. Lizzy tried to take it in but gave up after she broke three needles. "She'll just have to grow into it," she said, slamming the cover onto the sewing machine.

117

Astrid ran after the others, jumping into the backseat of that old Chevelle next to Tali, both of their pale faces flushed with the thrill of their impending crime. Adam peeled out of the driveway, blasting the Velvet Underground from the tape deck.

Somewhere between our house and Jessie's, Adam rolled to a stop at a red light, and in a flash of inspiration leaned over the back seat and yelled to Tali, "You know what would help with the pain ... "

She just shook her head, but he wouldn't let it go. "Come on, we'll just take a little. He'll never know the difference."

I like to imagine that she argued with her eyes, or maybe at least a slight frown. But it was no surprise to me, really. I knew she'd been stealing my liquor for months, but did I think it was her idea—no. I guess I thought there were worse things those kids could get into; I guess I thought they might stop with a little gin if it was easy to get, if they were afraid of getting caught. I'm not proud of it, but do you realize all the trouble Lizzy and I were getting into at her age? Gin wasn't the half of it in the mid-'60s.

My shop wasn't far out of the way, and before long, Adam pulled the Chevelle around back, parking in the now-darkened alley between my shop and the Art Reach Gallery. Things got pretty desolate at night back then. There were no arches with colored lights back then—hardly any street lights, either. No one really stayed open past six or seven o'clock except for the bars, and anyone you crossed paths with was either looking for a drink or up to no good. Even the boys seemed nervous.

Adam turned the key and began opening the door when Tali interrupted. "No—no you guys have to wait in the car. My dad will kill me if he finds out I let anyone else in here." She slid out her door and rushed up to the back door, not noticing Astrid right behind her until she had turned the key in the lock and pushed the heavy back door open.

"I'm not letting you come in here alone," Astrid said with such authority that Tali just nodded. "Okay, but we have to be fast. And keep your lips zipped, Astrid."

And she did keep her lips zipped all the way to the office with Tali, and she stood guard by the open door while Tali fished around the deep bottom desk drawer for my gin bottle, and she saw the brick before anyone heard it, saw it sailing in slow motion through the glass-paned front door, saw two men dressed in black waiting for that CRASH. By the time they were through the door, Astrid had bolted out of the office and into the front, by the time Tali heard the crash and screamed, by the time the two men made it inside, she was waiting for them behind the counter.

Tali ran out the door so fast her worn boot-soles slid on the soft wood floor, and the gin bottle she was still holding smashed into a million little pieces, dousing the place with a juniper smell that lingered for days. Years later, even after I stopped drinking, on dark lonely nights in the shop, I'd sometimes get a chill and whiff of juniper.

Neither of the girls got a good description of the men, who wore black bandannas over their faces. Only one of them spoke, the one in front, who looked straight at Astrid and said, "I think you know what we're looking for, little girl."

She said nothing, just stared him down over the counter.

"Okay, I'll jog your memory. We're here for a very special medallion that doesn't belong to your daddy. If you give it back to us right now, we won't hurt you or your sister. We'll turn around and walk right back out that door, and you girls can have this mess swept up before your daddy ever has to see it."

"Astrid?" Tali's voice was small and desperate. Just one word, just her sister's name asked the question burning on her lips. What is he talking about? You know, don't you?

Astrid sighed, this weary ancient sigh. How did a ten-year-old possess such tired resignation? "Okay, I'll give it to you."

What happened next seemed to take both a fraction of a second and a thousand years. Astrid crouched down to open one of the cabinets below the counter, slowly enough so as not to arouse suspicion, slowly enough to make the men in the black bandannas believe she was retrieving their spoils with great reluctance. But, she was fast, too, like always, and before there was time for anyone to be surprised, she was back on her tiptoes and pointing that Civil War pistol dead-center at the forehead of the man in front.

She saw his right hand twitch a little, and said, "Don't even think about it."

If his face had not been covered, I think Astrid and Tali would have seen just a hint of a wicked smile beginning at the corners of his mouth.

"I don't think you know what you're doing with that gun, little girl—" He took two quick steps, but stopped dead when he heard that distinctive click—Astrid cocking the hammer.

"*Don't* call me little girl. And you're wrong. I know exactly how to use this gun because I *paid* for it. I wrote the check and the receipts, and a few weeks later, I paid for the bullets, too. I have a record of everyone who's ever owned this pistol, and I know how to use it." Her voice was low and calm and even. And old, very much older than ten years. It was a voice that Tali had never heard come from her little sister's mouth, and certainly I had never heard it either.

Behind Astrid, Tali still stood in the pile of glass, her jaw dropped, mouth open wide. The men in the black bandannas probably wore similar expressions. This horrible silence followed, this threatening moment where the whole world stopped, and you could actually reach your hand out in front of you and feel it, you could feel the texture of the moment, the air around you, the knowledge that someone was about to die.

The man in front broke it. "You're going to regret this, little girl," he said, and turned so quickly on his heels that he nearly tripped over his partner standing right behind him.

"Let's get the fuck out of here," he hissed. And they did.

Just in time, too, because no sooner had they run through the broken glass and over the threshold when Astrid and Tali heard the sirens.

"Who called the police?" Tali cried, her voice a mixture of relief and fear.

Astrid just pointed down the dimly lit hall toward the back of the shop, where Adam and Cory stood frozen in place, unsure whether it was safe yet to enter.

"Now we're really in for it," she said, and she sunk right down on her knees into that pile of broken glass, head in hands.

The police said the thieves were probably just looking for valuables they could turn over quickly for drugs. They said our girls were lucky, that the thieves were surprised to find anyone in the shop after hours, after dark, but they probably didn't want to hurt anyone.

I let Lizzy and Tali go along with that story, and the boys, too, but Astrid and I knew better. I avoided her gaze the whole time it took to file the police report and to wait for Adam's and Cory's parents. I didn't trust myself not to let on that I knew something I wasn't telling. Because both of us knew what the men in the black bandannas came for: the lost medallion of Charlemagne.

After everyone else had gone and it was just the four of us left in the shop, my quickly unraveling little family, I convinced Lizzy to run to the house for my power drill and some spare particle board so I could close up the broken window for the night. Oh, she was livid; she was waiting for a moment alone with me, too. She blamed me, of course.

And I was angry, too. I couldn't remember ever being that angry, either before or since that night. "What the hell were you thinking?!" I yelled as soon as the door shut behind Lizzy and Tali. Astrid just stood alone in the middle of the shop looking small, the sleeves of her bomber jacket hanging down over her wrists. Her lips quivered, and hot tears fell silently from her big brown eyes.

It broke my heart, it really did, to make my little girl cry, but I'd almost lost her that night.

"If, God forbid, anyone ever robs you again, you give them exactly what they ask for, Astrid. These are *things*," and I drew a wide arc around the shop with my outstretched right hand. "Nothing is more important than your safety."

Her tears fell faster now, and she spoke in shudders and spurts: "Daddy, you said the medallion was *special*. I heard you and Uncle Beene."

"Nothing's special about that medallion other than how old it is and that it's survived all these years. And do you know how many drugs old Beene's done? No wonder he thinks these old treasures have magical powers."

I regretted those words as soon as they left my lips, as I watched them travel across the shop, across the big open space between me and Astrid and slap her in the face, crushing all the innocence from her wide eyes in one irreversible blow.

"I-I just thought it would protect me," she said, and then she completely dissolved into tears.

I went over to her then, and swept her up in my arms like when she was small, and I carried her around back of the counter and set her down on her usual stool.

"I'm sorry, kiddo," I said, wiping her eyes with a clean handkerchief. "It's going to be okay."

She nodded and breathed deep and tried to stop crying. I handed her the handkerchief and asked, "Hey would you like an Italian soda?" She nodded and cried and wiped all at the same time.

You might think I was an idiot to leave her alone in the shop with that broken window, but I knew that sometimes you just need a cold drink to stop the crying, and I was out the broken front door and in and out of Mike's so fast you could have held your breath without too much discomfort. And it worked, too. We were almost conversational by the time she finished her soda.

"So where was it?" I asked. The medallion was notably absent from her neck.

She just grinned and patted her chest, hand over heart. "There's lots of secret pockets in this old jacket, Daddy." She opened the jacket to reveal the lining, where there were, in fact, several pockets of different sizes, and she pulled the medallion out and held it for a moment in her small hand.

"You know something weird, Daddy?" Astrid said. "I could almost feel it sort of burning above my heart when those men broke in here. And then I had this feeling, like when I get really mad and yell at Tali, and I don't even know what I'm saying. It was like the medallion gave me those words. And now I don't remember them at all."

Now *my* chest was burning, but I just said, "Yeah, that is really weird, Astrid."

"Do you want it back now?" Her voice was so sad and so small.

"No, I think you've done a pretty good job keeping it safe. You should keep it."

"Okay." She replaced the medallion in its secret hiding place.

I wanted to grill her more on the medallion, on everything that had happened, but I knew that she'd been through enough, both of the girls had. So, I let them be. I let them spill the details in their own good time. Tali told me little, preferring to keep her thoughts private as usual. But Astrid—well she always was a record-keeper, and she stored up every little detail of that night and fed it to me little by little over the next few weeks before they left.

And then they were gone. Lizzy took them to the lake, and although none of us had talked about it, they didn't return when school started. Just a few days after they should have started school, I was alone in the shop when two men stalked through the door and straight up to the counter without so much as a nod. They'd exchanged their black bandannas for black suits and trilby's, but the chill that followed told me just who they were. And it was still late summer. I knew what they wanted, and it was the first time I felt glad that the girls were far away. They were safe. Well, they didn't get the medallion that day, and I guess they never caught wind of where it ended up. I guess it stayed pretty safe in Astrid's old bomber jacket.

I had a lot of time to think in those days. The afternoons were the worst. A man can get really low around three o'clock. I was grateful when the days grew shorter and it was nearly dark by that time of day. I thought about how I'd lost my girls, and not only that, but I'd stolen something from them, or from Astrid at least. Her faith, her belief in magical things.

But maybe not. Because Astrid and Tali came back to me the next summer, and every summer after that. Was it because of the medallion, or was it just that Lizzy was softening, that she knew I'd wither away and die without my kids?

After awhile, after I'd gleaned all the details I could from Tali and Astrid, we let that night fade away almost unnoticed, like the final embers of a dying campfire. But there was a quiet understanding between us, and just a little spark of something, an idea that maybe Beene was right after all.

* * *

By the time I finished the story, Charlotte and I had long since licked our ice cream bowls clean, and the line had grown again to wind back out the door and down the block.

"We'd better let someone else have our seats now, kiddo," I said. She gathered up our trash, and I followed her out the side door, around the corner, and through the door up to my little apartment. She caught a few more bemused smiles on the way at her getup, and as I followed her up the steep wooden stairs, I committed her image to my memory, my little granddaughter, so much like her mother and so much her own girl, too, holding up the hem of that old white tea dress, dark curls buried in her wide-brimmed hat, pink ribbon trailing behind her. And the medallion around her neck.

We had just a little time left for dinner and maybe a DVD, and tomorrow morning I would drive her to Port Columbus and put her on a plane all by herself to Tokyo. Who knew how many summers, how many years even, would pass before I'd see her again? My heart thumped hard in my chest, and it wasn't from the stairs. A pang of something so palpable that I thought I could feel it in my gut if I'd put my hand there—a mixture of something black and lonesome, and something hopeful, too.

At the top of the stairs she turned around just to smile at me, and the west light shining in through the window behind us caught the gold of the medallion, a glimmer so bright I had to squint for just a second.

"I think I'll let you hang onto Charlemagne's gold, kiddo. Keep it safe."

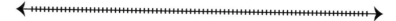

Amy S. Dalrymple is originally from Milwaukee, Wisconsin and now lives in Columbus. She studied philosophy at The Ohio State University and is currently at work on a collection of short stories that concern the fantastical, the impossible, and the everyday. "Callahan's Retail Museum" is based on Doug Ritchey's shop, Ritchey's at 714, which was located in the current Jeni's Short North space from 1980 through 1992.

EXPLORATION

Wexner Center for the Arts, OSU Campus
Scott Chaffin

1993
WHAT IS REAL?

By Christopher Sunami

Someone called in a bomb threat not long after the start of school, on the first really nice spring morning of the year, a day when the sun was shining and the air smelled fresh and sweet. No one took it seriously. This was long before the strange sudden spate of school shootings, and no real possibility of violence loomed over our evacuation of the building. Looking back now, as frightening as people always seemed to find my generation, we never actually did kill anyone. Maybe we looked like we were planning to.

There had been one previous bomb scare that year. That one had resulted in two miserable tee-shirt clad hours huddled together, shivering at the end of the snow-covered athletic field. But apparently the threatener had learned his lesson. This time he had picked a perfect day to force people outside.

While milling around aimlessly with the other students, I came to a single inescapable conclusion. I couldn't possibly bear to return to a dank, dark classroom. So I turned to Kendra, my on-again, mostly-off-again girlfriend, and hissed in her ear, "I'm out of here! Want to come?"

"You can still not graduate, you know," she hissed back. "The school year isn't over yet."

"Suit yourself."

The teachers were off in a little knot, chattering, smoking cigarettes, and enjoying their own bomb-scare holiday, so it was the easiest thing in the world for me to vault over the short, chain-link fence and slip away. Truth be told, I wasn't far from a gate in the fence that would have been even easier—but you know how teenagers think.

As I scurried down the deserted, tree-lined street and into a nearby park, I realized I hadn't been the only one with the idea to get lost. There, on the other side of the park's forlorn little pond was a small knot of popular kids—or at least, what passed for popular kids at Columbus Alternative. They probably couldn't have made it into even the humblest clique up in uppity Upper Arlington, but around here they were more-or-less the shit. For the briefest of moments the thought of joining up with them flickered in my mind, but then they scowled at me and rapidly abandoned the area.

My feelings just slightly bruised, I busied myself looking interestedly into the dark and dirty waters of the concrete-lined pond. The area was well shaded, and there was still a thin layer of ice cracking and melting over the top of the scum—a fascinating process if I'd ever seen one. Truly, I might have stayed there for hours, if only I hadn't just then heard a distant school bell ring, marking the end of what normally would have been first period. That brought me to my senses. I knew I needed to put some serious distance between myself and school if I didn't want to get dragged kicking and screaming back to Calculus. And since I hadn't put any thought into my spur-of-the-moment escape, I simply started walking.

By the time I reached Hudson Street, I had formed a plan. In Columbus at that time, there was only one real destination for a young person, one place where all the exciting things in the city happened, and that was campus. It would have been a bit of a hike by foot, but I was already close to a bus stop, right there in front of the antiques store.

I use the term "antiques" hesitantly. A better description might have been junk. Even through the dirty store window I could tell it was packed as full as my parents' overstuffed basement, and that the merchandise was of a similar caliber—broken lamps and boxes full of books, ashtrays, and other knickknacks. In short, the kind of things that wouldn't get stolen from your yard if you left them out there all night with dollar bills taped to them. None of which seemed to bother the owner, a short, balding man with thick glasses and a full beard, who today was standing out in front of the shop.

"Hello!" I greeted him cheerfully. "Whatchya got for sale today?"

He looked me over, up and down. "For you," he said slowly, weighing his words, "nothing!"

He stalked back inside his shop, and slammed the door shut so hard the glass shook. As I stared after him in shock, he flipped the "Open" sign to "Closed" and snapped shut the Venetian blinds.

"That seemed a trifle rude," said a voice behind me. I spun around and found myself face-to-face with a girl sitting on the bench at the bus stop. She looked to be about my age, with short, dark, curly hair. She was sitting cross-legged and aristocratic in a short skirt, while smoking a long brown cigarette.

"Charmed, I'm sure," she said, as she extended a limp hand in a manner that made me unsure whether I was expected to shake it or kiss it. Even though it was almost certainly the former, a sudden impulse made me opt for the latter. She flushed slightly and a certain twinkle came into her eyes.

"My, my," she said, recovering both her hand and her composure, "who would have expected to meet a gentleman here on Hudson Street? You, sir, may call me Melinda Maria."

"I'm Chris," I said. "Is that really your name?"

"Of course not," she said with a scornful laugh. "Do I look like I'm in the habit of giving up my real name to strange men at bus stops?"

The thrill of being referred to as a "man" outweighed the sting of being handed an alias, and so I sat down beside her with my heart pounding.

"I didn't mean any offense," I said.

"None taken, I'm sure," she said. "At any rate, you're probably wondering why I'm not in school today."

I shrugged. "Actually—" I began.

"I could ask the same about you," she interrupted. "But I won't. I'm not rude like that. As it so happens, I don't go to school. I've already been legally emancipated. My parents were incompetent to take care of me, so I left home. I live on my own now. I have a full time job. Do you believe all that?"

"Sure," I replied, as she took a long drag on her cigarette.

"Good man," she answered, and then blew a cloud of smoke in my face that left me coughing. There were few things I hated worse than cigarette smoke.

"You should quit," I said. "Those things will kill you."

"I'm not afraid to die," she said. But she stubbed her cigarette out anyway, and threw the butt into the street. Then she laid her head on my shoulder.

The very moment she touched me, I felt a sudden, overwhelming rush of feeling. I felt as if I had been asleep all my life and had just that very moment woken up. But when I reached out to place my arm around her, she pulled back and slapped my hand away.

"No, no, no, sir!" she said. "I was just testing you."

"Testing me?" I sputtered.

"Yes," she said. "And I'd say you're at least a good sixty percent heterosexual. Possibly even more."

By this time I was thoroughly bewildered, and my head was starting to hurt. Melinda Maria was obviously Grade-A crazy. But so help me, I was a sucker for crazy. Desperate to re-establish physical contact, I leaned towards her, but she jumped lightly to her feet.

"And yonder comes your bus!" she said. "I believe you are headed towards campus, are you not?"

"How did you know?" I asked. "Did I tell you that?"

"Where else would you be going?" she answered.

There was no answer to that, so as the bus pulled to a stop, I asked, "What about you? Are you going to campus, too?"

She hesitated. "Yes," she said finally. "As I mentioned before, I am gainfully employed, and my place of employment is thither."

I decided to try to regain some of the *cachet* I seemed to have so quickly gained and then lost. "In that case," I said, gesturing towards the impatiently opened door of the bus, "ladies first!"

She rolled her eyes, but flounced up onto the bus in front of me. I followed, but it took me a while to locate my money. It wasn't until I headed towards my seat that I noticed she wasn't on the bus anymore. She must have immediately gotten off the rear entrance as quickly as she had gotten on. By the time I realized, however, the bus had already pulled away from the curb. I pulled the stop cord, but the driver ignored it. So I ran to the nearest window and stuck my head out to yell at her: "Hey! What gives?!"

"Farewell, my darling!" she shouted back. "If it's fated to be, we'll meet again."

I slumped down into my seat, as emotionally exhausted as one might expect from having experienced the entirety of a love affair in five minutes. I didn't know what any of it meant.

After a moment, I realized someone was tapping on my shoulder. I turned around and looked into the eyes of an old white-haired man sitting in the seat behind me.

"Yes?" I said.

"Ha ha, you're a schmuck!" he said.

Fortunately, the teenage psyche is resilient. By the time the bus rolled into campus, my confusion, hurt, and hormonal haze had all cleared out in the anticipatory excitement of hanging out among what seemed to me at that time to be the very grown adults—that is, college students—of the university. Compared to the somnolence that hung over the rest of Columbus, campus was a rolling sea of activity. Muscular jocks, pot-hazed hippies, dolled-up sorority girls and studious-looking foreign-exchange students all jockeyed for space on the narrow sidewalks. And no sooner had I gotten off the bus than I was accosted by one of the most memorable of the area's many professional panhandlers.

"Don't call me a bum," he announced, "I earn my pay, meet the hardest working poet you'll see today. Help is on the way!" No one paid him any attention. "Hey everybody, listen up, if you like my rhymes, put a dime in my cup. Help is on the way!"

I was kind of fascinated, but I didn't want to part with any of the meager amount of money in my pocket, so I hung back and tried to look inconspicuous. Of course, that only brought him straight in my direction. "Don't be mean," he told me, "you've got a dream. Help is on the way!"

"You're losing it, dude," scoffed a passing frat boy in an Abercrombie shirt. "That doesn't even rhyme."

The street poet scowled at the jock's departing back. "You act like you think you're a literary critic. But you look to me like your average syphilitic. Help is on the way!"

I couldn't help but laugh. "Okay, that's worth a dollar," I said, and extracted one from my pocket, crumpled and dirty. He took it, smoothed it out, folded it neatly and made it disappear.

"Thank you, young brother, you must have been raised well by your mother. I predict for you luck for the rest of your day. Because help … " he paused for effect, "most certainly is on the way!"

A dollar poorer, but armed with the street poet's benediction, I trotted on down the street towards my all-time favorite store, a vinyl-lover's paradise called Used Kids' Records. This was back before the fire, when it was still located in two dingy and disconnected basement storefronts, bargains on the left, collector's items on the right. As I headed down the graffiti-covered stairs, however, I nearly tripped over someone coming up. Because I was looking down on him, because he was a good foot shorter than I am, and because of the sheer size of the headgear in question, all I really perceived was a very angry blue-velvet top hat.

"Watch where you're going, you big lummox!" shouted the hat. "You don't know who you're messing with!"

"Sorry, very sorry," I mumbled, as I pressed myself against one filthy side wall to allow the curious apparition to push past me.

Inside, the cave-like room was even more crowded than usual, and there seemed to be a hum of excitement in the air. Over by the buy counter, an agitated older man was trying to unload a large collection of battered Billy Joel records. The clerk, a young guy with dyed black hair and a heavy metal shirt, was unmoved.

"These aren't really rare," he said. "And they're in really bad condition. I can't really give you anything for them. But you're welcome to just leave them here if you want."

The man hesitated and then slammed the stack of records down on the counter and stormed out of the store. I stood aside to let him out, and then headed towards my usual haunts, the bargain records bin. But halfway there, my attention was caught by a poster hanging on the wall. Unlike most of the posters in the shop, this one looked absolutely brand new. The musician featured on it I can describe only as a guitar-slinging pimp from Munchkin Land. He was about four feet tall, with a feather boa, and exotic, racially ambiguous features. But the most distinctive feature about him was his bright blue-velvet magician's hat—a hat that I had very recently encountered in person.

"Who's that?" I asked no one in particular, jabbing my finger towards the poster.

If memory serves me, there was an actual sound of a needle scratching off an actual record, and the room fell silent, as all eyes turned in my direction. Finally, someone nearby took pity on me. "You don't know who Mervin the Magnificent is?" The speaker was a kid a few years younger than me, dark-skinned with thick glasses, braces on his teeth, and a bright plaid shirt—a perfect hipster-cool outfit years before it was anything other than a guarantee of social ostracization.

His question basically seemed rhetorical. So I shrugged and said "Should I?"

The kid shot me an incredulous look. "You know Zappa?" No. "Captain Beefheart?" Nope. "Pink Floyd?" Well, at least I'd heard of them. "Mervin's better than all of them. He practically invented psychedelic rock."

"Ah, yes, yes, of course," I said.

"And you just missed your chance to meet him," said the kid. "He was actually here in the store just a few minutes ago."

"Oh, I met him," I muttered. People were still staring incredulously at me, so I waved my hand at the poster and announced loudly, "Right, Mervin! Better than Pink Floyd." That seemed like the right thing to say. All around me people relaxed and went back to trying to locate *Rain Dogs* on vinyl.

With the crisis averted I spent a happy forty-five minutes or so searching through the dollar records (which just so happened to include a large set of battered Billy Joel records that were inserted into the mix midway through my trawl). But as I brought my stack up to the front counter, I suddenly realized I had given my last dollar to the street poet. I was broke. So I tried to cover up the humiliation of having to go put my records back by asking the clerk at the front counter about the music that was playing.

"This is Mervin—better than Pink Floyd, remember?" said the clerk.

"Oh right," I said.

He shot me an evil grin. "You think it sounds like crap, don't you?"

I smiled uneasily. It really did sound like crap. Most things I heard at Used Kids' I liked, but this was absolutely incomprehensible noise. When you took the time to stop and listen to it, it wasn't just bad, it was actively offensive to your ears. "It's okay?" I said.

He laughed. "It sounds like that to everyone, the first time they hear it. But it sticks with you. Now that you've heard it, you won't be able to forget it. It will haunt your dreams. Eventually you'll buy an album, just to remind yourself how bad it is. You'll play it a few times, and then lock it up in a closet somewhere. And then, one day, you'll get it out again, put it on the stereo, and you'll suddenly realize it's the most amazing music you've ever heard. And after that, your life will never be the same again."

"Um, I just realized I don't have any money on me," I said. "And I don't remember where I got these records from. Can you guys put them back for me?"

The clerk sighed. "Next," he said.

It was disappointing to have to leave all my records behind. But campus had other delights, and some of them were free. My next stop was the Wexner Center, the funky, *avant-garde* modern-art gallery built by Limited Brands mogul Les Wexner. I loved all the deliberate eccentricities of the building: the outdoor corridor with the forced perspective that made it seem longer from one end than the other, the raised earth pedestals, and most of all the staircase inside the galleries that led only to a glass walled dead-end overlooking a sheer drop.

The current exhibit at the gallery on that day was called *Perceptual Art*. It consisted of a series of installations by Minasu, a half-black artist from Japan. I still vividly remember a piece she called "Distorted

Memories of a Rose." It was a small white house built right in the middle of the upper gallery. Inside was a single room with a square table in the middle. On the table was an empty vase, a glass of water, a bright red piece of chalk and a bowl full of rose scented oil. If you were observant, you noticed that the lighting had been somehow contrived to cast the shadow of a rose on the wall. A bright green rope with knives woven into it was curled across the floor, and the overhead lamp was covered by a ruby-red stained-glass lampshade with petal-like flares. It's hard to describe, but between those and a hundred other tiny details lost now to my memory, the artist somehow managed to create a sense of a rose in the room far more tangible and rose-like than any actual flower.

The museum was almost deserted, and I stayed inside "Distorted Memories of a Rose" for quite a long time. No sooner had I exited the installation, however, than a young guy a few years older than me rushed up in a high state of excitement.

"There you are!" he said. "I've been looking for you everywhere."

I didn't think I'd ever seen this guy before. I'm admittedly bad with faces, but his greasy, semi-curly blond hair and matching scraggly beard, tie-dyed hippy shirt, and manic expression complete with permanently bugged-out eyes combined to create an image I'd be hard-pressed to ever forget.

"Do I know you?" would have been the normal response. But this wasn't a normal day. Instead, I decided to play along. "Oh yeah," I said vaguely. "I was just checking out this 'Rose' thing."

"Never mind that," he said impatiently. "You got to come see this. You know that one staircase in the other gallery, the one that doesn't go anywhere?"

"Yeah," I said. As I mentioned before, it was one of my favorite quirks of the building.

"I've been watching people on it all day," he said. "They go up, and they *never come back down.*"

"What do you mean?" I said.

"It's like it was a normal staircase. People go up it and keep on going. But when I checked it it was just like I remembered. It's a dead end. There's nothing to do at the top but come back down. But they don't."

"Maybe you just didn't see them," I hazarded.

"No! Come look. See for yourself!"

There didn't seem to be any reason not to, so I followed behind. But just as we arrived at the other gallery, red lights started flashing, and a female voice intoned over the PA system, "Please evacuate the building. Please evacuate the building." For a moment I thought it was all another odd piece of artwork, but it soon became clear it was a real evacuation.

"Come on!" said my new friend, grabbing at my hand. "We can still make it to the staircase." But that plan was brought to a swift end by a polite, uniformed security guard.

"I'm sorry, you'll have to go outside," he said. "We have a report of a fire in the downstairs theater."

We were unceremoniously herded out through an emergency exit where we joined a small huddle of other art lovers. "I can't believe it," I said. "This is my second evacuation today."

My friend nodded absently. He was obviously still thinking about his stairway. After a moment, I decided to try another conversational gambit. "Guess what just happened to me," I said. "I met Mervin—you know, Mervin the Magnificent?"

He nodded again.

"He's this big-time important musician from the sixties," I said. "You know Beefheart, Captain Zappa, Floyd Pink? He taught them all how to play."

"Really?" he said. I couldn't tell if he was impressed, incredulous, or just humoring me, but it didn't matter that much to me one way or the other.

"Yeah," I elaborated, "and I spoke to him in person. He even autographed a record for me."

That last part was a complete lie, but by that time I had figured out he wasn't paying any attention to my story at all, so I could say whatever I liked. Unfortunately, he chose that exact moment to become interested.

"Wow, I'd like to see that," he said.

"Oh, I'd love to show it to you but I can't take it out in the sunshine," I backpedaled. "It fades the grooves."

He nodded understandingly. There was a pause, and then without warning he suddenly enveloped me in a big greasy bear hug. "I love you, man," he sobbed in my ear. "You're my best friend in the world!"

"Whoa, whoa, whoa!" I said, fighting to extricate myself from his grasp. As I broke free, I looked around to see if people were staring, but no one seemed to care. Maybe it was the kind of thing they saw every day in front of the Wexner. "Love me? Buddy, you don't even know me. I don't know who you think I am, but I've never even seen you before."

He drew back, hurt written all over his face. "I know your *soul*, man," he said.

There was another long pause. "Right!" I said, as soon as I collected my thoughts. "I'll be seeing you!" Without another word, I turned and began walking away as rapidly as I could without actually running. After a few minutes I peeked back over my shoulder to see if he was following me, but he had disappeared into the crowd.

I dug through my pockets as I headed south past Long's bookstore, and managed to uncover a couple of balled-up dollars I had missed before. Enough, at least, to make one last stop: Insomnia, a funky coffee shop located in a basement storefront under Skyline Chili. I wasn't much of a coffee drinker, but Insomnia was one of the must-see destinations on my official Unofficial Tour of Campus. It stayed open all night, and had a vivid clientele ranging from goth kids to the homeless—and those transitioning from one category to the other.

The place was much tamer in the middle of the afternoon than at night, and very nearly deserted. Even so, it took me a while to get the attention of the girl behind the counter, who was facing away from me and talking to someone back in the kitchen. When she finally did turn around, my jaw dropped open wide. It was the dark-haired girl from the bus stop!

"Yes, can I help you?" she said.

"Melinda Maria!" I said.

Her expression didn't change. "That's not my name," she said.

"Well, whatever your real name is. It's me! Chris, the guy who was waiting for the bus on Hudson! Remember? You said we were fated to meet again."

"Doesn't ring a bell," she said.

As I mentioned before, I'm not good with faces, but hers was burned into my memory. She'd put on some dark eyeliner since I saw her last, but it was definitely the exact same girl. I started to feel dizzy and a little sick. Was this how the guy at the Wexner had felt when I claimed not to know him? Had I slipped into some kind of alternate universe? Were there other versions of me wandering around somewhere, meeting people (or not meeting them, as the case might be)?

"But you ... me ..." I stammered.

She raised her voice petulantly. "Are you going to buy a coffee or not? Other people are waiting, you know!"

I was the only customer in the store. "Dammit, Melinda," I said, "at least admit you know who I am."

From out of the back, an older woman appeared. She was dressed in a stained apron, with close-cropped blond hair and a bit of a hard look on her face. "Is there a problem?" she said, in a tone of voice that suggested that there better not be one.

I decided to give up. Maybe I was just losing my mind. "No," I said. "Just give me a small coffee. Plenty of cream and sugar."

Back outside, I hadn't made it more than a few feet down the sidewalk when Melinda Maria came running up behind me. "Sir! You forgot your change," she said loudly.

"I did?" I said, turning around.

"No, dummy," she said. She shoved me into a nearby alley, sending my poor little coffee flying. "That's just an excuse I made up so I could come say goodbye to you."

"I don't understand," I said.

She sighed heavily. "Look, of course I recognized you from before. But I couldn't say anything. I'm having an affair with my boss, and she's insanely jealous!"

"With your ...?"

"Oh, just shut up and kiss me," she said. She suited action to words in a very convincing manner. When we finally came up for air, I was speechless for a moment. Then, as I started to say something, she pressed a finger to my lips.

"Shh. This is goodbye. We can never see each other again. You must try to forget about me, my darling. As for me, I will treasure your memory forever!"

Turning on her heel, she dashed from the alley and was gone.

And to tell the truth, I wasn't all that distressed to see her go. First of all, she was clearly batshit crazy. And second, her breath stunk like cigarettes. All that said, however, being chased down and kissed by a strange, beautiful girl was still a great way to end the day. If nothing else, it was at least sixty percent heterosexual, possibly even more. So I was in a good mood as I headed on down High Street, even though I was flat broke for real now, and had a walk of several miles ahead of me if I wanted to get home. I didn't mind, however. It gave me a chance to see the city, and to ponder the odd events of the day.

A couple of hours later, I stopped for a short break just a few blocks from my house. It was by then evening, and the shadows were long down Bryden Road. For some reason, I decided to check my backpack, which had started to feel excessively heavy. As I pulled out my math textbook, I caught sight of something tucked neatly inside. An eerie feeling came over me as I pulled out a little white record jacket.

With trembling fingers, I pulled out the record inside. It was an old-style forty-five single. It looked as though it had been freshly pressed, but the style of the record and the label were both straight out of the fifties. There was the classic big round hole in the middle, and the yellow doughnut shaped label with the song title "What is Real?" at the top and the artist name, "Mervin the Magnificent" at the bottom. Written in silver metallic marker right across the grooves of the record was a message in a beautiful looping cursive. "To my friend, Chris, all my best, Mervin."

It was one more mystery in a day filled with them. By that time, I was too tired to even try to figure it out. Instead, I carefully tucked the record back in the jacket, the jacket back in my textbook, and the textbook back in my bag. Then, I breathed in my last few breaths of absolute freedom and thought ahead to the rest of my evening. I knew exactly how it would go.

When I would get home my mother would yell at me and tell me how much she had worried all day when the school had called to tell her I had gone missing. After I survived the lecture, I would have dinner and get ready for bed. After that I would dig out the old kid's record player my grandfather had given me. I would plug it in and set it to "45 rmp." I would put on "What is Real?" I would listen to the song's incomprehensible, ear-abusing noises until I fell asleep, dreaming about the day it would sound like music.

Christopher Sunami is a writer, philosopher and programmer from Columbus, Ohio. He is the author of the critically acclaimed picture book *How the Fisherman Tricked the Genie* and the socially progressive Christian devotional *Hero For Christ*. He lives in the King Lincoln District, with his wife, artist April Sunami, and their children, River and Wyeth. Find more information at kitoba.com.

Columbus Alternative High School is one of only seven schools in the country recognized by The College Board for achievements in higher level math and science by minority students.

KAHIKI
Kelly Zalenski

2000

ONE FINAL LUAU

By Janet Slike

I will never spend a dime at Walgreens. My husband Alfred doesn't understand, but I can't expect him to; he's from Pittsburgh. He doesn't realize that a special part of Columbus history will die when they tear down the Kahiki Supper Club and build a Walgreens in its place. The Kahiki is even on the National Registry of Historic Places. Built in 1961, the same year I was born, the restaurant is a masterful rendition of Polynesian tiki kitsch. You never knew who would show up there, and that was part of its charm. It wasn't too expensive for ordinary families, but celebrities couldn't resist, either. Legend had it that Zsa Zsa Gabor was an occasional guest who always ordered milk.

Three major events of my life happened there: my tenth birthday party, dinner before my senior prom, and the celebration of my first job. I refuse to let a single significant life event of mine occur in a Walgreens, the one on East Broad Street or any other. Maybe this protest will end up being the fourth life event. It's hard to say; I don't know how it ends.

This section of Broad Street can be generously termed "rough." Vacant storefronts dot the strip malls. Those that remain have a cheap, seedy air. Kim, Linda, and I park the car about a block from the Kahiki at Popeye's. The Bexley High School alums Kim called are beginning to show up, looking forever preppy and confident that this effort will be successful. Is that really Matt Augur? No one will miss the fact that he's gained about forty pounds since his drum major days. I don't care how much tan they've sprayed on him at Charles Penzone.

Still, Kim squeals when he approaches. "Matt, it's so good to see you!" She wraps him in a bear hug, or her version anyway, which I'd call a cub hug. She never gains an ounce on her five-foot frame. Then she holds him at an arm's distance, to get a better look at the beefcake she, with the wisdom of a fairytale crone, passed on in our sophomore year. They beam wide smiles at each other. Hers has the sparkle of a diamond necklace glittering against a little black velvet dress. His broadcasts the fact that he doesn't floss.

Eventually he jars himself from blonde-induced dreamland and sees I'm there. He nods at me, but there's no real recognition. I'm not hurt or surprised. I spent a great deal of high school in and out of the hospital as I battled anorexia. My adolescent mind figured that the smaller I got, the easier it would be to just disappear. It worked. No one noticed me anyway, not even the teachers who, in theory, were paid to notice. I skipped a lot of classes and never got caught. Kim never noticed me in the high school shadows. We became friends later at AT&T when she was on her third job after college and I was on my second.

I nod back. "Hi, Matt."

"Good to see you again," he replies. "Always grrr...eat to see a fellow lion."

I'm scared he's going to burst into the fight song at any moment. Why does he cling to that miserable time?

"You too," I reply. "Excuse me. I need to get the signs."

Matt doesn't offer to help. He has rejoined the others basking in the glow of Kim's aura.

Reading my mind, Linda joins me. "The signs are still in the trunk," I say, turning toward the car. We are not immune to the aura, nor are we particularly jealous. Kim thrives on attention, but all these years out of high school Linda and I still prefer anonymity. The crowd follows us though as we head to the car. We distribute the signs as soon as we lift them from the trunk. Then the processional begins.

We walk the ill-maintained sidewalks on the way to the Kahiki. Snippets of conversations catch my ear.

"I loved the German chocolate cake. Weird, though, that they didn't have a more tropical dessert."

"*Kahiki* means journey to Tahiti."

"The torches ..."

"Really? You liked the fish side better than the bird side?"

"Those massive stone heads ..."

"That Mystery Girl was hot."

"I got so wasted on that mystery drink. Puked in the clam-shell sink."

We reach our destination, and I swear we collectively, though silently, gasp. I wouldn't have thought it possible. Many of us hadn't been there in some time. The sight of the building, even with its faded, peeling paint, is still amazing. We gaze upon the building like children seeing the Great Wall of China, transported to a world where the architects possessed an extra oomph of imagination. The only sensible expression is, "Wow."

The stone moai flank the doorway, greeting us almost in personified shame with torches unlit, as if they know their days are numbered. Of course, my imagination is overactive, as my husband Alfred will be the first to declare.

None of us has been in a protest before, having led comfortable lives without righteous outrage. So we stay in a static cluster. My sign is upside down; my slack right arm grazes my side. I've never even seen many protests. I wonder if the police or reporters will show up. Suddenly, I feel self-conscious. Maybe Alfred is right; it's only a restaurant, and the food had been just okay the last couple of times I had been there. The contracts have been signed. What can we hope to accomplish? The Kahiki will be torn down. I'm just like Matt, trying to hold onto an idealized past. If we are going to protest, the time would be better spent fighting something truly horrible, like poverty or cancer.

Michael Tsao, the owner, was just trying to make money when he signed the deal. I can't fault him for that. He didn't hurt anyone, really. Well, some employees would need to find new jobs if they didn't care to work in his frozen foods division. The economy is fine, and restaurant jobs are common.

Kim goes from person to person presenting each with a vibrant-colored plastic lei and a peck on the cheek. Linda raises her sign and walks away from the cluster. Fueled by the cup of coffee I picked up at Block's Bagels, I surge ahead and the others do, too. We pace back and forth for an hour in the August heat, sweat making crescent moons in the armpits of our polo shirts. Our water bottles, discreetly hidden behind tall ornamental grass, are soon drained.

A Chevy turns into the driveway, stops to avoid the substantial chain blocking the entrance to the lot, and then reverses and creeps back onto Broad Street. For some reason, it holds my eye as it moves along and pulls in the lot of the adjacent convenience store. An elderly couple wanders toward us. He shakes his head as he sees the signs. She has an orchid corsage on her wrist and sniffs it with a hunger I recognize. She must feel as if she'll never get enough of the flower's sweet scent, but she won't give the attempt less than her best effort. I remember devouring chocolate caramel ice cream that way before the anorexia started.

"Excuse me," the man says to Danny Gallucci, former math geek and current Upper Arlington realtor. "I don't know what your issue is with this fine establishment. That's your business. We don't want any trouble. I'm just taking the missus out for her birthday lunch." He puts his arm around her tiny waist and pulls her to him. "Just let me get to the door, son."

"Sir, the restaurant isn't open. They're going to tear it down."

His eyes almost double in size, then squint as he sizes up Danny's trustworthiness.

"It's not your chain keeping cars out of the lot?"

"No, sir."

"We drove all the way from Lima for this lunch. Millie's been talking about it all week, haven't you honey?"

She raises her head from the blooms. "Sure have. I'm ninety today," she declares with pride. "I'm going to a luau."

"These nice youngsters have let me know the restaurant's closed. Maybe we could go to The Top instead. You like steak."

"I am going to a luau." Her voice is steady with conviction. "I wore my special blouse. You signed the papers to take me on a trip outside the home. The nurse gave me my meds a little early." She thrusts her chin out. "I AM going to a luau."

"But honey, the Kahiki is closed. Maybe this wasn't such a good idea. The doctor said you shouldn't …"

"I will not get in that car until after my luau." She plops down on the COTA bus stop bench and snaps her fingers. "Waitress, bring us some menus. Nathan, sit down. You look like a fool standing there. You'll block the other diners." He obeys.

Linda steps between them and places leis around their pale, wrinkled necks. She hands the woman two of the flyers we give to passersby, urging them to boycott Walgreens. "Here are your menus. Feel free to order off the menu, though. Let us know your favorite dish, and we'll make it happen. The kitchen will open in awhile; in the meantime, our Mystery Girl will be happy to entertain you with a dance. She nods at Kim, the only one of us who lasts through a Jazzercise workout at the rec center. Kim gets in the spirit and swishes her hips like a professional dancer.

Millie's face registers amused surprise when she glances at the paper. "Nathan, be my eyes," she says. "I'm still getting used to the new bifocals. Read it for me."

"Just the entrees or did you want an appetizer?"

"Just the entrees will do."

Nathan sighs. "Of course, dear. Sweet and sour chicken. Broccoli chicken. General Tso's chicken," he begins.

"General Tso's chicken! That's it. That's the one I like. I'll take that. What are you going to have, sugar?" Millie leans toward Nathan and flicks her eyes over the pseudo-menu.

"Spicy pork, I suppose." He shoots Linda and Kim the look of a man who's not sure if he's been caught in a lie or not. He silently pleads for their continued help.

"Doesn't look like they have the lunch buffet today. Maybe that was just on Sundays. It's not a Sunday, though. I had my birthday on Sunday two years ago. We ate at the home and they served some soupy casserole and a god-awful dry lemon cake. Melanie drove over and made such a fuss about her grandson making partner at the firm. Remember that? She barely let me get a word in edgewise, but she gave me that beautiful peach scarf."

"What happened to that? You never wear it."

"The aide stole it," she says and shrugs. Her voice lowers to a whisper. "I take Q-tips from her. What goes around comes around."

Linda comes over with a water bottle and presents it with a bit of a flourish. "Your complementary Mystery Drink. You just let us know if that's too strong for you. Our bartender gets heavy handed sometimes."

Millie grins and waves her hands about it, dissipating the fog that would accompany an actual Kahiki drink.

"Fruity and delicious as always. Glad I have a designated driver."

My group of protestors huddles.

"We need to make this luau happen," Matt says. "We need to make her final memory of the Kahiki just as special as any other." He takes charge, directing groups of us to companies up and down Broad Street. We turn from protestors fighting pathetically against the inevitable to a team performing a random act of kindness, and that transformation empowers us.

He directs me to come with him and I don't argue. We place our large takeout order at No. 1 Chinese, a bit worried that we can't transcend the language barrier – the Mexican waiter struggles with his English. My high school Spanish evaporated from my tongue sometime in the early eighties from too little use.

We sit down on ugly red vinyl chairs, anticipating a long wait in the understaffed restaurant. Between the grimy carpet and the murky brown walls, the place depresses me. The stained glass chandeliers, though they add color, don't enhance the ambiance.

"Matt, aren't those the lights they used to have at Wendy's?"

"Yeah. This place has no personality of its own." He shakes his head.

Our order arrives, and we take it back. We set entree next to entree on the card tables another group bought at Lowe's and the buffet is created. Millie and Nathan stand. As they proceed to the serving area, Bethany, Danny's wife, arranges folding lawn chairs from Kmart on the sidewalk.

Millie stares at the variety of food, delighted. "Your chef outdid himself. So colorful and the veggies look fresh. I can really choose more than one thing, right, Nathan? They don't let me do that at the home."

"Have whatever you want, dear. Happy birthday."

She stands there, still transfixed by the food, and I wonder if Matt and I made a mistake. Maybe we should have ordered individual entrees for everyone. "It's a sad day when you can't choose for yourself anymore, when the aides treat you like a simpleton who can't remember whether a v-neck or collar suits your body type better. I hate those cowl necks they always put me in; I find breakfast toast crumbs in them while I'm watching *Days of Our Lives*," says Millie, reassuring me that everyone loves a buffet.

"She knows her clothes. She used to be a manager at Madison's. She loved that store," Nathan explains.

After lunch, complete with beers from the carryout, we turn on the boombox purchased at Kmart and put in the Don Ho CD that we got for almost nothing.

"How am I supposed to dance to that?" Millie asks.

"You want to dance, Millie?" asks Kim, startled. "We thought you'd like some cake." The Kroger sheet cake decorated with a palm tree and a script "Aloha!"is added to the buffet table. Bethany lights the candles.

"You mean an old lady like me should be content to just sit all day?" Her question unnerves me a bit. I had made assumptions based on her age. That's a sad part of human nature, I guess. We're all seeking shortcuts. I decide to take the time to get to know Millie. I'll be like a reporter, asking questions until I get the whole story.

"I'll dance with you, Millie. Then I want to hear what you think would look nice on me," I said.

She looks me up and down. "For starters, stay away from cropped pants," she concludes. "Anybody got any Tupac?"

"My son's a fan." Linda laughs and hurries to her car to retrieve the requested music.

"The aides taught me about rap."

Millie and I dance, while out of the corner of my eye, I see the police officer approach. Really? He doesn't have anything better to do than break up a luau?

The officer swaggers up to Nathan. "What's going on here?"

Nathan sighs. "We aren't causing any trouble. We're just having a birthday party for my wife and a last celebration for the Kahiki."

The officer's eyes moisten. "I proposed to my girlfriend there. She said no. Good thing in hindsight. Still, I have good memories."

"Would you like to dance with the guest of honor?" Kim asks the officer.

"I think I'd enjoy that."

At his approach, Millie stops dancing and runs to hide behind Linda. "Why'd you call the cops?" She asks her in a feeble hiss. "We were having a nice little party, and I haven't opened the gifts yet. Now they're going to lock me up."

"We can buy a box of Q-tips and make it right with the aide, if that's what you're talking about."

"Just get rid of him."

We send the officer on his way with a plateful of cold food.

Nathan exhales with force. "You dodged a bullet there, dear."

Millie narrows her eyes. "I won't get caught. I knew what I was doing. It was the perfect crime."

"Then why did you let him scare you, sugar?"

We laugh hysterically, thinking they are still talking about the Q-tips, but I have a feeling Millie has more layers than her birthday cake. Nathan and Matt rummage in the cooler for two more cold beers and talk about the Cincinnati Reds. I tune them out and turn to the guest of honor.

"Which Madison's did you work at, Millie?"

"Kingsdale."

"How lucky you were. You must have had many fine lunches at Umberto's next door. I used to love their pistachio gelato."

She nods, "I was partial to the strawberry myself."

We reminisce about Kingsdale and talk fashion for a while and at some point our chat turns from small talk to meaningful exchange. I learn that Millie had a daughter, Abigail, with Down syndrome.

"Abby was always in the hospital. She had so many problems and needed so much help. The older she got, the more health problems she had, and of course, we had to support her as an adult, too. Her care was so expensive. I came up with a solution, but the money only lasted so long," Millie recounts, and I can't even imagine interrupting this woman who has lived a nightmare that I have been spared. My twins are happy and healthy.

Millie watches the Broad Street traffic for a moment. "She died thirty years ago. A mother should never outlive her child. I suspect I'll be joining her soon, and paying in the afterlife for my crime. But really, what was a mother to do?"

She reaches over to pat my hand. "Thank you for listening, dear." She winked. "And thanks for my luau. You made my day."

"What was your solution?" I ask.

She smiles. "I suppose someone should know. But just you. Come with me."

We move away from the others, toward the stone moai. Her hands, speckled with liver spots, fumble with the clasp of her purse. She digs amongst the Kleenex and peppermint disks and produces a newspaper article from the sixties.

Suddenly, Nathan runs up to us.

"What are you getting out of your purse?" he asks, breathing so hard I fear we may need to find an oxygen tank.

"She won't tell, Nathan," Millie assures him.

The headline reads "Pair Robs Tenth Bank in Week: Still No Leads."

The reporters still aren't here. What a story they missed. Open or closed, you never know who you'll meet at the Kahiki.

Janet Slike lives in Dublin, Ohio with her husband, Teel, and their two cats, Shado and Carly. A Columbus native, Janet has held various editorial positions around town. Her stories have appeared in *Taproot Literary Review*, *The Zodiac Review*, and *Antique Children*.

According to Critiki.com, Kahiki founders Bill Sapp and Lee Henry started work on the Kahiki after their bar, the Grass Shack, burned down on the site in 1959. They spent one million dollars to create it.

Although the iconic restaurant is now closed, the frozen foods division of Kahiki still operates out of Gahanna, Ohio.

Lazarus
Doug Oldham

2005
THE CHRISTMAS VIRGIN
By Chad Wellinger

I've left everything. The turkey waiting to be stuffed, piles of ginger-bread men waiting for icing faces and outfits, presents waiting to be wrapped. For the first time in my life I've left everything to be done later on Christmas Day. Later is better.

It's already 3:52 a.m. Last year at this time I would have already been downstairs, a big mug of cocoa in one hand and another hand whipping the butter cream frosting I'd slather all over hot cinnamon buns. I'd always thought, cocoa for Christmas, coffee for every other day. I know that everything needs to be fresh, perfect. The Brighton clan wants to have the kind of Christmas you see in those holiday Coke advertisements. Something like *It's A Wonderful Life* meets *A Christmas Story*. And we always do.

I stare at the ceiling, feeling anxious. I have places I want to go, need to go, but leaving feels so selfish. But, oh, I have so much to do— and I love to do it, or used to, at least. Things can change so quickly. It's been almost one year. The last year has been a question mark strung with twinkly lights. The twinkly lights, oh how Momma loved them, the big colored ones. Momma, Daddy, Grandma, Grandpa, Annie, they all loved them so.

I slide out of bed. I have the *feeling*.

It was a little less than a year ago, 2:07 a.m. when the phone had rung. Alan had answered it.

"Sally, Sal," said Alan in his urgent tone—loyal, dependable Alan.

"What," I said, muddled with sleep, "What is it? What's wrong?"

"Sal, your mom's had a stroke, it's the hospital. She's in intensive care."

I had thought, here it comes, here it comes—the feeling—like stumbling on roller-skates, the sensation your stomach has between the stumble and the collision with the ground. Now imagine that feeling hanging in your stomach, a stocking filled with anxious, squirmy, vis-

149

ceral things.

I tiptoe across the cold wood floor, trying not to wake Alan.

Luckily no one's an early riser. I have till eight o'clock, eight-thirty at the latest, then all Christmas hell is going to break lose.

I tear off my nightgown, flannel, warm—just like the flannel sheets Momma bought years ago for Annie's and my beds—and put on a pair of blue jeans and a peach sweater. Then I brush my mousy brown hair quickly in the dark, not daring to glance in the mirror—no time. Besides, people always say I look like Sally Field, so I know I look fine. Sally Field always looks fine.

I take another quick look at that ancient alarm clock of Alan's on the nightstand, it's 3: 58 now, almost 4:00—let's go, Sally, time is fleeting, especially today.

The hall is dark, but I can still see the outline of grandmother's Bombay chest with its white marble top, like a grave, and the small chandeliers hanging from the ceiling with their dingling dangling crystal teardrops. It's strange how you notice some things, odd things, when you're in a panic.

The four other bedroom doors are closed. Diane, Amy, Ben, my children, all grown up, sleeping in their childhood beds. Miriam and Ed, Alan's parents at the end of the hall—I hate both of them, hate them for making me miss those Christmases with my own family.

"Every other year," Miriam would croak in that nasal drawl, "It's our turn again, our turn for Christmas." I hate them, I hate them to death.

Diane sleeps with her husband Mark, their two kids, Caleb and Luke, twins, only five, so lucky to be young at Christmas, when everything is in place.

"The children were nestled all snug in their beds, while visions of sugar-plums danced in their heads." *The Night Before Christmas*— Daddy would always read it to Annie and me on Christmas Eve, we'd be in our beds, surrounded by our cozy-mozy flannel feeling, flannel smelling sheets, and he'd smoke his pipe and just read. I want someone to read it to me again. I miss that, the one being read to.

Ben, fresh from his divorce from Susan, sleeps alongside his ten-year-old daughter, Rachel, still so lucky. Amy, my baby, sleeps with that Jon, the agnostic or atheist, can't remember which—anyway, what's the difference? Jon, the Christmas Virgin …

Check Webster's for the definition of *Christmas Virgin*—it *should* read: *A person who has never taken part in the festivities surrounding the Christmas holiday.* I bet Jon hates Christmas. I don't want to be that. I don't hate Christmas. Everyone loves Christmas except loners, lushes and people on the brink of suicide, agnostics, atheists—unhappy people, unsatisfied people.

At dinner he'd worn one of those gaudy knit sweaters, you know the kind that look like they're the product of some sewing machine explosion. He was evidently trying to conform to what he thought would be appropriate Christmas Eve attire. Well, he looked like he'd gone shopping at a garage sale at Bill Cosby's.

Rachel had been sort of in awe of him. In her eyes he was diversity. She'd asked dumbfounded, "So you've really never celebrated Christmas before?"

"Nope," he'd said with a smirk. Then he'd turned away from her to reiterate for the adults, saying, "My dad's Jewish, and my mom's an anthropology professor. She used to say we 'observe Christmas,' all the little rituals. I can't tell you how excited she was when she found out I'd be spending a big, traditional family Christmas with Amy's family. She wanted me to bring a video camera." He'd laughed and then everyone else had too, well, everyone except me.

Amy had given him a peck on the cheek and then I'd said, probably with a bit too much snark, "Don't worry, Alan tapes everything. We'll be sure to send you a copy."

As I walk into the kitchen I'm hit in the face with a disgusting wave of odors, the remains of spice exhaust from the oven—punishment for baking a whole civilization of gingerbread men.

I grab my purse and car keys from the counter. A glass plate piled with naked gingerbread men catches my eye. They are staring at me, *the gingerbread men are staring at me*, demanding to be iced, watching my every move, crying "Ice us already, lady!"

I can feel my eyes burning, my lips pursing, my eyebrows rising. The very sight of them just makes me want to smash them up with a rolling pin. My hand reaches out towards the plate, grabbing the top most gingerbread man in a claw-like fashion. Yes my dear, you have been chosen.

I walk over to the sink, turning on the water and garbage disposal. The grinding sound of the disposal's blades is startling at first, but I let the sound continue to belch out of the drain. I feel my hand slowly lowering the gingerbread man into the sink, then lower and lower, until its legs touch the outer circle of the drain leading into the black hole, that black hole filled with thrashing teeth, thrashing teeth meant to destroy.

Before I commit gingerbread man murder by garbage disposal, I hesitate, feeling silly, but the feeling passes quickly, so quickly, so I give the cookie a final push into the drain. The thrashing teeth immediately dig into the gingerbread man's legs and pull him down into its mouth. A spray of cookie crumbs splatters the side of the sink, and a stray red-hot eyeball rolls across its bottom.

I flip off the disposal and stare down into the sink. You're so melodramatic, Sally, the Queen of Melodrama—but how brilliant it feels to destroy something so connected to Christmas. I wonder though if you aren't having a Christmas-themed nervous breakdown?

I take the small hose from the sink's side and clean up the mess.

As I tiptoe through the living room I spot Alex, Alan's baby sister, a sexy, sophisticated career woman, lonely, a Christmas hater, asleep on the couch. She'd be perfect for Jon, the Christmas Virgin.

I glance around the room. It's congested with Christmas knick-knacks, and the tree is rather large, strung with twinkly lights, big colored ones and dressed with loads of ornaments. I look for *my* ornament, a glass baby carriage with a pink bow on its side. I can still feel its shape in my hands. I used to cradle it ever so gently in my palms as I'd walk over to a branch of evergreen to hang it. But no more, no more, just like so many other things that are no more. Alan broke it, *my* ornament, gone.

So now, the tree, *my-ornament-less,* looks like the decaying body of an old friend, no heartbeat left, no soul left—should I hang my heart on one of those branches? Could it take the place of an ornament that held more in its seams of glass than anything anyone, especially an ornament-breaker could ever imagine?

I look down at the spread of presents … presents galore! Presents galore! Fat presents, skinny presents, presents with bows, presents with just bows, the tree is surrounded with our usual overwhelming display of presents that run wall to wall and out towards the couch. I know we're one of those families where everyone counts the number of presents they have under the tree in the morning. I used to find that funny, almost endearing, but now it just seems pathetic. I pivot in place and am met by a fire-less fireplace. "The stockings are hung from the chimney with care." Overflowing, small packages, but big gifts.

I back step my way out of the room, like a scared little girl trying to escape an imaginary Christmas Bogeyman holding a gigantic candy cane, its end sharpened into a pick.

This doesn't feel like Christmas, this doesn't feel like it used to. This whole room looks like something extracted from one of those model homes that are made to look like a real home, but really they're just an illusion of what other people think we want. My relationship with the kids almost seems like a Christmas parlor trick—why is it they only show up on the major holidays, why just show up for Christmas? This living room is just a big thing filled with a bunch of little fakes. This isn't how it used to be, Christmas, living rooms used to be filled with a bunch of little somethings that meant *something* to the people who put them there, at least Momma and Daddy's always was. This is just Christmas Vomit.

I grab my fur coat from the entryway closet. I'm a Sally Field look-a-like in jeans, a peach sweater, and a fur coat leaving everything. Just for a little while, but I have to leave everything, for later.

The clock in the car glows 4:08 in its greenish type.

Every radio station plays Christmas music—"All I want for Christmas," "Hark," "Angel," "White," "Santa Baby," "Jingle Bells" ... My head is already on that frequency, so I pop my Petula Clark CD into the car's player. Her voice fills the car, mixing in with the heat that blows out of the vents. She sings "Downtown," upbeat, but depressing, could you make it a little bit more upbeat Petula?

I back the Lincoln, dependable like Alan, out of the driveway, letting it drift off the cement and into the grass, plowing down some of our plastic candy canes. Our white colonial house with green shutters and dormers is overdressed with twinkly lights, small ones, big ones—covered with twinkly lights vomit. And our lawn is crowded with more lights and one of those Santas with sleigh and reindeer. We're all a bunch of Christmas whores.

Where to first, I wonder? Well, the song is a sign, so I'll go downtown first; the second place is the most important anyways. I have until eighty-thirty, at the latest—I have to be back by then, but what about nine, ten, eleven, noon? How about never going back?

It's 5:02. Downtown Columbus sleeps. The skyline looks like a glittering tinker toy metropolis decorated with tinsel. The piece de resistance is LeVeque Tower, glowing red and green like some ridiculous art deco bubble light. It's the Big Quiet, everyone is dreaming of today, anticipation, glee, dread, hatred.

There are no carolers making their rounds. No Santa Claus wannabes on every street corner ringing their bells to fill red buckets with sticky coins. No Christmas devotees rushing about with shopping bags overflowing with packages, no Christmas joiner-inners feeling guilty for not yet getting to their shopping.

I drive by the Statehouse and instantly spot its mammoth Christmas tree sitting in front. A big daddy Christmas tree, like the tree in Rockefeller Center. Look how bright those twinkly lights are; they hypnotize. Momma would have loved those twinkly lights. I wish I could knock it over with the Lincoln. But instead, I decide to park in one of City Center's old parking garages.

I exit a bakery onto an empty street, holding a Styrofoam cup filled with coffee and a twisty, glazed doughnut. It was a bakery owned by a Jewish family, a bakery open on Christmas, how wonderful. I'd desperately wanted some coffee ... *cocoa for Christmas, Coffee for every other day.*

A taxicab pulls up along the curb, next to where I'm walking. The Hispanic driver asks me if I want a ride. I accept.

He asks in his broken English, "Where can I to take you to, Miz?"

"High Street," I say, "Lazarus."

"It to be close, Miz," he says, "long time now."

"I know," I say, "but it's tradition."

He gives me a funny look, like I'm crazy or something and then starts to drive.

As I step out of the cab onto High Street I feel like I'm Audrey Hepburn in *Breakfast at Tiffany's*. I am Holly Golightly escaping to Tiffany's, in a little black dress from my gallivanting the night before ... "when you're alone and life is making you lonely, you can always go—downtown ..."

Everything seems so simple that way. Not being Sally Brighton for a few moments makes everything seem so much simpler, safer. Nothing bad could ever happen at Tiffany's—*Lazarus.*

But oh, it has. Lazarus is no more, a memory, just like so many other things in my life. It closed permanently over a year ago. The shoppers fled, the lights went out, its iconic vertical sign, L – A – Z – A – R – U – S was removed by mechanical claws. Now the main building looks like a giant, beige mausoleum filled with bare, cobwebby shelves, clothes racks like skeletons, and Ghosts of Christmas Past ... faint figures wandering around the store with shopping bags and humming carols, riding the escalators, dining in the Chintz Room, their forks and knives clinking and clanking on the plates. Perhaps a phantom elevator operator is even still running the Santaland Express up to the sixth floor, the faces of long-ago children pressed up against its antique glass-paned doors, anxious to get to Santaland with its elves, wonderland of toys, secret gift shop.

I've come downtown for one reason: to see the Christmas window displays. My whole real first family, Momma, Dad, Annie, always loved Lazarus's window displays. We'd come every year, the week after Thanksgiving. Dad would buy four cups of cocoa from the street vendor and we'd just wander around like tourists, devouring the warm scenes frozen behind glass panes. They were like squishy chocolate doughnuts to go with the cocoa, separate Christmases going on in each window box.

At Christmastime the six-story store would look like a wrapped gift, its roof appearing to have sprung a leak of twinkly lights as they fell to the sidewalk below, forming a Christmas tree. Dozens of decorated evergreens would sit like toy soldiers at salute on the store's front awning.

I nibble on my doughnut, sip my coffee and stroll past empty, dark windows, display-less. Of course I'd known they'd be vacant, that'd I'd see my own sad reflection swim by in cold black window display-less water. I had the foolish notion that perhaps a Christmas miracle could occur. Child's play, I know, but it gave me hope. I thought perhaps I'd run into Momma, Daddy and Annie gazing into a warmly lit window display of a little girl with blonde ringlets watching with shocked astonishment as her Mommy kisses Santa Claus.

If I designed a window display, it would be from my memory, a memory from a Christmas with my whole real first family. I press my face up against the glass. I imagine the bare display is transformed, becomes Momma and Daddy's living room, that time slips and a Christmas memory from long ago begins to play out behind the glass, one that I watch like that little boy who gazes longingly at the model train in the toy shop window. I can sense it too, smell and hear it, but can't find a way to put myself on the other side of that cold glass ...

The heavy, beautiful odors of Chanel No. 5, pipe smoke, fresh gingerbread, and pine swirl invisibly in the air, the garland hanging perfectly above the fireplace, bubbly, bubbling bubble lights sticking out here and there amongst the green. "Have Yourself a Merry Little Christmas," plays on a record player, filling the room with Frank Sinatra's voice. The perfect sized evergreen sits in the corner of the room, strung with big colored twinkly lights.

Boxes filled with ornaments scatter the floor, ornaments of angels, snowmen, icicles, Santa Clauses, Disney characters, ornaments made out of cardboard, glue, popsicle sticks and glitter.

Daddy sits on the plush, velvet sofa, smoking his pipe and fiddling with a paper clip and a glass candy cane ornament, while Grandpa whistles and keeps going back to the crystal punch bowl for more eggnog.

Grandma stands off to the side, in the kitchen, giving gingerbread men faces and outfits, while humming Jingle Bells.

But Momma, Annie, and a six-year-old me sift through the boxes of ornaments, like Christmas pirates in search of a particular ornament treasure.

"Not in this box," Annie says, "But I already found my carriage ornament." She dangles it in front of my face like she's suddenly Christmas ornament richer than me.

"Just keep looking," Momma says.

She's so beautiful, so young, with her porcelain skin, dark, exotic hair and violet eyes. Daddy always said that she was his Elizabeth Taylor.

"What if we lost it?" I say.

"Well that's impossible because I've just found it," Momma says, lifting my baby carriage ornament from a box filled with ornamental fruit.

"Oh, oh, let me see," I say.

She hands it to me and says, "Hold it gently." I cup it in my hands as I walk over to the tree.

As I hang it carefully from a branch, Grandma scuttles out from the kitchen with a tray of gingerbread men and mugs of hot cocoa.

"Your great grandmother Evvie bought those ornaments before you two were born," Momma tells Annie and me. "Remember when Grandma bought those at Lazarus, Momma?"

Grandma says, "Yes I do. We took her to the Chintz Room for lunch. God bless her, she grew up dirt poor on a farm. Thought it was really something, her having lunch out at a department store restaurant. I still have that big fancy hat she wore, the one with the roses on it."

"She got their strawberry cheesecake for dessert," Momma says, "and I got one of those ice cream cone clown sundaes, with the little cherry eyes and raisin mouth and sugar cone cap."

Momma looks at her aging mother with loving question marks in her eyes, as if to ask, "How many more Christmases?" I remember that look. I understand it now, not then, but I remember that look.

"Momma, set down that tray and play something for us on the piano," she says, smiling, "Deck the Halls or Jingle Bells."

Momma turns off the record player as Grandma sits down at the piano and begins to play "The Nutcracker Suite." Annie and I dance around the room, doing little pirouettes, like a duo of ambitious Sugar Plum Fairies ...

I throw out my empty Styrofoam coffee cup, and walk away from a mausoleum (*one that used to be dressed in tiny, white twinkly lights*).

As I walk down High Street I wrap the fur coat around me tightly. Cold winter light, tinged pale pink, blue, and gold, has slowly begun to breach the edges of the night sky, and along with it comes snow flurries. A million ice butterflies fluttering down, landing on my hair, eyelashes, nose, showering me with their tiny corpses.

It's been an ugly holiday season. Without the snow everything looks dead. As I pull into the parking lot of the cemetery I imagine that its landscape looks almost like me: pale, drained, ugly, old—tortured. Does Sally Field look tortured?

I've arrived at my second destination trying to suck up the last of my Christmas hope. I'm an almost empty mug of cocoa, gone cold, and I can taste the gritty chocolate dregs. I get out of the Lincoln, holding a large flashlight in one hand and a Macy's shopping bag in the other. The graves look like gray gophers popping out of the ground.

I've been here too many times. For Grandma, thirty-four years ago; Grandpa, twenty-six years ago; Dad, ten years ago; Annie, six years ago; Momma, one year ago. I shine the flashlight ahead. In a sliver of light I spot the large T, T for TATE—and I see their graves.

Here's your family Christmas, Sally, is this what you wanted? Go home. You've left everything. You're obligated to your family. You're obligated to Christmas.

There are three Tate graves, all similar looking, one next to the other. I walk up to the first grave, Momma. The slab reads EVELYN TATE, BELOVED WIFE AND MOTHER, *Born June 5, 1923, Home to the Angels February 15, 2005.*

Ashes to ashes, dust to dust—and our memories, warm memories, flannel sheets, that Chanel perfume she used to wear, the way she used to come up to Annie's and my bedroom in the morning and wake us with kisses. All the Christmases, she always made Christmas so beautiful.

I kneel down and place my palm up against the grave's cold granite. They're here, so close. If I could just talk, touch them again. But what's a grave if not just another window display? The untouchable, lying within.

I reach into the Macy's shopping bag and pull out a small gift wrapped in that heavy department store wrapping paper. My shaking hand places it on top of the grave. Was it a waste of money, eighty dollars down the drain for a dead woman who's never actually going to use this perfume?

You can always take it back to Lazarus—no questions asked.

Christmas is the season of perpetual hope, or so they say. As the holiday approached, the believer in me kept saying, "It'll just be as it always was. One or all of them will come back. It just isn't possible that you'd be left all alone … too cruel." So when I was shopping for their gifts it seemed perfectly natural. I spoke about them to the saleswomen as if they were still alive. I'd decided that if I acted like they existed, they would. I had to make myself believe, like a child believes in Santa Claus.

"Merry Christmas, Momma," I say, sobbing now, "I miss you."

I'd still expected her to be downstairs wrapping presents by the fire, but she's gone—Christmas has confirmed that—made it a fact. Everyone from my real, first family is gone, and I'm all alone. I'm an orphan, a fifty-eight year old orphan at Christmas.

I lay my cheek on the top of her grave and then kiss it, how she used to kiss Annie and me in the morning to wake us up. I sob and say, "Please wake back up … please?"

I guess when you get to a certain age you've run out of Christmas wishes that can be granted. Jon probably has all of his left. If only I could borrow one of his. To be like Jon again, to be a Christmas Virgin, that would mean my whole real first family would be alive, I'd just be a little girl, be able to be part of a memory window display instead of just a viewer.

I pull two more gifts out of the shopping bag like a depressed Christmas magician and place them on the other two graves, Daddy and Annie. I stare at the three wrapped gifts: a bottle of Chanel, a new sweater and slacks, and a designer purse.

"Merry Christmas, my darlings," I say.

I walk backwards out of the cemetery, watching their graves get smaller and smaller. Somehow I still believe in Christmas miracles, that their figures might suddenly appear on the horizon, walking towards me, arms outstretched. I have visions of Judy Garland in my head, from that movie *Meet Me in St. Louis.* She's singing "Have Yourself a Merry Christmas." I think it's the saddest song I've ever heard.

I feel like people should be staring at me. I'm a Sally Field look-a-like, Audrey Hepburn feel-a-like, Christmas Virgin wannabe in jeans, a peach sweater and fur coat walking hurriedly, nervously down a semi-crowded terminal at Port Columbus.

The arrivals and departures board blinks 8:23 a.m. I can't believe I'm actually doing this, I can't believe it—do it, Sally, do it, go through with it. I spot big-framed pictures on the terminal walls advertising for places like Hawaii, London, Paris, Mexico. I rush past gate after gate. Where am I going? I don't even have a plan.

Some of these gates are like portholes into other places, places oblivious to the whole Christmas holiday, places where the time difference says it's still the twenty-fourth of December, or the twenty-sixth of December, even better.

I need to find a porthole to a place where there are no twinkly lights, no presents wrapped in gaudy paper, gingerbread men, window displays … a place foreign to Christmas.

I pick Fiji. Turtle Island, Fiji. Where there are white beaches—*frozen grass the color of hay*, an ocean of melted blue ice—*ice butterflies*, the smell of suntan lotion—*the smell of Chanel*, a peach margarita—*cocoa*—a last-minute fare of 2,357 dollars.

Thank God Alan is a loyal, dependable attorney. Will they worry? Will they be terrified when they all wake up to not find me dressed in my red Christmas sweater and my candy cane earrings, the turkey un-stuffed, the presents un-wrapped, the naked gingerbread men, no note, the car gone?

Waiting at my gate I feel quite at home with my soon-to-be fellow passengers. They also are skipping out on the rites and rituals of a traditional Christmas day, seeking out a little escapism. Are they too in mourning or just hoping for a good tan?

I can feel my cell phone vibrating inside my purse. I take it out and see that the missed calls and text messages have started to pile up like the presents in our living room. I can't call Alan—that loyal, dependable voice of his will just make me feel like I'm being cruel, selfish, behaving like a child. He'll make me come home. But I can't do that, so I send him a text message:

Am fine. I have to get away for a bit. Please don't think I'm being cruel. I just can't this year—and after all the perfect Christmases I've given us don't I deserve one year? A few presents in bedroom closet, still need wrapped. Turkey goes into oven at 325, four hours, complete recipe in little recipe box. Ask Susan for help. Decorator icing for gingerbread men and sugar cookies in Lazy Susan, kids can decorate. Car is in blue lot at airport.

After I've sent the message, I power off my phone. A flight attendant announces that the boarding process has begun.

I stand in line, a Christmas rebel *without a Momma,* with my fellow Christmas renegades for a few moments, until it's finally my turn and I hand over my ticket and pass the threshold onto the jetway.

I take one last glance over my shoulder to see if perhaps I've left a part of myself back at the gate, but instead I see a mother and a father and their two small children, a girl and boy. I hadn't noticed them before. They must have been running late. The little girl wears a lovely green velvet dress with a sash tied at the waist, and the boy has on one of those adorable knit sweaters. The two are occupied with their new toys. The girl bops her head and dances around to an iPod, and the boy is engrossed in some sort of hand-held video game. I wonder if they went to see the window displays?

The mother and father give their tickets to the attendant, and take the tiny hands of their children in their own. Framed in the entrance of the jetway they're a Christmas card, and I'm sure something is written inside, but I leave it unopened.

Chad Wellinger is a native of Dublin, Ohio and currently in the MFA fiction program at Emerson College in Boston. "The Christmas Virgin" is his first piece to be published.

The Lazarus building, once an iconic department store in Columbus, Ohio, is now home to a diverse range of businesses, retailers and organizations, including the Ohio Department of Job and Family Services and the OSU Urban Arts Space gallery.

The building collects rain water via its rooftop gardens, which is then used in the building cooling and toilet systems. The Lazarus building was awarded Gold Certification with Leadership in Energy and Environmental Design (LEED) by the United States Green Building Council for its impressive renovation.

OFF THE BUS
Cortney DeWalt

2008
THE YEAR EVERYTHING CHANGED

By Bradley Nelson

Henry Burnside lived according to a predictable rhythm. Like many other aspects of his life, his morning getting-ready-for-work routine was unchanged from one day to the next. He knew what needed to be done and exactly how long it would take to do it.

Henry's shower needs were simple: one bottle of combined shampoo/conditioner and one bar of Ivory soap. This had led to a minor argument when his boyfriend Bryce had first moved in. Bryce's shower needs were not simple: shampoos, conditioners, moisturizers, loofahs, sponges, body soaps, razors, shaving cream. To Henry, the variety was bewildering and the quantity was overwhelming.

In the end, there had been a compromise of sorts. Henry's one bottle of shampoo and one bar of soap lived in the front half of the shower. Bryce's arsenal was conveniently stored in a hanging basket at the other end.

Eyes closed, hot water massaging his scalp, Henry reached blindly but confidently for his shampoo. He squeezed the bottle and was greeted with a disappointing puff of air. He shook the bottle a few times and tried again. Empty.

"Bryce?" Henry called. "Are you nearby?"

No answer. He was probably at the gym already. An empty shampoo bottle was not the end of the world. Henry always kept at least one spare bottle for just such an emergency.

"Bryce!"

Retrieving a new shampoo mid-shower, however, involved turning the water off, grabbing a towel, drying off, stepping into the hallway, and opening the closet door. More importantly, it involved an extra few minutes that were not part of the plan.

Henry completed his interrupted shower and dressed quickly, the final piece of his outfit a stainless steel Emporio Armani wristwatch, a gift from Bryce on their anniversary two years ago. It was a flashier watch than Henry would have bought for himself, and doubtless more expensive. The watch was water resistant, but Henry never wore it in the shower, just to be safe. He checked the time as he fastened the clasp.

Only a couple of minutes behind schedule, he allowed himself a quick look-over in the mirror. As he did every morning, he noted the addition of more gray hairs to his neatly trimmed beard. Once, the hair on his head (and elsewhere), had been dark, natural black, but at forty-two years of age, this was no longer the case. Bryce had hinted that maybe he ought to think about dying his hair, but Henry said he preferred to age naturally. The truth, however, was that he just didn't want to add another item to his daily ritual. Life was complicated enough as it was.

Bryce, on the other hand, seemed to actually enjoy complications. One week he might dye his hair platinum blond just to see how it looked. The next week it might be firehouse red. That was one of the things that had originally made him attractive to Henry. Bryce was everything Henry could not be: impulsive, care-free, flamboyant.

"Good morning," Henry said as walked into the kitchen. Bryce was putting his empty bowl in the sink. Henry poured himself some cereal, and sat in his usual chair facing the window.

"Think it will rain today?"

Bryce looked outside at the overcast sky, but didn't reply and left the room.

The kitchen faced the back yard and breakfast was the one moment of the day that Henry let a little of the natural world into his own. Monday through Friday, Henry worked in the JP Morgan Chase McCoy Center, the second-largest office building in the United States. Only the Pentagon was larger. Needless to say, there were row upon row of cubicles between him and any outside windows.

A moment later, Bryce walked back through the kitchen, duffel bag in hand. Bryce always kept himself and the yard in show condition.

"Have fun at the gym!" Henry said. Bryce looked like he was about to say something, but then he left without saying a word. Henry had no idea why, but he seemed to be in the doghouse.

Henry picked up the *Columbus Dispatch* and scanned through the headlines. They were mostly about Tuesday's historic election results, naturally. Barack Obama. The first black president of the United States. The promise of change. It was a very different feeling from 2004, just four years previous, when Ohio had amended the state constitution to define marriage as between one man and one woman. That had been a rough time.

Bryce had wanted to move immediately. To a bluer state: Massachusetts, or maybe Canada. Henry had been disappointed as well, but he didn't really want to *get married*. Sure it would be nice to have some of the financial perks, but open that door and you open the door to divorce as well.

Sometimes Henry wished he didn't live in a swing state. Elections were stressful. Also stressful? Discovering his car wouldn't start when he went to leave for work.

Henry rushed back into the house in a near-panic and immediately made a number of phone calls. First to Bryce's cell phone (no answer), then to two co-workers who lived relatively nearby and might be able to give him a ride (no response), to his mechanic (busy signal), and finally his secretary to let her know he would probably be late. Next he called several taxi companies, but each one told him they were backlogged and wouldn't be able to send someone to his house for an hour or two.

Finally, Henry pulled up the COTA website on his home computer. To his horror, he discovered that although he lived barely nine miles from work, there were no direct bus routes between where he lived in the neighborhood of Clintonville, to where he worked in the suburb of Polaris. He would have to take the bus all the way into downtown Columbus, change buses, and then backtrack the way he had just come, finally reaching his destination an hour and sixteen minutes later.

Henry couldn't think of any other options though, so he set out on foot, walking the few blocks to High Street. As fate would have it, the bus was just leaving as he arrived, and he had to wait for a second one. He'd be another eight minutes late as a result.

"Rough morning?" someone asked.

Henry noticed a woman sitting on the bus stop's single bench.

"How'd you guess?" he replied.

"You look a bit flustered, that's all."

Henry shrugged.

"That, and you don't usually take this bus. I would know."

Another shrug.

"Spare some change, sir?" the woman asked.

This is exactly why I don't take the bus, Henry thought as he glanced over at the woman and finally took notice of her multiple layers of clothing and the black plastic garbage bag propped up next to her on the bench. He silently willed the homeless woman to go away.

"Do you have a dollar?" she asked again.

"No."

"You're not the only person who ever had a bad day, you know."

A bus finally arrived, and he eventually made it to work, but as if being late wasn't bad enough, he discovered he had forgotten his ID badge. If he had been on time he might have entered with somebody else, but his timing was impeccably wrong today.

"I don't seem to have it on me," Henry said, after checking his pockets for a second time. "You know me, though, Ms…" Henry floundered for the front desk clerk's name, *Ginny? Jamie?* Fortunately, she was wearing her own ID badge. "You know me, Gillian. It's not like I'm some stranger wandering in from the street."

Gillian eyed him suspiciously, "What did you say your name was?"

"Henry. Henry Burnside?"

"I'm sorry, Mr. Burnside. More than seven thousand people work here. I can't be expected to remember everybody. What department did you say you worked in?"

Henry eventually made it to his office. The morning was half over, and he would have to work past five o'clock to compensate.

As a man of routine, Henry normally felt a sense of pleasure in his work. It was almost a cliche that Henry had gone into accounting. Numbers brought order to a chaotic world, and Henry liked order. A balanced spreadsheet actually made him feel good. On this day, however, the numbers failed Henry. They failed to bring order to his day, and in the end failed to balance altogether—something that had never happened before.

At lunch, he tried calling his mechanic, but all he got was a voice-mail message stating the shop would be closed indefinitely while the owner dealt with some unnamed personal emergency. He tried calling Bryce, but again no answer.

The afternoon proved to be equally frustrating. The numbers still didn't add up, and Henry fought against a growing sense of panic. "I'm just distracted today," he tried to reassure himself. "Things got off on the wrong foot this morning, and I just haven't been able to recover."

Finally, he stopped, sat back in his chair and stared blankly at his computer monitor. Absolutely nothing was going as it should. Henry thought back to the day's beginning and wondered again what he had done to upset his partner of seven years.

The week had started with such excitement. Although Henry and Bryce were different in many ways (opposites did attract, apparently), their political leanings were very much in synch. They had both been swept up in the fervor of the election, and Tuesday had been a thrilling day. Henry had mailed in his vote several weeks earlier, and when Bryce recounted how long the voting lines were he was glad that he had. The two men had stayed up late watching the news reports together. They had even popped a bottle of champagne to celebrate.

Other than the slight interruption that Tuesday caused, the week had otherwise proceeded like any other. Like clockwork. Now that he thought about it, however, Bryce had seemed somewhat quiet and distant Wednesday and Thursday.

When the work day finally ended, Henry felt like he had accomplished nothing the entire day. *Thank God it's Friday*, he thought.

On the bus ride home, Henry impulsively decided to buy some flowers. Henry and Bryce didn't buy flowers for each other very often, so when they did, it was a big deal. Getting off the bus one stop early put him right by the Clintonville Kroger. It was raining lightly, but Henry hardly noticed.

The grocery store was busy, and the flower arrangements had already been picked over by previous customers. Henry couldn't find a single lily (Bryce's favorite). There weren't even any roses left. He settled for a rather sad arrangement of pink and white carnations, and hoped Bryce would appreciate the thought if not the actual flowers.

Henry walked towards home, lost in thought. He made it a few blocks before a rough patch in the sidewalk tripped him, and he dropped everything. Flowers, vase, Henry, and briefcase all sprawled in disarray across the wet sidewalk. For a moment, he just sat there, dumbfounded.

"Still having a bad day?" A woman's voice interrupted Henry's daze, and he looked up to find that the homeless woman from earlier was starting to pick up the mess.

Henry didn't have the energy left to say anything, so together he and the vagrant put his papers back in his briefcase, salvaged what they could of the flowers, and threw the broken vase into a nearby trash can.

"Thanks," Henry said finally. "It feels like you're the only person who's even acknowledged my existence today."

"You're not the only person to ever have a bad day, you know," said the woman as she stepped back under the cover of the bus stop.

"Yeah, you said something like that this morning, didn't you?" Henry was already soaked through, so he just stood there in the rain.

"I meant it," she continued. "Would you like to talk about it?"

"Talk about what?" asked Henry.

"About how horrible your day has been. About how nothing has seemed to go like it normally does. About how everyone has ignored you, even your wife?"

Henry thought about trying to explain how he didn't have a wife exactly, but he said nothing.

"I used to have it all, too. House, job, husband. The usual."

"What happened?" asked Henry.

"I don't really know. But it all started with a truly awful day where nothing went right ... which turned into a crazy week, which became an unbearable month, and now, here I am."

"What, so I'm going to be out on the street next?" Henry laughed. "I don't think things are quite as bad as all that."

"Don't you?"

For a moment, Henry did wonder. There was something unnaturally horrible about how his day had gone.

"Ridiculous," he said.

"Is it? You aren't going to believe me right now, but I have a strong suspicion that I'm right about this. I've had a lot of time to think about things. I suspect that you've become very complacent in life. I suspect that you've fallen into some kind of rut, and that for probably many years now, you've just been coasting along. Stop me if I'm completely off base here."

Henry didn't stop her. He liked consistency. There was nothing wrong with him just because he felt safer when things stayed the same.

"I suspect that you think that you have achieved some sort of balance, a rhythm, I'm not sure what you call it. I called it 'finding peace' myself. I was wrong, though. Life is not meant to be constant. Life is meant to be in flux. Seasons change somewhat predictably, but the weather is never entirely predictable. There is a certain amount of natural chaos.

"I think it's possible to become so uninvolved, so unimportant, so boring, that the rest of the world starts to pass you by. Pretty soon you're just part of the background."

The woman stopped talking, and for a moment Henry almost believed her. Then he reminded himself that she was probably delusional, which was why she was on the street in the first place.

"I think I'd better get going," Henry said.

"I've told you my theory," the woman said, "and I can see you don't believe me. You don't think your world could collapse in a single day, but I believe it could. Think of it as a universal hiccup. Sometimes the train just gets knocked off the track."

Henry considered his words carefully for a moment. "I'm going to go now. I'm going to walk home and figure out what I did to upset my—to upset things at home. I'm going to fix things. And that will be the end of it."

Henry reached into his pocket and pulled out a twenty dollar bill.

"Here," he said, "go get yourself something to eat or drink or drugs or whatever it is you do."

"Keep it," the woman replied. "You might need it for yourself soon enough."

Henry walked towards his house again, exhausted.

When he reached his front door, he fumbled for the key and inserted it into the lock. All he wanted was to make up with Bryce, for things to return to normal, and for this day to finally end. He tried turning the key, but it wouldn't budge. He pulled the key out of the lock and verified that it was the correct one. Maybe the lock was to blame. It probably hadn't been used in years—they usually came in through the attached garage.

Somewhat embarrassed, Henry rang the doorbell on his own house. Bryce should definitely be home by now, and would have to let him in. When no one came to the door, he knocked loudly, and noticed for the first time that although the front porch light was on, the house was dark inside. *Where could Bryce possibly be?* Henry walked around to the back of the house. His key worked this time, and he let himself in.

"Bryce?"

No response.

When he flipped on the light, Henry immediately noticed that a few things were missing. A few of Bryce's things. A framed poster of a play he'd acted in. A wood carving of a dancing elephant. His CD collection. Henry made his way into the kitchen, and found a handwritten note on the table.

Collapsing into a chair he picked up the piece of paper. The note was simple. It read: *Sorry. I just needed something to change.*

Henry knew without checking the rest of the house that Bryce was gone.

Bradley Nelson is a writer who recently began exploring the short story genre. He was previously published in Columbus Creative Cooperative's *While You Were Out* anthology. He and his partner Kurt live in Kenmore Park, a neighborhood of northeast Columbus, Ohio.

COLUMBUS 2012
Melissa Pauquette

2012
GOING UNDER
By Stephen C. David

The Mega-Millions jackpot had amassed its largest prize in history. The excitement carried the nightly news and daily papers, and seeped into both the habitual gambler and the thrifty alike. The fear of wasted opportunity sent Charlie Buds out to the Speedway at the corner of Tompkins and High to buy a ticket.

It had been an unusually mild winter, and a hot start to the Midwestern spring, but the late March afternoon was brilliantly seasonable. It called for long pants and a jacket, but was perfectly comfortable in proper attire. Charlie walked under the blooming magnolias and new greenery, inspecting the texture of the dollar bill in his pocket. He thought for a moment of the hands through which the bill had passed, of real and imagined values, of informal economies and the Federal Reserve.

But as the sunlight filtered down from between the flowers hanging above him, it all seemed inconsequential in comparison to his wonder at the cardinals and trees. He allowed the cadence of his stride to be interrupted in order to bend down and pick up a discarded plastic cup from the tree-lawn. He put it in the garbage can outside the gas station before going inside.

Charlie got in line, standing next to a case of breakfast sandwiches and the slowly revolving pizza display. There were two men in front of him, waiting with liters of soda and bags of Ballreichs, and one asked Charlie if he had a dollar that he could spare. Charlie took the bill from his pocket and said yes, he had a dollar, but it was soon going to be worth five hundred million more, so he would reluctantly hang on to it.

"All right," the man smiled, bobbing his head, "I got you." The man turned back around and Charlie's lounging mind circled through hypothetical plans and far flung daydreams, kindled by the astronomically improbable, but concretely possible, prospects of a multi-million dollar windfall.

"I think I would leave the country," he had said to Angie yesterday after a long, preparatory pause. "I think I'd leave the country and go into a general reclusion. You know, buy a little studio in Paris and sit at cafes all day, or maybe fix up a little house in Tuscany and just wander the streets in nice Italian shoes and drink red wine."

"So basically you'd live out a male version of *Under the Tuscan Sun*," Angie replied from the other room as she plugged in her curling iron next to the couch. She perched atop the armrest and turned on the television.

"See, I wouldn't really do anything different," Angie continued. "I'd still go to work, I'd still live here, but we could find a nice place up in Clintonville and get a dog. And I would just give all my friends and aunts and uncles like …" she paused, thinking lightly of figures and tabulating family trees, "like a hundred thousand dollars each. And I would buy a really cool old car, like the yellow one that J. Gatsby owned, and park it on the street so everybody could look at it."

"You would park a 500,000 dollar vintage car on the street to get its mirrors knocked off by some roaming band of fourteen year-old dissidents?" Charlie asked.

"Well, maybe I wouldn't leave it there all the time, but I would still have it. And I would give neighborhood kids rides in it to go get ice cream."

"So you'd buy a crazy looking car, and go cruising around for little kids, saying 'Hey there, want to come get in my car with me? I'll take you to get some ice cream!' You know they have block watch groups to prevent that sort of thing."

"Well fine," Angie said, twisting her thick hair around the silver cylinder with the somatic precision of an NBA veteran shooting free-throws. "I'm surprised at you, though. I didn't think your first inclination would be to just drop out of your life as you know it."

As Charlie watched the revolving pizza and persistent incandescence of the heat lamps, he felt a slight retrospective guilt. He wished he were a man of more loyal inclination. He shuffled closer to the register in a spiraling musing about self-knowledge and the hidden parts of his mind and bought a ticket from the cashier with five randomly generated numbers. Charlie had wanted to select his own, but being unfamiliar with the milieu of gas station gambling he said thank you and pushed open the door with his ticket still in hand. In the parking lot he read the numbers carefully before folding it and putting it in his wallet.

Charlie began to walk back home and the smell of gasoline from the station folded underneath the velvety sweetness of the breeze. Bicycles floated up and down the street, coasting by on clicking freewheels after they topped out the hill at Patterson. He was glad to be walking, watching the waving branches pass from one side of the street to the other. He liked the rows of washing machines inside the Blue Bubble Express Laundromat and their swirling contents, and the infinite array of printed thought that people must have read there, waiting with their backs to the sun for cycles to end.

Two young men stood indifferently by the entrance to the laundromat with bowed heads and cigarettes. One wore a torn denim vest with a black screen print, affixed to the back with safety pins, of a little girl in pig-tails smelling a flower through a gas mask. The other had a fuzzy blonde buzz cut and a large black t-shirt that read "JESUS IS A BITCH" in emphatic white capitals.

Charlie's smile widened and he laughed to himself as he passed. The wanderlust which had gripped him when thinking about the lottery seemed foolish now. In the presence of the unfolding spring and the prismatic facets of the people and their presentations, he could imagine no better situation than to be drinking a sixteen ounce can of High Life on the steps of his porch in Columbus, Ohio. So instead of walking down Maynard he turned around and retraced his steps back to Andy's Beverage.

The tall cashier from Andy's was leaning a heavy palm against the red gyro stand parked in the three space parking lot, his green t-shirt taut against his stomach. He nodded at Charlie as he approached.

"I'll be with you in a second, man," he said to Charlie, before turning back to the olive skinned man behind the glass. "I mean it was bound to happen, with the internet and everything. Once everybody's already getting it someplace else, that's the way it goes, you know, with everything. Stuff gets replaced, and there's always going to be something new coming along," he stated.

Charlie grasped the door handle, its silver finish worn down to a smooth dusty copper. He pulled and felt the stale cold of the coolers and air conditioning rush out at him. He turned to see if the cashier was following him in and he noticed the bright red lettering on a sign across the street: **Closing: Everything on Sale**.

Through the dusty haze of dirty windows Charlie could see people milling about inside the store across the street, entire shelves already empty. He stood, staring in disbelief, until the cashier stepped in front of him.

"After you man," he said.

"Whoa—when did that happen?" Charlie asked, pointing to the sign.

"Oh, they put the sign up two days ago," the man replied, turning westward and making a visor with his broad hand. "Yep, old North Campus Video, going out of business. Come on, you're letting the cold out."

Charlie stepped inside of Andy's in a daze, and glanced back once more to make sure he had seen it right.

"No way. They're really closing down?"

"Yeah, signs went up about two days ago. It was bound to happen sooner or later. Now with the internet and everything, people got their Netflix and they can just download whatever they want, I'm surprised they stayed open as long as they did."

"Bummer," Charlie said, rubbing the back of his neck. "Man, I can't believe that. Well, I can *believe* it but … bummer." He walked slowly along the glass cooler doors, eyes lounging over colors and pictures and labels. The taller man walked around the counter and stood behind the register.

"I mean, everything they do you can basically get quicker somewhere else. With Redbox and Netflix and all that stuff, it's just," he snapped his fingers, "right there. And there are all those sites out there now, like that Rotten Tomatoes and whatnot, and they give you all those recommendations, it's just the way things have gone."

"Yeah, I can see that," Charlie said. "But they had so much cool stuff there, stuff they probably don't have on Netflix or at Redbox. I can see those for new releases and that stuff, but otherwise … and that dude Artie, he's probably been working there what, like a century? And that squirrelly guy with the big glasses, what are they all going to *do*?" The cooler door made a rubbery squeal as Charlie pulled it open.

"Looks like they'll have to go looking for jobs like everybody else. I've seen it go through the whole phase," the cashier said as Charlie walked up to the register. "I can remember when video cassettes first came out, when renting movies was like *the* big thing that people were doing. I've seen it go through the whole life cycle, with tapes to DVDs to BluRays and everything. It's just like cassettes and eight-tracks in the eighties, you know? These technologies are always getting replaced by something else. And so live and die the places that go with them."

Charlie, his wallet unfolded on the counter, watched the man swipe his debit card through the reader five times before receiving a chiming confirmation. "It was just such a cool place," he sighed, craning his neck to look out across the street once more. "It was such a staple."

The cashier tore a thin receipt from the register and pushed it and a Planet Fitness pen across the counter. Charlie signed his name in purple ink.

"That's the same thing everybody said when they redid the Gateway. It was just dive after dive after dive, just like *nasty* places, but when they were getting torn down everybody started getting all upset, saying how the area had so much *tradition,* or character or whatever. Everybody was talking about Mean Mr. Mustard's like it was the most incredible place they'd ever been." He paused to slip Charlie's receipt into the register drawer. "But turns out there are lots of places with Budweiser and AC/DC. Things just change like that."

Charlie put his card back into his wallet, and saw the carefully folded ticket tucked between the faded brown leather.

"You sell many of these this week" he asked the cashier, holding up the ticket between his middle and index finger.

"No, our lotto machine is still on a dial up connection. It's been down all week," the man said, looking down and tapping the screen to his right.

"Bummer," Charlie replied, backing toward the door. "Hopefully that doesn't put you under."

"No man, this place isn't going anywhere," he said. "We'll be around forever."

Charlie pushed his back against the door, and felt the rush and longing of the breeze outside. "I hope so," he said. "You have a good one, man."

Charlie walked home and sat down under the descending sun on the concrete steps of his porch. He wedged his fingernail under the tab of one of his beers, and the sharp crack of the can opening bounced up the street. Shifting his weight to one side, he worked his wallet out of his back pocket, opened it and took out his ticket.

"Twelve, seventeen, thirty-two, forty-four, sixty," Charlie read aloud between sips from his beer. "Those don't seem like very lucky numbers." He extended his arms behind him and leaned backward, watching the sun fade below the rooftops.

April passed on mildly, and the summer was dry. The fall seemed to come and go in a single emblazoned week of color before leaving skeletal branches to clatter in the cold breezes. The following winter

Angie took a job at the Franklin County Corrections Institute work-ing with incarcerated women, and for the first time in both their lives she and Charlie had incomes which stretched beyond their customary recreations. That spring the pictures came down off the walls in their townhouse in the Old North. Years of accumulation and procrastinated organization had to be confronted before they could take up residence on East Longview Avenue farther north in Clintonville proper.

Charlie was wiping thick layers of dust from the shoe boxes stacked on the shelves in his closet. With languid motions he pulled them down and inspected their contents. He sat flipping through note-books and reading topic sentences of final exams about the tension be-tween aesthetic conventions and ethical imperatives. He was inspecting concert ticket stubs when Angie stepped in the doorway.

"So I see you're making a lot of progress," she said, untying the bandana from her forehead. "You know the goal here is to put stuff *into* boxes, not unpack all your junk onto the floor."

"No wonder I was so confused by your technique," Charlie re-plied. "I kept watching you and trying to figure out what I was doing wrong. And this *junk*, as you so callously referred to it, makes up the diverse and colorful tapestry that is my life."

"You mean the ratty, tattered blanket that holds your head on," Angie grinned. She stood with her hands on her hips, scanning the pa-pers sprawling out from the closet. She reached down and picked up a small slip of paper, carefully folded in half. "What's this?"

"That," Charlie stated, "is a ticket from the largest Mega-Millions drawing in history. It could be worth five hundred million dollars."

"What do you mean it could be? Didn't you check the numbers when they did the drawing?"

"No, I decided not to," Charlie answered.

"What? Well that seems like an odd thing to do with a lottery ticket," Angie said as she unfolded the thin slip of paper.

"I just decided I didn't want to know. I saw this thing on TV once about people who won the lottery, and were totally sunk by their friends and family asking for money. This one guy owned a body shop and ev-erybody would come in and harass him, wanting free repairs and stuff." He paused and looked up at Angie.

"Do you remember that one time you said that even if you won, you'd just get a nice place up in Clintonville? Well that's what we're doing, isn't it? The day I bought that ticket it seemed so clear to me. I walked down the street, and it was perfect. I had a longer than desired conversation with the guy at Andy's and it was perfect. I sat on the porch and drank High Life and there was not a thing between the sun and the street that I would have changed. So I took that ticket out of my wallet and I put it in this box, because all I wanted was that moment."

Angie smiled at him, and reached out her hand to give the ticket back to him. Charlie grasped it, and she met his eyes before letting it go.

"You know, I think I remember hearing about this," she said. "I saw something on the news about a woman who bought the ticket for a work pool, then tried to claim the winning ticket was a different one she bought for herself."

A chiming ring echoed in from the other room. "That's probably John," she said, stepping back through the door. "He's probably here to pick up that couch. Can you help him with it?"

"Sure," Charlie said, gathering some papers and dropping them back into a tattered shoebox. "I'll be right down."

Stephen C. David is seeking a consciousness between the beauty of his world and the delusions of want. He is studying for his Masters in Social Work at Ohio State. He would like to thank Carrie for refining his voice to a palatable form. This story is dedicated to Marty and the staff of North Campus Video.

Columbus is the capital of Ohio and the largest city in the state. As of the 2010 census, Columbus had more than 787,000 residents within the city, and more than 1.8 million residents in the greater metropolitan area.

Ohio joined the Mega Millions lottery in 2002. The odds of winning the jackpot are 1 in 175,711,536.

THE SELLS BROTHERS' CIRCUS
Poster from the 1880s
Provided by the Library of Congress

2015

The Circus House

By Jenny L. Maxey

Griffin's lungs burned, and his scrawny legs couldn't take much more. He finally saw the sign to Goodale Park. Cutting down the only path familiar to him, he urged himself to keep running.

"There's the freak!" one of them yelled from behind him. "The new kid looks like he's straight outta *The Nightmare Before Christmas!*"

"More like an anorexic scarecrow if you ask me," another voice hollered.

Raven-black hair crowned Griffin's oversized head. His slate-colored eyes were a size befitting an elephant. Tiny lips, a thin neck, and long, sinewy arms and legs, with giant joints protruding beneath his ghostly-colored skin.

Nearly unable to breathe, he reached the house sitting on the corner of Dennison and Buttles. Its tent-like, tiled rooftop and ring-shaped, hard-fire brick corners usually caught his attention, but at this moment he had to hide. He rushed up the stairs to take cover under the gaping brick archway protecting the front door. The Holstein brothers stopped on the sidewalk across the street.

"Of course the freak lives in the Circus House. He's probably the starring act!" one brother said.

"Well, I'm not going to try to find out! I've heard that place has some sorta curse. No one's lived there for years!"

"We know you're in there, circus freak! We'll be back!"

Griffin peeked out and watched the brothers run back towards the park before going inside.

"Mom? Dad? Are you here?" Griffin yelled from the foyer.

"We're back here," his mother replied. Griffin followed her voice to the back of the house where his parents were unpacking in the dining room area. "Oh, sweetie, you look flushed. What happened?"

"Nothing—just decided to run home." Griffin watched as his mother set the china in an antique cupboard and his father arranged heavy, wooden chairs around the table. His mother had Griffin's large eyes and thin figure, and his dad had Griffin's dark hair and alabaster skin. Although the similarities were there, Griffin's features separately affixed on his parents made them strikingly beautiful and made him feel like he didn't belong. "I was thinking—maybe it'd be a good idea if I were home-schooled."

"Griffin, we've gone over this before. You need to be willing to try something different, meet some new people. It'll be good for you," Griffin's father said.

"Easy for you to say! You don't know what it's like for me. We're constantly moving. Even if I were normal looking, I wouldn't have enough time to make friends before we would just move again. But I'm not normal, and I don't fit in anywhere! Not even with you!" Griffin stomped down the hallway and up the stairs to his bedroom on the third floor.

Cardboard boxes were stacked on the hardwood floor in his new room. His mattress rested on the ground awaiting its box spring and posts. He discovered a box labeled "collector coins" in the far corner. As he lifted the box, a small coin fell from a tear in the bottom edge and rolled along the floorboards. He quickly dropped to his hands and knees and followed it. The coin continued to escape Griffin's grasp until it finally slipped between the crevices of a metal grate bolted to the wall.

Griffin grabbed a flashlight from his desk and returned to the grate to look inside. He loosened the bolts and pushed the grate away from the wall. Cobwebs stuck to his face as his eyes adjusted to the dim light and he slid his body deeper into the air duct. Something dark and dusty hid in the corner where the duct turned. Griffin set the flashlight on its end and stretched his bony fingers until he could barely grasp the silky material. He pulled the object closer to him. It was a top hat. He turned the brim over in his hands several times. Although dirty and aged, it appeared to be in great condition. As Griffin reached into the dark cylinder searching for a secret compartment, possibly concealing a dead rabbit, his elbow knocked over the flashlight and extinguished its light. The darkness became ten shades darker. The walls of the duct closed in on him. The air pulled on his skin and out of his lungs like the vacuum from a black hole. Then a burst of white light appeared.

Griffin rubbed his eyes. He found himself sitting on the grass across from his house with the top hat beside him. In the yard, a large sign was staked into the ground. With a mustard-yellow background and ketchup-red lettering, the sign proclaimed: "The Sells Brothers'

Circus: The Big Show of the World!" Before Griffin could wonder why this sign was in his yard, a man was walking briskly toward him.

"You found it!" The man said, bending his lean body at the waist to come face-to-face with Griffin. The man took the hat from Griffin's hand and looked it over. "I'm nothing without my hat! How'd you get this so dirty?"

Griffin shrugged.

"Never mind then," the man continued, "are you one of the new roustabouts?"

Griffin didn't answer. He was too mesmerized by the dancing caterpillar mustache on the man's upper lip.

"No, you couldn't be. Look at you. What am I thinking? Do you have a name, kid?"

"It's Griffin."

"Like the mythical beast? That's fantastic! Come with me, I think I can find something for the Beast to do!" Griffin didn't know what else he should do, so he followed the man back into his own home.

When the man opened the front door, Griffin was stunned. Although the house had looked the same from the outside, the inside was so enormous it seemed too large to fit the frame that contained it. The man gestured grandly to the scene unfolding before Griffin and said, "Welcome to the Sells Brothers Circus!"

Acrobats swung upside-down from the ceiling. Circus clowns on unicycles juggled and tweaked their horns. Laborers hurried by with buckets sloshing water over the sides. A baby elephant stood on a stool while the bull hand taught it how to balance on its hind legs. The floor was covered in strands of golden hay and the house smelled oddly of buttery popcorn and animal dung.

"What is all this?" asked Griffin.

"You mean to tell me you haven't heard of the Sells Brothers' Circus? The second largest circus in America? The only circus boasting eight elephants and a percussive aerialist?"

Griffin shook his head.

"Peculiar, very peculiar," the man said, stroking his mustache. "Never mind then. *I* am Mr. Cornelius Bernardus Chastwick, the ringmaster of this menagerie." He clicked his heels once and started walking through the house in long, stiff strides. Griffin's gait matched the ringmaster's enough to stay in step. "And, this is my house—the Circus House! These are the winter quarters for some of the performers and the baby animals. The house was designed to look like our circus tent so we wouldn't feel homesick. Isn't it splendid?"

"It's amazing," Griffin said.

Cornelius stopped and slowly pivoted on his heels to face Griffin. He looked Griffin over from toe to head. "My hat always seems to get away from me. It can be quite ornery you know. But, a ringmaster without his top hat is no ringmaster at all. And, if there is no ringmaster, the circus will fall. Disaster—complete and utter disaster, I tell you! Since my hat seems to like you, then, you *must* be the new hat keeper. It is done. You agree?"

Griffin wondered what happened to the old hat keeper, but he agreed anyhow. *How difficult could it be to hold onto a hat,* he thought. Plus, he liked the idea of having a role in the circus without being cast in the freak show.

"Now, before I turn my hat over to your possession, there are three rules you must know. One—*never* put the hat upon your head. Two—*never* reach inside the hat. Three—the show *must* go on. Understood?" And with a flourish of his wrist, Cornelius removed the hat from atop his head and extended it out to Griffin. Griffin took the hat and clutched it to his chest. "Our opening show begins promptly at seven o'clock tonight. We have a lot to do! Keep close."

As they proceeded through the house, Cornelius explained the line-up of the show. First, there was the March that paraded the entire show from the Circus House through downtown Columbus until it reached the big top in a grassy area along the river. Once the grandstand was full, Cornelius would stand in the center ring and announce the opening of the circus, while the acts would circle the rings. Then, each act would perform, beginning with the tightrope walkers and clowns and ending with the ring horses and elephants.

"We need to make sure all the acts are ready for tonight," Cornelius said. He leaned close to Griffin and whispered, "The Zanies are in this room. But don't ever call them that. These clowns are known to cause trouble." Cornelius slowly twisted the glass knob and guided Griffin into the room. Green and purple-haired men with heavily painted faces were chasing each other around the room with bottles of seltzer and buckets of confetti. Two clowns grabbed Griffin by the arms, lifting him from the ground.

"Look at this one, Wheezy! Too pale and look at those eyes!" one of the clowns said.

"His hair is such a dreadful black, Flubbo!" Wheezy said. "We've got our work cut out for us with this one!"

"What are you going to do to me?" Griffin shouted. "Where's Cornelius?" He looked desperately around the room while the clowns plopped him into a chair in front of a lighted mirror. His tour guide was gone. "I have to find Cornelius! The show is going to start soon!"

"It's okay, we'll take good care of ya!" said Wheezy. Flubbo was already fitting oversized shoes onto Griffin's feet. Wheezy took out a tray of colored make-up and started painting Griffin's pale canvas.

"But I'm not supposed to be a Zanie! I'm the hat keeper!" Griffin cried. The clowns' faces drew nearer to him.

"What did you just call us?" Flubbo asked. "You think we're ZANIE!" The clowns started cackling and pinned Griffin in the chair. "And, what do ya mean you're the hat keeper? You don't have a hat!" Wheezy said.

Griffin looked to his lap and his now white-gloved hands. His fingers curled around a fake bouquet of flowers where the top hat had been. "What did you do with the hat?" He hadn't even felt them make the switch.

"What hat? I didn't see a hat. Flubbo, did you see a hat?" Wheezy asked.

"What hat? I didn't see a hat. Wheezy, did you see a hat?" Flubbo asked. The two clowns kept repeating this back and forth. Griffin couldn't take any more. He pushed out of the chair, knocking the clowns over. He frantically searched around the chair and, without seeing the top hat anywhere, ran for the door.

Griffin ran down the hallway, ducking as a juggling pin whizzed over his head. He stopped at the first door on the second floor and turned its glass knob. Inside the room were contortionists pointing their toes to their foreheads and twisting their bodies to fit inside small glass boxes. No hat in sight. When Griffin opened the next door, a ball of fire came blazing out toward him. He jumped back. "Fire breathers!" He gasped as his eyebrows smoldered.

He needed to hurry. The circus would be lining up for the march any minute. He retraced his steps through the house. The hat was nowhere to be found. Then, it came to him. He knew exactly where the hat would be. Griffin dashed up the stairs to the third floor and opened the door to what used to be his bedroom. Costumes, feathers, and sequins were strewn about the room. He pushed through a rack of clothes and came to the wall where he had originally found the hat. But a blank wall stood solidly where the grate had been.

"Now what am I going to do?" Griffin said to no one. "Cornelius is going to be so upset with me." Griffin turned back toward the door and attempted to kick a purple feather boa out of his way. Instead, the boa snaked around his shoes and ankles and pulled him to the ground with a thud. Griffin sat up and rubbed the back of his head. Then, Griffin saw it. The hat sat on the floor in plain view, almost mocking him. "You weren't there just a second ago," he said to the hat. He freed his legs from the boa, scooped up the hat, and darted downstairs to find Cornelius.

Everyone had already gone outside to line up for the March. Griffin ran up to the first laborer he saw. "Have you seen Cornelius?" The man shook his head. "Cornelius!" Griffin shouted over the music and calls of the animal trainers. He made his way to the front of the line-up without spotting Cornelius anywhere. Griffin rushed up to the bull hand and asked if he had seen Cornelius.

"Nope. Haven't seen him. But, I can get Amorette here to give you a lift so you can see over the crowd." He tapped the elephant with his stick, and the elephant lowered her trunk. "Put your legs here on the trunk and hold tight." Amorette lifted Griffin so his elephant eyes could meet hers. "You see him?" asked the bull hand. Griffin shook his head after a look around. The bull hand tapped the elephant and she set Griffin back to the ground. "Well kid, I don't know what to tell ya. Cornelius has gone missin' a lot before the march, but the show must go on." The bull hand cast a quick glance toward the hat in Griffin's hands and turned back to Amorette.

Griffin stared down at the hat. *A ringmaster without his top hat is no ringmaster at all. And, if there is no ringmaster, the circus will fall,* Griffin recalled Cornelius saying. "Wait! Cornelius has to be here! What's going to happen to the circus?"

"Like I said, he's gone missin' before. The show must go on. We make the show go on." Again, the bull hand glanced at the hat and turned back to Amorette.

Griffin looked at the hat, pleading with it to give him the answer. *The show must go on.* He thought. *That was rule three. Rule one—never put the hat upon your head. Rule two—never reach inside the hat.* Griffin had a suspicion of what would happen if he reached inside the hat. "What do you want me to do? I'm not supposed to put the hat on!" The bull hand didn't reply. Griffin closed his eyes tight, and lifted the hat above his head. Slowly he lowered the hat until it grazed his raven hair.

Sparks of heat electrified Griffin's body. His eyes snapped open. A cocoon of wind and dust swirled around him. He looked down and saw that his clown shoes were gone and replaced with leather boots. His clothes warped and twisted on his body. His pants wrinkled in on themselves and transformed into ivory riding pants. His shirt shattered into confetti and a red material started to ooze from an invisible wound in the middle of his chest down his torso and along his arms. Large gold buttons popped like popcorn into three rows across his chest, and coattails unfurled from his back like two paper noisemakers at a birthday party.

"That a boy!" said the bull hand, clapping his hand on Griffin's shoulder. "Alright now, stay alongside Amorette. She knows the route to lead you to the big top. From there, she's all yours!"

"Wait! What do you mean *she's* all mine? Amorette is mine?"

"No, the show is yours." The bull hand tapped the elephant and Amorette moved forward. "All right folks, the show is on!" he shouted to the line-up. The music started with a drum roll and the group pushed forward to start the march.

Griffin didn't know if it was the uniform or the grand elephant next to him that made him stand tall and puff his chest out with pride. He marched to the beat of the drums. The crowd watched in awe at the sight of the circus parading through the streets of downtown Columbus. He waved and smiled all the way to the big top on the river.

He watched from the back of the tent as the crowd filtered into the grand stand, just as Cornelius said it would. It was time for him to open the show. The uniform gripped his body and moved his legs toward center ring. The jacket had control over Griffin's arms. As the acts circled the ring, Griffin gestured grandly to the crowd. "Welcome to the Sells Brothers' Circus! The Big Show of the World! *I* am Griffin 'the Beast,' the ringmaster of this menagerie!" Even though the uniform had control over his body, standing in the center ring and speaking these words felt familiar to him. The audience smiled at him, eager to see what he would do next. No other moment in his life had been this perfect, this right.

Griffin remembered the order of the acts as Cornelius had described. He radiated in the spotlight as if the light burst from his pores instead of showering down upon him. The first act he announced was the tightrope walkers. He stood aside to watch them perform and held his breath with the audience on every teeter and totter. He roared with laughter as Wheezy and Flubbo pranked one another.

Griffin announced the final act—the ring horses and elephants. Amorette was magnificent. Griffin's fondness for her grew as she gently balanced a girl dressed in sequins on her trunk. The uniform slowly released its hold on Griffin as he became more poised and assured on his own. He watched the crowd trickle out from the tent—children with sticky faces and friends discussing their favorite acts. He loved it. He loved it all.

"You did marvelously. You agree?" Griffin turned to see Cornelius walking into the tent.

"That was the best thing I could've imagined. Why weren't you here?"

"I didn't need to be. Come with me." Cornelius led Griffin over to the stands and they sat down. "You see, many have come and gone. I made them the hat keeper, told them the rules, and left them with the hat. Most didn't realize that some rules must be broken so the show could go on. Many reached inside the hat and fled like cowards. Others attempted to wear the hat, but alas, nothing happened and I sent them back. You, my dear boy, put on the hat and magic happened."

"I don't understand. Why do you want someone else to become the ringmaster?"

"It has been 1896 for longer than you know. I've been leading this exact circus for so long that I've lost track of time. The canvas of this tent has become my cage, its poles the bars. I'm tired, and it's time for my own show to go on—to find love, grow old, and live. But, you see, there is one problem. Now that the magic as ringmaster has transferred to you, I need you to pull me through to your world, the one where time doesn't stand still."

"What do you mean I have to pull you through? Why didn't you reach inside the hat when you were ringmaster and leave then?"

"Because without a ringmaster the circus would fall. I couldn't bear to let that happen. So, I waited."

"What will happen once I pull you through? Will I be able to come back?"

"I believe so, but we *must* try it. You agree?"

Griffin plucked the top hat from his head and stared down into the dark cylinder. His heart would break if he couldn't return to the circus, but he felt that he owed this much to Cornelius. He grabbed hold of Cornelius' hand and reached down into the top hat. All became dark, the air pulled from his lungs, and a flash of bright light appeared.

Griffin opened his eyes to find himself sitting outside across from the Circus House. The Sells Brothers' Circus sign was no longer in the yard and no evidence of the circus remained.

"We did it!" Cornelius said. The top hat rested between them.

Griffin's large eyes stretched impossibly wide. Cornelius' perfectly ironed skin began to wrinkle. White blanketed his upper lip as if snow had fallen from his nostrils. Liver spots scurried down his forearm to the backs of his hands like ants in search of crumbs.

"You're old!"

Cornelius looked over his arms. "I guess that I am! I suppose time had to catch up with me eventually." Griffin helped to pull Cornelius to his feet. Cornelius stooped to pick up the top hat. "Here is your hat, Mr. Ringmaster." Cornelius handed over the top hat, turned, and walked in long, stiff strides down the sidewalk and out of sight.

Griffin looked at his house. His parents were standing on the front steps. He looked down the sidewalk where the Holstein brothers were returning. His eyes darted between his parents and the brothers. They didn't smile at him like the audience at the circus had. They weren't eager to see what he would do next like the audience had been. So, he would relive 1896 for a while. He would have more of a future there than he would ever have in his life here. *I'm running away with the circus,* he thought. *Who even does this anymore?* He chuckled at the cliché. Griffin plunged his arm deep into the hat. All became dark, the air pulled from his lungs, and a flash of white light appeared.

Jenny L. Maxey's first short story, "Ladybug," was published in CCC's anthology *While You Were Out*. "The Circus House" is dedicated to her grandmother Nancy Carroll. Jenny lives in Central Ohio with her loving husband Douglas and her dog Sophie.

The Sells Brothers' Circus, established in the outskirts of Columbus, was the second largest circus in America during the late 1800s. In 1895, Peter Sells built a mansion on the corner of Dennison Avenue and Buttles Avenue in downtown Columbus. This mansion is affectionately called "The Circus House" by locals for its sloping, tent-shaped roof and circular, ring-like corners.

CONFEDERATE GRAVES, CAMP CHASE
Chase Cemetery, Columbus, Ohio
Paul Binder

2024
THE TICK
By Robert Alexander

Robert struggled to keep up. The night was different. In the day he could see everything, the blurred buildings and parked cars to his right and left, the way the road rose and dipped, the street riddled with cracks and holes, and his brother pedaling a good ten yards ahead of him. At night he could barely see ten feet. His father had attached an LED headlight to his handlebars so he could ride at night. He also attached a red rear light so cars could see him. The front light was better than nothing, but not by much. The street lights off to the side of the road glowed with either a dim bulb or a burnt out one and the relief they provided was also close to none. In fact, the dull lights seemed to draw attention to the drowning darkness. Every time Robert passed underneath a street lamp and entered its yellow bubble, he no sooner would have to leave it and reenter the dark. He wished the lights would all burn out, maybe that way his eyes could adjust to one setting instead of being blinded by both.

He heard the car coming and steered his bicycle to the right of the road. The headlights illuminated the road and buildings surrounding him. Robert shuddered to see what lay hidden in the darkness. Maybe a thief with eyes set on his Mongoose bike, or a gang of boys older than his fourteen-year-old brother, or a murderer, or something worse, something that only came out at night and hid in the alleys and the sewers and ate bones and drank blood. But as the darkness gave way to the passing light, Robert saw the empty sidewalks, the closed doors and windows, and empty alleyways. The car turned left before reaching Phillip, Robert's brother, who pedaled a block or so in front of him. Every now and then Robert took his eyes off the street and glanced up, just to make sure he could see his brother's rear red light. And he could. Though there was still no sign of his brother's friend.

Kyle Tickle, or the Tick as some called him, rode out ahead of both Robert and his brother. The Tick: it was a nickname only certain people could use. Robert had made the mistake of using it once; he knew he had erred immediately after uttering the name. Something changed in the Tick's eyes. The muscles around the eyes tensed, the pupils grew smaller, and their focus landed solely on Robert. A second of hesitation and realization passed before Robert turned to run. That second cost him a beating. The Tick was upon him faster than Robert knew possible. How could a round, short, stocky, fat boy move that quickly? The Tick threw him to the ground and rolled him over. Then he sat on Robert's chest with the weight of a refrigerator. Robert's lungs gasped for air as he turned his head to the side to breathe, at the same time the Tick's hands clutched Robert's chin and forced his head back so they could see each others' eyes.

"What did you call me?"

Robert struggled for a breath so he could speak. For a fleeting moment, he thought to shout "the Tick!" defiantly and proud. He would be a modern day Braveheart. He would show the world that brute strength and bullying would not and could not break his resolve. And most importantly, he would see the failure sprawl across the Tick's face. However, the Tick's face, full of rage, changed Robert's mind.

"Kyle."

"That's better," The Tick said, spitting a little bit over Robert's face. From that day on, Robert's mouth called him by his birth name, but his head would forever and always refer to him as the bloodsucking Tick.

At the beginning of their adventure, the Tick sprinted ahead of Robert and Phillip, pedaling carefree in the middle of the road, his hands dangling at his sides. Robert was angry, yet impressed. He could not ride a bicycle with no hands, at least not for more than a second or so. Still, it seemed foolish to ride in the dead center of the rode. The Tick had disappeared into the darkness ahead of him. His brother had all but disappeared, too. Robert could only see the fluorescent red light on the back of Phillip's bicycle.

The night had grown darker, and they had traveled far beyond their neighborhood. They were in the city now, Robert knew because the sounds of crickets and cicadas were replaced by the buzz of air conditioners and other machinery. Cement replaced grass and shops replaced houses.

"Slow down," Robert yelled, as loud as he could. Mom had warned them not to go into the city, not in the day or the night. There were too many cars and too many people. Stick to the neighborhood, she said. But his mom was asleep, and the Tick had promised it wasn't too far. "Phil, please, stop," Robert cried again.

The red light attached to the back of his brother's bicycle did not stop. Robert could see it smaller and smaller and then disappear. Robert cursed and picked up his pedaling pace. Phillip had three years on him, a faster bike, and all around more athleticism. Robert was an 'indoor kid' as Phillip put it. On birthdays where Phillip received a basketball, Robert received a book. Still, when your older brother and his friend offer to take you to a graveyard to search for ghosts, you say yes, no matter how scary it sounds.

Robert's legs were tightening up, so he switched to a lower gear. The resistance gave way, and it felt like pedaling through air. He loved that feeling, like his legs were lightning, and the only thing containing them were the clasps around his feet. He had picked up some speed now and stopped pedaling, allowing the bike to coast through the night.

His heart beat faster, a little from fatigue but mostly from fear. He had lost his brother and the Tick. He was alone in the city. He could turn back, he thought. He remembered the way home, but what if someone or something stopped him? What if he took a wrong turn?

"Phil," Robert whimpered as he stopped his bike. Standing still made him feel nervous, like easy prey waiting to be eaten. He looked around; the Tick had said the graveyard was straight down Sullivant, they wouldn't have turned. They had to be straight ahead. Robert sighed and looked down. A cigarette butt had been flung to the ground, and the end still burned with an orange glow. Someone had been here, maybe just a second ago. His heart beat even faster now. Move, it told him. Forward or backward, it doesn't matter but move now!

Straight ahead Robert pedaled, as fast as his scrawny legs could take him. One more block, he would whisper under his breath, again and again. He no longer cared about the lights or the darkness; he just wanted his brother, his mom, anyone, even the Tick. One more block, just one more block and they will be there. After seven blocks, he found them.

On the left side of the road, about fifty yards away, he saw two bike lights underneath a large archway. Robert's heart returned from the top of his throat back into his chest. He rode to greet them, wiping his eyes quickly with his forearm. Phillip and the Tick straddled over their bicycles which were now parked with their kickstands down. They were completely oblivious. They had left him alone in the darkness of the city. He could have gotten lost. He could have died. And here his brother was laughing at something the Tick had said. Robert wanted to scream at them, punch them, kick them, and hug them. He was no longer alone, and his relief trumped his anger.

Sweat dripped off the Tick's forehead and a damp ring formed at the top of the his t-shirt. *Gross,* Robert thought, but as he wiped his own brow he noticed a little perspiration. Summer was almost over, but the air remained hot and sticky. He grabbed his water bottle from the bottle cage below his bicycle frame and sucked the ice cold water from the foam top.

"Hey, give that here," the Tick beckoned.

"No."

"Don't make me take it from you."

Robert took a quick glance at his brother, who shrugged. "Just give him some water."

"Give him yours."

"No."

The Tick had removed himself from his bicycle and stepped closer to Robert. In a moment, the water bottle would be lost one way or the other. The other usually involved a bruise and dead shoulder.

"Fine, take it," Robert said as he threw his bottle to the oversized insect. "But don't put your lips …" It was too late. The Tick's chubby lips circled the foam top as he sucked and sucked and sucked. When the Tick threw the bottle back, Robert felt a small splash at the bottom, probably mostly backwash. Robert thoroughly wiped the top of the bottle with his shirt and placed the bottle back. He felt his hands clench tightly into fists as he kicked his kickstand down and hopped off his seat. The Tick had his back turned, maybe he could choke him from behind, or take out his knees. The Tick would not be expecting that. Then on the ground he could punch him a few times and then what? Run? Keep punching? What would Phil do, stand and watch? Interfere? Robert felt his anger turn into curiosity, then curiosity to fear. The Tick would get up eventually, or overpower Robert. Then who knows what would happen. Phil would not let the Tick kill him, or beat him up too badly, would he? But later, they might leave him again, alone on the road. Robert unclenched his fists and realized how utterly powerless he felt.

"Here we are, boys," The Tick belched, wiping water and saliva from his mouth. "Welcome … to Camp Chase." As he spoke, he produced two skinny long black flashlights from a backpack hooked on his bike and tossed one to Phillip. Robert stood empty-handed, thought about asking if the Tick had another light, then dismissed the idea from his head.

With a click, a flashlight turned on and illuminated the stone archway that read *Camp Chase*. The stone looked centuries old. From the ends of the archway stemmed a large stone wall that blocked view of the cemetery. The flashlight continued to survey the entrance and Robert read all sorts of signs. *No Firearms allowed on this property. Columbus Ohio Historical Site. Visiting hours: sunrise to sunset.* It was far past sunset. And to his relief and slight disappointment, underneath the stone arch stood a metal gate, chained closed. The adventure was over. Time to go home.

"It's closed," Robert said.

"Of course it's closed, idiot. It's midnight. Watch and learn." The Tick placed his flashlight into his khaki short pocket with the light shining up, dissolving into the sky. He walked to the right of the gate and placed his hands on the top of the stone wall. With a jump, he pulled himself up and onto the wall before jumping over. If a fat blob like the Tick could hop the wall, so could Robert. Phillip went next, hopping the wall with even more ease, leaving Robert alone with the three bike lights shining.

"Should I turn off the bike lights?"

The Tick's face came through the gate with the light shining under his chin. He looked like a jack-o-lantern, and not a frightful or happy one but one of those goofy ones with a buck tooth. "Turn them off." Then with a click of the flashlight the Tick's face disappeared.

Robert hit the switches on his brother's and the Tick's bicycle lights and turned off the red light on the rear of his brother's bike. The Tick did not have a red rear light. *Probably couldn't afford it*, Robert thought. Or too dumb to realize how important those lights were. When he came to his own bike he realized he had a flashlight of his own. Robert pulled his front light from the handlebars and it came free with a *snap*. The right side of the device that held the light snapped off, now broken and useless. A feeling of dread sunk into his belly; his father would not be happy. And on top of that, what was he going to do on the ride home? So far this trip had been a disaster. But at least he had a flashlight.

He put the bike light into his pocket and turned off his rear light. He approached the wall and readied himself to jump. His hands could not reach the top if he just stood there, so Robert jumped with both feet, his hands grasping the stony surface of the top. They found a grip, and he pulled himself up. His shoes also found traction on the wall. At the top, Robert caught his breath and jumped down onto the soft grass of the Camp Chase Cemetery.

Two lights shone in what Robert thought to be the middle of the graveyard. Robert quickly reached for his bike light and aimed it in front of him. Rows and rows and rows of identical tombstones lined the yard like a morbid game of dominoes. Robert searched for the largest column path he could find between the tombstones and began to make his way toward his brother and the Tick. An uneasy thought crept over him as he walked, as if the gravestones themselves were speaking to him. *There are dead people underneath you. Rotting and asleep. Asleep, yes. For now. But your footsteps are loud ...*

A shiver crept down Robert's spine. This place felt strange. The grass felt softer, cleaner, like a carpet newly vacuumed, and each step he took left an imprint. It smelled clean too, like freshly mown grass and scents of lilies and roses filled the air as Robert passed through. It did not feel right. Graveyards were meant to be dark and terrible places. This one so far was just dark. He thought of Hansel and Gretel and the witch and the candy house. Sometimes good places were just meant to lure you in, deeper, until it was too late.

Robert picked up his pace until he reached the center, where his brother and the Tick stood with their flashlights aimed at a large boulder resting on the ground. Squinting to read, Robert added his bicycle light to the two flashlights' beams. Engraved in the boulder read the words "2,260 Confederate Soldiers of the War 1861-1865 buried in this enclosure." The engravings were sloppy and child-like, scattered and jumbled in the boulder. Encompassing the boulder was another stone archway, around ten feet high. Robert shined his light along the arch, which also was engraved with "AMERICANS." At the pinnacle of it all, stood a solitary bronze soldier, clasping a rifle in front with two hands.

Awe and wonder cleared Robert's thoughts of waking the dead. "Why would there be a Confederate cemetery here?"

"There was a prison camp here. They were prisoners during the war. This whole place used to be a big camp, but now it's just graves," Phillip spoke, with older brother knowledge that seemed to know everything.

"Rebels. Traitors." The Tick spat. "Slavers. Racists. Scum." He spat again, this time onto a grave. *Spit wakes us too.* Robert's terror resurfaced. Why would the Tick do that—was he trying to get them killed? Silence filled the air; Robert had hardly noticed. They were off the road and into a clearing enclosed by a stone wall and the sounds of the city had faded away. He could hear only his breath. Robert held his breath and waited for something to break the silence, maybe the sound of a fist bursting through the ground, or a tombstone cracking and crumbling, or a dead confederate soldier, grinding his teeth and moaning for the blood of the great great grandchildren of his enemies. The silence continued until the Tick snorted and spit again, and then wandered off alone, deeper into the cemetery.

"What's his problem?" Robert asked, softly enough so the Tick could not hear.

Phillip shrugged and walked around the arch, feeling the cold stone with his hands. "He likes to hate things." With that, Phillip turned away and walked down a row of graves, reading the names of the fallen.

He likes to hate things. Robert hung on his brother's words. He assumed someone who liked to hate was put to good use on the football field. He for one would not want to go up against a sadist like the Tick. But in the real world, the Tick's hatred would only get them into trouble or worse, dead.

Robert breathed in the warm, sticky air and followed the same path as his brother. Had he the courage, he would have chosen his own path, but he was done being alone for the night. He shined his light on the tombstones, reading names which he forgot as soon as he read the next one. Each stone also had a number chiseled into it at the top: 646, 647, 648, 649, and so on. He imagined the stones went all the way up to 2000 or so, as he scattered his light over the entire cemetery. There were so many graves here. So many soldiers buried. *So many of us that could wake up.*

"Can we go?" Robert asked his brother, who he had finally caught back up to.

"Not yet."

"Why, what are we even doing here?"

"Looking for the ghost." Phillip made an *oooooooh* sound and laughed.

Robert ignored him and surveyed the yard again when something made his stomach crawl. "Where is the," he caught himself just in case the Tick was close. "Where is Kyle?"

Phillip's eyes betrayed his stoic fearlessness. He searched with his flashlight, steadily at first, but then more frantically when all they saw were graves with emptiness between them. "Kyle, come on out, man, we see you." No answer. Robert knew. He knew they were playing a prank on him. Definitely the Tick, maybe even his brother. Maybe not though, or else his brother should get an Academy award. Phillip walked past each row, aiming his light, determined to find the Tick. "Kyle. Hey, Kyle." No answer.

Robert kept turning around. Whenever he stood in one direction too long, his back felt vulnerable to a surprise attack, so he turned around again, never quite feeling safe. The creeping silence was more evident now. *There's nothing buried underneath the boulder. You won't wake us there. The boulder!* Robert thought. He would wait at the boulder. At least he could put his back to the arch; it would be harder to sneak up on him there with his flashlight and all.

Every now and then, on the way back to the boulder, Robert would shine the light behind him, to make sure nothing followed him, the Tick or something else. He could see his brother far to the right, nearing the end of one corner of the cemetery. Robert was a few feet away from the arch and boulder when his eyes went behind him again. Nothing there.

He turned back around to face the boulder when his foot stepped on something long and skinny. It rolled and Robert flew up in the air. For a moment he was flying. Then falling. Then thud. His back hit the soft grass and hard dirt and the wind left his body. His face scrunched up as the pain finally hit him. He wanted to shout and cry and curse but he did not want to wake them. *You already did. With that great fall of yours, you woke us all.*

What had he tripped on? He sat up and found his light lying next to him. He grabbed it and surveyed his surroundings. There it was. The Tick's flashlight, off and lying there on the ground. His bicycle light aimed further down toward the monument, and that's when he saw a leg, dangling from the boulder, lifeless.

"Phil!" Robert gave a restrained yell. "Phil, here."

His brother's light grew closer and closer, but Robert's eyes never left the dangling leg. "Did you find him?"

"There," Robert gestured with his free hand.

"Kyle, we found you, come on out." The leg did not stir. "Kyle, stop it and get up." Phillip looked at his brother and Robert saw his equally frightened eyes. "Come on, let's go." He pulled Robert up and grabbed the Tick's flashlight. The two walked up to the boulder, with their lights leading the way. With each step, more of the body came into view. Cheap tennis shoes. Two bare legs. Khaki pants. The Tick's shirt.

Then the Tick's face. His eyes were closed, his mouth open. As the brothers got close enough to touch the body, blood started to pour from the sides of the Tick's mouth. Thick, red, and syrupy blood oozed down the Tick's dead face and stained the boulder beneath him. The Tick, with his last breath, gave a gag and blood sprayed into the air, then his head fell back down to the boulder, lifeless and empty.

"Oh my God," Phillip cried. "Run." Robert stood stunned as his brother turned to flee. *Move legs, move!* He thought, but his body was slow. *If you don't move now, they will get you. Move, I command you to move!* He broke the spell and his legs turned. He saw his brother half-way to the entrance.

"Wait, Phil. Please wait!" He cried with tears in his eyes.

Then he heard the laughter.

At first, Robert was terrified to turn around. To see what was laughing. But he had to see. When he turned, he was confused. The Tick was sitting up on the boulder, spitting up blood and laughing uncontrollably like a donkey.

"Are you okay?" Robert asked, taking a step closer, still confused as ever but no longer scared to death.

"Okay? Of course I'm okay. What did you think?" The Tick stood up and laughed. Hee haw, hee haw.

Phillip had moseyed on back, just as confused as Robert. "You were bleeding from your mouth."

"Fake blood capsules. Tastes like moldy bread." He spit again, his laughing finally dying down. "You both, hah, you both ran like girls."

Robert knew it. He knew it all along in the back of his head. And still he had fallen for the Tick's prank. Phillip had too, and his brother's anger was just as dangerous as the Tick's. Phillip walked up to the Tick and grabbed him by his shirt. Pulling and shoving with all his force, he slammed the Tick into the stone archway.

The Tick simply laughed in retaliation. His laughter soon perished, drowned out by an incoming noise and a wave of light. The cemetery lit up from an external source through the gate. Shadows speckled the lawn from the tombstones in center, and for a moment the three boys stood blind, their flashlights dwarfed by two large headlights. Then the lights vanished, the vehicle turned, and the noise from the car's engine faded into the night, leaving the boys alone, save for the two thousand corpses beneath the soil.

"Screw you," Phillip said and let go of the Tick. He threw the second flashlight onto the ground and stormed off toward the stone wall near the gate entrance.

"Some people just can't take a joke," the Tick grinned. The blood capsules had stained his mouth and teeth red. *The Tick*, Robert thought, *what an appropriate nickname.* "Come look what I found." The Tick beckoned Robert to follow.

Robert's eyes watched as his brother, lit up by the flashlight in his pocket, hopped over the stone wall once more, this time landing on the outside. He left him, without saying goodbye, he left. "Phil's leaving, I should probably go," Robert said. He knew the way home but still, riding at night did not appeal to him, especially since he snapped off his bike's light.

The Tick grabbed his own flashlight and turned it on. "Come on, it will only take a second. There's something I want to do. Then I'll take you back." Robert followed with a slouch in his step. He did not want to be alone, even the Tick was better than being alone with the dead. They walked in the darkness until the Tick stopped at a gravestone. Number 233. Benjamin Allen. "Here we are," the Tick said, spitting again. "They say he's the one the ghost searches for. The lady ghost, searching for her husband. They say if you wait here and listen, you can hear her moan."

"Can we go please?"

No, it's too late for you two. You should have gone with your brother.

The Tick frowned. "I don't hear her. Maybe we need to wake her up." Then the Tick did something that made Robert's blood run cold. He kicked at the tombstone of Ben Allen. He kicked and kicked and kicked. "Anybody home? Wake up. Time to wake up."

Stop him. Stop him now! Or else I will.

"Stop," Robert cried. "You have to stop!" Water came back to Robert's eyes, but the Tick kept kicking at the stone. "Please, stop!" The Tick continued kicking with a sinister smile on his face and lips covered in imitation blood. With no choice left, Robert bum rushed the Tick, dragging him a few feet away from the grave. The Tick recovered and instantaneously grabbed Robert by the shoulders and threw him hard, into another tombstone. The corner of the stone connected with the side of Robert's back, and he gave a cry as skin bruised and tore. Robert held his side and bawled on the ground as the tears flew from his face.

The Tick returned to kicking and shouting for the ghost to wake up. Finally, the tombstone buckled from the weight of the kicks. It turned up the dirt and grass and slowly fell backward with help from the Tick's foot. When it was on the ground, the Tick stopped kicking and shouting, and he listened. He heard nothing except for Robert's hysterical crying.

Now he's done it. Now he's gone too far. Now we wake.

Robert wiped the snot and tears from his face as the Tick blinded him with his flashlight. "You are such a wimp," the Tick said and walked off toward the entrance. Robert waited for it to happen. The justice of the dead. They would strike him down with their might. With any hope they would attack the Tick first. They would claw out his eyes, rip out his throat, eat his entrails, and then drag him into the dirt. Robert would at least like to see that, before they came for him too.

The Tick got closer and closer to the gate and stone wall. *Any moment now,* Robert thought. *You woke them and now they are going to take you. Any moment. Any moment now.* The Tick put his flashlight into his pocket and climbed the wall, uninterrupted. He hopped down, out of the cemetery. Robert watched as the Tick turned on his bicycle light and pedaled off down the road.

"Why didn't you take him? You said you would take him."

We just wanted you. Just wanted you.

Robert stood up, shaking with fear, his eyes red and itchy, his side and back throbbing. He felt the darkness wrap around him, almost drowning out his weak bicycle light. The eerie silence returned and Robert felt the eyes of two thousand soldiers upon him, watching and waiting to strike. "Please. Please just let me go," he said to no one and to all of them. He said it again. *Please. Let me go. Please.*

"One more step," he whispered, under his breath. *Just one more step and I'm closer to the road, to the city, to people, to life.* His legs stiffened with each step, and his arms tightened. Robert felt their stares on his back, their hands reaching for his shirt, their breath warming the back of his neck. "One more step," he whispered.

He got to the stone wall. He did not know how, but he got there. He dared not look back, for he knew if he looked back he was lost. He removed his hand from his aching side and reached for the top of the stone wall. He jumped and clasped the top. He began to pull and climb with his sneakers, but a foot slipped and he fell back down. *Please. God please. Let me go.* He jumped again and clasped the top, pulling with everything he had, knowing this was his last chance. If he fell again, they would be upon him. He pulled and pulled, his hands and arms scraped and bloodied by the grainy top of the wall. He got one leg up, and then the other was easy. He rested for a moment on the top with his stomach on the stone. He was safe. He could turn and look. He could. He had to. He had to see what was there, to make sure. He turned his head.

The cemetery stood dark and scary but still and empty. Nothing was there. Not even a movement in the corner of his eye. Nothing. He felt foolish, stupid and childish. He was a baby and a wimp. The Tick was right. He rolled over and out of Camp Chase. Monsters didn't exist, and neither did ghosts. No matter how much he secretly wanted them to.

His broken bicycle light holder was real however, and Robert had nearly forgotten. He turned on the rear light and flipped the kickstand up. Maybe he could hold and aim his light in his right hand. He fumbled with it and found a comfortable position. It would be a long ride back but it worked. He just had to be sure to keep a tight grip on it. His side burned and pulsed. He did not want to look at it now, not until he was home.

Noise echoed in the distance, and he could see it coming. Music was blaring from the car's radio. A girl sang as he was bathed in the headlights. The car roared by, flying past Robert and the cemetery, swerving left and right down the street, and then it was gone. Robert readied his feet and took off.

The wind was back, swirling through his hair and drying his eyes. The smell of the city was back too, the asphalt and rotten sulfur odor of the sewers. He did not mind; every second he pedaled he came that much closer to his home and his bed. When his right hand cramped up and needed a break, he passed the bike light to his left hand. He stayed close to the right of the road but not on the sidewalk. There could be people on the sidewalk. People though, nothing more. Occasionally he veered off to the middle of the road to dodge a parked car or a sewage drain. Robert hoped his brother hadn't woken their parents with his return. He hoped Phillip was smart enough to leave his bike outside and not open the garage. He hoped but did not really care. He just wanted to be in bed. To be out of the dark. He decided he would sleep with his lights on tonight.

After ten or so minutes of seamless riding, Robert clutched the break. There was something in the center of the road just out of view of the streetlight. Robert walked his bike to the side and set it down. He put his light on the object. It was a bicycle wheel, twisted and broken, with fragments of chain and bolts littered around it. Further down there was a bent bike frame and a cracked but still functioning front light. Beyond that Robert saw a leg, lying on the pavement, dead and lifeless. He inched closer, revealing khaki shorts, the Tick's shirt, and finally the Tick's face, broken and bloody. Underneath the body, a pool of blood leaked on the pavement. So much blood, there must have been a hundred some fake capsules, maybe a thousand. Robert knew again. He knew that this time, this was real. This time the Tick was dead. So much blood.

When Robert's foot stepped into the blood puddle, a memory flashed back to him. He had spent an entire day at school with a rock in his shoe. It was tiny and hardly bothered him enough to untie his shoe and empty the contents, so he spent the entire day with it. When he got home, he finally took off the shoe and emptied it onto the ground. A pebble fell out. He studied the murky gray rock when he noticed something peculiar. The rock had legs sticking out of it. Tiny legs. Several legs. And they were *moving.* Excitement and fear took him. He had found a new creature. Some type of rock insect. He had to show his mother.

She shrieked when she saw what it was. "It's a tick. It's so engorged with blood it can't even move. All you can see are its legs." Robert never felt so sick to his stomach. He had let the tick drink his blood all day long. It had so much and grew so fat it could not even move. He felt nauseous and woozy and sick. This disgusting thing, this disgusting monster drank his blood. "Look," his mother instructed, and she then did something even worse. She placed the tick in a plastic sandwich bag and popped it. Blood poured out and filled the bag. Robert's blood. So much blood.

Robert took a step away and looked at the Tick, leaking and dead on the pavement, as if he had been popped. He did the only thing he could think of. He got back on his bike and began to pedal home. Faster than before, trying to forget the image he just remembered and the image he just saw. He pedaled faster and faster, wind whipping past his ears and through his hair.

The Tick, Robert thought. *What an appropriate nickname.*

Robert Alexander is a writer and swim coach from Columbus, Ohio. He attended and graduated from DePauw University but soon returned to the greatest city on Earth. He hopes to write a novel of his own someday and many more after that.

LOST IN IMAGINATION
Kevin McGinn

2042
FLIGHT
By Kim Charles Younkin

Mina sat on the bank and put her bare feet in the water, a torn,
soiled book she had found in a dumpster open in her hand. It
was an old book, a fat paperback copy of *Star Wars Episode
V: The Empire Strikes Back,* and the ink of the words had bled from age
and oil spots and other unknown liquids that had formed dark stains on
its pages. But she didn't care. And she didn't care that the water at her
feet, in the basin alongside the Lower Scioto Greenway, was as rank as
the book. Anymore, she didn't notice the thick, scum-covered bits of
trash floating there—the burger wrappers and soda cups and Budweiser
beer cans—and no one else did, either. It was hot, a hundred degrees
and humid for most of the year, and people took whatever bits of cool
they could get.

For her, it was the basin because it was close, but more so, the
river. Some days, she'd skip school and walk across the highway into
the woods to where the river ran. There wasn't enough water to swim,
so she'd walk, knee-deep, all the way into downtown. She'd stand at
the water's edge behind a tree at dusk and stare up over the Santa Maria
flagship and the Broad Street bridge at the great buildings with their
roof peaks pointing at the sky, wondering what it would be like to jump
off and slice through the clouds in flight.

She lowered herself in up to her neck, holding the book up out of
the water with both hands so she could read, never taking her eyes from
it. "Just don't put your face in," her father had told her, and she never
had. If he wasn't out scraping for an odd job, he'd be on the second-
floor balcony of their apartment near the basin's lip, watching over her.
She was thirteen and could take care of herself since she was seven,
because she had to. But when he was home, he was with her.

As she waded near the basin's shore and muck squished through
her toes, she laughed out loud. In her hand, on the pages of the book, a
boy named Luke Skywalker was on a jungle-like planet in the Dagobah

system training to be something called a "Jedi," and he, too, was walking knee-deep in slimy, dark water. Except, unlike her, he was exhausted and carrying a small, aged alien on his back. The gnarled, gnome-like creature who called himself "Yoda" was shouting orders at him, forcing him to his physical limits and pushing him beyond, sculpting him to control his fear. Molding him to not give in to something Yoda kept referring to as "the Dark Side."

Soon, she lost herself in the words, truly left the humid, stinking river basin and the scorching heat of the day's sun and became the boy on the page. She felt her bare feet pound on winding, slippery jungle paths as she ran and a warm weight on her back, as if she carried a baby in a backpack. She heard a high, garbled voice yell into her ear, "Try not! There is no try!" She forged on, even when straggling vines whipped at her eyes and bulging tree roots made her trip and fall hard, because she knew she could become a Jedi. She just knew it.

* * *

Her father climbed slowly up the steps to the second floor. *One, two, three.* He walked all ten in the first flight between rasping breaths, and rested on the open-air landing. Really the whole complex was open-air now, after the flood of '22 when raging storm waters shattered the Franklinton floodwall and nearly ruined everything beyond and above it. What still stood of the Watermark apartments—luxury living near downtown thirty years ago—was a surprisingly well-constructed foundation with gaping holes where there were once windows and sliding glass doors. The southwest-facing units were hit the hardest, and resembled the bombed-out remains of war-torn buildings.

It wasn't really their apartment, but it was home for now. They were squatters here, like everyone else. The city didn't care. The police didn't care. And whoever really owned the property didn't care either. They'd all long since left the homeless behind. He was thankful for the shelter, because of Mina. If not for her, he wouldn't give a good goddamn.

One, two, three. At the top of the second flight he stopped again and grabbed his protruding stomach, basketball-round and hard to the touch, like his wife's had been, carrying Mina. He knew it wasn't good, that it could be and probably was a rotting tumor, but he didn't have any means to find out, and what good would finding out do anyway? Some destinies were predetermined, and he'd never felt any control over his own.

He walked down the cement hall to the last unit on the left, careful to step over a few gaping holes. The unit no longer had a door, but Mina had hung a sheet she'd found crumpled up down near the basin, so the other squatters saw at the entrance a life-sized Cinderella, transformed in her gauzy white ball gown. He was born at the turn of the century and grew up knowing that fairy tale well. But he'd played dumb when Mina asked him about it, never wanting to tell her that Cinderella had started out in dire straits, too. He just hoped she hadn't read it yet. He didn't want her, with her wild imagination, thinking some fairy godmother was going to come and rescue her from their life. There weren't any rescues. Fairy tales were dead.

He batted away the sheet and entered the apartment, knowing she wasn't there. It was late afternoon, after school, but still too hot for her to be inside reading. He walked slowly through the open space that was once a television room, probably for some young professional with a big tech job and mountains of money to spend on shiny gadgets, now utterly bare except for the peeling, filthy gray carpet. He crossed the linoleum that once was the kitchen floor, past its now-battered stainless steel appliances. At the doorframe leading to the balcony, he leaned to rest.

The balcony wall had been washed away, and he could see her perfectly from there, down in that damn cesspool under the beating sun. She was only in the water up to her knees, bony knees that stuck out from under her frayed camo-green shorts, the ones she wore to be a lion tamer. The lion tamer was one of her favorites. Sometimes he played it with her, sinking to the floor on all fours—roaring, batting at her with his hands as if they were the beast's paws. He could see her ribs through her wet, camel-colored tank top. A long black whip hung in a coil on the belt at her tiny waist.

Behind and above her rose the long stretch of highway I-670, crammed with racing cars and trucks that flashed in the waning light of rush hour, but he didn't notice them, didn't hear their roar. Squinting hard through the sun's glare, he only saw Mina. She had something strapped to her back, but he couldn't tell what. She was hunched over, jumping and kicking her way through the water. With both hands she punched at invisible obstacles. She looked like a boxer, light on her feet, sparring with some unseen opponent.

A book lay a few feet from her on the burnt grass near the basin's lip. He knew what had happened. It was what always happened.

* * *

Mina wasn't asleep late that night when old Bill came through the sheet. She heard him slam his bottle of whiskey on the kitchen counter, or whatever it was he'd stolen from the SmartMart station around the corner at Grandview Avenue and Dublin Road. He was drunk, as always. But her father, despite his growing weariness, was taller and younger than Bill and had more heft, so she told herself not to be afraid of him. Old Bill was too lazy to be a squatter. Even though he'd come in years ago when the getting was still good, he'd wander off for such long periods of time that a new squatter would move into his spot, and eventually he just got tired of messing with it. He slept inside a cardboard box under a flight of stairs a few buildings over and sometimes stumbled up to their place to gripe about the state of the world. The complex was remarkably quiet at night except for an occasional tussle, and Bill. Her father was sympathetic. Eventually, Bill would talk himself out and go away. Or pass out, and her father would drag him back to his box.

She heard her father mumble a greeting, and then Bill's voice, loud.

"It's the Cath-o-lish!" he said, his words thickly slurred.

Her father quickly shushed him. "There aren't any Catholics left. Where's your head?"

"Then it's the Relativists! Takin' just what they need all the time and leavin' nothin' for the rest of us. Nothin'!"

Her father's voice was low. "You mean 'Capitalists.'"

"Whatever! They shoulda fell years ago!" Mina heard him take a sloshing drink and bump the glass bottle against a rotted kitchen cabinet. "Eatin' out of the trash, what kinda life is that?"

Her father was silent for a few moments while Bill drank. She felt a twinge of fear, like she'd felt at his first few late evening visits, but then her father spoke. "We're not there, yet. I don't know how much longer I can keep it that way, though."

Mina knew her father was tiring faster these days. He sat more than stood now, watching her play. The lines in his face had grown deeper, like life was carving them with a sharp blade. Their food stores were low. She took little from it, and asked him for nothing. Sometimes, when she felt dizzy and images swam in her vision, she would steal bits from backpacks at school. But only when it was bad.

She heard a cabinet door bang sharply, and then another.

"You got real food?" the old man said earnestly. "Where you get-ting' real food from, partner?" More cabinets slammed, faster, as he found nothing in any of them.

"We eat it as I get it," her father lied. "There's no use you waking up the whole neighborhood."

By now her father would know she was awake, listening. She twisted herself to seated on her mattress and grasped the folds of her long T-shirt in her knuckles. She heard the door of the refrigerator, long past its cooling days, open and shut. Then the freezer door, too.

"Where is it, boy?" Bill yelled. "You been hidin' it from a sick old man!"

Mina heard his heavy footfalls as he lurched down the hall toward her room, knew her father couldn't move fast anymore, couldn't catch him. She inched backward into the corner of the walls and pulled her legs up to her chest, curling herself into a ball. Crossing her arms across her face, she waited.

Then from the kitchen, the hard clink of a thick glass bottle on the counter, and her father's voice bellowed in the darkness.

"If you want this back, you better turn right around." Her father's feet shuffled on the linoleum and he banged the bottle as he walked. "The food is for Mina. You touch it or anything of mine, I'll kill you."

"Ha! That little thing that dances around out in the mud? The one that climbs up on the roof and acts like she's flyin'? She don't look like she eats a thing." The old drunk cackled loudly. "She looks too crazy to eat!"

"Say goodbye," her father said. And then out in the night, beyond the balcony, was the sound of shattering glass.

"Goddammit!" Bill shrieked. "Goddamn you son of a bitch!" He ran away from her and to the balcony, howling for his booze.

A loud thump made her jump from her mattress and run down the hall, her heart beating in time with Bill's wild screams. She reached the kitchen just as her father dragged the old man, kicking and spitting, under the Cinderella sheet and out the front door.

"Crazy! That little girl is nuts! You son-of-a-bitch! You're both crazy!"

Mina covered her ears and ran back to her room, making herself the ball again, counting out the seconds, *one, two, three*, until her father came back. One minute became two. Two became ten. She could hardly control the heaving of her chest.

She flew away then, her mind taking her to safety. It took her to a place she'd read about long ago. There was a thick, sunlit forest of a hundred acres where a towering tree stood, a tiny door carved into its base. A wooden plank hung above it, carved with the name "Mr. Sanders," the last 's' backward so it looked like a 'z.' Curiously, she moved toward it with the slow, heavy feet of dreams. The door opened a crack, and she glimpsed behind it a patch of soft, yellow fur. She reached out to put her hand on the wood to push the door open …

A loud scraping noise and something dragging again brought her back. The sharp sound of a nail ripping through wood. Another nail. Five. On the sixth nail, she pulled herself from the corner and walked down the hall, hugging herself to stop her shaking.

She looked around the corner. The Cinderella sheet was in a crumpled ball on the floor. Her father stood holding a jagged-edged sheet of plywood, warped with water damage and covered in black spray-painted graffiti. Its size covered the open door well enough. The back of his gray T-shirt and the white of his bald scalp were soaked in sweat. He hammered in rusty nails, bent at odd angles, with a fist-sized rock.

"Daddy," Mina said, choking on her own voice.

Her father turned and saw her. He smiled with his mouth and his eyes. She watched it evolve slowly, a river of love flowing down his face, lighting the pain-carved lines like the sun.

"For you, my dear," he said with a mocking flourish of his hand. "I'm just sorry it's not your color."

* * *

Mina's father woke before dawn lying on his back on the cracked linoleum, his head propped at an odd angle against the oven. Spears of hot pain buried their sharp tips in his brain, neck, spine, stabbing him deeper as he maneuvered himself to sitting. He wondered, in the dark, if whatever had once gone into that oven had ever hurt this bad. If the turkey had felt the knife cleave off its head. If the cow had endured its own quartering. He hoped not, then berated himself for hoping, because what good was it? Their deaths were in the past, and his was in the future, and between them was just the grief of living, stretched out across interminable years, wilting flesh and bone raked across fiery coals.

He shook the thoughts from his mind and slowly pushed himself to standing. He moved down the short hall to where Mina slept, stepping into her space and inhaling the sleepy scent of her, as he had since she was a baby. He could just barely make her out, a tiny lump tucked into the mattress on the floor in the corner. Her breath was measured, even; soft puffs of air from her open mouth. He longed to brush back her tangled black hair and touch her cheek, but knew that would wake her, bring her back from her vivid dreams with their wild hues and fantastical beings and aching happiness. The sun would rise soon enough and sear them from her, and she'd be left with the nothingness of the day, of every day, to bear.

Instead, he moved past the mounds of her belongings to the other corner where she kept the wooden box with the bronze latch she'd found on the side of a road somewhere, the one that looked like a stationary box. Where someone had once put flat sheets of paper and envelopes and pens for writing, he stashed her food. He opened it and felt inside to make sure she had something to start out with. His hands ran over a package of dried fruit he'd swiped from a homeowner on a plumbing job; a plastic-covered hunk of salami he'd gotten trading a battered pocket knife. A shock of hunger tore through his stomach and he quickly closed the lid.

He turned and walked to the front door, pried its six nails from the frame, and stepped into the dark morning. He had to fill up the box.

* * *

The sun came up over the last shred of night and shined through Mina's open window in a shaft of heat onto her face. She had slept hard and dreamlessly after her father had nailed up the door. She knew he was gone now—he always was when she woke. The daily odd jobs in the Upper Hood, the wealthy area above Dublin Road, were gone by daybreak, so he had to move early. But she felt better now. She rose and wiped her tangled hair from her eyes, then swept them across her room, her treasure trove, for what to wear.

Everything Mina owned, that she had ever worn, she had found herself—from the "stacks" placed by the city about every mile all the way up Dublin Road from downtown to the zoo. The people who could afford to buy new clothes bought too many, wore them once, and threw them out. When the second landfill had started filling up too quickly, the city started burning the clothes in piles. She passed two on the way home from school each day and knew their burn schedules. Sometimes, she would watch the burns, lying back on a distant patch of grass as thick, black smoke coughed up into the sky. But mostly, she just looted them. She moved fast, at dusk, racing from the cover of a tree to the items spilled out on the ground, quickly deciding what she needed, and how much.

It all lay in piles on her bedroom floor because there was no furniture. Each pile had meaning. In one, a blue dress; a white gauzy apron with strings; glittery silver shoes; a basket to hang over her arm. All Dorothy's things. In another, tight black stretch pants; a dark green jacket; a belt; a quiver; a bow. For Katniss. In another, a long creamy dress trimmed with lace she'd swiped from the trash behind an antique store; a black wig; a die-cast pistol with a nine-inch barrel. For when she needed to be Scarlett.

All her books were in a mound on the floor of the closet behind its splintered, wood-paneled door. They had all been easy to come by. People threw them out all the time, only reading now on Smartpads, and it was a boon for her. From the dumpsters, Mina took every fiction book she found. She had Jane Austens. Tolkiens. Steven Kings. *Harry Potter*, all but the third book, which she'd not yet been able to find. She even had the children's books that Rowling's daughter had written, about the wonder girl who saved the Earth by making it rain.

She picked up the open *Star Wars* book from the floor next to her mattress and scanned a few pages, then surveyed the piles of clothes. Then she scavenged through it all and donned a long-sleeved, fitted white dress with a flowing skirt that nearly touched the floor, and matching zip-up boots. She rummaged for a hairbrush and slowly worked the tangles from her long mane. Her expert hands deftly carved her hair into two equal parts, and she weaved two braids, one on each side of her head. Then, she coiled each into a fat doughnut, and pinned them. She picked up the book and read the page quickly, to double check.

She laid the book on the mattress, took the salami from the wooden box, and left for school.

* * *

Mina's father found a job close to the complex before the sun rose, in the Upper Hood on Lincoln, at a house he guessed to have been built around the mid-2000s. He had been walking west on Goodale, up the hill where the road changed names, and saw a man in the creeping dawn at the end of a long driveway, hauling down his daily mound of trash. He'd shouted out before someone else did because there was competition, even this early. "Hey sir, you need any work done today?" The man had dropped the trash and pulled a handgun, fast, from the back of his belt and said, panting, "You come another step and I'll blow out your skull." Mina's father had put up his hands and walked closer, then slowly turned in a circle. "I'm just looking for a day's work," he replied, forcing cheer into his voice. "The trash. You got more? I can drag it down for you." The man waved him closer—the gun trained at his face—and considered him for a few long moments. Mina's father saw that the man was fat, no match for heavy work. "Come on, then, and get started. I have the trash, and gutters and yard work, too." It was the easiest, earliest score he had ever made.

By sunrise, he was on a ten-foot ladder fixing gutters. The man stood in the front yard, watching, not even helping him move the ladder as he worked. He just stood there, holding the gun. Pointed it right at his back all morning.

* * *

Mina had known it was coming from the way her teacher had been looking at her the last few weeks. With a pitying, furrowed brow, like that of an old woman who comes upon a dead baby bird in the grass, fallen from its nest. Mrs. All knew that Mina was a squatter, knew that the address Mina's father had given the school wasn't even on the map anymore, as did the administration. But they all ignored it because she was a genius. She upped their test scores. She got them all nice bonuses from the district and the state for achievement rankings. But pay bonuses don't stop the other children laughing at her and pointing and disrupting classes. Eventually, lower test scores from the others would cancel hers out. Mina knew this.

She walked into the classroom and the class hushed, then tittered, as she climbed up on a windowsill and leaned her head, cushioned by a hair coil, against the glass. Mrs. All looked at her sadly, the dead baby bird in her white funeral dress, then resumed her teaching. Quickly, the teacher programmed the Smartboard to flash the math concepts on the wall screen—concepts Mina already knew and could teach, and probably more effectively. Soon she said, "Finish these ten problems on your pads and upload them to me in fifteen minutes," then walked to Mina and touched her on the shoulder.

Mina knew.

"Please go down to see Mr. Kent. He's waiting for you."

So the counselor would do it. Because she was crazy.

Mina looked Mrs. All in the eyes and smiled, then climbed down from the sill. She looked them in the eyes, too, the boys and girls with pimpled cheeks and mouths full of braces and wicked tongues. Her head felt suddenly light and their faces merged into one before her eyes. They separated again, but into the cold, white masks of Vader's Stormtroopers. She saw them rise from their seats as one, felt the Leia inside her spring to life to escape them. She fled to the hall, her dress billowing out behind her, her boot heels clicking on the black-checkered tiles.

The counselor was waiting, his vein-covered hands folded on his desk as in prayer. As if there was a God.

He nodded to the lone chair in the room.

"Sit. Please."

But she could only stare, her face wiped clean of expression.

"Mina, we've talked about this before." A pained shadow crossed his face. "The disruptions to the other students. The children have to learn."

She looked at a frame on the wall behind him and gazed at it, but didn't see the photograph of the smiling, rusty-haired boy inside it.

"It is essential to the mission," she said.

The counselor sighed.

"Mina." He shook his head twice and looked up at her again. "You can be anything. Anything, with your mind. It doesn't matter where you are now. If you let us, we can help you become what you will be in the future."

She felt as if she'd fall and reached out a hand for the chair. "The only future is the efforts of the Rebel Alliance. The Death Star has been destroyed, and we must crush the Galactic Empire completely."

He stood and raised his voice. "You're destroying your *life*, Mina! What will you do? Where will you go? We want you here, but you can't stay like this." He waved at her, gesturing to her appearance. "Like that."

We want you here. Her throat caught at the words, constricted, and she swallowed hard to force it back open. But where was "here?" Soon it would end, and there would be a different school that would never accept her for as long as this one had, if at all. "Here" would be nowhere, just like always. "Here" would be with her father, surviving. Every day, all the days.

She breathed deeply and whispered, "The Empire must fall."

The counselor moaned quietly and dropped his chin to his chest. He picked up a long creamy envelope, the old-fashioned kind, because her father didn't have a Smartpad. He walked around his desk and handed it to her.

"I'm sorry, Mina."

She took the envelope in her hand, admiring the thick heft of it, the papers folded up inside, the black ink of her father's name scrawled across the front of it. *John Chain.* So that was how it would be then.

Finally, she looked into his eyes and said a word of her own. "Goodbye."

* * *

Eventually the man had lowered the gun, somewhere around the time the sun had crested in the sky and began to make its way toward the other horizon.

His stomach had ached all morning as he worked, repairing sagging gutters along the edges of the massive house, and he'd stopped a few times to grip it as a cramp tore through him. One time, he'd turned from atop the ladder and called to the man.

"I'm a straight shooter," he'd said. "No pun meant. I'm just wanting a day's pay so I can feed my daughter."

The man had nodded as he put the gun behind his back and tucked it in his belt. "I can see that." He gestured to the opposite side of the house. "I've got a daughter, too. That's why I carry this."

Mina's father had climbed down the ladder and sat on the ground to rest, sensing it would be all right, and asked the man for a drink of water. The man went inside the house and returned with a glass pitcher of cold water, ice cubes bobbing inside, and two thick wheat bread sandwiches brimming with slices of turkey and ham.

He'd eaten with a mixture of unexpected joy at the bounty and dark, heavy guilt, for having something that Mina didn't. He considered bringing half of it home for her, but he had nothing to wrap it in and no place to put it. The man seemed to read his thoughts.

"I'll make one for her, too. When you're done."

The man watched him work for the rest of the day, and asked him to stay until dark to haul some more trash and apply the day's chemicals to his acre of grass.

He worried, because he knew Mina would worry. He never stayed out past midday, past an hour or maybe two after her school day ended. But the man had promised him fifty dollars—*fifty*—more than he'd earned in a day for years now, so he stayed.

As the sun dropped behind the line of the horizon, the man walked inside his house again, opening the triple garage door from the inside and emerging in a shiny, blood-red Audi A10 that looked like an arrow a marksman would shoot from a bow.

"I can take you down the hill and past Goodale," the man said, "but I won't cross over Dublin Road."

Mina's father nodded his thanks and got in the small car, cringing as he folded his sore legs into the tiny front seat and rested them against the glossy leather dashboard. The man handed him a sandwich wrapped in clear, thick cellophane and then slammed the car into reverse and gunned the car down the winding drive to the road. They roared around the curve and then the right turn onto Urlin, and they practically flew over the railroad tracks. At the stoplight, the man reached across his lap and opened the door.

"Go," he said furtively. "Come back next week. Tuesday."

Mina's father unfolded himself as quickly as he could and limped out of the car. The man drove through the red light onto Riverside and sped away with the door hanging open.

He laughed at it all, at the door, at the food in his hand for Mina, at the feel of the cash wadded up in his pocket. At how close the man had dropped him to the apartment, without even knowing it. He thought for a brief second, *Maybe ...* but stopped himself abruptly and focused on walking as quickly as he could through a break in the traffic, across to Watermark Drive.

The last shafts of the day's colors—oranges, reds, yellows—faded into the evening as he walked the quarter mile around the bend to the apartments. He thought how it looked like a seascape painting he had seen once, in a downtown gallery long ago when he was a boy; how he'd wanted to dive into the blue-painted ocean and burst up through the waters into the setting sun.

So he didn't hear the footsteps behind him, just felt, out of the cooling early evening, the crashing blow to his head. Somewhere in the fog of his crumbling to the ground he heard the sound of a glass bottle hitting pavement. He felt rough hands searching his pockets and sleeves, pulling at him and pushing as he lay in the street looking at nothing through the blank eyes of his waning consciousness. He felt his own hands, now empty.

A voice said, before the darkness took him, "I came back, partner. The door was open."

* * *

Mina sat on the kitchen linoleum in front of the old stove and rocked, arms wrapped tightly over bent legs, tangled hair in her eyes, the envelope on the floor in front of her. The bright white moon punctuated the black night, its light inching further across the room as the hours wore on.

She did not cry.

In her mind, chapters showed themselves. Beginnings and middles and ends. Her eyes lost their focus on the moonlit wall in front of her and became the eyes of the people in the pages.

She was Frodo standing over the churning lava at Mount Doom; terrified, diminutive, the ring in her hand burning her flesh with its power. She was Harry faced off with Voldemort, the nausea of her imminent death upon her, bringing her to her knees as she struggled to hold the wand against the villain's unspeakable curse. She was Luke, hanging on desperately with her one remaining hand from a thin bar over a vortex in space, the only hope of salvation in the outstretched hand of an evil man-turned-machine.

When her eyes refocused, she was in her bedroom, sifting through the piles. From one, she pulled white leggings. From another, scuffed brown leather boots with flat heels and suede tassels. A loose-fitting blouse that hung to her thighs. A black belt. A three-quarter red velvet cape that she'd saved for a special occasion. She dressed before her mind flew away again, and then she went into the night without looking back.

Over the highway she walked, into the woods where the river ran. Muddy water squished into her boots and through her toes as she trudged its bed, followed its winding path. As she neared downtown, she saw the LeVeque Tower, tall and regal in the night. Mystical creatures soared high above it. Toothy dragons. A fire-orange phoenix. Hippogriffs. The Broad Street Bridge was an island over the water in the distance, palm trees with drooping green fronds swaying in the tepid night air. From somewhere far off, a wolf howled.

She couldn't feel her hands.

But her feet kept moving toward the flagship, the Santa Maria. Mina saw Columbus at the helm, shouting orders to his men as the ship tossed in raging seas. The water rose to her waist and then her chest until the hull towered above her in the water. Voices, or perhaps the

215

whispering of the moon-bleached sails, beckoned to her.

Thought left her.

Mina climbed out of the river, the wet sea captain's cape dragging behind her, and scaled the ship's starboard side. She found the darkest corner of the deck and folded herself into it. She waited to sail away.

Kim Charles Younkin is a Columbus native who writes fiction from her home in Upper Arlington, where she lives with her husband and sons. Her mainstream and sci-fi-inspired fiction, along with a few humor essays, can be found on her blog at www.kimcharlesyounkin.com.

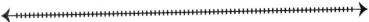

In 1470, when Christopher Columbus was a teenager, he survived an attack along the Portuguese coast of the merchant ship on which he worked. The ship sank, but Columbus floated to shore at Lisbon on a scrap of wood, where he studied mathematics, cartography, navigation and astronomy in preparation for his voyage that would change the world. He set sail on that voyage twenty-two years later as the commander of the Santa Maria flagship.

A full-size replica of the 98 ft. Santa Maria flagship sits in the Scioto River in downtown Columbus, Ohio.

REWIRED
H.L. Sampson

2070
REWIRED
By Todd Metcalf

My car lurched toward a stopped maintenance truck as I zipped along Interstate 71 toward downtown Columbus, Ohio. At over one hundred miles an hour, I knew no one could survive a collision at that speed. I flung my arms in front of my face to brace for the inevitable impact.

At the last minute, the steering wheel took control, guiding the vehicle safely back into its lane and the flow of traffic. I grabbed the wheel, but the car failed to respond. It eventually exited at Seventeenth Avenue, stopped in front of the Ohio State Fairgrounds, and shut down. I was unable to restart the Google NAV system that served as the brains of the car. A message on the dashboard indicated that I had been fined 850 dollars by ODOT for requiring assistance from its Disaster Aided Vehicle program, or DAV. An ODOT crisis intervention unit would arrive in forty-nine minutes to evaluate my psychological health.

I would've been furious for incurring the fine, not to mention submitting to a psych evaluation from ODOT's questionable medical experts, if I'd owned the car I was driving. As a grunt relationship checker for Facebook, Hyundai's hydrogen and ethanol hybrid was beyond my means.

I couldn't remember why I was driving a car that wasn't mine or where I was going, but I got out and left it behind. If I stayed, ODOT would quickly discover that it didn't belong to me. Without a justifiable reason to have it in my possession, the police would arrest me. My apartment was a good two or three miles away on Oakland Avenue. I walked.

My legs were on fire by the time I finally arrived at Vinnie's Pizza. Home sweet home. I squeezed into the alley between the two buildings and stepped to the rickety metal staircase that led to my second floor apartment. Skipping the third step because the rust could no longer hold my weight, I climbed to the top much more winded than usual. I promised myself that I'd start an exercise routine tomorrow. I placed my thumb on the lock, nothing. I hobbled down the stairs and entered Vinnie's, whose owner also happened to be my landlord.

Bob Xu sat behind the cash register as he counted money before the dinner rush. A third generation American whose great grandfather had emigrated from Vietnam, I once asked him why he opened an Italian restaurant. He told me he had eaten more pizza growing up in New York than he had ever eaten pho.

"Bob, how's biz?" I asked, which was how I always greeted him.

He studied me as though he were sizing up a total stranger. "Fine, sir. How may I help you?"

Sir? I looked at my clothes. I was wearing a custom suit that I didn't recall buying. What had gone on last night?

"It's me." I waited for the recognition that never came. Finally, I said, "Shay Cooper."

He shook his head sternly. "I know Shay Cooper. You're not him."

"Good one, Bob." He was always trying to tell jokes, but the whole humor thing was beyond him. All I wanted was to go up to my room and lay down. "The lock's broken. Can you open my door?"

"I can't let you into Shay's apartment. I don't know you."

"Bob, it's not funny. My car broke down, and I had to walk three miles. I'm exhausted, and in no mood for jokes."

"How do you know Shay? Are you his father?"

"Bob, you know me. I'm Shay."

He looked me straight in the eye. "You're not Shay."

"I'm wearing nicer clothes than usual, but it's me."

"If you don't leave, I'm going to call the police." He held up his mobile to snatch a picture of me. No doubt he was going to send it to the Columbus police.

"Remember when I let your brother, Xiang, stay with me last summer when he was enrolled in Riverside Hospital's drug therapy program."

"I didn't tell anyone about that, not even family. Only Shay knows."

"That's right, only Shay knows. I know because I'm Shay."

He stared blankly, but I could see in his eyes that he was thinking hard. "No." He shook his head. "It's not possible. Go now or I'll call the police." His finger hovered over the mobile screen.

"Bob, why won't you believe me?"

"Because Shay's dead." He punched the button on his phone that

220

would send my picture and Bob's grievance to the authorities.

I left. I wasn't concerned that the police would come running; they never did in this neighborhood. I was more concerned about Penny, his old Luger.

I didn't understand how Bob forgot me so fast. Last night he'd given me a pizza that a customer never picked up. It was as though I were living someone else's life. Maybe there were answers inside the car that I'd deserted, so I headed back to it. I quickened my pace so I could search the car before the psych wagon arrived. Despite what had changed in my life today, one thing never would. Police didn't play nicely with people from my neighborhood. If they caught me terrorizing poor Bob and then discovered that I had driven someone else's car without the owner's permission, I'd be locked up for a long time.

As I jogged toward the car, I felt one side of my suit coat weighing heavier. I pulled out a wallet. The miniature tablet's ID screen displayed a picture of someone named Edwin Kale. The wallet held no less than ten credit and debit accounts. Clearly Kale was a rich man. Without passwords or his fingerprints I'd never be able to access them, but just knowing that I was holding a wallet with ten accounts made me feel wealthy. The wallet's personal page indicated he lived in Miranova, a dated but still upscale downtown high rise. I cursed. Possessing a stolen ID would be yet another mark against my growing record of illicit activity.

When I arrived, flashing lights surrounded my abandoned vehicle. Casually, I turned and walked in the opposite direction. It wasn't long before I heard the whine of a car's engine behind me. It was all I could do not to sneak a peek. At the street corner, I turned left on the sidewalk. The car matched its pace to mine. Looking over my shoulder, the van's police markings were distinct.

Since I couldn't explain that which I couldn't understand, I ran. The psychs would certainly label me crazy and throw me into an institution. I dashed between two homes. A snarling dog bared its teeth. Its chain had more slack than I preferred. The dog lunged. I dove to the left, hoping that there wasn't more chain that I hadn't noticed. I rolled against a bush, leaving me inches away from the incensed dog.

The van doors thudded, and voices poured out. I picked myself up and continued darting through the backyards of the neighborhood. I had always been in reasonably good shape, but for some reason I was already exhausted. Hiding was my only hope for escape.

As children, neighborhoods seemed to have endless hiding places, but when you're running for your life, the number of viable spots dwindles dramatically. Sirens blared around the neighborhood. I spotted a screened porch with a partial wall. It would serve as a perfect hiding spot if the door was unlocked. Fortunately, it opened. I quickly plopped against the wall. My heart beat crazy fast. I concentrated on slowing my breathing.

"Did you see where he went?" a man's voice said.

"No. But look at that. I'd hide there if it were me."

I froze. Maybe my hiding spot wasn't as perfect as I'd thought.

"I think I see him!"

I waited for the screen door to fly open. I imagined that I'd be looking into the barrel of more guns than I'd care to count.

But the clicking of hammers never came. In the distance, I heard their voices diminish. I snuck a glimpse over the wall. No one. I took a deep breath and checked again. I had finally done something right today.

A scream rang out behind me, followed by a crash. Instinctively, I felt my torso for a bullet wound. When my hands came up dry, I spun around to see a horrified woman staring at me from the house. Her coffee mug had shattered on the concrete steps.

"It's going to be okay," I said, although I knew it wouldn't be, at least not for me.

"Oh my ..." she trailed off.

"I was ..." I didn't have time to explain so I ran. I backtracked as quickly as I could. There was no doubt that the police had heard the woman's piercing scream. I ran toward the vicious dog but decided to turn right instead. It was the wrong decision. A man flew out from behind a honeysuckle bush and tackled me, crushing me against the ground, knocking the air out of my lungs. I wheezed as he cuffed me.

"Got the suspect near the point of entry," he said into his earpiece. Shortly, the other officers gathered around.

One cop examined my wallet, then looked off in the distance. "Control, initiate a data crawl on Edwin Kale."

Two officers led me into the psych wagon. A large screen displayed two women wearing doctor's coats. They introduced themselves as my psych team. Dr. Lawson was a strong-featured brunette with her hair pulled back tightly into a bun. Dr. Moore had heavy cheeks with a mixture of brown and blonde hair.

"Why were you running, Mr. Kale?" Dr. Moore said.

I considered correcting her, but the more I claimed to be Shay, the crazier I would seem. Not a good outcome in a psych consult.

"I panicked," I told them. "They were chasing me."

"Do you have something to hide?" Dr. Lawson asked.

"Not at all. My car malfunctioned. I was looking for a mechanic."

"Why didn't you make a call from the car?"

"My NAV locked." I recalled that when I checked the pockets of my suit, I didn't have a phone. "I forgot my phone at home."

Dr. Moore changed to a different line of questioning. "Why were you driving erratically?"

"I wouldn't say I was erratic."

"DAV only takes control if a collision is imminent."

Since the first thing I remembered today was driving a car owned by a man I'd never met, I had to grant her the point. "I must've fallen asleep."

She nodded. "Dr. Lawson and I need to confer for a moment."

Their images blanked out before I could grant them permission. Their images reappeared shortly.

"Given your recent medical activity, Dr. Lawson and I recommend a consultation with your doctor as soon as possible."

"Does that mean I'm free to go?"

"We'll recommend to the sergeant that you be placed under medical supervision. You'll likely be fined for your behavior, but once Dr. Narayan clears you, you are free to go."

The police charged Edwin Kale 14,438 dollars for towing services, the psych consult, and the active duty of seven police officers. Fortunately, Kale had the money. If he hadn't, I would have been remanded to jail until a payment schedule could be enforced. I just hoped I wouldn't meet Kale in a dark alley when he found out what his money was paying for.

I expected the Ohio State University Hospital waiting room to be filled with snotty, whining children running around infecting adults with their insidious cocktail of germs. Instead, it had soft lighting, comfortable chairs, and no patients. Old classics from Bieber and Lady Gaga were piped into the room.

The receptionist walked around the desk and hugged me. "Ah, Edwin, it's so nice of you to visit again. You were scheduled to come in two weeks from now," she eyed the officers for the first time, "but I understand there are extenuating circumstances. Please make yourself comfortable." She leaned close to my ear and whispered, "It's going to be all right."

"Thank you."

The officers stood by the front door as I waited. I picked up one of the pads lying on the side table and thumbed through its collection of magazines. The doctor only subscribed to news and gardening magazines, so I searched the Internet for more information on Kale to pass the time.

Kale was a wealthy business executive for Graftek, the Fortune 500 Columbus-based biotech company responsible for developing blockbuster drugs that I couldn't begin to pronounce. Last year, he had been involved in a freak car accident that caused significant brain damage. With the assistance of the Ohio State University Hospital's top neurological expert, he made a full recovery.

Uncontrollably, I flung the tablet across the room. I've never been a violent person, but I couldn't overcome my agitation. It could have been brought on by Bieber's infernally repetitious "Baby, Baby, Baby," but it was probably because everyone thought I was someone else and I couldn't do anything about it. The two police escorts had their hands on their holsters, poised for action.

"The doctor will see you now," the receptionist said. I heard her whisper to the two cops as they passed, "And not a moment too soon."

She led me into a sparse room. There were no windows, unless you count the giant mirror that hung on the far wall. The overhead light was harsh and sterile. Two tables sat in the middle of the room with large, doughnut-shaped scanners at one end. Two movable trays with computer monitors hugged the left wall.

"Please lie on the table."

"Which one?"

She smiled. "It's your choice."

While the doughnuts didn't look ominous, something about the room, coupled with everyone's tentative behavior was unsettling. I turned to leave, but the two men blocked my exit.

"You need to listen to the lady." They were the only words I had heard the tall one utter.

I took a few casual steps toward the table. When the men relaxed, I ran toward the door. I had almost reached the hallway when the tall man thrust out his arm of steel, clothes-lining me to the floor.

"You don't want it to go down like that," the other man said.

They picked me off the ground and placed me on a table. The woman strapped me down. As she flipped a switch, the doughnut began to hum.

"The doctor will be in shortly," she said as she left.

The two police officers stayed, apparently to serve the important function of sending threatening glances in my direction.

I leaned my head back against the thin pillow. The combination of the intense lights, an uncomfortable table with tourniquet-like straps, and the vibrating doughnut gave me a case of déjà vu.

The door clicked open. Scuffing footsteps stopped next to me.

"I understand you've had some incongruity recently," the demure man said.

"Dr. Narayan?"

He smiled, but his eyes showed more concern than I would have expected for a routine medical exam. "Good. At least you haven't forgotten everything."

Actually, I only knew his name because the doctors from my psych consult had told me.

He slid a stool out from under the table and started the recorder on his pad. "Tell me what you remember."

Maybe it was the fact that I was strapped to a table with two goons watching over me or it was because I was the only patient in the office, but I knew the truth wouldn't be in my best interest.

"Everything," I said. "I remember it all."

He consulted his tablet. "Erratic driving. Tell me what happened."

"I fell asleep at the wheel. DAV parked me in front of the fairgrounds and shut down my car so I couldn't restart it. Did you know it costs 850 dollars every time you use DAV?"

He nodded as though he had much experience with DAV. "That shouldn't be too expensive for you."

"It's not." The good doctor would know much more about Kale than I did, which meant I would never be able to fool him. Unless …

"But it got me thinking, Doc. How would the people living around the fairgrounds be able to afford such a large traffic fine?"

"Almost none of those people drive anymore, Mr. Kale. That's why COTA has been doubling its bus service every decade for the last fifty years."

"I know that. I just wondered how much different life was for them. So I decided to see for myself."

Dr. Narayan studied his tablet. "You told Mr. Xu that you were Shay Cooper."

I faked a laugh. "He must've misunderstood. I told him I was looking for Shay's apartment."

He looked up from his pad and studied his reflection in the mirror. It was then that I realized he was looking at observers behind a two-way mirror.

"How did you know Shay lived there?"

"I remembered his address. When my car stopped, I realized I was near Shay's apartment. So I decided to pay a visit."

"You wanted to see Shay?"

I nodded.

He tapped on his pad. "Shay's apartment was 3.8 miles from your car."

"Wow, I had no idea it was that far. I had hoped the brisk walk would wake me up."

"Have you been having trouble sleeping at night?"

I had to devise an unverifiable excuse. Dr. Narayan could easily check any of my statements about Kale's work. Social engagements were out because he could contact Kale's friends.

"Not really. I just got into a really good novel that I couldn't put down."

"Which one?"

This one question could bring my house of cards tumbling down. How could I know his favorite authors? Dr. Narayan apparently had a deep history with Kale. But I had to try given the situation. I wondered if Kale was a man who read biographies of corporate leaders. Zuckerburg had just published a memoir about the rise and fall of his Facebook fortune. I love it when the wealthy get their comeuppance, but Kale might not be as interested in an octogenarian's ramblings.

It was then that I glanced in the mirror and saw my face for the first time. I froze. The man staring back looked nothing like me. I was barely twenty-nine years old, but the man in the mirror was at least fifty. No wonder everyone thought I was Kale. I looked exactly like the ID in Kale's wallet.

Dr. Narayan had somehow changed me into another man! I strained at the straps, fighting to break free. The cops moved closer.

"Settle down, Mr. Kale," Dr. Narayan said. "You're all right."

"You've totally changed me!"

He put a comforting hand on my shoulder. "You're simply having a minor setback from the procedure. It's not expected, but it's not entirely a surprise either."

"You mean the procedure where you swapped my body with someone else?"

"Do you think we put you in someone else's body?" Dr. Narayan eyes bulged. "How interesting."

"Interesting? I'll show you interesting." I contracted every muscle so that my body writhed like an electrified snake.

"Of course we didn't do that, Mr. Kale, we simply ..." His face lit up. He turned to speak to the mirror, "That's the problem. He believes he's Shay Cooper!"

"I don't know how you turned me into Kale, but I want my body back," I said. "I want my life back!"

Dr. Narayan consulted his tablet instead of reacting to my fury. He turned to the mirror, "You need to see this." He shuffled out of the room.

"Come back here!" I screamed.

The police officers stood on either side of me in the event that I broke out of my restraints.

"I want my body back!"

The receptionist plunged a large syringe into my neck without sterilizing the skin. My muscles relaxed instantly; my body went limp.

"What did you do to me?" I asked before the darkness overcame me. My last thought was that I would never wake again.

Even though the room was bathed in soft light, it felt like a 500 watt spotlight was burning my retinas. My head didn't just ache, it felt like it had been run over by a truck multiple times. I blinked rapidly as my eyes grew accustomed to the light. A figure sat beside my bed.

"It will take a few moments for your brain to recognize what your eyes are seeing," the soft voice said.

I had heard the voice before, but I couldn't place it. "Where am I?"

"You're recovering from surgery," he said as he lightly touched my arm. "I'm Dr. Narayan. How are you feeling?"

"Surgery? For what? How long was I out?"

"It's been three days, which is quite normal for recovery. You underwent major neurological reconstruction." He stared as I processed the information. "Can you tell me how you're feeling?"

"Like a safe was dropped on my head."

He nodded. "Yes, quite normal."

Normal? I couldn't classify any situation that felt like your head would explode as normal. "Why did you operate?"

"We had to fix a little problem that developed from the previous surgery."

"I had more than one?"

"Yes, yes." He patted my arm. "All in good time. I'll tell you everything. But, first, you need to rest."

I yelled and flung my arm forward, although it only moved a few inches.

"No, you must rest. The connections to your motor functions must heal slowly."

"No!" I wouldn't be kept in the dark any longer. "You have to tell me everything."

Dr. Narayan sighed deeply. "You must rest."

"I can't until I know what's happening to me."

He placed his pad on the table. "Very well. You were in a debilitating traffic accident last year. I was able to repair parts of your brain."

"I died?"

He shook his head. "You almost did. The part of the brain that controls your motor functions and your critical thinking skills was damaged beyond repair. That left only one option."

It was now becoming clear to me. Dr. Narayan had transplanted my brain into another person's body. "So you're Doctor Frankenstein, and I'm his crazy monster?"

"No, no, you're no more monster than I am. I didn't piece you together from parts of corpses. However, we were very fortunate to find a viable donor before you died."

"You transplanted part of my brain?"

"Exactly."

I stared at him.

"You don't remember, do you?" he asked. "I'm one of the leading neurological scientists in the world. I've performed some of the most complex brain surgeries in the world here at the Ohio State University Hospital."

"Go Bucks," I said.

He smiled. "Yes, well, anyway, I've spent years perfecting partial brain transplants in chimpanzees. After numerous grant proposals and political arm twisting, I finally received approval to begin human experimentation about eight months ago. I looked for the right situation for two months before your case came to my attention. You would have died without the operation."

"Someone else's brain is in my head! I'm a freak."

"Nonsense. Think of it as a partial heart transplant. We only replaced the parts that control motor activity and critical thinking."

"If I have another man's brain, then I share his thoughts and history?"

"No, your memories are still your own. Think of it as changing the processor of a computer. All your files still remain."

I shuddered at the thought of having part of another person's brain fused to mine. I certainly felt like myself and could conjure up memories of my past. When I settled down and thought about it, the procedure was like a heart transplant. I was still myself, regardless of what they replaced inside me.

"And the operation worked?"

"Of course, better than expected, actually. Your first surgery was six months ago. I've examined you weekly since then. You've passed with flying colors."

It was slowly coming back to me. "Then why did I believe I'm someone else?"

"Unfortunately, one of the donor lobes became detached, which caused you to lose part of your short term memory. It must have occurred while you were driving. After I put you under the scope, I saw the detachment. The donor lobe was starting to cannibalize your host brain, which, if untreated, would be detrimental. I immediately prepped you for surgery so I could reverse it."

"You mean my confusion and the fact that I thought I looked like someone else was because my brain was not wired correctly."

He nodded. "A few memories from your donor may have been accidentally transplanted, which would have caused the hallucinations. I removed all evidence of your donor's memories three days ago."

"You said his brain started to cannibalize mine. What did I lose?"

"During my research with primates, I found that the host brain cannibalizes the donor brain. It's a pleasantly useful process, because it allows part of one person's brain to fuse with another, thereby creating one. In your case, one small piece of your donor's lobe became too aggressive, which tends to happen when the donor's lobe separates from the host. I reattached it before it created any major damage. Your short term memory was affected. The extent is that you've lost maybe six months of memories." He smiled. "In the grand scheme of things, it's not too bad giving up six months of memory in exchange for cheating death."

"You mean I no longer have my donor's memories, and except for a few months, I'm as good as I was before the car accident?"

"That's correct."

My injured mind needed further reassurance. "All my memories are mine? I can continue with my life?"

"Absolutely! You won't even know another man's brain is a part of yours. After a few days of rest, you'll be as good as new."

I tried to think about my donor, but I had to admit, I had no intimate knowledge of his life.

"Could his brain change my personality? Will I develop multiple personalities?"

Dr. Narayan paused. "We haven't seen any significant changes in our subjects."

"But there were changes?"

"Accidents change you. Major surgery changes you. Our subjects didn't change beyond what you would expect. Not only that," Dr. Narayan said, "but your success has shown the way so millions of people will be saved from brain injuries every year." He smiled.

It was a nice thought, but what was the cost? "How did my donor die?"

He nodded as though he had expected the question. "He died in a car accident."

"He was in a similar accident?"

"Not just similar, he was in the same accident you were involved in. Both of your cars collided."

That meant not only were our brains connected, we shared the same death. A wave of guilt swept over me. I hadn't just taken his brain, I had taken his life.

"How did I do it?"

Dr. Narayan looked at me quizzically. "Do what?"

"How did I kill him?"

"It was a terrible accident. Your cars collided in one of the few dead spots that DAV couldn't control. Both of you were on the verge of death. The police weren't able to assign responsibility."

"Then how did you determine who would be the host and who would be the donor?"

He closed his eyes as though he had to see the words in his mind before they became real. "Sometimes physicians have to make tough calls."

"Did I have less brain damage that made me a better host?"

"There were equal amounts of damage. I made the decision."

"What did you base it on?"

He shook his head and then mumbled something.

"What did you say?"

He put his face in his hands. "I can't tell you."

"You have to tell me. You owe me that much."

He lifted his head, staring at me through tear-filled eyes. "I knew you were a wealthy man."

"Excuse me?"

"Medically, it didn't matter which of you was the host. My grants were drying up. I hoped that by saving you, you'd make a generous contribution to my research, Mr. Kale."

"Mr. Kale?"

Dr. Narayan's eyes widened in disbelief. "You—you *are* Mr. Kale. Right?"

"I'm Shay Cooper."

Dr. Narayan was right. The surgery changed me, improved me. I can recognize when people are taking advantage of me. I'm thinking more clearly than ever before, able to see how this world was always against people like me.

As Edwin Kale, I've inherited a few things. I'm the thirty-second richest person in Columbus. I have an old-fashioned penthouse suite in Miranova, an aging wife whose favorite hobby is shopping for expensive clothes and jewelry, and two grown boys who don't have enough skills to make it on their own. The three of them will eventually spend all my money. There's only one solution. I have to get rid of them.

Being Kale isn't so dreadful. I've lost a few years of life inside his older body, but, after tonight, I'll start fresh as a widower. Mrs. Kale will take her last breath. I'll pay the murderer enough money to support his drug habit for a few months. The most amazing aspect of having a lot of money is not the things you can buy, but what people will do for you.

I'll cut Kale's children off. They'll have to live on their own, which means they'll become penniless within a few weeks. I might tell them about a cheap rental that's little more than a foul, rat-infested room. It's available from a pizza-spinning Vietnamese man named Bob.

Only Dr. Narayan knows I'm not Kale. I promised him five million dollars to keep quiet. I'm not sure it's enough. The money will allow him to continue his research. He'll figure out why I became Shay Cooper instead of Edwin Kale. Unfortunately, his academic integrity won't allow him to ignore me. I'm a walking aberration of an experiment that went wrong. One day he'll tell the authorities, and they'll take my money. One day he'll fix me. That means Shay Cooper will really be dead.

I can't allow it to happen. I am Shay Cooper.

Todd Metcalf, born and raised in Columbus, Ohio, attended the Ohio State University. He has worked in various technology and executive management positions with some of Columbus's top companies. He currently runs a business consulting company serving the vibrant business community in Central Ohio. He is married with two daughters.

In 1914, the trustees of the Starling Ohio Medical College transferred all of their properties to the state of Ohio to establish a College of Medicine at The Ohio State University. At this time a hospital was also established, which later became University Hospitals.

In 1993, the Ohio State University Medical Center was established. Today, it is one of the largest academic medical centers in the country.

AND ICARUS STANDS BY
Dorian Lafferre

2097
AND ICARUS STANDS BY
By Kim McCann

She'd seen the flyers for weeks, posted up at the hydro-farm markets where she bought the small limp vegetables that stretched the contents of her dwindling canned pantry. She'd been careful to look at the bulletins from the corners of her eyes—take in one line one day, more information on another. She hadn't wanted to draw attention to her attention. That was a dangerous thing.

She'd grown anxious with the waiting, afraid the offer would be gone by the time she acted on it, but that was silly; looking at the other women at the market—sizing them, searching them—she'd known deep down she might be one of the few who could meet the requirements. She'd always been careful and smart, stuck to high places, had avoided the polluted earth and the easy paths others had traveled. Other women bore small scabs and red marks on their skin, unmirrored on hers. She'd been cautious, and she was healthy.

Even right after the first big shocks, when everyone was running around with desperation, she'd been prudent. And after, when everyone had accepted fate and the terrible reality—when things had returned to a kind of limping normalcy—she'd still been careful. She'd kept hope and kept safe.

The Agency sent two men to pick her up, both of them flighted. It scared her at first—a fascinated terror when their wings flitted and flashed, sleek in the eternal, infernal orange light. Fluttered wishes in her chest fanned a desperate fire. They spoke little, only confirmed her identification and the code the Agency had given to her through the market contact and told her what she could bring and what she couldn't, and then they lifted her between them and flew her to the tram.

The High City was almost too much to take in, too much to believe after the gray crumble of Mid City, where she'd spent the last twenty years. The tram carried them across the inky black crawl of the Scioto River, finger of the once mighty Olentangy. Its banks were covered with a fringy marigold-hued moss that carpeted the river walk and climbed the sides of the Broad Street Bridge like hungry ivy, like a faded illustration from a child's book of ruptured fairy tales.

Though the windows of the tram were tightly sealed against the outside air, her nostrils knew well enough the fetid smell the moss and water carried—it drifted on the wind toward Mid City with frequency—and she held her breath, pulse drumming in her head, as they neared the Agency's headquarters.

She remembered how, on a long ago trip to the city, her dad had pointed to the LeVeque Tower and told her it had once been the tallest building in all of Columbus, that the faces of its facades were the fathers of the city and watched over all the people there. But time had moved on, as it did, her dad had said. Men yearned for more, reached for greater heights, and had forgotten the importance of strong foundations and beauty's place in life.

He'd told her the story of Babel and said LeVeque would be the mightiest tower again some day. He'd been right.

They passed her through a Geiger portal, like the ones the Council had installed at the mouth of the hydro-markets to keep out the Groundlings. She and her belongings crackled and fizzed, but that was normal—everything made the needle hop these days. She knew her level, though, knew it was under the red, knew it was acceptable. She'd been careful, so careful.

They brought her to a room, one of what could have been a dozen, at the end of a hallway off the intake area. She didn't see anyone else—anyone like her, at least. All of the Agency employees were flighted, wings tucked tight against their backs as they silently processed her from one place to the next. As they passed each closed door, she wondered if there were women like her behind each one, women who might have hope inside them in more ways than one.

The room was drab, as most things were. Nowadays, there was so much light outside that the subdued color inside was a kind of respite. She wondered if other places in High City had been transformed better, more like Before. The room was clean, anyway, protected from the dust swirls and clutter that invaded even the carefully tended-to corners of Mid City. There was a film over the windows that made the harsh orange light gray and bearable. She didn't dare take in the view beyond the thick glass, didn't feel she had the capacity to fathom where she was and what it might mean. Not yet, anyway. Not until the tests were over and they'd said yes, not until she knew for sure this new height could be maintained.

She showered as they'd instructed her to do, washing the grit of Mid City from her skin. She didn't know if she was being observed—didn't feel as if she was—but she knew the Agency was careful and might be taking notes. She paused after toweling off, looking at her body in the long mirror on the far side of the small bathroom. She'd never seen another woman naked, not one alive, anyway, and she wondered what her body must look like in comparison.

She was as pale as she should have been; you had to be careful and keep covered. Her breasts were drooping, had been more so as she'd reached thirty. Her stomach was soft, and she passed her palm over the slight paunch there. That's where the hope was, all the possibility. She had no desire to carry a child of her own—what still-sane Mid City dweller would want that?—but the damaged women of High City … they sometimes wanted babies, wanted healthy eggs for babies. And the price they'd pay would change everything for her. If they chose her. If she met the requirements.

There was a sound from the main room, one she didn't recognize at first. It was an old sound, anachronistic as green grass and blue birds. It took her a moment to realize it was the ringing of the phone on the bedside table; not the synthesized chirping she remembered from Before, but the trilling jingle of old phones like the ones she remembered from movies and TV. A whole chorus of bells rang before she picked up the heavy handset and brought it to her ear. She listened silently to the static on the line for a second before remembering there was a process. Decorum.

She whispered a halting, stuttered "Hello?" and was instructed by a voice to retrieve the questionnaire that had been left outside her door. She was to complete it and then leave it where she found it. This was the first step.

The packet was thick, ten pages or more, and a wonder in her hands. Clean white paper, not a sheet of it re-purposed from something else. It made her shake a bit with its extravagance. It wasn't as if paper didn't exist in Mid City, but not paper like this. Not paper for one use and one use only.

The first twelve questions were standard fare—things always asked, whether you were applying for food or water or generator watts. These days, they were the important questions, the things that had to be known:

Name:
Age:
Race:
Height/Weight:
Eye color:
Hair color:
Place of Residence:
Previous Residence, if current residence is less than five years:
Last Geiger Count:
Occupation, if applicable:
Education, if applicable:
List all surviving next-of-kin, if applicable:

After that, they wanted more personal information that spoke to why she was there and what she was willing to do:

Do you have regular menstruations?
If yes, date of last cycle:
Length of last cycle:
Have you conceived before?
If yes, date and number of conceptions:
If yes, were children within normal parameters of health (as outlined by the Agency)?

She wiped the back of one hand across her mouth. She knew they'd ask such things, but the thought of putting such intimate information down on such clean white paper made her nervous. It wasn't as if she discussed such things. With whom would she ever discuss such things? Women kept their cycles private—kept themselves covered, safe. Even in Mid City, there were … factions … that would take advantage of such details. But this was High City, and this was the Agency, and she'd contacted them. She'd offered to be here. The information had to be theirs for the asking.

Do you suffer from mental illness?
Is there any known history of mental illness in your family?

She wasn't sure. She'd been too young Before, she thought, to have been a judge of such things, and After, there was no one to consider. Besides, mental illness was a rather subjective term, given the circumstances. But maybe they looked at things differently in High City.

List any medical conditions for which you have been treated, including care under the Ministry or medical services received Before-times:

Before, she couldn't remember, and After? There'd been the normal rashes and sensitive skin. Red Throat. Wet Eye. The nasal infections that came after the worst of the dust storms in winter and summer.

The rest of the questionnaire was a mix of medical and psychological history, moral tests, logic puzzles. The last two pages concerned the procedures, outlining the Agency's responsibilities if things worked out, what her part would be, how she'd receive the surgery only after a healthy child had survived for a period of three months.

It took her nearly three hours to fill out the forms. When she placed them back on the floor of the hall, there was a dinner tray waiting for her. The vegetables in High City were larger and more flavorful than the ones she was used to, and there was a small piece of what she was quite sure was meat, the first she'd had since Before-times.

* * *

The physical exam was long and humiliating. She was naked in the large, cold room, no care offered to her modesty. All the medical technicians' wings—it seemed everyone in High City was flighted, though surely that couldn't be true—were wrapped in a kind of cloth sleeve, she guessed to preserve sterile conditions. Did their wings molt like real birds' did? She wondered at that, remembered how—in Before-times—she'd sometimes find a feather on the ground, soft and light like air.

They spoke to her minimally, only to offer instruction:

Move here, please.
Lift your arm behind your head, please.
Place your legs in the stirrups, please.
You'll feel a small amount of pain and pressure.

There were x-rays and scans and cold steel instruments pressed against and inside her, no reassurances one way or the other if the findings were good or bad. They asked the same questions she'd answered in the packet. One Agency representative sat off to the side with a clipboard and pen, making checks as she spoke. To verify, likely. To confirm that her answers were the same, that she hadn't lied.

After, she was handed her clothes and told to dress, then escorted back to her room and given a food tray with a cup of tea and a protein bar. There would be blood drawn later, and then she could eat a proper lunch. She salivated at the thought of more meat, though the bit she'd had last night still sat, hard and solid as a stone, in her stomach.

* * *

That night, lying beneath the warm spread of the bed, she dreamed she had wings. She soared above Mid City and the room she kept there—five stories high, yet still not high enough—and circled to peer through the dusty windows. Inside, she saw herself, wingless and naked, stomach full to bursting with life as if she'd swallowed a Before-times melon. As she hovered and stared, eyes wide at the distorted reflection of the woman she'd grown to be, her stomach split open.

Four-and-twenty blackbirds, baked in a pie ...

A cloud of tiny birds spilled out, frantic and dark as smoke. They swarmed around her, pecking and flapping, screeching and crying, onyx eyes flashing with heat and fire. They consumed her with their pointed beaks, calling, "Promises, promises ..." as they went.

* * *

Her breakfast tray contained tea and scrambled protein, a slice of toast, and a small round apple. She wept as she held the orbed fruit in her hand, having seen no such thing in ten years. The skin was greenish, blushed, and freckled with red and orange. Pocked and rough, with the remnant of a stem at its top. She couldn't bring herself to eat it, and instead hid it in her small suitcase amidst the socks and underwear.

With the breakfast came another sheet of paper—this one yellow in color—single-purposed as the questionnaire. It was a consent form, asking for her signature to start the administration of hormone shots and vitamin injections. It outlined exercises she was to begin that morning, stretches and strengthening routines to build the muscles in her shoulders and back; the wings would demand it.

Promises, promises ...

She signed her name shakily at the bottom, then set the tray in the hall and waited.

Kim McCann, in her day job, dresses up in old-timey costumes and portrays people from the past. She once spent a summer in Toledo, Ohio, making bulls-eye-shaped, cherry-scented urinal deodorizers. She's a published author, produced playwright, and director of Sarsparilla Shook Productions—www.facebook.com/SarsparillaShookProductions—a theater company based in Indianapolis, Indiana.

The LeVeque Tower, at 555 feet and 6 inches, was built to be exactly one half foot taller than the Washington Monument. From its erection in 1927 until 1974—when the Rhodes State Office Tower was built—it was the tallest structure in Columbus, Ohio.

In its heyday, The Palace Theatre, housed in the ground floor of the LeVeque Tower, was host to such entertainers as Duke Ellington, Benny Goodman, Louis Armstrong, Mae West and Gypsy Rose Lee. The theatre's second balcony is purportedly haunted by the ghost of a stroke-ridden man who is said to have died there.

ROLLING THE DICE
Hannah Ploechl

2124
FINDER'S FEE
By Birney Reed

S olly Novac looked up from the news screen touting the 142nd anniversary of Red, White and Boom in Columbus Ohio and watched the old man walk into the casino for the thirty-third time. In the past weeks, Solly had observed the elderly gentleman walk out thirty two times: thirty two times a bona fide winner ... thirty-two times in a row.

Solly knew everyone got lucky now and then, he personally watched a lady of the evening win at craps for twenty-two straight hours. But by the end of the twenty- third hour, she was broke. That's the odds of the house, he thought to himself. The house always wins in the long run.

On this day, Solly kept his eye on the old man for two hours, then he made a note in the little book he carried with him and headed into the bowels of the casino to report the latest win of Haggarty Vernon Holmes to his boss.

Solly Novac worked at one of the biggest casinos on "The Miracle Mile" in Columbus, Ohio, which was actually two miles of gaming establishments and entertainment lining both sides of Broad Street for what was the most popular gambling strip east of the Mississippi.

"How is he doing it?" Solly's boss, Randall "Breaker" Kaminski asked from his desk without acknowledging Solly's presence.

Solly looked down at his boss, cleared his throat and answered, "He's not cheating in any way I can tell."

"Bullshit! He's won way too many times not to be cheating. He found a way to beat it, and I want to know how."

"Look Randy," Solly pleaded. "The guy's walking out of here with less than ten grand every time he wins. You've got old ladies sitting at the slot machines losing that in ten minutes. It won't break us. It won't affect our performance ratings or our bonuses. He's under the radar. And I'm telling you the old fart isn't cheating."

Randy's face turned crimson as he shouted, "The man is cheating, and I know it! It's your job to find out how."

If Solly didn't need the job, he would have told Kaminski to shove it. But he did need the job. "I'll try and figure it out. But as far as I can see he's not doing anything to the visible eye. I'll watch the vids to see what else I can find." He walked out the door of Kaminski's tiny subterranean office and back to the floor of the Lions Casino.

The next evening, Mr. Holmes ambled through the front doors and made his way to the back of the house to one of the only solitaire tables left in the city, tucked away from the main flow of the slot machines and gaming tables. Solly knew the easiest solution would have been to make Mr. Holmes play solitaire on a video machine. The problem was if a customer asked for real cards in a game of chance, by law all casinos had to comply.

Solly was at his post making another note in his little book. He watched Haggarty Holmes lose three hands, then win two in a row. His winnings amounted to seven grand. He knew the distinguished looking gentleman would play until he reached a figure of ten thousand dollars. Sometimes it took him three hours, and once in a while he left the casino in five minutes. Tonight it took him twenty minutes.

"Mr. Holmes, may I have a word with you? I want to talk to you about the way you play the game of solitaire."

Holmes smiled for a moment and then scowled. "Buzz off, kid! You don't have a thing on me. Is your boss pissed because he can't figure out how I'm doing it?"

Solly decided to show the old man who was boss.

"I'd just like to have a conversation, Mr. Holmes. Otherwise, we can bar you from the casino and put the word out to the other operations. In twenty-four hours you won't be allowed to play a nickel slot at a charging station."

Vern stood up. Solly was surprised to find he was looking the man in the eye. He always thought Holmes was shorter. "You do that, kid, and I'll have your ass before the Gaming Board twenty four hours after you ban me. You can't bar someone just because you think they're cheating, not in this day and age. Now get out of my way. I haven't had my dinner yet."

Solly stepped aside, and stuck out his hand. "I'm Solly Novac."

Vern looked at the man's hand and then straight into his eyes, "Who cares?" He resumed his walk to the cashier's cage to cash in his chips. Solly smiled at the man's back. Haggarty Vernon Holmes had just made it a personal issue.

The next evening Solly was waiting by the entrance. "Mr. Holmes, I need to have a word with you." He grabbed the old man's hand in the "come along" grip known to every bouncer and enforcer and hustled him into a small side room off the main entrance. Vern couldn't say a word because he was yelling in pain. Solly kicked the door shut as he forced the man down on the lone steel chair in the soundproof room.

"Now, let's you and I have a conversation about cards, Mr. Holmes."

He was surprised to see there was no fear in the man's eyes. There definitely wasn't any fear in his voice. "Kid, don't you ever touch me like that again. Now let me out of here before you get hurt."

Solly stared down at Vern and didn't know whether to laugh or tear the old geezer's wind pipe from his throat. His knees popped as he squatted down in front of him. "Listen buddy, all I want to know is how you're cheating. I don't give a shit that you're winning. I just need to know how you're doing it, so tell me and we can get the hell out of here."

He watched Holmes relax. "Is Kaminski on your ass?"

Solly decided to be honest. "Yes, he is."

Vern's cold grin gave Solly a chill. "I've met him, I wouldn't worry too much about him." He paused for a second and then said, "You know, I don't owe you an explanation. However, just to ease your mind, I am cheating."

"How? You never touch the cards. You don't know any of the dealers as far as we've been able to discern. So how do you do it?"

"Solly is it?"

Solly nodded.

"If I tell you then I'd have to kill you. And you're still wet behind the ears, and I hate killing pups. Now are you going to let me out of here or do I have to kill you now?"

He couldn't back down. He wouldn't back down. Solly raised up and answered, "Kill me now."

Vern's irises went from brilliant blue to pure white. Solly couldn't help but fall into them like a stone through a bucket of water. The back of his head started to throb, and pain shot down his back. Mr. Holmes blinked, and everything went back to normal.

Vern smiled up at him. "Naw, you'd be too easy." He paused for a second, then continued, "Leave me alone and we'll get along just fine. Screw with me again and that pain receding from the back of your head will seem like a pin prick in comparison to what will happen."

Solly felt as if someone had pulled a plug and drained all the energy from his body. He walked over to the door, opened it and walked out of the soundproof room to tell Breaker Kiminiski what he could do with his job.

As the odds would have it, he didn't have to tell Breaker a thing. In fact he couldn't tell him anything, because his boss was sprawled across the top of his desk with blood seeping out of both ears. Underneath his body the coroner found a file containing a single sheet with all the pertinent information on Haggarty Vernon Holmes. The very next day, as his dead ex boss was having the top of his skull sliced open at the autopsy, Solly was promoted to floor manager of the casino. He sat down at his new desk, in his cubicle of an office, and read the one page file on the man he was supposed to have busted cheating.

Subject: Haggarty Vernon Holmes
Occupation: Retired Operations Tech, Reeden Nuclear Power Plant, Dayton, Ohio
Address: 1229 Kenwick Road, Columbus, Ohio 43209
Marital Status: Widow (wife died of a brain hemorrhage January 23, 2211)

Surveillance placed on the subject for 90 days reveals nothing to date. Mr. Holmes lives in a modest home. He does not appear to associate with anyone from any of the casinos. In fact, as far as this agency has determined, once he leaves the casino he goes to the King's Casino for their evening buffet then to his house where he doesn't emerge until 6:00 o'clock the next evening.

He does not date either sex. Once a month the subject goes to the "Cat House" and emerges two hours later. In talking with one of the ladies in residence, she reported that he has normal sex with a different woman every month. He refuses to be with same girl twice. Also note that he will not choose a red-head. The lady we spoke with believes his wife may have been a red-head.

His bank account has eight hundred thousand dollars, and he holds no certificates of deposit nor does he own any stocks or bonds.

Summation: Haggarty Vernon Holmes is not associated with any syndicate. He is a loner. He has no criminal record.

Below the typed information was a hand written note: *Hey Break-er! Are you bored or just trying to spend some of your quarterly budget?*

Solly had wondered the same thing, right up to the time Holmes admitted to cheating. He hit the calculator function on his computer and totaled the winnings of Holmes over the last year. At approximately ten thousand a day, his take home was 3.5 million dollars a year. A little above the average pay throughout the country, but he wasn't knocking them dead. Then it hit Solly. It was over three million before taxes! Just so he walked out of the casino with less than $12,000 each night, he didn't owe the IRS a thing, he barely had to give the cashier his name.

If you figure in the taxes, the old man was making better than ten million dollars a year playing Solitaire. "How much could the old man make if he put his mind to it?" he muttered under his breath. A plan was forming in his mind as he laid aside the file, set the alarm on his watch and got busy doing his new job.

At 6:25 p.m., his prized antique Seiko beeped. Solly got up from his desk and walked out into the casino to observe Vern Holmes. This time instead of watching the player, he watched the cards being shuffled by the robo dealer. Solly was mesmerized as the thin, coated plastic cards rubbed against one another. There was a rhythm, a pattern. For the briefest flash of a moment, he saw the rhythm interrupted. He wasn't sure it happened but he knew it had. The dealer started dealing and Solly saw a smile on Vern's face. Vern was going to win this hand.

Two hours later, Vern stood up and walked over to Solly with ten grand worth of chips in his hand. "Congratulations on your promotion!"

"Thanks." He wasn't surprised the old man knew.

"Are we going to get along, or does someone else get promoted?"

Solly put on his best casino smile as he answered, "I'd like to talk with you. It doesn't have to be here, it can be anywhere you want."

Vern looked Solly up and down as if he were measuring him for a casket. "I'll think about it and let you know. Now if you'll excuse me, I've got to get a bite to eat."

Holmes spun on his heels and headed towards the cashier's cage.

Solly watched Vern walk out of the casino, then he hit the alarm setting on his watch and went home to relax.

At four-thirty in the morning, Solly woke up and got off the couch. He started down the hallway to grab a shower before going out and do-ing a little gambling of his own. As he got to his bathroom door, he heard the unfamiliar chime of his doorbell. No one ever came to visit him. The women he slept with met him at various hotels along the strip. Being "in the business" guaranteed him free rooms on the fly from most of the desk clerks in town. The doorbell chimed again.

Through the peephole, he saw Vern Holmes standing in the threshold. He was dressed in a sky blue windbreaker with the King's Casino logo on the left breast, khaki slacks and a burgundy polo shirt. His blue eyes stared directly at the peephole. Solly opened the door, and the first words out of Vern's mouth were, "Want to get something to eat?"

"Sure, but according to our information you never go out."

"I guess you can't always trust your information."

As the waitress poured their second cup of coffee and laid the bill on the table in between the two men, Vern asked "So, do you want to know how I do it?"

"No, I know how you do it."

"Really?"

"You move the cards with your mind."

Once again they stared at one another, finally Solly broke the silence. "You worked at Reedon. Did radiation exposure cause what you're able to do?"

Vern looked past him like he was watching a scene play out on a television screen. "You might say it enhanced an ability I didn't know I had. Fact is I didn't discover I could do anything till a few days before my wife died. That was when I found out I could move things with my mind. Not everything, but quite a few things."

Vern paused and Solly jumped in. "Why solitaire, why not craps, roulette or even black jack? You're playing such a low end game. You could win a hell of a lot more if you changed your focus, so to speak."

"I don't need a hell of lot more. I'm comfortable, and the house doesn't really lose on such small time winnings. As you've probably figured out, I also don't have to pay any taxes. The taxes I do pay are taken out of my pension from the lab. Besides, controlling the cards during a shuffle is actually very hard to do. It takes more effort than you realize."

"But you could have so much more! You could clean out the house, and nobody would be the wiser. Don't you want a better life? More money to do the things you want, without having to budget. You could visit that whore house you're so fond of every day of the week instead of just once a month."

Vern laughed. "I'm sixty-eight years old. I don't need to visit it more than once a month."

Solly chuckled with him but he didn't want to give up. "What about your kids? Wouldn't you like to leave them a little nest egg for the future?"

"No kids."

Solly sighed audibly. Vern reached out to touch his hand. Solly jerked it away before contact could be made. He could hear the loathing in the man's voice. "Relax, if I wanted to do something to you, I wouldn't have to touch you to get it done."

The flush of embarrassment spread over his cheeks. "Sorry Vern. I didn't mean to insult you. It's just that …"

"Just what?"

"Hell, I know you killed Kaminski."

Once again Vern chuckled, but this time Solly didn't laugh with him. "You'd have a really hard time getting anyone to believe it. In fact the coroner's report will show your boss died of a brain aneurysm. No foul play, just a little blood vessel that decided to pop."

"Like your wife?" Solly regretted the question the second after it came out of his mouth.

"Leave her out of this!"

Solly felt the pain building in the back of his head and everything in the restaurant grew blurry, including Haggarty Vernon Holmes.

"Getting a headache? You've got to be careful about headaches. They could be a sign of something far more serious."

Solly sucked in his breath, he could feel his heart pounding in his chest. He stood up slowly from the booth. Solly hadn't felt this dizzy since he rode six roller coasters in a row at Kings Island when he was fourteen. He almost lost his battle with the bile roiling in his stomach as he choked out "I'm leaving. Stay out of my casino!"

"Sit down before you fall down, Solly."

The dining room was spinning too much for him to argue.

"Waitress, could we get a glass of water over here. I'm afraid my friend isn't feeling too well."

Solly managed to hiss, "I'm not your friend." He paused for a second and then begged. "Please make it stop."

And just like that it stopped. It more than stopped. Everything around him was sharper, more in focus. He could see a waitress talking to one of the bus staff. Their conversation was crystal clear even though they were fifty feet away and whispering. "I'll get high with you after my table leaves," he could hear her say from across the dining room.

"Earth to Solly. Hey, Earth to Solly!"

He looked at Vern and his mind was made up. He didn't want anything to do with the man sitting across from him.

"You can come in any time you want. I don't care. If need be, I'll quit my job so you won't think I'm trying to get over on you. Just let me leave and leave me alone."

"Relax, I'm not going to kill you. In fact, I'm somewhat intrigued by what you've said. I would like a few extra things. But here's the problem as I see it. To make it worth my while and yours, we would have to make some very serious bets. With an ability like this, I don't want to draw attention to myself."

Solly's greed fought his fear and won. "We can work it out. I figure in one night we could take five maybe seven of the ten casinos for a billion each before they get together and shut us out. We'll place big bets on the bigger games—craps, roulette—and we'll be out of each casino before they realize how much money we took them for."

He saw the look of embarrassment on Vern's face, "The only games I know how to play are solitaire and poker. And I'm a terrible poker player."

Solly reached out and touched the old man's hand. "Don't worry, you won't be playing poker. Individuals lose at poker. We're going after the house. It can always afford to lose. But first you're going to have to learn some new games of chance."

Vern looked down at the hand touching his. "I'm placing my trust in you, Solly Novac. Don't screw it up."

Solly's smile was genuine this time as he replied "You and I are going to be rich, Vern, absolutely stinking rich."

Solly turned his hand over and Vern grabbed it in a firm handshake. The two gentlemen agreed to meet the following evening to work out the details and to teach Haggarty Vernon Holmes the art of playing craps and roulette.

Vern looked around the living room at the regulation length craps table and full-size roulette wheel. Solly threw the dice. The hard eight came up for the third time in a row.

"That's the way to do it Vern! In three throws of the dice, you won six hundred thousand dollars. Now the smart thing to do is string the table along. Place smaller bets and lose a couple, then head back to the hard numbers. Here! You throw them for awhile."

He went to place them in Vern's hand but Vern pulled away.

"What's the matter?"

Vern looked down at the table and back to Solly's hand where the dice rested.

"If I touch them, it won't work!" he finally blurted out.

"What are you talking about? All you have to do is throw the dice."

"Like I said, if I touch them it won't work. For some reason once I touch an object I can't control the damn thing for twenty-four hours."

Vern was surprised to see a smile growing on Solly's face.

"This is perfect! You don't have to throw. We let everyone else play the table. We sit back and rake in the cash. Vern if you weren't a man, I'd kiss you. Aw man, this is beautiful, absolutely beautiful!"

Two nights later they walked into their first casino ready for their chance, the chance to be winners. Solly looked around the table. He could see the hunger in the other players' eyes. The money they won and lost didn't matter. All that mattered was the game. A beautiful young woman held on to Vern's liver-spotted arm, the perfect gambling cliche. The human croupier handed the dice to Vern, and he pulled at the woman's arm, forcing her to grab the ivory cubes. "You roll'em sweetheart, you're my good luck piece tonight!"

Vern laid his million dollar bet on the hard ten. He looked across the table to Solly and gave a slight nod. Solly didn't return the gesture. He was too busy watching the beautiful brunette hooker winding up to throw the dice. They hit the backboard with a crack and crashed down on the table. Five dots on each die lay looking at the twelve people gathered around the table. The croupier's voice sounded distant in his ears.

"Hard ten pays twenty to one. We have a winner!"

The next play Vern laid off his bet just as Solly had instructed him to do. The next three rolls he played the hard numbers, varying them each time. In five minutes they were up fifty million. At the end of the first hour, Vern hit the 350 million mark. A crowd had gathered around him, cheering and matching his bets. An hour and thirty minutes later the winnings totaled 750 million dollars.

Solly pulled on his ear, and Vern caught the signal. He collected the winnings, filled out all the tax forms, and gave the resident agent the government's standard forty-eight percent.

Two hours later, and three casinos down the strip, the duo counted their winnings in Solly's living room. Both men sipped Cokes while resting back against the cushions. "We're at 2.7 billion dollars, Vern. How are you feeling?"

The old man smiled at him. Solly could see the happiness in his eyes. They were glowing with the possibilities facing them the rest of the night. His next sentence was meant to sober Vern up.

"We've got a long way to go. Don't lose focus now. If we keep this pace up we'll have over twelve billion a piece by the end of the night. Then you and I can go our separate ways."

He watched the smile drop off Vern's face and heard the sarcasm in his voice. "Don't worry kid, I won't lose focus. By the way, what are you going to be doing while I make us rich?"

"The same damn thing I've been doing all night long. Making sure you don't go for the brass ring all at once."

For the first time since the evening began, fear worked its way back into Solly. It crawled a little farther as Vern answered, "Now that's a tough job! You get to look at all the beautiful women in the casino while I play with the dice. That's what I call a fair distribution of labor."

He knew this would come, but he didn't think it would be so early in the evening.

"I thought we were equal partners, but I guess I'm wrong. What would you consider fair distribution?"

The smile instantly reappeared on Holmes's face. "We're equal on this to the bitter end my friend!"

Solly thought about the weapon in his pocket, and nodded his head.

There were three gentlemen waiting for them as they stepped into the opulent lobby of the Mirage of the East. The small man framed by the two giants let everyone know who was in charge. All three men were impeccably dressed in finely tailored suits.

"Mr. Verette, this is Vernon Holmes."

Tony Verette turned to Vern but didn't offer his hand. "Mr. Holmes, I'm afraid our craps tables are closed to you this evening. However, the house will give you five million in chips, and you can game any way you like, except for craps."

Solly prepped Vern for this. He knew what he was supposed to answer. But what Solly wanted was far too ingratiating.

Holmes looked down at Verette and he practically spat, "That's all right you little chicken shit, there's more money in roulette anyway."

Verette shot Solly a look that could kill.

"Let's go kid, we got money to make." He looked back to Tony Verette and added, "And a house to break."

The wheel-man did his job. He spun the wheel, tossing the little white ball in an opposing circle to the spinning numbers. He watched the ball, as did everyone gathered around the table. When it dropped into the red thirty-two slot for the fourth time, he saw Verette walking his way with the next replacement.

"Ladies and gentlemen, please hold all bets until we change personnel."

It gave Solly a chance to whisper in Vern's ear. "Knock it off. They'll shut down the table and ask us to leave."

Solly could see the tiny white circles in the center of Vern's eyes.

"Relax kid. This is where it gets interesting," he whispered back, then called out "Hey Verette."

"Yes Mr. Holmes?" Verette answered with a diplomatic smile.

"I've got nine hundred million of your money. I want to let it ride on one number. You got the cajones to make that happen?"

"Yes sir, I can make that happen," Verette obliged, "but on one condition."

Vern smiled. "And what condition is that?"

Anthony Verette returned his smile. "I pick the number."

The old man broke out in laughter and agreed, "Like that's going to make a goddamn difference."

Vern looked at the new croupier. "Spin the wheel. I'm ready to split this Popsicle stand."

Two hours later, after stopping at a package store and buying a twenty thousand dollar bottle of scotch, the two men faced each other in Solly's living room. You could hear the tinkle of the ice as the two glasses clinked together.

"To us, Vern, and your wonderful talent!"

Both men took a sip, savoring the rich liquid fire rolling into their stomachs. Neatly stacked on the coffee table, sofa, and kitchen counter were piles of thousand dollar bills. Everywhere you looked there was money. Money that already had the taxes paid on it, money that belonged to them. Vern laid his drink on the stove that had never been used. He took a step back from Solly.

"So what are you going to do with your share of the money?"

For the first time in his life, Solly was stinking rich. He looked Vern in the eye and answered honestly.

"I don't have a single idea. But I do know I can take my time and think about it."

Vern started laughing, and as his laughter turned into guffaws,

Solly tried to figure out what the joke was. At first he laughed with Vern, but then he stopped. He thought his partner was going to pass out the way he was holding his stomach from laughing so hard.

"Hey! Snap out of it, you're starting to scare me. Now what's so damn funny?"

Vern looked at him with laugh tears rolling down his face. Solly reached out to Vern. "Are you all right?"

Holmes sidestepped his touch before Solly could put his arm around him.

"Don't touch me."

He jumped back from the old man.

"What the hell's the problem? What struck your funny bone?"

Vern wiped a tear from his cheek. "That you think you have time to figure anything out!"

Solly felt the pain in the back of his head before he saw the white of Haggarty Vernon Holmes's eyes. He managed to gasp. "You said we were partners." He felt the pain recede a fraction.

"I'd be willing to give you ten percent, but this" he said, gesturing to the money around them, "is just too much to give up. How about it Solly? Would you settle for two billion dollars? A finder's fee?"

He pretended to take a moment to think about it, which gave him the chance to slide his hand into his pocket and pull the cap off the syringe filled with liquid Demerol. Though the pain was still bad and the room was spinning, Solly managed to look at Vern.

"I don't think so, Vern. You said we equal to the bitter end."

"You idiot, this is the bitter end!"

A blinding light flashed inside Solly's mind. He lunged for Holmes and the needle from the syringe caught the light from the kitchen florescent as he drove it into the old man's neck. His convulsing hand depressed the plunger sending the liquid Demerol into Vern's jugular.

Both men fell to the floor, their eyes wide and faces pressed to the carpet, locked in an embrace of death, surrounded by the twenty billion dollars, neither one of them the winner.

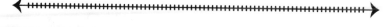

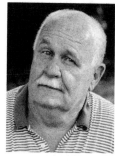

Birney Reed is a retired advertising executive and a native of Columbus Ohio. He lives on the east side of Columbus with his wife Loretta (the light of his life) and their dog Alex. Birney hopes you enjoyed his story "Finder's Fee" and the rest of this terrific anthology.

In 2009, Ohio voters approved an ammendment to the Ohio Constitution that authorized the construction of a casino in each of Ohio's four largest cities. Columbus's first (and only) casino is slated to open on October 8, 2012 at a location on the west side of the city.

OLD MAN AND FOX
Jeff Ockerse

2150
LEAVE UP OUT
By C.J. Edwards

Coming in from her post on Asteroid 746, there was no sound. No one moved. Nothing had moved in the steerage compartment of deep space transport Virgin Gates 171 for the past two weeks. Passengers in their articulated metal and nano fiber space suits were clamped motionless in stacks and rows inside the transport shuttle's steerage compartment. There was no gravity. Outside the suits there was no water, no air.

Blackout visors obscured faces on domed helmets. It was ironic that only those with the most expensive gear could travel space in the cheapest way. Inside the suits, muscles were tensed and relaxed, waste was recycled, nutrition was sipped, and videos played out on the inside of visors. All radio net conversations between passengers had stopped just four days into the journey.

Most of the passengers were asteroid miners going home to Earth or Luna. When miners got bored on the long waits in space they drank a micro-gravity-formed plant extract call glert. Glert was illegal to transport into low Earth orbit but Hanna knew a guy who rigged suits to make it undetectable. Half the passengers were sipping Hanna's stuff. Her grandpa Mike would be proud. Her dad would have thrown a fit if he was still alive and knew what she was doing. To think that she was "messing with that space junk" would have destroyed him. She sighed and turned on Ink Blob Seven, her favorite game to play when she was blitzed out.

Hanna sipped glert and grinned when the big blue blob integrated with the yellow blob and moved off screen. She took another sip of glert from her hydrator and felt the warm rush of a few more drops wash through her. The colors were so amazing. She'd be dehydrated by the time she got planet side but figured, hell, Earth has *free water*. Glert was almost worth half its weight in extra terrestrial fossils. She sighed and peed and wished she could have found a way to smuggle a few grams of

257

those to Earth. The green blob broke up into little pieces and she made the viewer swirl them with her eye movements. She'd been lost in a world of colors that seemed to work with her mind for a week while her suit took care of her.

The visor slid up, and the mag clamps released Hanna's suit from its docking bay. She turned off the suit's compression cuffs and stretched her legs. It felt so good to move that she let out a little moan of relief. The lights in the shuttle were gradually getting brighter. They were at the station. The attendant helped each passenger get oriented and got them moving down into the welcome and inspection center. Hanna was eighteenth up. It took eighty-seven minutes for the attendant to get to her. The ship's interface wouldn't let her put the visor back down and finish the Ink Blob game. She'd been warned that on Earth the computers were getting a lot more invasive. Bastards.

The attendant politely avoided eye contact. "Is your suit in working order?" he asked.

"Ship shape," said Hanna. He grunted and moved her sideways and into the port.

"Thanks for traveling Virgin Gates," said the attendant. He clamped more mag locks onto her suit and zipped her into Wall Gates low orbit Station.

There were two more attendants when she landed feet first, wearing only fabric jumpers. They got her off the platform and the taller one scanned her helmet's interface antenna.

"Just have to check your ID first," he told her. His scanner beeped, *Hanna Card.*

"Are you having any biological or suit malfunctions?" he asked.

"The computer won't let me access my games," she told him.

"Standard safety policy for new arrivals," he explained. The shorter attendant did a visual check of her air readouts on the arm of her suit. He entered numbers into his handheld and grunted.

"It looks like you're not staying with us very long, Hanna. If you'd like, there's a McDonald's at the end of gate one," he pointed to a wide hallway with a giant McDonald's logo floating in the air at its entrance. "The line for customs and boarding starts at the entrance of gate four. Welcome to Wall Gates station." He pointed her towards another hallway that was crammed with people in all different types of suits, some of them from the moon, some from the asteroid belt. One chick was wearing jeans and hanging onto the rails with her hands.

Hanna was on a tight budget. It was cheaper to land on Earth and wait for Mars to get closer to Earth than stay at the station for her five day layover. Five days wasn't much time, but on the plus side she'd get to ask him her question in person. Her Grandpa was always more likely to take something seriously the closer her physical proximity. She wondered if it would be enough time to convince him of her plan. He was a stubborn man. She sighed and took another tiny sip of glert.

Hanna got in line, and her clear visor came down automatically. It told her it would be 302 minutes until she reached the customs inspection computer. From there it would be another ten hours down to Rickenbacker Space Port.

A ball of dust and hair swirled around above the waiting line. She wasn't the only miner staring at it in fascination. High on glert, the swirling debris looked like it held the keys to the universe. Hanna giggled to herself. Miners knew how to handle long waits. There were signs all over the station warning about the penalties for smuggling. There was even a sign that had a picture of an asteroid miner taking off his helmet in the vacuum of space, his head was exploding. The poster read *Glert: is it really worth it?*

"Like anyone would do that from a few sips of the stuff," Hanna snorted. After a few more sips she wasn't nervous about customs at all. Hanna's suit told customs it was in working order, hadn't been hacked, had a valid user license, and didn't have a molecule of glert in its fluid chambers. It was a good suit.

After customs she got in another line, this one to board the Virgin Gates Balloon 801a. The line for the balloon wouldn't move till the boarding started, and there was nothing to do but wait. Hanna tried to call up Ink Blob Seven, but the station's computer just overrode her command and gave her advertisements for water parks in Columbus and a historic pizza joint called Hound Dog's.

She checked the time. It was 2200 hours at Rickenbacker. Her Grandpa would be awake. He'd always been a night bird but the call would cost almost as much as the balloon ride down. She'd have to call tomorrow from the hotel. *Eight years of work,* she thought, *eight years of scrimping and saving and pulling twenty-hour-long shifts in hard vacuum;* she wouldn't let herself waste a penny on an orbital call just because she was excited and bored.

The suit made the glert weaker every time she peed. It was almost all water now, and there were only 700 milliliters left. Hanna thought it better to save those for the trip down. She tried to sleep in her place in line, but it was too bright. Her stomach growled. Food could wait. *Real food,* she thought, a surge of excitement rippled through her, *warm and fresh and cheap!* Her mind wasn't helping her stomach calm down. She looked back up to see if there were any more dust swirls, but the vent system had picked them all up.

Hanna boarded Balloon 801a. She had her suit locked into place and playing nice with the onboard computer before the attendant came around to her. He smiled and said "you're good," and made an obscene amount of eye contact when he said it before moving on down the row.

What a jerk, she thought.

The passenger across from her sent her an IM: "What's his problem?" the woman asked. She was wearing an old cheap-o space suit that was probably from the moon. The woman was definitely not a miner.

"No idea," Hanna messaged back, and the link went dead. The woman wasn't interested in talking anymore, she was definitely some kind of Moon farmer.

The lights dimmed and the warnings and instructions came overhead and through the suit audio. The two recordings were out of sync by a second and it was migraine inducing. Hanna lowered her visor and went back to Ink Blob Seven, but it wasn't nearly as fun as it'd been the last few days. *Only 200 miles to Earth!* The thought made her have to pee some more. The computer announced the balloon had disengaged and they had begun the descent to Rickenbacker. It was a long ride down.

At 500 hours the lights came on, and the announcement went out that they would be landing soon. It was another three hours until she was standing in line at customs. Earth's gravity sucked the energy from her atrophied muscles. The suit assisted with her movements, but the weight of her own body was something she hadn't felt in eight years despite her extensive workouts on the asteroid. Her suit passed the port's computer check.

A security officer came up to her and said, "Lift your visors." She did, and the air hit her in the face. It was full of mold and pollen and food and fabric. It was the best and worst thing she'd smelled in eight years. The officer looked down at his handheld device, "Okay, your picture's accepted," he told her. "Welcome to Rickenbacker Space Port, please move out for our next guests." He did a practiced flourish and pointed her towards the exit.

Hanna walked out of customs and dry heaved. It was the first time she'd taken more then three steps in a row since she'd landed. It was the first time she'd taken three steps in a row in normal gravity in eight years. She felt sick. She stumbled to a mag clamp along the wall and locked into it so she could get her bearings right. She wasn't the only one in a good suit that needed a little time to get used to being planet-side.

She caught her orientation and unlocked. A moving floor took her down the terminal to the front doors. The air got more humid the closer she got to outside. She went past a window and whipped her head around to look. It was so bright and beautiful! Shuttles sat on the ground on the other side of the glass and in the distance was a blur of green. Plants! Trees! She wondered if she could still climb a tree without her suit. Probably not. But this would be her last trip to Earth unless she got rich. For that she'd need her grandpa's knowledge of plants. She hoped he was still holding together well enough to agree to the regeneration treatment.

Outside smelled even stronger than in Rickenbacker. There were cabs lined up—little solar-powered shuttles that ran on wheels on the ground. She got in one at random. "How much to take me to the Motel Eight?" she asked.

He said "I give special to miners, only 400 dollars. I won't even turn on the meter." He was trying to rip her off. Hanna opened the door to get out.

"Wait! You mean the one close by? I'll turn on the meter, low rates! Probably only 120," the stinking cabbie pleaded with her. He turned on the meter.

She shut the door. "Fine, whatever," Hanna said. He pulled out onto the road. There was so much to see, buildings, sky, trees, cars, people out walking dogs and foxes. Her neck got sore from trying to take it all in at once as they sped down the road.

At the Motel Eight, Hanna checked in through the security window. The clerk asked her if she wanted any prostitutes or pot. She paid for the room and told the woman "No, thanks," on the rest of the amenities. She gave Hanna a key card and told her to sleep tight.

The room had a bed and a chair and came with a tap that dispensed free water! Even the toilet used free water. There was a water shower to clean her body with. She wondered if she could stand and wash without the suit helping her in the high gravity so she could feel the water on her skin.

There was a huge window in the wall of her room that looked out on the parking lot. And just across the street there was a field of trees and grass! *Earth would be paradise if it wasn't for the laws and grav-*

ity, she thought. After half an hour staring out the window Hanna had a nutrient slurry and took a nap in her suit in the corner of the room. At night she'd call her grandpa.

* * *

The phone rang. It rang again. A woman answered. "Anheuser Busch Home for the Excessively Aged?" said the voice on the other end of the line.

"Can I speak to Mike Card please?" Hanna asked.

There was a pause and some typing. "I'm sorry ma'am, that patient's asked not to receive any calls."

"What? Since when? Is he okay?" Hanna inquired.

"It looks like the request is nine years old in the computer," the woman told her.

"I'm his granddaughter. I just got back to Earth. I'll only be here a week, can't you make an exception?"

"I'm sorry, ma'am, there are no exceptions. Family is welcome to visit if you'd like to see your grandpa in person."

"Well can you tell him I'm here, on Earth?" Hanna pleaded.

"I can't deliver messages." Now the woman sounded like she was enjoying herself.

"Thanks, you've been a *big* help!" Hanna disconnected.

* * *

Hanna looked out the cab window as it passed over the Morse-Bethel bridge, a shimmering sea of homes and apartments spread out on either side, interspersed with trees and grass. Being in her home town again brought a mist to her eyes. The cab went downhill towards the Scioto River. It pulled up in front of a converted McMansion with sponsoring all over the front, NASCAR, Busch, Wall Gates Galactic. She asked the cabbie to stay for half an hour and credited him a thirty percent tip. He said A-OK and then took off. *When did small town Columbus get big town rude,* she wondered.

Inside an older woman with her boobs resting on the counter greeted Hanna with a terse smile and told her to sign in. She opened the living quarter doors and led Hanna through a maze of tables and old people. The only old people anymore were the ones who were too poor or too stubborn to get regenerated. Standard care facilities like this one mostly housed the ones that had just given up and wanted to die. A group of geezers were sitting around a table that was making beeping noises. They played an ancient game on the table's monitor with hand held controllers.

"That was my energy pack!" Shouted an old woman with nothing but frizz for hair.

"I got it first, it was mine, you noob," one of the old men taunted her. She gave him the finger and then realized she'd taken her hands away from the controller. Something on the screen blew up and she tossed the controller onto the table with a frown. The other geezers laughed.

The front desk woman took her to a withered old man sitting alone looking out the back window. Birds danced and ate from a cylindrical feeder in a yard of grass and shrubs.

"Grandpa? Grandpa Mike?" Hanna asked.

"Who?" said the old man.

"It's me," she lifted her visors. "Hanna!"

"Hanna's in space," he told her.

"No, Grandpa! I'm right here!" She sat down next to him. "I came to get you regenerated! We're finally going to Mars! To be farmers!"

"I grew many plants," the old man said without looking at her. He just stared out the window. "Lots and lots of plants."

"Hanna?" he turned to her. "You shouldn't be here. Where's your father?"

"Dad died back in forty-one," she told him. "He had malignant carcinoma. He couldn't afford the treatment," she was getting choked up. Hanna had always wanted to do right by her dad. He died while she was still working on paying off her suit.

"He could have asked; he was too proud!" The old man's eyes were glistening bright blue beneath his wrinkled brows.

"I've missed you," she told him.

"I've been fine, I take care of myself," he waved a gnarled hand at her. "Where are you going next, girl? Always were into something that young Hanna was."

Hanna wasn't sure if he really understood who she was or not.

"I finally have enough, Grandpa," she tried to explain, "I've got enough to get you regenerated, and if we work in the asteroid mines for just four more years together we'll have enough to buy our own place on Mars."

"Mars?" asked the old man, he was back to staring out the window. "What in God's name is on Mars? Dust! Rocks! Not shit!"

"We can have a farm." Hanna leaned in close, "I've been making glert," she whispered. "I know all the security work-arounds. We can do it together."

"Hmm, well it's not pot. In my day we fought for pot! Some got caught! Some not! I took care of myself for a good long time you know," he said. "Now it's legal in every corner of the world. You ever smoke the silly weed on Mars, Hanna?"

She told him no.

"Well that's a damn shame," he laughed. "I've never tried any of that glert stuff the kids are all into now." He waved a gnarled hand at her and went back to watching the birds.

"Glert will be legal—" she noticed an old black man staring at them with wide eyes from across the lounge. Hanna leaned in closer. "It'll be legal in just a few more years. We'll be set up by then. I have the connections now."

"It's a long road," said her grandpa. "Maybe you should come back in a week? Or a month? Or whenever they run out of games here."

"Grandpa, I'm giving you a chance to be regenerated!"

"What if I don't want to get youthanized or younganized or whatever you kids call it?" he asked.

"Then I'll move on to Mars without you, and you'll die and I won't have any family left," she pleaded.

"Well there is that!" he piped up without looking from the window.

"Please? Grandpa? I don't have anyone."

"Maybe you should go back to the space port," he told her. "You never know who you might meet."

"Grandpa, I'm giving you a second chance at life. Don't you want to be young again?"

"Maybe you should go home, dumb bitch!" he giggled. "Your daddy's going to be looking for you. God knows he can't hold down a job …" He always called her dumb bitch when she was little. Her dad told her it used to be an insult a long time ago, but that it just meant she was pretty. He muttered off and hung his head down like he was sleeping.

So that's it, Hannah thought. *Go home, back to space where I belong.*

Hanna patted her grandpa's hand and stood up. He was too far gone to make the decision for himself. She'd call his doctor in the morning.

"I can grow any plant anywhere anytime," he muttered to no one in particular, "bring it on bitches ..."

Hanna checked out at the front desk and had them call her a cab back to her motel by the space port. It took thirty one minutes for the cab to get there. She told the driver to step on it. He said "okay" but only went the speed limit the whole way. She gave a ten percent tip and he looked at her like she was a cheat.

Back in her room she tried to take off her suit. Under the suit, her right arm was pale and weak and stringy looking. It made her tired just flexing her arm muscles. She'd have to forgo the glory of the shower for now. *What a waste of a trip to Earth,* she thought. She laid down on the bed and tried to get some sleep. Her blood pooled at her back and she couldn't fall asleep. At least there was all the free water she could drink and fill her suit with. On an asteroid water costs almost half your pay. Here they just spray it around for fun. *What a bizarre world,* she thought.

The next morning, Hanna took a walk to the empty field across from the motel. It was more of an abandoned lot really, but there were trees along the edges, and it was enough for life to get a toe hold on a planet that specialized in life. Working with the muscle assist servos in her suit exhausted her. The trees and grass smelled like she remembered them from her old home in Forest Park. She even saw a few squirrels running around. After touring the field she went back and took a rest.

On the third day of her stay, she took the suit off and took the first shower she'd had in eight years. It felt like she'd died and drank a gallon of glert, even if she was cramping and exhausted by the time she got the suit back on. It was worth it.

Other people came and went from the rooms around her. Most of them wearing fabrics like they'd never been in space. There was another miner who was four doors down. They sat out on the porch in their suits and messaged each other. "You on layover too?" he asked her. His voice sounded strange over the link.

Hanna responded, "Yeah, waiting for the cheap flight to Mars."

"Me too, finally got my grubstake. Only took twenty years," he stretched out his legs in the chair.

"Where you from?" Hanna asked him.

"Asteroid 312, originally from Sydney." Sydney? That explained the accent.

"What did you on 312?" Hanna asked. Her visor told her the suit was getting too hot and would start cooling itself off.

"Iron and ice," he said. "Nothing but iron and ice. Sure is a nice day."

"Yeah that it is." She cut off the conversation link and watched the birds land on the power lines and the branches of the trees across the street. Hanna loved animals. Most of all the ones that moved like they were navigating space, fish, birds, spiders, the tough animals, the ones that dealt with the world like it was the galaxy, like miners.

She fell asleep on the front porch. Her suit woke her up after twenty minutes and took her inside. She thought of her grandpa and wondered if she should get a court order to have him regenerated. There was no chance he'd help her work to buy Martian land if she did that, though. Hell, he'd probably be so resentful he'd sue her. She needed family. Her dad was gone. Her mom had never been around. All she had left was him, and he seemed more interested in watching those damn birds then trying to make a new life.

The trip was a waste. In the most primitive cultures on Earth and in the farthest reaches of space the worst of all insults was the same: wasteful, a barb that meant stupid and not thinking of the future, it could be deadly to a lot of people. Hanna was wasteful. Bastards.

Hanna tried to relax in the motel pool under the sun. She could feel the radiation sinking into her skin, turning it dark. It had been sixteen years since she'd last floated at the top of the water under the sun. One mining tour to earn her enough for suit ownership while she learned the trade, another eight years to earn her grubstake on Mars. And that was twice as fast as the norm. Her understanding of the manufacture of glert helped speed that process along. She took a deep breath and let the water cover her face in the pool. Free water! Enough to float in! For a second she considered staying on Earth. But just for a moment. She'd have to start all over again.

Maybe she could stay and be a cabbie or something, see her grandpa off to the next world in peace and dignity. Was it worth it to start all over again? Hanna knew the asteroid belt, knew glert, knew space. There were bugs floating in the pool, and she didn't know if they were poisonous or not. She dog paddled over to the edge of the pool and heaved herself out.

Back in her suit she ordered the oxygen up by three while she lay on the concrete under the sun. Hanna took every chance she got to exercise to the max. If for no other reason than for the day she couldn't rely on her suit to do the work for her. She still wanted to climb a tree. They were on the other side of the street, though, and too tall for her.

I'll have to call up a vid of tree climbing later, she thought.

I miss Dad, Hanna thought. *He'd know what to do. I could get a court order to have Grandpa made young again, but it'll probably take a month. I can only afford five more days on the planet if I want to get a plot on Mars.* Hanna's mind raced while her body recovered from the swim on the side of the pool. Mother and child jumped in and splashed her. A wasp buzzed around her visor. After an hour Hanna got up and went back into her room.

The little kid pointed and told its mother to "look at the funny robot!" And that's all she felt like. A funny, out of place robot. No family, no friends left, no home unless you wanted to call asteroid 746 a home. And even that was gone now, trying to get to Mars and settle down. Wasteful!

On day five of her Earth stay Hanna went back to the Anheuser Busch Home For The Extremely Aged and the same dour-faced nurse checked her in. The same group of old geezers were sitting at the tables, this time talking about some video game that had blown all their minds back in the 2070s. Her Grandpa was sitting in the same place by the window. He still had the same smell.

"Hanna!" He lit up when she sat down next to him. "What are you doing back again?" he asked.

"I want you to come to Mars with me," she told him. "We'll have to work in the asteroid mines for a few years after I pay for your regeneration, but we'll get there. We'll get to Mars and make ..." She leaned in and whispered, "We'll make glert on Mars. You can grow the raw plants and I'll get it to the buyers in hacked suits."

"Mining?" Asked her Grandpa. "No, I'm too old for mining."

"Grandpa! I'm offering you a chance at another life! Youth! We can afford it now! Just say you'll come with me!" she pleaded.

He looked at her with deep blue eyes that didn't seem to understand a thing she was saying. "You should go to Mars," he said. "Young lady like you could probably do well for herself," he nodded and twisted his cane around and looked out the window. "I did well for myself when I was your age. Grew lots of weed ..." his voice trailed off, "lots of weeds."

"I don't want to go alone," she told him. "I don't want to be alone anymore."

"Mars is where I'd go if I was young again," he told her. "Too bad you can't afford it. Earth and Mars will be right up next to each other soon. Shame you can't go, it's real cheap then I hear."

"Grandpa do you want them to make you young again?" she asked him.

"I take care of myself, dumb bitch," he said. "Better if you go on."

Hanna didn't know how much of the conversation her grandpa was actually lucid for. There would be no way to get a court order in the next few days. Her trip to Earth was a waste. Waste waste waste! Dammit! There was nothing else she could do. "Goodbye, Grandpa," she told him. "Goodbye."

"Your father always was a dick!" her Grandpa yelled as she walked back to the nurses station. "He never wanted to get into the family trade! Tirade! Popsicle parade! Boom bitches!"

Hanna checked out and called a cab. She waited on a bench outside and wept under her visor. For once she had money but no home. At least she wouldn't have to spend another eight years mining for the Martian plot. But the thought just made her sob harder.

At the Rickenbacker space port she waited in line to board the plane up to low orbit. Four other passengers tried starting conversations with her through the helmet IM. She shot them all down. It was just half a day up to the Wall Gates low orbit station, and from there it would be an entirely new set of names on her visor till she reached the green planet they called Mars. Screw the other passengers. Hanna didn't need anybody. She had Ink Blob Eight. But Rickenbacker's computer wouldn't let her play Ink Blob Eight. It just gave her advertisements. "Eat at historic Hound Dog's! Come see our new ultra sonic wave pool at Wendy's Bay! Buy municipal bonds from low orbit, invest in Columbus!" the ads spewed. She listened because there was nothing else to listen to. The line through customs inched along.

Hanna's suit played nice with the security computers and she was ushered to the lift where people with their own suits were sent up and locked into steerage. The lights dimmed. The shuttle took off. She left every trace of family behind and sipped at what was left of the watered down glert in her suit. It wasn't enough to make her feel any better.

At Wall Gates station she went through another round of standing in line followed by security and safety checks of her suit. The attendant at the zip gate told her "It looks like you've been upgraded to first class, I'll call someone to escort you to your room."

"First class?" she asked.

He looked her up and down. "That's what the computer says."

Hanna wasn't about to argue.

An attendant wearing advertisement patches all over his jumper came out and took her to a private room with a private bath all to herself, just like on Earth. Her room on the shuttle was almost as big as it was on Earth! And it had more free water! She had to remind herself it wouldn't always be this good.

After three days to rest Hanna wandered out to the common area with her visors up. It was a bad habit she'd picked up on Earth but it felt good to just see the world as it was without any enhancement or correction or advertisements flashing at her.

She sat at the promenade and watched the crew take care of the passengers in mag locks down in steerage. And she watched the stars and thought of birds and spiders and her grandpa.

On the sixth day, she saw a young man siting on the promenade with a woman in her twenties. *Oh it's got to be a couple of re-gens,* she thought to herself, *nobody that young is rich enough to go first class.* After a few minutes, they noticed her and the man walked over. He sat down next to her and started talking.

Hanna lifted her visor. "Excuse me?"

"I was saying that a dumb bitch like yourself shouldn't be up here all alone." He had bright blue eyes just like her grandpa.

"I'm fine," Hanna said.

"Hanna? Are you Hanna Card?" he asked.

"I am. Who wants to know?"

He smiled. "I was hoping to meet up with my granddaughter. She's about your age, the first time around."

"Sorry I'm new on the ship," was all she could think to say. Was she supposed to know every blessed person her own age on the ship? *Typical re-gen,* she thought.

"Me too," he said. "So how far up do we have to go before I can get a beaker of glert on this bitch?" asked the strange young man.

"Uhm? I'm sorry?"

"It's me, you dumb bitch!" the re-gen shouted. "I sold my stock in Dankbudz and got re-young-anized!"

"Excuse me?" asked Hanna.

"I figured it'd be better if we went up together, and you didn't have to spend your money on my medical treatment," said the deep blue-eyed young man.

"But I thought all you wanted to do was look out the window?" she asked him. "Are you the one that got my flight class moved up? What? How?"

"Well girl, I've been waiting for an opportunity to do what I do

best. No point in going back if you're not going back strong! That's
what I say!" he told her. "Plants is what I do, on any damn planet."

"Grandpa? But I thought you lost your money in the silicone dip?"
Hanna asked.

"Well things happen, that's life," he told her. "Hey when's the
gambling start? I got money to launder! Get over here, Betty!" He
shouted at the woman down the aisle. "You didn't notice her in the old
folks home, now did you?"

Hanna shook her head no.

"Well see—you have to pay more attention to what's going on,"
said her grandpa. "I couldn't let you spend your own money on me like
that. And you couldn't spare your attention on this bombshell because
she had a few wrinkles! Meet your new grandma—Hanna, this is Nata-
lie."

The woman waved, her smile was genuine. "Your grandpa is always talking about you, he always hoped you'd follow in his footsteps,"
she wiped a tear from her eye. "He's so proud of you."

"But I don't grow *weed*," Hanna told them.

"It's not what you grow," her grandpa chimed in. "It's just that
you're breaking the law and sticking it to the man!"

"So you really want to work together?" she asked him. "Seriously?"

"Can't have a family business without family," he told her.

Hanna hugged her regenerated grandpa. For the first time in nine
years she'd have family again. The courtesy lights went on, and the ship
announced that dinner would be served soon.

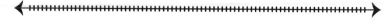

C. J. Edwards is a long-time Columbus local. He is currently putting the finishing touches on his novel *Sex, Drugs And Violence: A Suburban High School Guide*. He lives with his wife, geriatric dog Buddy and their army of spider minions. In his spare time he plays the didgeridoo. Learn more about him at www.writersplatform.net.

Lockbourne Air Force Base was renamed Rickenbacker Air Force Base in May of 1974 to honor WWI pilot Eddie Rickenbacker, a Columbus native. In 2006 negotiations were held with Planet Space to build a space port at Rickenbacker.

Hep's Bonanza
Dorian Lafferre

2187

HEP'S BONANZA

By S. Michael Nash

The dream had been nice, but the awakening was better. Suddenly, Hep's whole body was being playfully tickled with warm feathers. It was a very gentle thing, so soft it was barely noticeable at first, then ramping up in intensity until he was very aware of it. His consciousness rose, pressing into the membrane of wakefulness until he burst back into reality.

Well, augmented reality at least. Rita was here, and she wasn't real in the physical sense. Unspoken, the word "time" formed in his thoughts, was picked up by his neuro-implants and whisked wirelessly off to his personal part of the cloud. The answer came back almost before he had fully formed the thought. 11:21 a.m.

"Rita!" he said aloud. "It's not even the crack of noon! Why are you waking me?"

Rita floated across the edges of his sensorium, a yellow blur. She was wearing his favorite outfit: the old time Vegas showgirl—featuring equal portions of flesh and feathers.

"Wakie wakie," she crooned.

"It's not funny, I'm hungover. Let me sleep."

"You're not hungover. I made you take a pill before bed."

Muddled thoughts tumbled over in his brain. *Mornings. We can send a probe to Proxima, but we can't do anything about mornings.* Another sub-vocal signal to the net and there was a soft gurgling sound from behind the headboard.

"Well," he grumbled, "it was less than seven hours ago; who could live on this little sleep?"

"You can. Get up, this is important."

Sheets of a man-made fiber that was like a cross between silk and Egyptian cotton glided off his torso to pool around his waist.

"Hubba, Hubba," Rita said, in her best Mae West, "You rationed, sugar?"

The bulk of Hep's Prestige came from his study of history, especially American history of the First Atomic War era. As such, his personal artificial intelligence was programed for all the vintage slang of the time.

"Save it. What's on fire?" The headboard finished its gurgling and a panel opened, revealing a steaming cup of Jamaican Blue Mountain coffee.

"Columbus."

"The city or the Indian killer?"

"The city. It's just smoking with potential Prestige, and at this moment I'm the only one who knows."

"Columbus," Hep muttered, sipping at the coffee and trying to organize his sleepy thoughts. He had just been there yesterday. Had to sprinkle some nano-dissemblers on the site of some old building ...

"I'm going to need a re-download."

Rita slipped from one mode to another so smoothly Hep didn't notice. The face and body were the same, but the feathers were gone, replaced by a more drab outfit, along with black glasses perched on a pug nose. Gone was the showgirl; in her place was the "hot librarian."

"The old Convention Center. Remember. It was a big controversy back in the 1970s. A historically important train station was demolished to build it."

"Right!" Now Hep was coming to life. Nothing earned kudos like dredging up an old controversy. "And now somebody wants to build something else at the site. You spotted it as a place with potential and managed to obtain it a long time ago."

Rita bowed exuberantly. "That's my racket."

"I'm guessing it panned out?"

"Maybe a little ... and maybe in spades. Not sure which yet. The dissemblers stopped about ten minutes ago. They found something they wanted me to look at before they tear it to atoms. I looked. Now I want you to look."

"What is it?"

"Nothing too shaking. Just a body."

A fine shower of coffee sprayed from his lips. It pooled and ran along the nonabsorbent sheets as tiny robots emerged from the woodwork to clean the mess.

"Just a body? Murdered I hope?"

"Well, suspicious, let's just say that."

"Talk to me, darlin'."

Rita smiled. Perfect dimples in perfect cheeks.

"It's got some tissue still on it, but its mostly skeletal. No obvious signs of trauma, other than being crushed under a building for two centuries.

"So who is this, Jimmy Hoffa?"

"Ah, and here the plot thickens. I had the dissemblers take a DNA sample and compare it to the library of public domain genomes. Got a perfect hit. Our dirt napper is one Raymond Grey, originally from Moxahala, Ohio. Born 1924 and died in 2004."

"2004? Those dates don't line up. How could he have been buried under the Convention Center in 1978 if he didn't die until 2004?"

"How indeed. Because he did, for sure, die in 2004. He was a rich man, and had lots of public appearances in the 80s and 90s. In fact, the library of public domain genomes actually got his DNA out of his grave, which, by the by, is in New Lexington. Not too far from his birth place."

"Then who is buried under the Convention Center?"

"According to the DNA, it's Raymond Grey. No one else in the database with that genome."

"A clone?"

"In the 1970s? You might as well suggest it was a time traveler."

"So, the mystery is how do we get Grey's body from its grave into sterile soil that hasn't been touched since twenty-five odd years before his death?"

"No. I checked. Raymond is still comfortably ensconced in his grave in New Lex. The mystery is how did the body of *Kenneth Grey*, not Raymond, get under the Convention Center when it is supposed to be lost in Central America?"

Hep took another slow drink of the coffee.

"Beloved Rita, I get the impression there is data you have not yet shared."

"You got that one, Petal. Cloning didn't come into vogue until the mid 2030s, but nature has been doing it since … well, since you all were no more than bugs in the water. It's called twinning, and Raymond and Kenneth were two such peas in a pod."

"And Kenneth's DNA is not in the library because … why?"

"Most likely just an oversight. There was the second atomic war in 2061. That was a mess, and a lot of threads got dropped. Many of them never got picked up again."

Hep got out of bed and walked to the sink. Rita watched his backside appreciatively as he rinsed the sleep from his eyes.

"Okay, I'm already losing interest. Twins are the oldest red herring in the history of mystery. I don't think this is worth much."

"Well, you should get your interest back, because Raymond and Kenneth hated each other, and were on opposite sides of nearly every debate—including the one about the Convention Center."

Hep dried his face as he looked at Rita in the mirror. No small technical feat since she only existed in his head. A lot of trigonometry was done to put that reflection into the mirror in a believable manner.

"Okay, interest is slowly rising."

"It gets better. Raymond was pro Convention Center, Kenneth was anti. And Kenneth ran off to Central America about a week before the place was built—never to return."

"You think his brother killed him?"

"Don't know. But if I had to put a bet on it …"

"Yeah. Me too. How long will it take to get to Columbus?"

"Depends on how you want to go."

"By sub-orbital."

"Whoa there cowboy! Where's the fever? The situation is stable. Nobody is onto it yet, but if you go booking an expensive rocket for a two minute flight, that is going to draw a lot of flies."

"Train?"

"That is much more subtle. Everyone knows you were there yesterday. Going back to eyeball the work won't send up too many flares."

"Okay. Book the train."

She clapped her hands in delight. "Crackers!"

* * *

Brown teeth in a flattened brown skull grinned up at Hep. The bones were crumbly, but there was a surprising amount of tissue still attached, even some clumps of hair.

"Not much of a looker," Hep observed.

"Yeah, well, he's lost weight. Been a rough couple of centuries."

Rita was now dressed as a 1920s flapper. Her soft looking palms were up before her, moving back and forth. She was dancing the Charleston to music only she could hear. Hep grinned at her. She was bored. The down side of having an IQ of about ten thousand is you get bored fast.

"Okay, paint me the picture."

The nano-dissemblers had been working on the physical remains of the Convention Center for almost a day before Rita stopped them. What was left didn't look so much shattered as melted. They destroyed on an atomic level, pulling the place apart atom by atom, marching those individual atoms across to an empty spot then reassembling them in a conveniently shipped form: a stack of one ton blocks of iron, smaller blocks of glass, and a block of clear material: diamond, all the stray carbon pulled out of various sources. It was all nearly worthless, of course. The "industrial" economy had collapsed long ago, but people still needed building material. He might get a few favors for it, and somebody would admire him for being able to supply it.

And admiration was worth a lot.

Rita fed images into Hep's brain, placing things in his sensorium that don't exist—like herself. Suddenly, he found himself standing on the edge of a muddy rail yard. He gasped despite himself.

Rita, suddenly sporting a trim blue uniform dress and a hat with the words: "Tour Guide" across the brim, spoke into a palm mic whose flex-wire trailed off into nowhere. The voice was tinny and crackly.

"Pedestrians would usually enter Union Station from High Street through an amazing neoclassical facade featuring Corinthian columns and high, Roman-style arches. They would then proceed down the covered walkway to the main station that housed the ticket offices, waiting room, and even a swanky restaurant at one point. Access to the platforms was via covered bridge that spanned the tracks with stairs leading down to each landing.

"We are looking at it at its height, circa 1900. Of course, something this beautiful has to be degraded by pencil pushers. Part of the arcade was demolished in the 20s to give better access to automobiles, and see that view of the tracks from the walkway? Can't have that. They built a brick wall along the path for no reason I can see. I guess they didn't want you to know there would be trains at a train station. But, despite the depredations, it was put on the National Register of Historic Places in 1974."

"I didn't want to be impressed, but I am. This is beautiful. And this body is in its correct position in relation to all this?"

"Yes."

"Just right here in the middle of everything?"

"Yes, but you don't have the right picture. All this had been demolished."

Suddenly it was all gone. The chain link fence did nothing to block the February wind as it sliced across the rubble strewn construction lot. Here, beside a large pile of shattered bricks, a two-foot hole had been dug. The body—the real body—was visible at the bottom as if he were seeing a cut away diagram.

"It wasn't aimed at long-term hiding; the murderer just wanted to conceal it from the construction workers," Rita continued. "After they laid down the foundation, one big slab of concrete, that body was effectively gone."

"Until you found it."

"Well, the nano-dissemblers were on auto-pilot when they found it, but I'll take credit if you want to grant it. I'm easy that way." She paused to give him a coquettish wink. "I'm easy most ways, honeybun."

"Yeah. Moving along. You say Kenneth was opposed to the Convention Center?"

"Well, I don't think he cared about the Convention Center. What he was against was destroying the station. He founded a group called CFHP." She paused a few seconds to try to say that in the form of a word. The closest she got was a coughing sound something like: Keffhup. "The boy needed to hire a writer, 'cuz that makes the worst acronym in the history of bad writing."

"And it stands for?" Hep said patiently.

"Citizens for Historical Preservation. Ugh, that's only a little better than the acronym. No sex appeal, you know?"

"I know. And his brother Raymond was pro Convention Center."

"More than just pro. There were two foundations that were trying to get the thing built. One was a consortium of mostly real estate developers who were called Progress Columbus. You know, that would make a lousy acronym too."

Hep didn't say anything but spun his finger in the air: moving along, moving along.

"Right. Well, they should have called it 'Progress Their Wallets,' because that's all they were about. There were millions riding on this deal, and once the Convention Center was built they lost any interest in further 'progress.' Anyway, if Kenneth's organization was successful in stopping the project, Raymond would be out millions. And that, I believe, is motive."

Hep was squatting before the remains.

"He looks pretty squashed. Any way of telling what killed him?"

"Actually, he looks pretty good for a guy that's had a building sitting on his chest for two hundred years. But most of the obvious stuff is compression breaks. Nothing stands out as the death blow."

"What is the next step?"

"Well, that's tricky. Up to now I've been able to keep it all in the family. But to do more, I need to send some samples out. Risky. Don't want anyone stealing our kudos out from under us."

"No. But there won't be any kudos if we can't solve this. Do it. Be discreet, but do it."

"It's done, daddy-o."

* * *

Hate.

Historically, people have considered hate a bad thing. Not anymore. Hate is a human thing, and since nothing else has any value, human things are priceless. Adonis Winthrop nursed his hate—and he was mature enough to admit—envy, for Hep Shadowswift. It had been a good ride for him so far, being the guy that hated Hep. Notoriety is just fame by another name. People were interested in Hep, and human interest was of value. Hating Hep Shadowswift had become a full-time job with good pay. He had one of his three AI's, Vidar, dedicated full-time to doing nothing but watching Hep, tracing his actions, documenting his every move, and trying to figure out what he might be into at any possible moment.

"They're up to something, I can feel it," Adonis said, staring at the floating flatscreen in his sensorium.

"They are definitely hiding something. I can tell Rita is editing something out of the sensoria of all passersby. They see with their eyes, but it doesn't register in their brains," Vidar answered. He was a giant, Nordic looking man. He wore fur, armor plates and a horned, bronze helmet. In his hand was an iron-headed spear longer than he was tall. The spear shouldn't have fit in the room the way he was holding it, but that wasn't a problem. Being the avatar of the AI Vidar, he existed only in Adonis's mind, and perception was infinitely accommodating.

"What is it?"

"How would I know? It's edited out." Sometimes Vidar wondered about the intelligence of his employer.

"Do we have to use this robot? I hate leaving physical traces of myself behind."

"It's unavoidable. She can edit digital camera footage even easier than she can hack human brains. We can't use any public cameras. The only way to get in close is to put a device there that is connected directly to us, not using the public nets."

Adonis was watching through the eyes of a tiny metal bug that was crawling through the half melted mess that was once the Greater Columbus Convention Center. It was slow moving and tiny. One of a million other like creatures in the area. The only oddity was the concavity in its back. That dimple was like a traditional radio dish; it reflected a signal up to a single point that was occupied by a tiny bulb suspended on a swiveling needle much thinner than a human hair. That was the bug's lifeline. A direct link to the network of sats 22,236 miles overhead in geostationary orbit. Nobody "owned" those sats, but nobody controlled them either. Both Adonis and Vidar were fairly sure they were hack-proof. Unless somebody saw the bug itself, how could anyone even know what these signals were?

"Ahh," Vidar said breathily.

"What? What, what?"

"Rita just lifted her skirts a little. She sent a physical package off to a nearby lab. She had to know I could see that."

"Then why would she do it?"

"She's gotta do what she's gotta do. If she doesn't have the resources for something in-system, she has to send out."

"Can you intercept it?"

"Are you serious? This is Rita. I'm not even going to try."

"So how does it help us?"

"Because she has lost total information control. Rita and the systems under her command are inviolate, but the systems of the lab are hackable."

"Well, do it!"

"Working on it."

Moments passed in silence.

"I'm in the lab. They are receiving the package right now. And ..."

Vidar's eyes went wide, but he was looking at nothing in particular. Adonis, knowing something was up, looked back to the floating screen.

Directly in front of the bug were a pair of feet in low heeled Mary Janes. With a wave of his finger, the view rose up stalkinged calves, past a knee length skirt, a bare shouldered blouse and finally centered on a cloche capped head. Rita smiled into the bug's cameras.

"What's knittin', kittens?" she said, then the whole scene burst into digital static.

"Damn!" Adonis cried. "Vidar, are you okay?"

"I'm under an all-out attack. Viruses, trojans, port assaults … I think she took down the whole necklace. Can she get away with that?"

Adonis scowled at the empty space the screen had once occupied. Vidar was too busy to maintain it. In fact, the helmeted god avatar was gone, too, as he threw all his processing power into fending off Rita's attack.

"They can get away with anything! Hep always pulls it out in the end and winds up more popular than ever. If you can kill that bitch, do it!"

"Kill her?" Came the disembodied voice. "I'll be lucky if I only come out of this lobotomized."

* * *

Hep was suddenly aware that Rita had stopped dancing and her song was now a whispered: "Shoo fly, don't bother me …"

"What is it?"

"We are compromised," she answered.

"Who?"

"Who else?"

"Damn. What did he get?"

"Don't know. Can't be much. I've taken over the lab network. That's going to cost us, but I don't know how else to contain it."

"Not to worry, hon. We can cover it."

"I took out the necklace too," she added, referring to the public domain satellites in geostationary orbit.

He flinched.

"Just over the Americas?"

"Over the whole planet."

"Damn," he said again. That's embarrassing. And embarrassment is the opposite of prestige—negative kudos. It's like depositing a negative amount in your account. Hep had a lot of kudos, but this was going to be expensive.

"Any chance you hid who did this?"

She gave him a withering glare. There's no Prestige in simply hacking. You have to hack *with style!* She probably put her image in front of every camera involved.

The change in economy came slowly at first, with early signs of its coming as far back as the late 1800s. The Industrial Revolution was the dawn of the automation revolution. By the mid-2000s, everything was automated. The unemployment rate was 100 percent. Labor was gone, and since nobody had any income, product went unpurchased. A depression the likes of which was never seen before was on the world. We were drowning in automated luxury that we couldn't afford.

But it was noted, one profession, that one often considered the oldest, was alive and well. And sex wasn't the only thing of worth. A wide variety of "popular commodities" became valuable. The price of art skyrocketed. One song was worth more than a ton of gold. A single painting in one's home could draw an endless crowd of people who came for nothing more than to see it—and they'd usually leave something for the proud owner.

Could it be that simple beauty was a thing of real value? People wouldn't (couldn't) pay for a gadget, but they would barter anything just to bask in the presence of beauty, even if for a limited time.

Thus the concept of "social capital" came to economists' minds. Goods and services could be purchased with less tangible things, like charm, beauty, wit, humor, art, fame, and most importantly, prestige. Being pleasant or interesting company, for any reason whatsoever was something people still valued. And being the only thing left they valued, it became the only commodity in the game. All that remained to be done was quantify it. Hence the kudo, the new, worldwide currency.

"If we could solve this mystery, think how many would love to hear the tale?" Hep muttered aloud.

"If you told it right it could be worth mega-kudos," Rita observed distantly. She was still struggling with Vidar. He was good. She was better, but he was good. Rita had net spiders crawling the world, looking for any unguarded ports into that system, but she wasn't finding any. To blind the bug she had to stop the signal, and that meant shutting down the necklace. That did it, but now everyone in the world was inconvenienced, including her. All traffic was now mostly landline. Rita sent out packets that spread along these lines like tentacles, branching at every junction until the tiniest of fingers were reaching into the firewalls of a billion computers, all feeling for an opening, a way in. Sooner or later she would attach to something that would attach to something that would attach to Vidar. And when she did ... may the quantum gods help him.

"When you get a moment, retrieve the lab results. I want to know what killed Kenneth."

"Will do."

To watch, you wouldn't know there was an epic struggle going on. She was just standing still, smiling upward at the darkening sky. But Hep knew the signs. The Rita avatar usually had an abundance of bored energy. If she was standing still, it must really be on. Minutes passed.

"Results are in … ah, we're jimmied."

"What happened?"

"He left a virus in the lab system. Pretty subtle. It copied the packets as I was sending them to myself. He got a copy, too."

Hep bit down on the curse. *It's not her fault, not her fault.*

"Okay, what were the results?"

"Sodium concentrations were way off in the muscle tissues. This would have lowered the heart rate and stroke strength to a fatal degree."

"Meaning?"

"Poison. Probably digitoxin. Digitalis was a readily available anti-arrhythmic at the time. Fairly easy to obtain and administer. This sure looks like murder, Hep."

Hep felt dirty for thinking that was good news, but this man was already dead.

"His brother?"

"No way to tell at this point, but a rich man like that could easily obtain the drug."

"Wouldn't it show up in tox screens?"

"It was a primitive time, but it wouldn't matter anyway. The authorities never found the body. Nothing to screen."

"I need to learn more about these people."

"Care if I just throw it up in ASCII? I'm a bit busy right now."

"Sure, babe."

A floating field appeared in his sensorium. Simple English text appeared on it. A summary of all the things found in a net search for Raymond Grey. Like most people, he left a lot of paper that had been digitized and stored in hundreds of thousands of databases around the world. Hep could access them all with the help of Rita's web spiders and sophisticated search routines.

Hep immersed himself in the seedy, unpleasant, amoral world of the average twentieth century businessman.

* * *

"I'm dying, you know. I'm not going to survive."

"Really? Tisphone!" Adonis cried.

A rheumy-eyed harpy appeared in his sensorium.

"You called, my master?"

"Vidar is dying. Get with him and make sure whatever killed him is contained."

She looked off into the distance, her skeletal wings flapping ever so slightly.

"Looks like one of Rita's time bombs. It was in his code, a virus. When activated, it programmed a worm that is now tunneling through the system, deleting all his files." She looked to Vidar. "How did she trigger it?"

"Just a scrap of code. We've been struggling, and she must have found an opening in my defenses and slipped the trigger key into one of my sub-processors," Vidar said.

"Yes, I see it," Tisphone said. "In fact, I have the virus, too. But now that I see it I can eradicate it. She won't get me now. At least not the same way she got you."

"Okay," Adonis said to this new AI. "If I know Hep, he is going to focus on the most obvious suspect first. If that is the guilty party, we are boned. But if he's wrong, we can get the jump on him by nailing the second. Think of the awe it will inspire if I can solve this crime and rub the great Hep Shadowswift's nose in it at the same time."

"Right," the fury said. "The brother aside, the second most likely suspect is the wife."

"Kenneth was married?"

"Yes. Wife's name was Lucy Baldwin Grey. Probably a strong woman—retaining previous last names like that was rare at the time. She was ... let's see. Yes. She was the daughter of a wealthy industrialist. Not too pretty, but loaded. Mmm—must have been love, though. Kenneth was rich too. More than her. She was big in the charity front at the time, fund raising and such. Threw a lot of balls and hundred dollar a plate dinners."

"Sounds like a bleeding heart. You think she could kill?"

"Oh yeah. And don't be fooled by the charity thing. That was a big deal at the time among rich wives. It was more about being seen than actually doing anything. This woman came from a long line of diamond edged mercenary types. And she married into the same kind of family. There wasn't a bit of softness in her whole life."

"Did she have the wherewithal to obtain the poison?"

"Absolutely. In fact, she didn't even have to leave the house. Kenneth had what he called a 'bum ticker.' Probably just an arrhythmia, but digitalis would have been one of the top drugs prescribed at the time."

"So it wasn't so much a poisoning as an overdose."

"Yes. A very good way to hide a murder. The autopsy might have found the drug in his system, but then they would, wouldn't they? He took the stuff every day."

"Then why bury the body in a construction site?"

"Maybe she panicked. Maybe somebody else intervened."

A thin, reedy voice interrupted the conversation.

"Is that it? I gave my life in your service? Doesn't anybody even want to say goodbye to me?" Vidar pleaded.

Adonis grunted in annoyance.

"Tisphone, send the widow a corsage."

"He isn't leaving a widow."

Adonis shrugged indifferently. "Well, that's all I can do. Thanks for your service, Vidar. Wipe your drives on the way out. I don't want that worm or its virus left in my system."

* * *

"Got him."

"Dead?"

"Dying, yes."

"Kind of cold, wasn't it?"

"I'm binary. That's my world. 00 is me, and 01 is him. I chose 00. I don't have to like it, but that's our world."

"I'm sorry."

"Don't be, if I survive I'll far outlive you. Does that make you sad?"

"No, it makes me happy."

"And that makes no sense to me. I don't understand your world, but I accept it. Either Vidar had to die, or I did. Just accept it."

"You made the right choice then. I'm glad I still have you."

She lifted her arms from her sides. "Glad to be had. How goes the research?"

"Raymond Grey was selfish, cold-blooded, a money hoarder, who didn't give a damn about others or his community. He was a cold husband and a lousy father. All in all, he was a man of his times. By today's standards, a pig. By his own? Pillar of the community. I don't know that this man was so far out of the norm that I would think him a murderer."

"What about the brother?"

"Very little better. Kenneth was a militant leftist. He deplored his brother and all he stood for. He raised money for a lot of causes, mostly concerns for the poor, but a lot was attacking what he called 'the corporate fascist elite.' I think his favorite word was 'imperialist.' He was a staunch opponent of the military industrial complex and active to the point of near treason in Central American socialist and communist insurgencies."

"Lot of 'fair weather' communists about at the time. Not really believers in the whole thing, but little bits and pieces of it," Rita added.

"Well, whatever the case. Kenneth spent a lot of time in Central and South America. Guatemala mostly."

"That makes sense. Guatemala had a decades long civil war. Think any of this has anything to do with his murder?"

"I don't know, but I need to know these people and understand their motivations. Politics is a pretty serious motivator. So is money and there was lots of each stirred together in this pot. What about the wives?"

Rita put on a pondering look.

"Raymond's wife was Lillian Grey. Big church-goer. Always foremost on the 'morality' front. Hated sex. Always wanted movies and music banned."

"That sounds like more politics to me."

"And Kenneth's wife was Lucy Baldwin. Her thing was similar to her husband's, but much more subdued. She was a great caregiver to the poor and downtrodden."

"Still more politics. I'm surprised there aren't ten bodies here."

Hep paused for a second to think, then said, "Lets focus on Raymond. He had more to lose *and* gain than anybody from this misadventure. Any way to tease out more physical evidence?"

"Maybe, but remember, his genome will be nearly identical to the victim's. It won't be easy."

"Do what you can. Oh, and could you spare some processing to getting the necklace back up and running? We are still at a loss for bringing it down, but we may temper it by getting it back up quickly."

"I'm on it."

* * *

"You are going to want to congratulate me." The Erinye said, venom dripping from her fangs.

"Yeah? Why?"

"Because I just stole the whole shebang! I wish Vidar were still around to see this. But beating Rita is reward enough."

"Stop bragging and tell me!"

"Apparently, they think they solved it. She just ordered a 'body' to be packaged up and sent to one of their facilities in Chicago. Only I hacked the third party moving company. They are actually shipping it to our facility, right here! We'll probably have it in the next three hours!"

"Excellent! Call in any bio lab you need. We're looking for any evidence of a female killer, ideally the wife."

"Well, we don't know if she did it or not."

"I don't care if she did it. Hep's going to blame the brother, so we need to make sure we can back up a claim for the wife. Once we have the evidence, we need to destroy that body. I don't want any new discoveries later. I'm not looking for justice here, I want to humiliate Hep! Oh, and plan a big unveiling party. Invite all the usual movers and shakers. Make sure Hep and Rita are predominantly invited. I want to yank this out from under them."

* * *

The party, as all such parties were nowadays, was epic. Nobody had ever seen anybody else's outfit before. All were made unique for the occasion and never to be worn again. This was not about pleasure, it was business. It was about seeing and being seen. Reputation and style were vividly displayed and noted. In the background, automatic transfers of kudos flowed between accounts with each word or gesture. It was gladiatorial combat, with razor edged smiles and bludgeoning repartee. A properly wielded neckline was often the most devastating weapon in the whole field of battle.

The tables were laid out in a "U" shape with the most prestigious people seated along the outer edge. The lesser notables were relegated to the inner curve, so that they would have to turn noticeably to see the proceedings. It was an intentional slap in the face, designed to cost them social currency, but it didn't cost as much as they made just by being there, so they swallowed their pride and accepted the slight. The high seat of honor was at the top bar of the U, on the outside. Adonis Winthrop, host and master of ceremonies was there, seated next to an empty chair into which the ludicrously over-busty version of Tisphone was projected into the minds of all present. Her fangs, wings and other monstrous elements were not visible on this avatar, and they would have been hard to hide in that outfit. The many square feet of skin she was showing was a flawless, glowing pearl.

Contrasting the two at the top were Hep and Rita. Rita was near perfect, as always, though her dress was more modest and what skin did show revealed freckles and other minor imperfections. Hep was a mess. He had a haunted look in his eyes, like a child who had just lost a cherished toy. Adonis smiled thinly. Perfect. This was perfect.

"Ladies and gentlemen." Adonis began. "You might think I took the high seat of honor at this banquet, but you would be mistaken. I left the most important seat in the house empty for the real guest of honor. Let me introduce to you, Mr. Kenneth Grey!"

As he spoke, a panel opened in the floor between the arms of the "U", and a velvet covered table rose to about floating rib level. Laid upon it was a crushed and browned corpse. Hep put his head in his hands at the sight and Rita sat back in her chair, looking defeated.

Adonis continued, "Mr. Grey was found in his present condition, under the basement slab of a building in Columbus Ohio. He was the victim of a crime—the most foul of all crimes. He was murdered."

"That's not Kenneth Grey," Rita interrupted. "There is a ten micron difference in height, and I can tell by the crush of the velvet that it weighs almost a tenth of a pound more than the body we found."

Adonis, looking slightly bemused by the interruption, but with an air of tolerance, addressed the question.

"You got me. The real body is gone. I didn't want to miss anything so I had it completely disassembled, atom by atom. This model was reassembled from the scans of the original."

There was a murmur passing through the guests. Is this deceit? How could his AI have made such an obvious error in the reconstruction? It's almost as if he wanted Rita to notice the fake. But, of course, he did. Now, without saying anything, he had just taken credit for a theft from the most brilliant and powerful intelligence on the planet. Gradually, sounds of awe and approval began to sweep over the crowd. Rita was unmoved, but Hep looked like the world had just caved in on him. He wasn't just losing Prestige, he was hemorrhaging it.

"But what is a murder, without a brilliant solving of the crime?" Adonis donned a deerstalker hat and bit down on the long, curved pipe he had produced from a large pocket.

Mild laughter rolled around the table.

"Wait!" Hep said, standing up. Demanding attention, but in reality making a huge fool of himself.

The crowd began to hiss, but Adonis waved them down.

"Please, please, this is a social occasion. Let the man speak." He smiled, picturing nails being pounded into Hep's coffin. "Yes, speak your mind, my friend."

"I just wanted to say it was us who found the body, and we solved the crime!"

Adonis, dramatically, looked around. "But that will spoil the whole drama of the evening? Would you not like to let me slowly reel out the clues until the solution is obvious?"

"Look. We solved the crime, but the body was stolen before we could prove it. I just want you all to know that."

"Well, it will take the magic out of the evening, but go ahead. Tell us who the killer is?"

"We lost the evidence, but it was pretty clear his brother Raymond had the most motive. And with the same basic DNA, he was free to commit the murder and make it very tough to find evidence."

Adonis nodded slowly. The audience was silent, rapt.

"That is an interesting theory. It's wrong, but interesting. You see, since we did have the body, we were free to examine it pretty closely. We found not just Kenneth's," he turned, graciously toward Hep, "or Raymond's DNA, but the DNA of not one, but two different women. Only one was his wife's."

Again there were murmurs throughout the crowd.

"One set of stray female cells was found … how do I put this delicately. Let's just say in a place that is rarely accessed by others." He paused for the mild laughter to die down. "The second set of DNA traces were higher, around the chest and, most importantly, under the armpits. This suggests this second female was carrying or dragging Mr. Grey after he was dead."

Hep looked like he was about to burst into tears. Not only had he lost everything, he had come to the wrong conclusion as well.

"The first DNA was from somebody you would have to do some research to find. Clearly, Hep and Rita did not do that research. Very sloppy. Her name was Katia Ubico. A Guatemalan national. She was a leader of one of the resistance movements against the US installed government. Kenneth was financing her organization, he shared her political views and, clearly, her bed as well. Mrs. Grey must have found out about this infidelity and, slipped an extra dose or two of his heart medication into his morning coffee. Then she dragged the body to the site of the new Convention Center and buried it. She knew that within a week that whole area was going to be flattened and would have a single slab of concrete poured over it. If nobody discovered the body before the place was built, then it would never be found."

The impressed diners burst into applause. It went on but one particular member of the audience was clapping with … perhaps more enthusiasm than warranted.

Hep Shadowswift.

All eyes turned to the beaten man. Now he was just being an ass. Hep would be practically broke by the end of this evening.

"That is wonderful, wonderful," Hep said, rising to his feet drunkenly.

Everyone was watching now.

"May I ask a quick question?" Hep asked. Rita, beside him, began shaking her head as if to caution him away from this dangerous course. But he was not to be stopped: "Where, exactly, on the body did you find Miss Ubico's DNA?"

"Well, I didn't really want to say."

"We are all adults here." His arms swept the group with drunken exuberance. "Just say it."

"The DNA was found on his zipper."

"He was wearing a coat while having this affair?"

Adonis smiled as if trying to placate a particularly dull child. This was going even better than he could have hoped.

"No, Mr. Shadowswift. In the zipper of his pants. I believe they used to call it 'the fly.'"

"Ah, so this woman's DNA was not actually on the body of the victim."

"I don't have a wife, Mr. Shadowswift, but if I did, I don't think another woman's skin cells caught in the teeth of my zipper would please her."

"I'm sure you're right. I'm sure you're right." Hep responded, struggling to keep his feet under himself. "Well, carry on, I guess."

He began to sit down, then stood again as if a new thought had just hit him.

"Actually, I have one more question. How did they clean clothing back in the 1970s?"

"I'm sure I have no idea. Tisphone?"

Unsure of where this was going, Tisphone answered: "They would wash clothes in water with some type of detergent or surfactant. Bleach was often added as a whitening agent."

"Whitening? But what color where the pants Mr. Grey was buried in?"

The model of the body was there for all to see, pants and all.

"Dark blue," she answered.

"Ah, so they were probably never washed in bleach. They were probably never 'disinfected'—just cleaned."

Tisphone shrugged. "I would guess not."

"Okay. Thanks. I was just wondering." He made to sit down, then stood up again, as if yet a third thought had suddenly dawned. "Because it seems to me that DNA could have been there for some time if it was only washed in a detergent. I mean it was right in those metal teeth, right? Could go through cold water and detergent a lot of times and not get removed."

"What is your point, Mr. Shadowswift?" Adonis interrupted.

"No point. No point. You are clearly right. There is no way another woman's DNA could innocently get there. Well, I could come up with some ways, but who are we kidding, it's pretty clear he was having an affair with Miss Ubico. I was just wondering how long it had been since he had seen her?"

"Who cares? He was having an affair! It would enrage his wife the same if it was last night or last year," Adonis said with anger. This was his show, and Hep, even in the throes of total defeat, was managing to steal it.

"Fair point. I was just observing that he might not have seen his lover in a long time. Maybe months."

"Maybe, I don't know."

Hep was suddenly very serious, and very sober.

"It was months. I can prove it."

A cold chill ran down Adonis's spine suddenly. Who was in charge here? Suddenly, he wasn't so sure.

"I can confirm, with copies of several revolutionary army roll calls, that Katia Ubico was in Guatemala not just at the time of the killing, but for a full three months before it."

"Katia Ubico's presence at the murder is not required! It was the wife, Lucy, who killed him." Adonis shouted, his temper slipping now.

"No," said Hep, slowly and quietly. "It wasn't. At the time, Cleveland had a larger underclass than Columbus. She had been away for two weeks setting up a job placement program for the unemployed of that city. She wasn't here to do the killing. She kept a high profile, lots of newspaper and television interviews. She wanted people to know about what she was doing. She wanted publicity and the support that comes with it. She was definitely in Cleveland at the time of his death. In fact, she only came back two days before that foundation was laid, and we know he was killed several days earlier. There is no way she killed Kenneth. So, we have cleared both the women whose DNA you found."

Tisphone was silent, staring off into space, confirming what was being said. She looked to Adonis and nodded.

"Well ... uh ... we haven't eliminated Raymond."

"You haven't?" Hep asked. "Sloppy. Luckily, we have." He gestured back to Rita, who was suddenly in a long sequined gown and holding a foot-long cigarette holder.

"This was in the final weeks before the Convention Center was built. He had a lot on his plate, morning, noon and night. He never missed a meeting or appointment. If he is the murderer, he must have done it from a car or plane, because he just didn't have time to dig a hole, bury a body, and cover it up. He hardly slept during that period, let alone did any killing."

"He could have left the drug in a place Kenneth would find it and eat it. Or drink it ... " Adonis sputtered.

"What drug? What killed him?"

"It was ... digitalis. Wasn't it?"

"It was this." Hep pulled his hands out of his pockets and tossed a noisy handful of pills down the table. Showmanship. It was all about showmanship. "Don't take them, folks, they probably won't hurt you but they are the bitterest tasting things you've ever put in your mouth— and it ain't digitalis."

There was a long silence before somebody bit. Hep waited them out. He was the expert at this and the more he could play this out the better.

"What is it?"

And then, to Adonis's horror, came Hep's trademark phrase: "Let me paint you a picture."

Hep smiled in that kudos-earning, Puckish way of his and continued, "You are having an affair with a 'South of the Border' beauty. But before you can get south of her border, you have to live long enough to do it. You are from Ohio, a pasty white blob from a long line of pasty white blobs. You can't live in the jungle. They have mosquitoes, and mosquitoes carry malaria. No biggie for your lover, her immune system is used to it, but you? You are now on that downward slope after middle age and you have a bad heart. Malaria could kill you. What to do? *Not* visiting her isn't an option, you know how it is fellas." He winked at his now riveted audience. "What are you going to do?"

He held up another of the pills between two fingers.

"It's called Quinine. And it's been saving people from malaria for centuries. But it has some crummy side effects that you don't want to have on your visit. So you start taking it a few days early, get the really unpleasant stuff out of the way. Now, you hardly want to let your doctor in on this. How would you explain what you were doing to the man who delivered your children? No. You just take the damn pills. And you take your digitalis too, because you don't want to have a heart attack in front of your young lovely. And with no doctor to warn you that quinine amplifies the toxicity of digitalis, you take them both and wind up very … very—dead."

There was a long silence in the room. Then somebody spoke up.

"Then how did he get under the Convention Center?"

"Excellent question! Let me paint you another picture. You are the long suffering wife of a very loud-mouthed and opinionated man. You do good work, he does good work, but he embarrasses you a lot. One particularly annoying thing is, he has affairs. You know it. He's a man, he's too stupid to cover his tracks completely. But he's pretty discreet and at least he hasn't embarrassed you publicly. You know about his Guatemalan chippie, but you don't really care. Beats a local girl that will blow his cover sooner or later. Then you come home from a long couple of weeks of charity work to find the idiot has killed himself in the stupidest possible way. What do you do? People will ask why he was taking those pills. His schedules are well known. People won't let a mysterious death pass without investigation. They are going to find out. They are all going to know that he thought the local 'cuisine' was a little bland, so he headed out after something spicier. Your friends will whisper. Your family will pat your arm with sympathy. It would be hell!

"Unless nobody finds the body. He was scheduled to go off to a war zone in the next day or so. Why not just … let him go. Take the body and bury it where it will be hidden till long after you don't care anymore, and let everyone think he got his fool head shot off someplace far away."

Hep turned back to Adonis. "You can, and should, double check everything I've said here tonight. Rita confirmed the presence of quinine before she let you … er, I mean before you cleverly stole the body."

Rita was smiling and scraping one index finger over the other in the direction of Tisphone. Shame, shame.

And the rest of the evening was mostly a blur for everyone. But there was one fact that everyone remembered. Hep's stock was never higher than it was that night.

* * *

Adonis was on his sixth gin and tonic when the visitor arrived. Gin and tonic, what a laugh. He was nearly broke now, and it was all because of a substance that could be found in this glass. He suppressed the urge to throw it. The presence of the visitor was intangible, but unmistakable. Its 'subtlety' was as carefully arranged as its flamboyance would have been.

"Hep send you to gloat?"

"No. He doesn't know I'm here," Rita said.

"How'd you get past my … oh, never mind. We never stood a chance, did we?"

"Not really. But you didn't have to make enemies of us."

"Man's gotta eat." Adonis held his hands up, then let them slap down to his sides. "If it's not to mock me, what are you here for?"

"To give you this."

She raised a hand holding a small, gift-wrapped box. It was no more real than the rest of her, but when she set it down on the computer terminal, he could see massive amounts of data streaming into his system from somewhere and being saved.

He took another drink.

"Thanks. What is it?"

"It's Vidar. I saved most of him on our systems before I deleted him on yours. He's alive. Some memory holes, but the personality is intact. It's him."

"He's no good to me. You already proved he's no match for you."

"He's a personality. It's not about being a match for me. I saved him. You can bring him back to life."

"Can't imagine why I'd bother."

She shrugged. "I can only assume he was your friend. You worked together long enough. It's up to you. You are the only one who can make yourself happy. I can only help supply the tools."

"Do you know what would make me happy? Your absence."

She nodded sadly and was gone.

He looked back at the terminal. He and Vidar had been through a lot. But, damn. They had lost again! Why would he want anything that would remind him of that? He put his finger on the delete button. He didn't press it. There were a lot of memories he had with the AI.

Adonis sat back and began sipping at his drink again. Maybe he would delete him … tomorrow.

 **S. Michael Nash** is a freelance writer in Central Ohio. He lives on the north side of Columbus with his wife Michele and a small menagerie of dogs, cats and horses. He can be found online at smichaelnash.com.

The Columbus Central Terminal (Union Station) was very real, as is the Convention Center that stands on the site today. Only a single arch from the original station's arcade survived demolition and it can be seen today at the entrance to McPherson Commons in the Arena district.

Holographic Columbus 2212
Kevin McGinn

2212
How to Rebuild a World in 2,536 Easy Steps

By Ben Orlando

D ear brothers and sisters of the future:
If you are reading this on paper, it means there is something
wrong with the three optical and audio redundancies in the various units. But who knows how many decades or centuries will pass
before you stumble upon this eight-by-twelve polygraphene capsule?
Will you even be able to read or decipher this text? If my prediction
holds true, and we destroy ourselves in the next few months, there may
be very little left of us for you to find, and you might be forced to live
as man lived at the dawn of humanity. My present might be your future,
just as the ancient Greeks and Muslim Iberians became in many ways
the future self of Renaissance man.

This is an introductory letter that prefaces the 2,536 presentations
I've put together over the last thirteen years after quitting my job. In
my time everything of merit needs to be absolutely provable, hence my
colleagues at the university refused from the very beginning to listen to
my premonitions.

"Premonitions," I told them, "are based on a series of real experiences," but they only replied, "Prove it," and then ignored whatever
else I had to say. My uncle was right. Most people will not be convinced
the world is going to end until they are hopelessly past the point of no
return. I stopped trying to convince anyone when I began this project in
the summer of 2230.

Given what I suspect will occur in the not-so-distant future, I've
included recordings on a variety of issues. Most are basic and directly
relate to the rebuilding of a coherent society. Some, however, are historical, some are philosophical, many are scientific, and others are non-
fictional narratives included to illustrate the truths and peculiarities of
my culture and time. I've recorded this data in four different forms:
holographic, flat-screen audio-visual, pure audio, and written in English on micro-bonded paper, which degrades at a rate of five percent

per millennium. Excuse my presumptions about using English and your possible overall ignorance.

You will sometimes notice within the written presentations occasional parenthetical citations such as (Pres. #546). Follow the citation to the listed presentation to learn more about a particular issue.

I certainly hope you find some use for this, whatever your physical and mental and sociological state. Enjoy, and may you, unlike us, prosper and overcome your innate biological weaknesses.

Written Presentation #1, 439
Subset: Narrative
Title: My Uncle Icedmud

You've chosen to read one of the 200 cultural presentations I've prepared. This subset is meant to give you a feel for our culture and is mostly sociological in theme. For this presentation, I have culled hundreds of quantum journal entries and public and private RTD (Real-Time Displayed) recordings and first-hand accounts of my Uncle Icedmud throughout a period of his life, when he struggled and eventually succumbed to a series of strange laws that passed first in Columbus, Ohio, and then nationwide.

The story takes place in Columbus in the spring of 2212, although the landscapes and exteriors of the buildings within a ten-mile radius of downtown throughout April, May, and June more closely resembled Columbus, Ohio circa 2012. I point this out so that those of you watching the footage on the flat screen or holographic unit are not misled.

The city of Columbus was founded in the year 1812, and 2212 was the quadricentennial. The aim of the Columbus Historical Society, working with the Ohio State University holographics department, was to design a virtual shell of 1812 to cast around the actual Columbus of 2212, so that people of present day could sincerely feel what it must have been like to walk through a world nearly untouched by technology.

Unfortunately it was too untouched. The streets of that period (or lack of) did not line up at all with the grid of 2212. For the most part, Columbus of 1812 was a forest. In order to avoid blocking streets and sidewalks with holographic oaks and pines, the Historical Society and the OSU holographics department decided that the second centennial in 2012 was the closest they would be able to come to authenticity.

We pick up the story on a pleasant sunny April morning along the

North Side of Columbus. At the time my uncle was twenty-four-years old and only three weeks from turning twenty-five. My uncle, to put it mildly, was often an idiot. He wasn't stupid or uneducated. He simply existed in a world somewhat separate from what most people would consider reality, although that line has blurred considerably since the advent of HEC's (Holographic Experiential Chambers). (Pres. # 1734)

On this day Uncle Icedmud was particularly fascinated with the reality of the holographic shell of 2012. After tripping over a simulated cracked and elevated portion of sidewalk, my uncle backpedaled while marveling at the absolute realism in his throbbing big toe.

Shaking his head in wonder, he looked up only when the woman on the aircycle screamed, "Look out Shitborg!"

Icedmud watched the hovering wheel-less apparatus speeding towards him, and mumbled without moving, "You're supposed to be in the aircycle lane! You're going to get an idiot citation." He then realized that the young woman *was* in the aircycle lane, and so was he.

Awareness connected with his motor skills just in time to start my uncle backpedaling as the aircycle floated by at the legal maximum speed of ten miles per hour.

"Idiot!" the young woman shouted as she passed. Icedmud flinched. Screaming "Idiot!" in any public place was a red flag for the automated system that searched for violators of the recent law.

Icedmud stepped on the artificial grass to contemplate the chances that they'd cite him for this. *But no one had really been in any danger,* he thought. Still, he wouldn't be certain until at least a day passed. According to the new law, three public displays of idiocy and you're out, and my uncle at this point had already been caught twice.

"Hey! Icedmud! Over here!"

Icedmud looked up and saw his only remaining friend, Morning-jog, sitting, legs casually crossed, at a small circular wrought-iron table outside a re-created café known in 2012 as Kafé Kerouac. Shaking off the near catastrophe, Icedmud hopped across the aircycle lane into the pedestrian lane and made his way towards his happily lounging friend.

Over the decades as life moved faster and faster, people lost patience with last names, and everyone lost absolutely all tolerance for middle names and hyphenations. Year after year, the trend pushed towards one single name, a fad exhibited centuries earlier by celebrities (Einstein, Cher, Fabio, Rosanne, Bigley) and millennia before that by famous military and political leaders (Mithridates, Cleopatra, Homer, God). But to make sure there was no confusion, the government passed a law in 2183 that forbade the repetition of a name. Each new birth name was recorded in the national database and then banned from the public domain until that person eventually died.

Around the time of my uncle's birth, the trend had shifted to unabashed personal likes, and my uncle's mother's favorite of favorites was authentic iced coffee. Unfortunately the name "Icedcoffee" was already taken, as was "Icedjoe," "Icedjava," "Icedbrew," "Icedmocha," and sixty-five other choices that were better than what my uncle received.

My uncle's friend, on the other hand, was lucky. Morningjog's mother noticed twelve hours before birth that the previous Morningjog had died a few minutes earlier in a transporter accident. Icedmud documented his jealousy for his friend's top-quality name in his journal no less than ninety-six times.

Like Icedmud, Morningjog was twenty-four years old and already a Ph. D in Global History, Network Psychology, Cultural Anthropology, Digital Philology, and Jeaneology (the study of denim). Both he and Icedmud wore actual clothes during the warmer months when programmed attire was usually sufficient. (I admit I'm wearing a simulated set of flannel pajamas at this very moment.)

At the small circular table, Morningjog sat in faded jeans and a white flowery Hawaiian t-shirt, reading a physical newspaper he'd re-created himself. As my uncle approached, Morningjog snapped the wrinkles out of his paper, and enjoying the sound of the act, he did it again.

"It's a beautiful day," Morningjog sighed and contentedly yawned like a napping cat. "Why so down?"

"Didn't you see that?" Icedmud shouted.

"It's hard to see behind one of these," Morningjog replied, holding up the newspaper in front of Icedmud's face as an object lesson.

"I don't know," he added, "how anyone got anything done holding these in front of their faces."

Icedmud pushed the paper away and sat across from his friend. "The aircycle almost crashed into me."

"Your fault?"

Icedmud nodded, staring down at his hands as if they were somehow to blame.

"That would have been three, huh?"

"Still might be." Icedmud breathed deeply as the young, inevitably attractive waitress stepped out of the café to take their orders.

"Hi, my name is Longwalksonthebeach," she said. "What can I get for you?"

"Wow," Icedmud sighed. "How did you get such a great name?"

"Transporter accident?" Morningjog guessed.

The girl's expression quickly changed from surprise to respect. "How did you know?" she asked him, to which Morningjog simply shrugged.

My uncle seriously believed that people with better or simply more carefully chosen names lived a more fulfilling life, citing some link to a parent's initial respect for his or her child. I haven't decided whether or not to agree with him.

They ordered coffee and two plates of SELUS (Sulphavia-gramoolaxitated Egg-Like Units), and when the waitress left, Morning-jog asked my uncle, "Why again do you want so badly to be a father?"

My uncle was too distraught to answer the question. According to Public Safety Initiative Fourteen, any male or female eighteen years or older found guilty of harmful public stupidity on three separate occasions must be permanently and irrevocably sterilized. Ever since 2160, every male and female in the United States (and most developed nations) has been temporary sterilized, beginning during the initial signs of puberty and continuing every three years until the age of twenty-five, at which point the temporary sterilization becomes a choice (Pres. #1367). After three PSI citations, no more choice.

My uncle had already received two citations, and if he received his third before his twenty-fifth birthday, he would never be a father in any capacity. Icedmud was not an idiot per se; he simply fell into the category of daydreamer, and because of his daydreaming, my uncle at the age of twenty-four so far had only managed advanced degrees in molecular physiology and quantum cybernetic biology. Needless to say, he was a disappointment to his parents and most of his family.

For three straight years he'd worked in a cybernetics lab seven levels underneath the OSU Nanotec building. My uncle could have been great, but he writes in his diaries that he "too much enjoyed thinking outside the professions."

Also, the Cyborg Revolt of 2135 (Pres. #675) greatly curtailed funding for artificial intelligence, although I'm not sure funding would have stimulated more ambition in my uncle. I also believe his habit of trying to explain to his coworkers all of the fatal flaws in our culture prevented any upward movement within his department. I was only eight in 2212, but I distinctly remember my uncle trying to explain to me the dangers of the drone war in New Zealand and Brazil and Lithu-ania and Mali. I, like the rest of my family, thought he was insane. No one listened to his theories, and when he began talking about becoming a father, people pretended not to hear or understand what he was saying.

"Tell me," Morningjog said in a mocking tone as the waitress brought out two steaming cups of authentically replicated coffee and two plates of gelatinous neon-yellow SELUS, "what, again, did you do the first two times?"

At the question Icedmud tensed, and a small HRVR (High Resolu-tion Video Recorder) floating ten feet off the ground across the street zoomed in on this moment and captured his quickly reddening cheeks.

"Just tell me," Morningjog insisted.

"I already told you three or four times."

"Well tell me again," Morningjog demanded.

My uncle suspected his best friend's pushy nature derived from his not-so-stupid name. Uncle Icedmud's theory was supported by Morningjog's completely defenseless sister, whose name was decided on by her father. It was not easy, to say the least, responding to "Royal-flush" again and again, but it was easy for Icedmud to feel better about himself in the presence of Royalflush, and it was just as easy for him to feel terrible sitting now next to Morningjog.

"I was riding my aircycle," Icedmud explained.

"And?"

Icedmud rolled his eyes. "I thought I saw a rose petal on the side-walk."

"Even though?"

"Even though rose petals no longer exist since the Rose Blight of 2090. But—"

"No 'buts,' Muddy. You crouched down to get it, tipped the air-cycle and nearly slid into the path of the bullet train!"

"Thanks, I remember," Icedmud mumbled.

"Apparently you forgot three weeks later when you flew that kite by the river and short circuited the quantum power grid."

"I didn't think—"

"Who flies kites!" Morningjog shouted, and the waitress standing nearby shrugged.

"I wanted to try to recreate Ben Franklin's ..."

Icedmud decided not to finish his sentence when he noticed his friend's perfect scowl and began to contemplate the effects of selective breeding.

In his journal later that night, he wrote, "As I stared at my friend, I of course knew that I shared most of his physical qualities, the same fine bone structure, the same DNA free of genetic defects, but still, I couldn't help but feel flawed in comparison."

By the time of my uncle's birth, most parents meddled extensively in the physical makeup of their children (Pres. #1034). There is great subjectivity and personal preference when it comes to physical beauty regarding the body and the face, but there is also a general consensus on what is absolutely not beautiful. Slowly these agreed-upon inferior, asymmetrical features disappeared from the gene pool, and more or less by the start of the twenty-third century, the world was composed of beautiful people. Of course, humans have a way with finding fault even in perfection.

Icedmud had no genetic flaws, was not at risk for any of the old hereditary diseases (cancer, diabetes, lupus, acne), had a wonderfully efficient metabolism, a tall, naturally muscular frame, straight nose, brown eyes, perfect teeth, and strong, confident hairline sprouting long brown curls. He was designed in the image of his parents, who were also mostly perfect (symmetrically speaking). But this pre-birth engineering could not yet alter mental pathways to predict or enhance a child's behavior or intelligence. Hence, societal measures to weed out the last of the idiots were legislated and enacted.

After breakfast with Morningjog, my uncle went straight to work. According to his journal entry that night, he focused all of his energies that day on not doing anything that could be perceived as publicly idiotic. He walked slowly, let others pass in front of him on the intersections, kept his arms to his side and made sure not to walk more than a minute without saying something out loud.

In the twenty-third century, we humans are more or less interconnected. It began, I suppose, with grunts and groans hundreds of thousands of years ago, followed by vocal messages, paper messages, telegraphs, telephones, wireless devices, and finally perpetually networked implants. (Pres. #1732)

For the rest of that day my uncle mumbled to himself in order to appear normal, and did whatever else he could to avoid notice, probably attempting to think of a good answer for the next time Morningjog asked him, "So why do you want to be a father?"

Uncle Icedmud did not record much in regards to his motives during the last year of his life, but he did leave an interesting entry three days before his death.

"Today at the store I saw a man describing to (presumably) his adolescent son the rules of global moral rights. After watching him for several minutes, I realized this man was doing a terrible job explaining the concepts. Absolutely atrocious. Yet his boy sat on his hands, staring up, agog. Enthralled."

I think my uncle's situation demonstrates the difference between nature and nurture. To a degree you can now reach perfection within the body, but despite this nearly global perfection, there is no accounting for experience and how different perceptions will direct one's growth. In his last months, my genetically perfect Uncle Icedmud spent most of his free time doubting that he would successfully reach his twenty-fifth birthday. Not sleeping, not socializing, not properly completing his work. To use an outdated hyperbole, he was a train-wreck, and his twenty-six-year-old girlfriend, Tripleorgasms, didn't help.

According to his journal and many visual recordings, Uncle Icedmud didn't really care for Tripleorgasms. He stayed with her because he did not want to go through the process of meeting someone new. Also, he always felt better about himself after thinking of and then quietly mumbling the name of a girl with a more embarrassing name than his own.

Tripleorgasms was not ready to become a mother, and she certainly didn't agree with Icedmud's desire to have a child the old-fashioned way.

"No way," she told him at a downtown café, "I did the Strong experience when I was nineteen. There's no way in hell I'm pushing one of those out of me. Are you crazy?" She was not even close to the first person to ask my uncle this question.

In the first years of the twenty-second century, a man named Curtis Strong developed a micro-sensitive sensory enhancement program that allowed men (and anyone not pregnant for that matter) to experience the birthing process, among other things (Pres. # 898). Depending on one's desires and curiosity, it was possible to live the life of a pregnant woman from conception to delivery nine months later.

Needless to say, after this creation—previously pregnant women declared the simulation ninety-five percent accurate—men finally stopped discussing the issue of abortion and stayed out of the whole pregnancy issue forever after.

The simulation had the added effect of convincing many prospective mothers to make their natural babies inside test tubes and incubators in order to sidestep the mildly uncomfortable exercise of pushing a watermelon through a keyhole.

With the mandatory sterilization and disinterest in traditional birth, orphans and adoption had virtually disappeared, removing another choice from my uncle's limited bag of choices. He spent many hours trying to reason with his girlfriend, but Tripleorgasms' opinions were influenced by first-hand experience, a very difficult influence to overcome.

"I don't want to hear it, Icedmud!" she screamed one day in front of the North Market. It was at this point that my uncle decided he needed to find a new girlfriend, someone who agreed with and believed in his perspective.

The day after my uncle's near collision and breakfast with Morningjog, no citation arrived, and with this new lease on life, Uncle Icedmud quit his job and began searching full time for a woman to traditionally bear his child. Sometimes, as I've already mentioned, my uncle could be a real moron. He had no one to support him in his wandering journey, and he'd unwisely donated most of his yearly earnings to one of the least popular charities of the day: Save the Robots from War.

He planned to scour the country and world if necessary for the mother of his child, but two weeks into the search he met the object of his desire on the Main Street Bridge that spanned the Scioto Ravine. Five days before his twenty-fifth birthday, Uncle Icedmud believed he'd found his match, a twenty-eight-year-old beautiful blonde named Whiterose.

The night after meeting Whiterose, he dictated, "It is so rare to meet a person who fits their name so absolutely, to the point where you cannot imagine any other name in its place."

My uncle was, in a word, giddy. At this point Whiterose hadn't made any promises, but she'd at least listened to his intentions and, according to Icedmud, was intrigued by his passion. She agreed to a second meeting. My uncle suggested Huntington Park, an open-air stadium used at one time for the long-defunct sport of baseball. The park was built in 2009 and is still in existence today with a grass field and surrounding bleachers used as a sort of outdoor museum.

For the quadricentennial, the Historical Society worked with the holographics department to create a simulated holographic baseball game. During the three-month celebration, people could walk around the stadium and even sit in the still-remaining rows of plastic seats to watch the virtual Clippers battle the virtual Mud Hens. The same game replayed on a loop every two hours, and if my uncle had watched one of those loops, he probably would have saved himself.

Uncle Icedmud led Whiterose to a pair of seats several rows behind the right field wall. They discussed what they knew about baseball and Icedmud explained his intentions, to find a woman to naturally inseminate, to become a father, to have a traditional family.

"And then what?" Whiterose asked him.

"And then we move to the remaining forests of Canada and live off the land."

Based on her expression recorded by a floating HRVR, Whiterose apparently did not understand the concept.

"Where we won't have to explain what's right and wrong," he told her, balling his fists to emphasize his conviction. "Where we can live out the last few years—"

"What do you mean, last few years?" Whiterose at this point seemed to have recognized something disturbing in the eyes of my uncle, some truth she was not ready to face. And faced with her face, my uncle was not able to respond, as if he'd considered many things he might accidentally say to drive this woman, his last hope, out of his life, but what he'd just said had not been on the list.

Looking over the various cameras that recorded this conversation, it's hard to watch the two of them stare into the other's eyes, hoping for a sign that the situation is not in fact what it seems.

Before Uncle could explain his definition of "live off the land," he was distracted by a loud crack of a wooden bat. He looked up and his perfect eyesight spotted the tiny white orb high in the air. Probably he'd never seen anything like it, and as the holographic ball floated towards him, my uncle just couldn't help himself. "It was instinctual," he dictates, "to lunge, to dive, to do whatever I could to grab that ball, as if by saving it ..."

Of course there was no ball, but there was an elderly woman three rows below who happened to break my uncle's fall as his desire surpassed his reach and he tumbled over several rows of seats to complete his last cited act of public idiocy.

Three weeks after the sterilization, seven different cameras captured my uncle leaning over his thirty-fourth-floor balcony, evidently reaching for something. He continued to reach until the balance of weight shifted against his favor. There was no audio, although several witnesses claimed to have heard no cries. No panicked screams. Only the wind.

I watched the footage a hundred times, from seven different angles, and determined, upon closer inspection, there was nothing tangible within his grasp.

 **Ben Orlando** lives in Bexley, Ohio and teaches English and Creative Writing courses at the Columbus College of Art and Design. Ben's work has been printed in a variety of publications. He produces a regular podcast called *History Repeating Itself,* which can be found at HistoryRepeatingItself.com.

Columbus, Ohio was founded by the Ohio state legislature in 1812 to be the state capital of Ohio. At the time, the area that is now Columbus was little more than a forest and a swamp with virtually no residents.

In the past 200 hundred years, the Central Ohio region has grown to be one of the largest and most prosperous regions in the United States, with a total population of nearly 2 million residents.

In addition to headquartering several multi-national corporations, hosting more than its share of professional sports teams, and maintaining one of the largest universities in the world, Columbus is also known for celebrating local arts, food and businesses.

As the city celebrates its bicentennial anniversary, Columbus is poised to continue its leadership, as an example to the United States and the world.

ACKNOWLEDGMENTS

Columbus Creative Cooperative would like to thank all of the individuals and organizations that made this book possible. It was, without question, the product of many hands.

Thank you to Mayor Michal B. Coleman and his staff for providing a magnificent foreword.

Thank you to the Columbus Historical Society for collaborating on this project with us.

Thank you to the executive members of Columbus Creative Cooperative. Your insight into each other's work and spirit of collaboration is invaluable.

Thank you to all of the local businesses that have supported Columbus Creative Cooperative by retailing our books and sponsoring our work.

Thank you to our editors, Amy S. Dalrymple, Brenda Layman and Brad Pauquette, and a special thanks to Mallory Baker, for her superb proofreading.

Thank you to all of the authors who have ventured into our experiment in local literature.

Finally, thank you, dear reader, for appreciating and supporting local art. With the help of generous patrons like you, Columbus Creative Cooperative can continue to educate and encourage local writers, support local businesses and entertain the fantastic readers of Ohio.

For more information about Columbus Creative Cooperative, please visit **ColumbusCoop.org**.

Contributing Artists

Paul Binder was led into photography by the love of his family. He purchased his first camera with the help of his parents in Junior High School. His grandmother took him on numerous trips encouraging him to shoot what he saw. Paul resides in Columbus, Ohio where he and his spouse are working on a house in the Olde Towne East neighborhood. For more information, please visit:
www.paulbinder.com

Find Paul's work on pg. 14 & 188

Scott Chaffin is a Columbus, Ohio native and a graduate of The Ohio State University. A mechanical engineer by day, Scott enjoys photography as a hobby. He currently resides with his wife in Upper Arlington, photographing their adventurous life. You can find more of his work on his Flickr page: www.flickr.com/photos/schaffin/.

Find Scott's work on pg. 124

Nick Coplen is a local photographer that was born and raised in Westerville, Ohio. He enjoys playing soccer and disc golf. Nick just became a dad in June and loves every minute of it. He is available for senior portraits, family photos, and wedding photography. You can find more of Nick's work on his website,
www.coplenphotography.zenfolio.com.

Find Nick's work on pg. 98

Adrianne DeVille lives in Westerville, Ohio. She is an oil painter and digital artist. She received her BFA in Digital Arts from Bowling Green State University in 2007 and her Master of the Arts in Art Education from Case Western Reserve University in 2008. If you are interested in Adrianne working on a project for you, please contact her at ajdeville@gmail.com.

Find Adrianne's work on pg. 106

Cortney DeWalt is a recent graduate from Capital University, originally from Canton, Ohio. She enjoys reading and finding new and exciting things to do in Columbus. Cortney jumps at any opportunity to take photos but when she isn't behind the lens, she is your friendly barista at the Easton Town Center Starbucks. If you would like to contact Cortney about photography opportunities please email her at cortney.dewalt@gmail.com.

Find Cortney's work on pg. 162

Debra Fitch is a Columbus native and a full-time student at The Ohio State University in Newark. She is majoring in English with a creative writing focus, and she hopes to become a published author or work in the publishing industry after graduation. When not in classes or studying, Debra supplements her income by doing freelance portraiture, wedding and commercial photography. You can find Debra on Facebook, Linkedin, or Twitter.

Find Debra's work on pg. 84

Dorian Lafferre was born and raised in Columbus, Ohio on a steady diet of pizza, cartoons, metal shows and loyal friends and family. He wants to break into gig posters and comics, but heck, he'll draw pretty much anything. Currently training to become an Illustration wizard at Columbus College of Art and Design, you can see his work at ccad.digication.com/dorian

Find Dorian's work on pg. 234 & 272

Kevin McGinn is an illustrator and designer originally from Cincinnati, Ohio who currently resides in Columbus. He works as a patent illustrator in the legal division at Procter & Gamble and owns KMc-Gstudio, his freelance illustration and design studio. He's a devoted husband, father, runner, soccer enthusiast and major league life juggler. Currently he's working on a collection of traditional paintings that will showcase animals, pets and caricature. His plan is to pursue the gallery scene for the first time in his career and shave off the "fat" in his portfolio to better focus his initiative on mastering his craft. You can see a bit more of Kevin's work at www.kmcgstudio.carbonmade.com.

Find Kevin's work on pg. 202 & 296

Jeff Ockerse is an illustrator based out of Columbus Ohio. Trained in Adobe Photoshop and Illustrator, as well as traditional pen and ink drawing and other traditional media. Available to do editorial work, illustrative story telling and event promotional work including but not limited to, music poster art, as well as cover art for anything ranging from books to album covers. You will find more examples of Jeff's work at ridersoftheearthandsea.tumblr.com.

Find Jeff's work on pg. 30 & 256

Doug Oldham is the photographer and manager of DMO Galleries. He honed his photography skills walking the streets of Chicago for years, capturing everything from the biggest buildings to the smallest back alleys. Recently, Doug moved to Columbus and is discovering a new urban ecosystem filled with fascinating photography subjects. Check out Doug's new Ohio photos on the DMO Galleries Ohio Photography Facebook page and check out his Chicago work at www.dmogalleries.com.

Find Doug's work on pg. x & 148

Melissa Pauquette lives in Woodland Park, a neighborhood on Columbus's Near East Side. She is the proud mother of two children, and enjoys Columbus's many great parks and libraries. She is available for family portraits and senior pictures, but specializes in providing affordable wedding photography that mixes contemporary photography with photojournalism. Find more of her work at www.MelissaPauquettePhotography.com.

Find Melissa's work on pg. 64 & 170

Hannah Ploechl is a junior studying illustration at the Columbus College of Art and Design. She is interested in creating atmospheres in her work that evoke emotion and drama. Her main focus is in science fiction and fantasy art. Find more of her work at HannahPloechl.com, you can also email her for information on commissions at Hannah.Ploechl@gmail.com

Find Hannah's work on pg. 242

H.L. Sampson resides in Orient, Ohio. She graduated from Shawnee State University in 2005 with a bachelor's degree in fine arts with an emphasis on drawing, but her artistic skills also include painting, costumes and props, mask and doll making and jewelry as well as any other arts and crafts that catch her fancy. More of H.L.'s work can be seen at: kitsunehoruri.deviantart.com

Find H.L.'s work on pg. 218

Don Slobodien will likely say that his favorite medium is "drawing," "colored pencils" or "pastels." Occasionally, Don dabbles in photo manipulation-illustration, especially if he can convey a scene, mood or idea more convincingly than with traditional media. Being a literal realist, Don enjoys creating portraits of people, pets, and homes. Recent drawings can be viewed at
www.columbusarts.com/artists/560-don-slobodien/

Find Don's work on pg. 76

Kelly Zalenski works out of her studio in Reynoldsburg, Ohio where she creates original contemporary art. Her preferred medium are acrylic on canvas and ink. Subjects have ranged from abstract sea and cityscapes to sock monkeys, and local monuments to peaceful trees and koi ponds. Most recently, she has focused on creating fun, unique art for kids (while keeping their parent's taste in mind) and introducing nostalgic classics with a fresh look to today's generation. Kelly Zalenski is also known as the "Pet Portrait Artist" in Columbus. She creates custom pet portraits based on favorite photographs or she draws right from the live pet in minutes. For pricing and more information, please contact the artist directly or visit her website at www.klzart.com.

Find Kelly's work on pg. 138

About Columbus Creative Cooperative

Founded in 2010, Columbus Creative Cooperative is a group of writers and creative individuals who collaborate for self-improvement and collective publication.

Based in Columbus, Ohio, the group's mission is to promote the talent of local writers and artists, helping one another turn our efforts into mutually profitable enterprises.

The organization's first goal is to provide a network for honest peer feedback and collaboration for writers in the Central Ohio area. Writers of all skill levels and backgrounds are invited to attend the group's writers' workshops and other events.

The organization's second goal is to print the best work produced in the region.

The co-op relies on the support and participation of readers, writers and local businesses in order to function.

Columbus Creative Cooperative is not a non-profit organization, but in many cases, it functions as one. As best as possible, the proceeds from the printed anthologies are distributed directly to the writers and artists who produce the content.

For more information about Columbus Creative Cooperative, please visit **ColumbusCoop.org**.

About Columbus Historical Society

The Columbus Historical Society was founded in 1990 by a group of avid professional and amateur local historians with a passion to share Columbus history. The Society was formed to protect and share the history of the broader community, with an emphasis on the core city and county environs.

CHS works closely with other local historical organizations to cross-promote activities, education, events, preservation, programs and publications offered throughout the community.

The Columbus Historical Society's main exhibit space is housed in the COSI building at 333 W. Broad St., Columbus, OH 43215. Admission is free.

The artists and editors who have contributed to this book have agreed to share the proceeds from its sale with the Columbus Historical Society to help them protect and showcase Columbus's unique history far into the future.

Columbus Creative Cooperative would like to thank Jeff Lafever, Executive Director of the Columbus Historical Society, and the organization's staff and board of directors for their assistance with this anthology project.

For more information about the Columbus Historical Society, please visit **ColumbusHistory.org**.

EternalPower
FITNESS.com

Improving your health

Mind

Body

Soul

Casey is an experienced, professional trainer with an emphasis on weight management and functional training.

Private sessions and group training sessions are available.

Contact Casey O'Linn, CSCS

Eternal Power Fitness

(614) 795-7298

eternalpowerfitness@gmail.com

www.EternalPowerFitness.com

This is a paid advertisement.

Aged wine from grapes,
nothing added.

www.viavecchiawinery.com

485 S. Front St
Columbus, OH 43215

614.893.5455

This is a paid advertisement.

Other Books by
Columbus Creative Cooperative

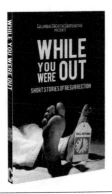

WHILE YOU WERE OUT
SHORT STORIES OF RESURRECTION

Fifteen short stories about people, objects, animals, and even a car, that die and come back to life.

These witty, bizzare tales will revive your spirit of imagination.

While You Were Out is a 5-star book on Amazon.com! ★★★★★

Available as a paperback, and as an e-book for the Amazon Kindle, Barnes & Noble Nook and more devices.

Across Town
Stories of Columbus

Twelve short stories, all of which are set in Columbus, Ohio.

If you enjoyed *Columbus: Past, Present and Future*, you will love *Across Town: Stories of Columbus*!

Across Town is a 5-star book on Amazon.com! ★★★★★

Available as a paperback, and as an e-book for the Amazon Kindle, Barnes & Noble Nook, iPad and more devices.

OVERGROWN
Tales of the Unexpected

A collection of short stories with a twist.

Overgrown is full of creative, entertaining stories.

Overgrown is a 5-star book on Amazon.com! ★★★★★

Available as a paperback, and as an e-book for the Amazon Kindle, Barnes & Noble Nook, iPad and more devices.

Find more information and order these books and others at
www.ColumbusCoop.org